CALLING MR. LONELY HEARTS

LAURA BENEDICT is the author of *Isabella Moon*. Her short fiction has appeared in *Ellery Queen Mystery Magazine* and a number of anthologies. For the past decade, she has worked as a freelance book reviewer for *The Grand Rapids Press* in Michigan and other newspapers. She lives in southern Illinois with her husband, Pinckney Benedict, and their two children.

Praise for Laura Benedict

'I dare you to read the opening lines of [*Isabella Moon*] without being swept away . . . Like Alice Hoffman, combines mystery with magic . . . Spooky, sexy and rich'
Elizabeth Hyde, author of *The Abortionist's Daughter*

'Haunting . . . This mystery / thriller will simultaneously tug at the heart-strings and scare the bejesus out of readers. In a word: unforgettable.'
Chicago Tribune

Also by Laura Benedict

Isabella Moon

CALLING MR. LONELY HEARTS

A Novel

Laura Benedict

arrow books

FT Pbk

Published by Arrow Books 2010

1 3 5 7 9 10 8 6 4 2

First published in Great Britain in 2009 by William Heinemann

The Random House Group Limited
20 Vauxhall Bridge Road, London, SW1V 2SA

www.rbooks.co.uk

Addresses for companies within The Random House Group Limited can be found at:
www.randomhouse.co.uk/offices.htm

The Random House Group Limited Reg. No. 954009

A CIP catalogue record for this book
is available from the British Library

ISBN 9780099509295

The Random House Group Limited supports The Forest Stewardship Council (FSC), the leading international forest certification organisation. All our titles that are printed on Greenpeace approved FSC certified paper carry the FSC logo. Our paper procurement policy can be found at:
www.rbooks.co.uk/environment

Printed and bound in Great Britain by
CPI Bookmarque Ltd, Croydon, CR0 4TD

For Pinckney,
who knew long before I did

Acknowledgments

It would be impossible for me to thank everyone who so kindly helped in bringing this, my second novel, about. But before I try, I must first thank the readers, booksellers, and reviewers who took the time to read and comment on *Isabella Moon*. I'm exceedingly grateful to you for making my debut such an amazing adventure.

The publication of *Isabella Moon* brought me many inspiring new friends, but I must mention fellow writers C. J. Lyons, Kelli Stanley, Karen Dionne, and Jordan Dane by name. I've loved sharing my debut journey with them and cannot imagine how I could have done without their advice, compassion, support, and brilliant insights. C. J. Lyons was also my official medical consultant for this novel, while Kelli Stanley clued me in to the mysteries of creating things from clay. And I must thank Bill "Speedo" Cameron for his spelling expertise.

Jennifer Talty kept me going with her energy and delightful quotes of the day when I found myself flagging; and I can only say to Joe Frick: "The twins are forever in your debt!"

At Ballantine Books: Mark Tavani, my talented editor, continues to amaze me with his ability to read my work and then help me to see it in fresh new ways. Also, Gina Centrello, Libby McGuire, Kim Hovey, Gene Mydlowski, Rachel Kind, Beck Stvan, Kelli Fillingim, Shona McCarthy, Paul Taunton, Michelle Taormina, Dana Leigh Blanchette, and Lisa Barnes, my charming and tireless publicist.

In the UK, Vanessa Neuling and Emma Finnigan have shown such care for my work despite my being so far away.

Susan Raihofer, my cool, calm, and collected super-agent, is always there when I call to bombard her with ideas or to fret about some little thing. She keeps me grounded and is always hopeful. Also at the David Black Literary Agency, Leigh Ann Eliseo takes excellent care of me in the audio world.

Dominic Cittadino, D.D.S., my favorite dentist, is nothing like the dentist in this novel (though he does tell a good joke!). He and his staff generously listened to and answered my frequent questions (thanks especially to the lovely and patient Marsha Gostowski). I'm in debt as well to Hope Jones, D.D.S., for her expert knowledge, continuing friendship, and delightfully wicked sense of humor.

Tandy Thompson, globe-trotting polyglot and most excellent human being, cheerfully translated various sections of dialogue for me and never once said, "You want him to say what?" Kermit "Pig Helmet" Moore was once again my invaluable crime and punishment consultant.

For background information about Santeria, I found the following books invaluable: *Santeria: The Religion* by Migene González-Wippler (Llewellyn Publications), and *Santeria: A Practical Guide to Afro-Caribbean Magic* by Luis Manuel Núñez (Spring Publications).

I must also mention Luanne Rice, whose encouragement, warmth, and brilliant example have sustained me and taught me to embrace unknown possibilities.

Special thanks to Jeff Jones, M.D., Erin Connelly, Cindy Marks, Anneliese Wilmsen, and Alexander Wilmsen. And much love to the three women who enrich my life daily: Monica Wilmsen, Teresa McGrath, and Maggie Caldwell.

I am always grateful to my parents, Judy and Jerry Philpot. They were especially supportive of me in the writing of this novel; Cincinnati is their home and they taught me to love it as much as they do. They advised me not only on the geography of the city, but its many nuances and personalities as well. I hope that they—and everyone else in that wonderful city—will excuse the few liberties I took in mixing imagined locations with real ones.

Pinckney, Nora, and Cleveland—I know I've said it before, but it bears repeating: You are my reasons for living.

PART I

What If?

CHAPTER 1

She was just plain Alice, and they never let her forget.

Roxanne and Delilah, who was called Del, knelt close to Alice by the light of a candle, the skirts of their stiff blue school uniforms crumpling against her. Del rested a hand on Alice's shoulder as though she might try to get up from the leaf-strewn ground and run away. But they all knew she wouldn't. Roxanne used a twig to stir some pungent concoction in a shell-thin African bowl she had brought from home. The odor suffused the copse like the fug from an ancient outhouse. To Alice, it smelled suspiciously like a baby's dirty diaper. There was something else, though. Something caustic and chemical-smelling that made her eyes water.

"I don't have to eat it, do I?" Alice said.

"Oh God," Del said. She hadn't wanted to go along with this whole thing in the first place. She was nervous enough about being in the park after dark. And there was something deeply wrong with what they

were doing, she knew. Witchcraft on television was fine, but this was something else.

"Of course not," Roxanne said, her voice patient. The bowl was heavy in her hands, though it hardly contained anything at all. If she were a few years older than thirteen, she would know it was heavy with her own desire—a desire that she could, at that moment, identify only as dimly sexual.

"Get her coat off," she told Del.

"Come on," Del said. "Don't be a baby, Alice."

She reached for the buttons on the front of Alice's pea coat, which was exactly like the ones she and Roxanne were wearing, though Roxanne's had a black velvet scarf tucked beneath the collar. Alice didn't help with the coat, but she didn't resist, either. Del flung the coat and the blue cardigan sweater with its Our Lady of the Hills crest onto the dormant grass.

Alice shivered in her blouse, hoping that she would be able to leave on at least her skirt and socks.

Roxanne nodded. Del's cold-numbed fingers tugged at the buttons of Alice's blouse.

"For pity's sake," Roxanne said. "Alice, you need to unbutton your blouse. You don't have to undo it all the way. Then you need to lie down."

Alice did as she was told. Roxanne put down the bowl and tucked the discarded coat beneath Alice's head. She brushed her fingertips over Alice's brow and smiled. Sweet, tender Alice. Though perhaps not so sweet, she whined sometimes. But at least she was Pure Alice, who had never been kissed—a virgin, as they all were.

"Now. Everyone be quiet," she said, picking up the bowl. Her hands shook a bit with the excitement of it all. She closed her eyes.

The words she spoke—seemingly to the sky, or the air in front of her—were unintelligible to the others. Her tone was one of supplication: a petition or a prayer, not so different from the prayers the priests said at mass. She tried for the same singsong in her voice, the same careful cadence. She'd added a few thoughts and words of her own to *the spell she took from the satanic witchcraft book she stole from the public library, thinking that they would make it more effective.*

The herbs in the mash were ones she remembered being used in a joyful Santeria rite that her mother had taken her to, when her mother was on one of her "spiritual quests." It was this blending of dark magic and the divine that she believed would give them what they wanted.

Alice squeezed her eyes shut, trying to ignore the cold, but she had to clench her jaw to keep her teeth from chattering. Del picked up the flickering candle in its fragile hurricane and held it close as much for warmth as to protect it from the unpredictable air around them. Roxanne pressed her fingertips against Alice's shoulder. She dipped the fingers of her other hand into the bowl, then touched them to Alice's bare chest.

Alice turned her face away from the hideous smell. Whatever was now on her chest felt like frozen sand. But she held still. She was doing this for all of them. Roxanne didn't recognize the depth of Alice's faith in her. Alice would die for her.

Del watched, wondering how Alice could let something so strange, so horrible, be done to her. Alice's face was as plain as her name, not homely, but fair and unfreckled, with high, broad cheekbones and too-thin lips. Alice's was not a threatening or even very expressive face. She smiled often, but her smiles were tentative, as though someone were always watching her and she didn't know if she should be smiling or not.

Alice reminded Del of a stray dog that had hung around their house for several months. She hadn't liked the way the dog flung itself at her feet, its belly exposed. It was a sneaky dog, pushing their elderly spaniel away from her kibble when it thought no one was watching, peeing on the rug when her mother let it inside, shivering, on snowy days. She knew she would probably go to hell for thinking so, but she wasn't sorry when a speeding pizza delivery car knocked it to the side of the road, its neck twisted.

She had never known Alice to be sneaky, or to do anything that would hurt or betray any of them. But there would be a first time, she was certain.

She watched as a woolly caterpillar inched its way into Alice's dull blond hair, its body curving gracefully as it moved. As it crawled toward Alice's cheek, Alice's lips and forehead contorted. Was she in pain? Del held her breath, thinking Alice might cry out.

"Roxanne!" Del said, stopping Roxanne in mid-chant.

Alice's eyes opened in a bald stare before rolling back to show two half-moons of white below their trembling lids. Even by the light of the candle, her lips looked blue; her body stiffened and began to spasm, lifting itself from the ground.

Before Roxanne could move away, Alice's left arm hit outward, catching Roxanne mid-stomach so that she gave a loud gasp. The bowl flew from her hand.

Del began to scream, then—remembering that they were in the park and anyone could hear—covered her mouth to stifle it.

Alice jerked, her teeth clapping together with each violent throw of her head, her small, flat breasts shuddering. Now it was Roxanne who stared. Alice was like a mechanical doll, broken, frantic and wild in its malfunction. She was fascinated. Everything about Alice was always so predictable, so studied. But she had become interesting.

With a final upward thrust of her torso, Alice's body was calm, but her face was tinged blue, her eyes slitted, still with just their whites showing.

As Del scuttled away to crouch beneath a tree, the candle dropped to the ground, shattering its glass globe.

"We killed her!" Del said. "Shit, Roxanne. We killed her!"

Roxanne tilted her head, watchful. A slow curl of breath escaped Alice's mouth and dissipated.

"She's breathing," she said. "Quit freaking out. There wasn't anything in there that could hurt her." She twisted around to find the bowl, but could see nothing in the gathering dark. "And now it's all gone." They would have to start over again because she hadn't finished. Just another few minutes.

"We have to get someone," Del said. "What's wrong with her?"

Roxanne was in motion now, stuffing things into her book bag.

"The only place anyone is going is home," she said. "Just don't tell anyone you saw her tonight. She probably won't remember anything anyway—damn it, Del, the candle!" She pointed to the ragged circle of burning leaves surrounding the still-lit candle. The flames were small and tentative, etching black stripes into the palms of the leaves around it.

Del found herself looking stupidly at the fire for several beats, knowing what was going to come next, imagining Alice's frozen body being consumed by the flames.

"Del!" Roxanne shouted.

Del swept handfuls of leaves on top of the burning ones, patting them with her hands. Were the leaves stoking the fire or stopping it? She couldn't tell.

"Help me," Del said. But Roxanne didn't move. Del buried the flames until just a few whispers of smoke rose from the pile.

"We have to go," Roxanne said. "Are you coming?" In the distance, they heard a shrill whistle, someone calling a dog or a child indoors.

"How can you be so hateful?" Del said. But Roxanne was moving away, confident that Alice would come to herself. She had homework to get to, and she was already thinking of the sketch she would do of Alice's face, that look of emptiness, of complete abandon.

Del ran, her book bag thumping against her back. At the edge of the park, she crossed Arthur Street without bothering to go down to the crosswalk at the corner. A passing car blew its horn at her as she stumbled onto the opposite sidewalk. She made her way up the hill toward her house, breathing hard in the cold night air, hardly believing what she was doing.

Every lamp in every house she passed seemed to be burning as though to expose her. A dog she didn't know emerged from one of the yards and jogged along beside her for a few moments. Glancing down, she saw that it was short-haired, light brown with large splotches of black—a shepherd, maybe, or some mix.

"Go home," she said, but it didn't even look up at her. She wondered if her fear had attracted it. She was afraid for herself. Afraid for

Alice. A dog like this—maybe even this very dog—might find Alice in the park. Her mind couldn't form the next horrible thought.

At the next corner, the dog stopped while she walked on. She looked back to see it staring after her, its breath lifting in misty bursts beneath the streetlamp.

Her father's car was in the driveway. It was after seven and she had missed dinner. When she tried to decide what she would do next, she could think only of Alice. How could she go into the house as though nothing had happened and eat the food that her mother left warming in the oven for her? How could she sit down and do her homework, watch Seinfeld or Saved by the Bell or some stupid movie and wait for the phone call from Alice's father, who would want to know why Alice hadn't come home?

She thought of how she'd let that caterpillar crawl into Alice's hair. She would go to Hell for what she had done, even though it wasn't her fault Roxanne was so mean.

As she slipped into the garage, she dropped her book bag gently inside. The smell of cooked sauerkraut came to her through the kitchen door, but she wasn't hungry. She tripped over her father's toolbox—the single-car space was stuffed full with boxes and bikes and workshop equipment—and felt something sharp graze her leg. Groping around the shelves by the door, she finally laid her hands on the flashlight they used for camping.

Del hurried toward the back of the empty park, praying that the pale glow she saw was some trick of the streetlamps or someone using one of the barbeque grills for a winter picnic. But she knew better.

"Alice," she whispered.

The flames clung to the ground in the copse like a brilliant orange blanket. Alice stood in the opening, silhouetted against the light. She cried out, holding her forearm to her eyes against the beam from Del's flashlight. In the moment before Del jerked the beam from Alice's face, she saw that Alice's skin and clothes were streaked with dirt and ash. Bits of leaves poked from her hair. Del thought of the caterpillar, but knew it was the least of Alice's problems. It was the wild look in Alice's eyes—a look of fear and anger and confusion—that caused her stomach to clench.

"Stay away from me," Alice said. "Go away."

"But it's me," Del said, slowing her step. She was more afraid of Alice than she was of the dog that had followed her up the road. But it wasn't actually Alice that she was afraid of. It was whatever had happened to Alice, whatever had changed her. The flashlight's beam caught one of Alice's legs, which were covered with dark streaks: blood, maybe, or feces?

"I saw you," Alice said. "I saw you run away."

"I'm here," Del said, trying not to look at Alice's exposed breasts, which were sharply divided by the stripe of noxious salve Roxanne had applied. "We have to leave."

The fire didn't seem to be spreading beyond the copse, but, still, she knew it wouldn't be long before someone saw it. There would be questions.

Alice wouldn't move.

"You just passed out for a few minutes," Del said. "It wasn't even that long."

"I was dead," Alice said, her voice flat.

"Let's go home," Del said. She didn't like this Alice at all. This Alice frightened her.

"You both left me here," Alice said. "And I was dead, but he told me to come back."

"Don't be stupid," Del said. "Just come on. We'll all be in trouble if you don't come." She was on the verge of leaving Alice alone again, now that she knew Alice was alive. It didn't matter anymore that Alice was the purest of them or that Roxanne had promised that the so-called spell would attract a guy for them, and only for them. She told herself that it was a bunch of bullshit that Roxanne had made up. If only Alice would be quiet about it.

"He came for us, but you didn't even wait to see him," Alice said. "Don't you want to know what he looks like?"

"Get your stuff," Del said. The fire had not yet reached Alice's coat and sweater and book bag. But it was Del, not Alice, who gathered *them. She buttoned Alice's blouse and stuffed her into the coat as though Alice were an idiot child. Then Del shoved the book bag and sweater into her arms, causing Alice to stumble backward.*

As they left, Del almost tripped over the lost bowl. She kicked at it, driving it several feet away.

"Stop! Roxanne will be mad if you lose her bowl," Alice said.

Roxanne, who was the one who said they should leave Alice in the park, the one who ran away first. Del had known Roxanne since they were both four years old, but she still didn't completely understand why Roxanne did some of the things she did. Her mother had told her that Roxanne "acted out" because she didn't know her father, and that she thought she was special because she was "artistic." But those seemed like lame explanations to Del.

"I wouldn't worry about Roxanne, if I were you," Del said.

Ignoring her, Alice ran to the bowl and tucked it into her book bag.

They walked in silence until they reached Alice's house, one of the grand old mansions overlooking Victoria Park's duck pond.

"Fix your hair," Del said. "You've got leaves and stuff in it."

Alice bent over and quickly brushed her hands through her hair. When she came back up again, she smiled at Del. There was a smear of dirt across her left cheek, but Del didn't mention it.

"Thanks," Alice said.

Del didn't respond, but turned away to walk home. She couldn't wait to get away from Alice, whose eyes had at last lost their wild look. It was seven-thirty and Del was finally hungry. She didn't ever want to see Alice again.

After she'd gone only a few steps, Alice called to her.

"He looks like an angel," Alice said. "A perfect angel."

CHAPTER 2

Week 16 4/7

Dillon got out of the steaming Escort and eyed the expensive-looking car crumpled against its front bumper. He prepared himself to give the asshole who was driving it the scare of his life. Scaring people was one of his chief pleasures, and he had decorated himself accordingly: even the tattoo artist (a nice piece of ass out in San Francisco) had been skeptical about inking the row of blood-dripping fangs across his forehead. He himself was particularly fond of the scrollwork goatee on his chin, but the righteous row of studs on his upper lip, along with the ones over each eyebrow, were, as they say, the icing on the fucking cake.

He'd been coasting down Gravois Street, a single finger on the wheel, enjoying the raw pleasure of the night wind through the Escort's open windows. The few hours before dawn were the best, the coolest of the day in what had been a hot Cincinnati summer. In his pocket were a fresh thirty bucks and a couple of hits of Ecstasy he'd picked up playing roadie for The Toasted Bobs. They'd sat around the club drinking a few after-hours beers, but he was hardly even buzzed. Certainly not buzzed enough to miss seeing a car right in front of him. There was a stop sign at the bottom of the hill, which he'd intended to ignore, but no streetlight, and the car had seemed to appear out of the darkness from nowhere.

Now they were both in the middle of the intersection and his chest hurt like hell because the stupid airbag hadn't gone off.

He got out and tapped on the glass to get the attention of the guy inside the other car.

"Man, where are your fucking lights, man?" he shouted. There were no witnesses, no other cars around except the ones parked curbside. The houses around them were dark.

At first he thought the man inside the car was dead or something, the way he was leaning into the car's steering wheel. Then he sat back, and, without waiting for Dillon to move, pushed the door open.

"What the fuck?" Dillon said, jumping back.

He didn't look to Dillon like someone who'd just been in a car accident. He looked calm, and was dressed in the kind of clothes guys only wore in magazines. Probably a faggot. Probably a fucking lawyer, too, driving a car like this. He could smell the leather from four or five feet away.

"Are you all right?" the man said.

"Where'd you come from?" Dillon said. "Where are your fucking lights? You could've killed us both!"

"Did you break something?" the man said, reaching out to touch his arm, which was crossed over his chest. "Maybe you should sit down."

Now Dillon was getting aggravated. The guy was acting like he was in charge, just like every other asshole in a suit. He jerked away.

"Shit," Dillon said. "This was your fault. And my car's fucking totaled."

"That's a shame about your car," the man said.

He couldn't bear to stand in front of this smug asshole who didn't seem to get that his only form of transportation, his only freedom, was gone and that it was *his* fault. Proving it would probably be a pain in the ass. People like this guy almost never had to pay for their fuckups. There would have to be police. He wanted to climb back into the Escort to see if there was a joint rolling around. *Calm*. He needed to keep his shit together and make this suit understand.

"I'll tell you right now that my insurance is no good," Dillon said. "So you're screwed right off the fucking bat. And they always blame the guy who does the rear-ending, even if it's the other guy's fault." At this, he gave the man a look that said he wasn't going to take the blame, that he wasn't somebody to be messed with. "You're not going to stick me with this bullshit."

"So, I take it that you don't want me to call the police?" the man said.

Dillon didn't like that he couldn't see the man's eyes in the dark, couldn't read him. He preferred not to get violent unless he was pushed, but he was ready.

"That would make your life easier? More pleasant?" the man said.

He couldn't tell if the guy was serious or was just taking his time, mocking him with his Eurotrash TV accent.

"I'm saying that if this shit gets all complicated, you're not going to get squat out of me anyway," he said. "So I wouldn't even bother."

"Hm." The man put his hand to his chin, thoughtful.

Dillon waited, breathing hard. It bugged him how quiet it was. Nobody on the street had turned on so much as a porch light to see what was going on. But it wasn't the kind of neighborhood in which people spent a hell of a lot of time outside. The house nearest to them was covered in graffiti and the only car in its driveway was up on blocks. Still, not even a random gangbanger had bothered to check out what was going on. It felt to him like a movie set where the crew was all out of sight, like one of those fake towns where the buildings were just fronts held up by wooden frames. He'd seen enough episodes of *The Twilight Zone* on the Sci-Fi channel to be a little freaked out. He didn't like the feeling.

He watched as the man walked to the back of the car (which he later learned was called an Aston Martin) and stroked its rear end like it was some kind of pet. It looked like the kind of car that would get carried away in a padded truck, rather than hauled up behind a tow. Following him, Dillon saw that maybe the damage wasn't so bad. The Escort was definitely totaled. There would be no fixing it and it had probably only been worth about five hundred bucks ten minutes earlier.

But the worst part was that the car didn't actually belong to him—it was registered in his sister's name. She was always doing nice things for him like that, covering for him, lending him a little cash when he needed it. This was one more thing he was going to owe her for. She was patient, though. Always patient, even when he really fucked up.

"I'll tell you what," the man said. In the glow of the Escort's remaining headlight Dillon could see that he was the kind of guy that chicks really went for, with expensive shoes and a hundred-dollar haircut that looked messy.

"I agree with you that we shouldn't trouble the police," he said. "What things of a personal nature do you have in the car? Do you have a screwdriver?"

"I don't know," Dillon said. "The usual shit. Why?"

In five minutes the Escort was cleaned out and he had the license plates off. It was a beautiful plan, and he wished he'd thought of it himself. Maybe the guy was some kind of mobster who did shit like this all the time. He didn't like messing with those kinds of guys, but he wasn't looking to argue. And it occurred to him that his sister's asshole boyfriend had probably come up with the money for the car, so maybe it wasn't such a loss. His sister would be sad, but he would make it up to her. She always forgave him in the end.

The Aston Martin fired up with the kind of muted rumble that those fancy European cars always made. He wasn't sure yet what the guy wanted from him, why he wanted to help him out. *Probably wanted him to suck his dick, and no fucking way was that going to happen!* After this was done, he planned to just take off, leaving the guy and the car behind. He was about ten blocks away from the apartment of a keyboard player named Beefheart who he knew well enough. He'd walked farther.

As the man drove the Aston Martin over to one of the opposite corners, it made a scraping noise against the pavement that lasted a few seconds, then stopped. He could see now that the Escort really had gotten the worst of it. The man left the Aston Martin idling and came back to where Dillon waited. He carried a container of lighter fluid in his hand.

"Let's not linger here," the man said. "You have a cigarette lighter?"

Dillon dug in his front pocket and held it out.

"No, you should have the pleasure," the man said. "But let's hurry, shall we?"

It had seemed like a hell of an idea when the guy suggested it: to burn up the car and report it stolen. The man handed Dillon the lighter fluid.

Dillon gave him a questioning look—what the hell was a guy like this doing with lighter fluid in his fucking expensive car?

"It's an excellent spot and stain remover," the man said.

"Right," Dillon said, taking the can.

He leaned into the Escort and squirted the fluid over the cloth interior and onto the soiled floor mats. He'd always liked the smell of lighter fluid. Once upon a time it had been a cheap kind of high, but that was baby stuff, and besides, it gave him a bitch of a headache.

He flicked the lighter at the edge of the driver's seat. It took a moment to catch, and he thought maybe it wasn't going to work and the guy was playing some kind of trick on him, and maybe this whole thing was a stupid idea. Then it caught, and there was a rush of heat in his face and he felt himself being jerked away from the car.

He and the man stood a good ten feet back, watching the interior of the car fill with smoke and yellow light. The sight of the burning car gave him an intense feeling of pleasure. In fact, he could feel an erection coming on in his jeans. Fire had never gotten to him like this before. He felt warmth on his face, and liked it. It made him feel alive, this fire. But he knew that if he stood there much longer, it would heat the studs on his lip and dry his eyes out so they felt like sandpaper.

Across the street, a light came on in one of the houses.

"Time to go," the man said, turning his back on Dillon. He moved toward the still-running Aston Martin.

Forgetting all about his earlier decision to get away from the guy, Dillon followed. He sank into the car's soft leather passenger seat. It wasn't the kind of car he'd ever imagined owning, but now that he was inside he could see the appeal of it. The seat seemed to mold itself to him, and the touch of the leather reminded him of his grandfather's pigskin bomber jacket that hung far back in the coat closet at his sister's place. He hadn't oiled down the jacket in a while—if he didn't get to it soon, it would begin to crack and eventually tear. Someday, he would have a motorcycle, and he would want it then.

"I could use a drink," the man said. "You?"

"Nothing open now," Dillon said.

The man backed the car a few feet, and pulled out into the road. Dillon looked back through the rear window at the Escort, which now had smoke billowing out the open door and passenger window.

"That's going to be one fucking mess," Dillon said. But it wasn't going to be his mess.

"I was thinking about driving out to one of the casinos," the man said. "Twenty, thirty minutes."

"Yeah," Dillon said. "But if you try to put a hand on my dick, I'll fucking cut it off."

The man didn't move in his seat, but kept looking at the road. Dillon didn't like his smile.

"That won't be a problem," the man said.

Dillon was drunk, but not drunk enough to miss that the building through which Varick led him sometime after ten o'clock the next morning was a pile of shit. A collage of peeling paint and faded work-safety posters covered the walls; the windowless steel doors they passed were dented, some almost scratched bare of paint. The hallways smelled of chemicals and rubber and mold. He didn't like the rustling noises he heard from the building's recesses. He hated rats—truth was, he was scared as hell of rats—and this place looked like Rat Paradise. Although he had definitely crashed in worse places, this didn't look like somewhere a guy in a thousand-dollar suit would live. He tripped over a piece of PVC on the floor and fell into Varick, who pushed back at him, hard, like he didn't like it. Still, Varick smiled, his teeth—teeth that weren't so pretty as the rest of him—bright in the dusty light of the hallway.

"Steady there, my friend," he said.

"I still feel like I'm on the fucking ship," Dillon said, as they stepped into a freight elevator. The casino they'd gone to, The Golden Galleon, had a dance floor that spontaneously tipped every few minutes, causing the dancers to suddenly get close to one another. The band was crap but he had danced, while Varick sat by looking bored, because the women in the place had been fucking hotter than he could stand. When one sweetheart with a skirt like a cheerleader's and a halter-top that barely covered what Varick had called her "assets" came over to the table, he couldn't refuse her. He remembered guiding her to the edge of the stage and kissing her; her lip gloss was sticky and tasted like a strawberry Popsicle. Then one of her girlfriends had come over and laughingly pushed him away and the girl he'd kissed started dancing with her, ignoring him. He remembered feeling embarrassed and a little confused, but Varick waved him back over and bought him another drink.

Now, Varick closed the gate on the elevator and took Dillon's arm to lead him to the back. "Can't have you falling out," he said. "Safety first."

It freaked him out the way the guy was treating him like some kind of kid brother. Maybe he was a fag after all, and he was just moving slow.

"No fucking way," he said.

"Is there a problem?" Varick said.

Had he spoken aloud? Shit. He was too fucking drunk. He rubbed at the row of studs over his right eyebrow—one of the piercings was getting infected, he could tell. Fucking cheap-ass piercing parlor over in some bum-fucked Kentucky town. He should've gone to his regular place.

Varick was looking at him. Again, that smile, a smile that wasn't quite friendly, but might be mistaken for friendly at first glance.

Dillon didn't see any sense in answering. He was pretty sure the guy wasn't a fag. If he was, there was a four-inch pigsticker in his boot to let the guy know his true feelings about the matter.

When the elevator clanked to a stop, Varick opened the gate and gestured for Dillon to step out. A giant number 7 was painted on the opposite wall.

The institutional green paint job in the hallway was recent enough that Dillon could smell the fumes. Stopping in front of a door near the end of the hall, Varick flipped up the cover on the keypad beside it and pressed some numbers. When he was finished, he pushed open the door and stood aside.

"Make yourself comfortable, my friend," he said.

CHAPTER 3

Week 16 4/7

"Just hold out your finger," Roxanne said. "She'll jump right on there."

She knelt down on the floor and held her arm out toward Del's five-year-old stepdaughter, Wendy, who was worried about the bright blue parakeet on Roxanne's shoulder.

"Will he bite me?" Wendy said, inching closer.

Roxanne didn't care for most children, but she could feel Del and her husband, Jock, looking on. The bird was a present for the girl and, to tell the truth, Roxanne kind of liked her. Even though she was a step-daughter, with her springy blond curls and hazel eyes, she looked re-markably like Del had as a child.

"That's some hostess gift, Roxanne," Del said. "It's just dinner."

"I'm sure I missed her birthday or something. Or it can be an early Christmas present, if you want."

Jock laughed. He was a lawyer, expansive and muscular in the way of former football players, with close-cut, dark hair and a broad, honest face that looked younger than his forty-something years. Though he was several years older than either she or Del, she liked the way he moved, with a confidence that spoke of utter control of himself and his life. (Fortunately, he didn't seem to be controlling Del—Del put enough pressure on herself for the both of them.) He'd gone to Cincinnati Collegiate, a prep school that served the non-Catholic wealthy in town, then to Duke, and was a widower by the time he and Del got together three years earlier. It was Roxanne's opinion that Del was way more insecure than she needed to be about Jock. Del had always been a worrier.

"Here, baby," Jock said, lifting Wendy into his arms. He touched Roxanne's shoulder with his hand and the bird hopped onto it. "There's your bird." He moved his hand slowly toward Wendy and she reached out to stroke its back with a tentative finger.

"You should name her," Roxanne said, getting up from the floor.

Del came over and put her arm around Roxanne and kissed her on the cheek.

"What was that for?" Roxanne said.

"Because you're thoughtful," Del said. She was very attached to Wendy, Roxanne knew, and Del had told her some minor horror stories about trying to win Wendy's trust early on. But she also knew better than to have illusions about her own thoughtfulness.

"You think about it, honey," Jock said. "You'll come up with a great name. Let's put her in her cage and find somewhere for it in your room. Tell Miss Roxanne 'thank you'."

He gently set the child down and slipped the bird back into its cage, where it immediately flew around and lighted, upside down, at its top.

"Thank you for my upside-down bird," Wendy said, looking up at Roxanne.

"You'll be a great friend for her," she said. "You can tell her all your secrets."

Wendy smiled and threw her arms around Roxanne's hips, then ran off after her father.

After dinner, they sat in the Florida room at the back of the house. The long wall of sliding doors was open to the unusually cool September evening and Roxanne had her favorite shawl—black-dyed Peruvian al-paca woven tissue-thin—draped around her shoulders.

"So, any juicy divorces you can talk about?" Roxanne said. She leaned toward Jock, who sat in the chair opposite hers. "Come on. I can keep a secret."

Jock raised an eyebrow, seeming to consider. Then he also leaned forward. "Let's just say Bob Kohler's not going to be buying up any more newspapers anytime soon. He'll be selling off a considerable number of assets." He leaned back and took a sip of his scotch. "But you heard it from somebody else."

"No, really?" Roxanne said. As an artist, she lived on the fringe of social-page society. People like the Kohlers had her sculptures in their homes—here and in Hilton Head or Majorca or Bermuda—and of-fices. But she preferred her life to theirs. If she became one of them, she knew she wouldn't be able to work—she would be too distracted. Work and art were the only things that meant anything to her.

"What is it?" Del said. She came into the room bearing a hand-painted tray laden with a pot of chocolate fondue and chunks of freshly cut pineapple and ripe strawberries. Roxanne watched her. Dear Del, who tried so hard to be the perfect suburban wife. She took everything so seriously; she had ever since they'd met in preschool at Our Lady of the Hills. It worried Roxanne sometimes, how Del seemed to be trying just a little too hard. Her parents weren't wealthy, merely comfortable, and she had definitely married out of her league when she married Jock. Roxanne wanted her to succeed, finally. Right out of college she had married a guy down in Lexington, but he'd spent most of their two years together stoned and unemployed. Del definitely deserved better. Roxanne just hoped she could handle it.

"Jock was just dishing on the Kohlers," Roxanne said. "He's so naughty."

Del put the tray on the low table in front of Roxanne and went to sit on the arm of Jock's chair.

"That's my Jock," she said, putting her arm around her husband's shoulders and kissing his head. As she moved, the square-cut yellow pendant around her neck that Roxanne had thought was a citrine caught the light and she realized it was actually an oversized yellow diamond. "Naughty to the core."

Jock grinned. Even after a year of marriage, he was besotted with her, Roxanne could see. That was a good thing.

While Jock was getting Wendy ready for bed, Roxanne sat at the island in the kitchen finishing a glass of wine and watching Del load the dishwasher. Del had designed the kitchen herself and Roxanne had helped her pick out the granite and distressed copper accents. Just a few months earlier, it had been featured in the *Enquirer* in a story about renovations in older Victoria Park homes. As far as Roxanne was concerned, Del and Alice were welcome to live in the area where the three of them had grown up, but it wasn't for her. She would have felt stifled here. There were too many things to remember—good things as well as bad—and she didn't need the distraction.

"I probably should've had Alice and Thad over, too," Del said. "Or, at least Alice."

"Why?"

"I think she's lonely," she said. "She said Thad's been out of town a lot. That's kind of weird for a dentist, isn't it?"

"Alice can take care of herself." It was true, despite the fact that Alice came off as needy to most people. But Roxanne had known her for more than twenty-five years. Alice was just a fact of life, like Roxanne's own black hair, which was lush and thick but tended to unruliness if she didn't mind it, like the calluses on her fingers and palms from working with clay. Alice was just there. Alice called when she needed her, and sometimes Roxanne would answer, sometimes she wouldn't. "I don't think Thad wants to be home."

"What does that mean?" Del said, turning off the faucet. She took a dish towel and carefully wiped the water from around the faucet handles and the edges of the sink.

"Well, they've been married seven years, and there's that seven-year-itch thing," she said.

"That's a harsh thing to say."

"Maybe," Roxanne said. "But I think she's taken things a little too far with that nose job and those Suzy Socialite clothes and those diets she's always on. I love her, but she's a freak. Sometimes, I think she's channeling Michael Jackson."

Del struggled to hide a smile. "I think she looks pretty good. But maybe the stilettos at the grocery store are a little much," she said.

They both laughed.

Roxanne had lunched with Alice just the previous Tuesday. Since her father had died and she'd come into her inheritance, Alice had seemed to turn away from her, which was, generally speaking, okay. She'd been obsessed for years with having a child, and for a long time had talked of little else. But she'd developed serious endometriosis early and the scarring was so bad she could never be pregnant. Roxanne knew it was probably unethical or unkind or un-something to not stick by Alice after the years of loyalty she'd shown her—loyalty that could never be repaid, so why should she bother, really?—but she found Alice's drift into self-obsession too bizarre and too time-sucking. She almost told Del what Alice was up to now, how she'd gone as far as inventing a lover for herself to make Thad jealous, but she couldn't bear how pathetic it all was. Why Alice simply hadn't taken an actual lover was beyond her. Del would eventually find out for herself. Alice couldn't keep a secret for long.

"Do you think he's screwing around?" Del said. "That would suck. She doesn't deserve that."

Roxanne shrugged. She'd had a go at Thad five years earlier but he'd shied away, pretending he didn't know what she was asking. In a way, she was glad he hadn't bitten. He'd turned out to be a bore, as far as she could see. But she had her suspicions about him. Nobody could be that boring.

It was a guilty habit, she knew, sleeping with married men. *Like mother, like daughter.*

Jock came in carrying Wendy, pink and smiling, fresh from her bath. "Mommy Del needs her good-night kiss," he said.

Wendy leaned out and took Del's face between her small hands and kissed her on the lips.

"Sweet dreams, honey," Del said. "Did you let Daddy brush your teeth? Two minutes, with the music?" She looked at Jock. "The dentist said it needs to be for two minutes, remember."

"Oh, yes. We brushed an extra minute just to be sure," Jock said. He gave Roxanne a grin that said that maybe he was having some fun at Del's expense, humoring her.

"Good night, Wendy," Roxanne said.

She was charmed by the child's animated, round features that gave her the look of a Mary Cassatt moppet. While she worked primarily in clay, she thought she might do a drawing of Wendy sometime—something especially for Del—or maybe of Del and Wendy together.

Jock said, "Tell Roxanne what you named your bird."

Wendy blushed and hid her head against her father's neck. She said something, but no one could make it out.

"I don't think she heard you," Jock said, teasing. "Go on."

Wendy turned around and quickly said, "Roxanne." She hid her face again.

"Oh, that's so sweet," Roxanne said.

Del laughed and Jock looked pleased.

"Let's go," he said.

Wendy waved to them, giggling, as he carried her down the hallway.

Del and Jock stood in the open doorway to watch Roxanne walk out to her car.

"You should come next Friday," Roxanne said. There was an opening for another artist and his work at Gallery on the Square where she often sold her own artwork. "Maybe bring Alice?"

"Yeah. I haven't seen Thad in a while," Jock said. "He's a good guy."

"Maybe," Del said. "We'd have to get a sitter."

"Or we could just leave her with the bird," Jock said. "With her new name, it will be like having Roxanne here all the time."

For the briefest of moments, she imagined living in the picturesque house that towered over her—at five foot one, nearly everything towered over her—with Jock and Wendy and all the furniture and Del's spectacular jewelry and the sleek foreign cars in the garage and Jock's muscled body beside hers in the antique bed in the master suite. But then she thought of the mass of clay that was waiting in her studio at home, of what was waiting inside it that she, and only she, could free, and she knew that she had finally reached a point in her life where it wasn't worth taking things just because she could.

"Yes. Just like it," she said.

Roxanne liked coming home to her house in Kenwood. She parked in the driveway because the single garage was packed with her work—a few complete pieces, but mostly abandoned sculptures she couldn't bear to part with. Her clients all imagined that she lived in some chic downtown loft. Nobody ever guessed that she had a place in the suburbs.

The house itself was a small architectural treasure: a cedar-shingled Arts and Crafts–style bungalow with a long, deep porch and several original stained-glass windows. Iron-trimmed lanterns, also original, hung on either side of the front door. It was a friendly house, as unlike as it could be from the austere, blond-brick, postwar apartment building she'd grown up in on the unfashionable eastern end of Victoria Park. There, she had shared the lives of her neighbors (as well as her mother's, and her mother's many boyfriends) through beige, plastered walls. She much preferred to be separated from other people by grass and concrete and trees.

She hung her wrap on the wrought-iron tree just inside the front door and locked the door behind her.

Even when it was empty, the house was never silent. The water pipes groaned and the many windup clocks she'd bought over the years and put in every room ticked in competing rhythms, filling the air with a kind of busy energy, and, in the spring, there were the sounds of birds nesting in the chimney. But the sounds were ones she could live with— alone. They were a vast improvement on the noises of her childhood: the constant traffic outside the apartment, the muffled slamming of doors, the fat kid, Barry, from downstairs, who played his trumpet in the parking lot every afternoon after school, even when it was snowing. The sound she missed the least, though, was the sound of her mother's voice with its ridiculous girlish lilt that she'd cultivated over long years of practice. Roxanne had learned to avoid that voice, beginning when she was old enough to make her own meals and snacks and let herself in and out the front door with a key that she kept on a string around her neck. But tonight, Carla—she could only think of her mother by her first name, the name by which she had been taught to call her since she was four years old—was on her voice mail.

"Roxaaayenne, honey," she said. "Chet and I are coming into town for a few days, but I don't know if we'll have time to see you. So don't be mad if you see us out because it's not about you, honey. It's about Chet's business. So please don't be mad, okay?" Then she heard Carla talking away from the phone, telling her bichon frise, Twinkle, to stop digging in her purse. "By the way, honey, do you still have that black evening bag I lent you, sweetie? I'd like to—"

Roxanne clicked "3" to erase the message.

"Chet" was her new stepfather, a recent surprise. She hadn't yet met him. Carla had long prided herself on avoiding marriage, and had even refused, at the age of seventeen, to put the name of the famously married music promoter she claimed got her pregnant backstage at an All-man Brothers concert on Roxanne's birth certificate.

There was a second message from a sometime client from Denver who was coming into town *without* his wife. She liked the image that she knew he had of her: a free-spirited artist who was generous about letting him into her bed and never made any demands on his time or emotions. Plus, he was cute and always made sure she was just as satisfied in bed as he was. But she was busy and wanted to get some work done. She erased his message, too.

When she'd first bought the house, it had had an enormous rotting sunporch tacked onto the back of it, but she had it ripped down, along with the house's back outer wall, and built a studio with broad windows that looked over the two-acre-deep stretch of wood sitting beyond the backyard. It was almost midnight, but she felt the aching need to have tools in her hands and her fingers covered in clay. Work made her feel alive, and, after being with Del and Jock in their perfectly manicured house and having eaten Del's perfectly prepared meal, and admiring their perfectly perfect child, she needed to spend some time not thinking and not admiring, but just being herself.

In the studio she turned on all the lights so that the night outside the window disappeared and she was alone with her own image in the glass.

But she wasn't quite alone because the room was filled with clay figures, mostly birds, but several children as well, each paired with a bird of prey.

When she first planned the series, she hadn't known that she would make the children blind. But the first one's eyes turned out smooth and blank, and she knew it was right. Several clients and interviewers had asked her what the blindness signified, and for a long time she told them that she didn't like to read things into her own work, that she preferred that people discover their own meaning in it. But a few weeks earlier she'd glanced over an interview proof from a college alumni profile she'd been a subject of and was surprised to find that she'd finally given an answer:

"They're blind because there are some things that children should never have to see."

CHAPTER 4

Week 17

Alice let herself into the shadowed kitchen and turned the dead bolt behind her. Feeling like a teenager sneaking in after curfew, she leaned back against the door and listened to the muted sound of the television coming from the media room deep inside the house.

Thad was still awake.

She slipped into the powder room off the kitchen and turned on the light. In the mirror, her face, usually so pale, was pink and warm, heated by all the wine she'd drunk at the restaurant. Taking a lipstick—Tawny Rose—from her bag, she smoothed it on her lips, but instead of blotting it, she used a tissue to blur the edges. Perfection was the last thing she wanted. She mussed her hair, lifting and scrunching it with her fingers. She wanted to look used, a little rumpled and sensual, as though she'd just left her lover's bed.

There was no lover, of course. She was only pretending so Thad would be jealous. Roxanne had told her it was a stupid idea. But then, Roxanne pretty much hated all of her ideas, and had, well, since forever. She had always suspected that Roxanne didn't think she was very smart. It didn't matter, though. She still loved Roxanne.

The *pat-pat* of her footsteps echoed just a bit as she passed through the kitchen. Every surface in the kitchen was hard—even the seats of the chairs nestled around the table in the nook at the end of the room. Hard and modern and shiny and new. She had had it designed to her taste, now that her father was dead. Her mother had died back when she was in high school, and for years she and her father had kept everything in the house unchanged. Now, she missed them both, but missed her father particularly. They had been a kind of team after her mother died, frequently traveling and dining out together. Then she'd married Thad, and she'd even insisted that they move into the house when her father's health began failing. It was her opinion that he'd died so young—at sixty—of a broken heart.

Just outside the media room, she paused to inch her body-conscious skirt around her waist so that it hung off kilter. Maybe it was too much? She slid it back a fraction. With a smile that she hoped looked casual, she went inside. It was all in fun, this game. At least she tried to tell herself that. If she thought of it any other way, it made her too sad.

"You're up late," she said, speaking up over the noise of the gang fight on the television screen.

Thad. Sweet Thad, with his soft blue eyes, cowlicked blond hair, and vague, nearsighted look that never seemed to clear, even when he was wearing his glasses. In their wedding pictures—she'd had the best one copied many times and put in all the guest rooms and the living room—Thad looked stunned.

She was sure that Thad loved her for herself, in a way no one else ever had, but Roxanne had warned her that he was only marrying her for her money. It was the one time she could remember getting in an argument with Roxanne, and she'd come close to throwing her out of the wedding. But she hadn't. She couldn't stay angry with Roxanne for very long.

"The boy can't believe his luck," her father had said after the wedding, clapping Thad on the back.

Now, Alice wasn't so certain. Thad seemed to be moving away from her, away from their life together. She wanted him back. She wanted that slightly drunk, hesitant young man who had made love to her the night before their wedding, brought to her hotel room by a pair of former frat brothers who had given him a choice between Alice and a hooker. She had surprised herself by letting him in, and, almost eight years later, she still wanted him. They were married and that meant something, didn't it?

Thad looked up from his recliner, blinking slowly. On the television screen, blood splattered across the face of a teenage boy in a woolen cap, and he let out an agonized scream. Thad turned at the sound of it, seemed to consider for a moment, then paused the film.

"You're home," he said.

She crossed the room to drop a light kiss on the top of his head, wondering if he would notice her perfume, and went to sit where she was certain he could get a good look at her. She wasn't naive enough to think she was a natural beauty, but she'd had a little work done. Her colorist said she wasn't ready for an allover dye job, so her light brown hair shimmered with golden highlights. While her freckles were regrettable, they seemed to go with her blue-green (more green than blue) eyes and she had recently had her lips enhanced. Of course, the nose job had been important, too. But it was truly the clothes that made this woman, and she knew it. It was her personal theory that every woman should have a seamstress properly fit her clothes.

She sat at a coquettish angle in the chair, stretching out her legs a bit to show them to advantage. But Thad was looking again at the television.

Men think about sex for six seconds out of every ten, Roxanne had told her, and Roxanne knew men. *There's something wrong with him.*

"Those women just wouldn't shut up about that silly book," Alice said, with an exasperated sigh. "You'd think they'd never read anything else but cereal boxes."

Thad's hand crept toward the remote.

"I can tell you about it later," she said. "If you want." *Ask me where I've really been, whom I was really with. No one wears shoes like these for a book group!*

He picked up the remote and clicked the television off. A warm glow from the automatic, recessed lights spread over the room. "You obviously want to talk," he said. "Was it your book group?"

"Well, you know how they are," she said. "It's really just an excuse to drink some wine."

In truth, she'd drunk nearly a bottle of Pinot Noir by herself. And there had been no book group, just her, sitting alone at a table at Les Deux Freres.

"Don't go if you don't enjoy it," he said. "You shouldn't waste your time."

He didn't like other people to waste their time, though she'd observed that he wasn't above wasting his own. Witness the evening hours he spent in front of the television. But she knew that the young women in his practice—the hygienists and assistants and clerks—didn't spend much time goofing off or gossiping. At least she hadn't noticed them doing so when she occasionally dropped by the office. Sometimes, she thought that maybe she was a little afraid of them. They were all so purposeful. Watching them work made her feel useless and not much better than if she were some decorative object on a store shelf.

"It's just something to do," she said. Her hand slid down her calf to adjust the strap of her sandal.

His eyes followed the motion.

"Something wrong?" she asked.

He gestured toward her feet. "What's with the shoes? Have I seen those before?"

The shoes. They were beautiful shoes. Italian. Though there hadn't been much leather for the shoemaker to fashion, they were so spare and delicate. A single, narrow copper-hued band crossed over the top of her foot and another rose from the footbed near the front of the spiked, four-inch heel and wrapped around the back.

"Oh," she said. "I got them down on the Square. What do you think?" It was a jackpot kind of evening. He never asked her about her clothes or shoes. Sometimes, he commented on her jewelry if it was especially noticeable, like one of the larger pieces she'd inherited from her mother.

"I knew a girl in college," he said. "She called shoes like those f-m-p's."

"Pardon?" Alice said.

"You know," he said. "Fuck Me Pumps." He said it clearly and distinctly and she thought his eyes held some kind of challenge.

She laughed, nervous, but held his gaze.

"Did you?" she said. She felt her heart beat a little faster.

"Did I what?"

"Did you have sex with her?" Alice said. "Was she wearing shoes like these?" She stretched out one delicately shod foot toward him.

What the heck, she thought. Thad watched her without answering as she came over to his chair and climbed onto his lap, sinking her knees into the recliner's cushion. Her skirt hiked up to the rim of her panties, which were boy-cut but constructed wholly of stretchy peach lace.

"Alice," Thad said, leaning back, away from her.

Ignoring his scolding tone, she worked her fingers into his damp hair. He was prone to taking showers at odd times. Sometimes, he showered two or three times a day. And he always showered after sex. She kissed his forehead so that her breasts brushed against him.

"I'm glad you like my shoes," she whispered, saying the words against his skin, pushing her hips against his stomach.

"You weren't listening, Alice," he said. When he took her arms gently and put them away from him, she didn't resist.

"What's wrong?" she said. It was a question she was tired of asking. "Too bored? Too tired? Too angry?" She ticked them off on her fingers. "What is it?"

"You're drunk," Thad said. "I can smell it on you."

"If you could do it with her, then why not me? It's not like you're going to get me pregnant or anything," she said. She couldn't keep the spite out of her voice.

"We're done here," Thad said. "I'm sick of your bullshit, Alice."

The chill in his voice alarmed her. It was as though she'd come home to find another man in Thad's place. They had had their disagreements, but nothing she had ever said had caused a reaction like this one. And he had never before cursed at her.

He started up from the chair, which sent her tumbling off his lap. But her shoe was lodged in the gap between the chair and its cushion, and when she pulled herself free, she slid to the floor. They both heard her skirt rip up its back seam.

At a different time in their lives they might have laughed, but now Thad's face wore a look of disgust that made her feel sick inside. Sick and angry.

Still, he reached out his hand to help her up. "Get up and stop acting like a brat."

Later, she would feel sorry and wonder how she could have done such a terrible thing (of course, he had certainly driven her to it), but at that moment, she wasn't thinking of the future. Closing her hand around the shoe, she drove its heel as hard as she could against his temple.

Thad fell back into the chair, grabbing at the side of his head, his glasses pushed to one side of his face. Though he wasn't screaming, and, in fact, wasn't making any sound at all, he was obviously in pain. She still held the shoe, as though she might hit him again, but her anger was suddenly gone. She couldn't believe what she'd done. She got up off the floor to try to help him, wanting to take it all back.

"Oh, my God! Thad," she said. "I didn't mean to!"

"Get the hell away from me," he said, pulling off his glasses. He squeezed his eyes shut. "Just get the fuck out."

She took a step toward him. "Let me—"

He stood up and grabbed her by her upper arms and she could feel the power in his hands. She knew at that moment that she was in some kind of danger, that he could easily kill her. It was there in his eyes. Was that what she wanted? Was she so miserable that she didn't care?

"You hate me, don't you?" she said.

The anger left his eyes and they almost looked tender to her, which gave her a second of hope. A thread of blood inched from his temple to his cheek.

"You're pathetic," he said. He pushed her away so that she stumbled backward a few steps. "Just get out, Alice," he said.

When she hesitated, afraid, he shouted at her. "Get out!"

She turned and fled to her room.

Alice sank down into the tub, the water lapping at the rounded tip of her chin. She'd had too much wine, but the shock of the past hour had brought her to a strange state of awareness.

It wasn't her fault their life was falling apart. All she'd wanted was a child. One child. But nothing had worked: the surgery, the hormones, the drugs. The endometriosis was still painful and the scarring massive. The unfairness of it all was starting to get to her. Del had Wendy and was planning more children with Jock. Roxanne—well, she still could. It wasn't fair! She wanted only what was due to her.

Before their wedding, they'd agreed that they both loved children. Then he began working long hours, wanting to get rid of the debt from dental school. But, thanks to her father's death, the loans were all paid off, so they started trying. For three years, they had tried to repair and heal her treacherous insides.

Then he started having trouble sleeping and told her he didn't want to disturb her and moved into another bedroom. He was slipping away, and she was powerless to do anything about it. He didn't love her anymore because of what she couldn't give him.

When the bath cooled, she got out and pulled the old-fashioned rubber stopper from the drain. She crossed her arms, massaging her triceps with her fingertips. Never in their marriage had Thad laid a hand on her in anger. As she dried herself—dried the body she'd worked so hard to take care of, to improve, the body that had become so useless to them both—loneliness settled over her.

She lay down on her bed, her head pounding. It seemed like a hundred years before that she'd lain in a different bed in the enormous house, isolated and afraid to make new friends. Back then, Roxanne had become her friend. Roxanne had rescued her, even when she was just six years old. Roxanne, who'd even fancied herself a kind of witch when they were young, had fixed a lot of things. But Roxanne couldn't fix this. She felt herself falling into despair, which she knew was the worst of sins. Thad definitely wasn't coming to her tonight. After what she'd done, he might never again.

She rested her cheek on the pillow, and listened to the traffic passing on the road between the house and the park. She closed her eyes.

What if? Her favorite game.

What if one of the cars out on the road slowed and pulled into the driveway? What sort of car would her lover drive? She hadn't thought of that before. She decided it would be sleek and black, like her lover's hair.

What if he looked like an angel?

Hadn't she had enough of angels long ago? She remembered the other angel, the one who had almost ruined their lives.

But she couldn't stop herself. She pressed her hand between her legs and felt the warmth spread through her. This angel wasn't pale and golden, like an angel in paintings, but like Michael, the Archangel, an avenging angel with a strong-boned face and dark, serious eyes. Eyes that would read her so completely, that would look so far into her soul, that she might feel ashamed at what he saw there.

What if his body were heavily muscled, with a hint of strain at his shirtsleeves? A man with scars, perhaps. A man who had lived.

What if he chose her out of all the other women in the world that he might have?

He would let himself into the house with the key she'd given him, and perhaps even walk past the media room, causing Thad to turn his head, listening, uncertain if someone had been there or not.

He would make his way up to her bedroom and stand in the doorway, watching her, wanting her. And she would be waiting.

CHAPTER 5

Week 17 1/7

In the bathroom Thad peeled back the bandage from his temple. The wound was no worse than one he might have gotten as a kid, messing around. Overnight it had changed from a throbbing mess to a yellow bruise with a web of dried blood and skin at its center. He touched it gingerly, and decided to leave it unbandaged. There would be questions at work, but he knew he could make something up.

If there had ever been a moment in their marriage when he had wanted to kill Alice, it had happened last night. Why hadn't he killed her? Because he was smart, and because he had too much to lose. Whatever had held them together, tenuous for so long, had finally snapped. He was free.

It didn't take him long to get cleaned up and to throw a few things in the carry-on bag he kept beneath the bed. A couple of his favorite shirts and some khakis, a navy sport coat, workout gear, his leather toilet kit (a long-ago gift from his father-in-law—venal bastard that he'd been, he'd had good taste), as well as his passport, an envelope of cash he kept in the inner pocket of a once-worn white dinner jacket, his Ruger 9mm (not out of need, but to keep it the hell away from Alice in case she got ideas), and the framed snapshot of Pilot, the Irish setter he'd owned when he'd married Alice. Why shouldn't he have believed her when she'd told him Pilot had pushed past her to jump out of the car in the grocery store parking lot and run off? He'd been that sort of dog. Lovable, but capricious.

Downstairs, the house was quiet. Alice, he knew, would be upset, embarrassed for a few more hours. She'd probably taken a sleeping pill. But he stashed the carry-on in the stairway leading to the basement and garage beneath the house, just in case. It wasn't so much that he wanted to leave without her knowing, but that he wanted to keep it to himself. He wanted to savor it.

He made coffee and poured himself some cereal. It was a celebratory day, one that called for steak and eggs and biscuits and gravy—the chicken gravy his grandmother had often made would really have hit the spot. He imagined for a moment making such a breakfast, waking Alice, seeming to forgive her, then not coming home that evening, leaving her more confused than she already was. The idea appealed. He thought of Alice lying in her bed, alone, her skin cool to the touch (her skin always seemed cool when he touched her—Alice had no warmth). He could wake her with a kiss, startling her, reassuring her. It would be almost like old times, when he'd been blinded by her father's money into thinking she was a real woman, a woman he could hold. In the end, though, he couldn't stand to hold Alice. Holding Alice was like trying to caress a stick—a beautifully dressed, manicured stick. Tucking into his cereal, he decided that he wasn't that much of an asshole, no matter how many times she'd treated him like a servant, sending him back out to the car to fetch her wrap, telling their friends that Thad just didn't understand that it was hard, hard, hard growing up with money, that it gave a person certain obligations. No, he wasn't such an asshole.

He wouldn't miss this house, with its dignified little shrines to Alice's dead parents, the pseudo-casual studio shots of Earl and Sheila Lambert, with a young, whey-faced Alice crammed between them. He wondered if Alice would have turned out better if the stout, smiling Sheila had lived.

"Do you still love me?"

Alice had crept halfway down the kitchen stairs and was leaning over the railing, wearing only a bra and underwear. Her hair was mussed from sleep, and her eyes were red. She was human, he knew, but he couldn't scare up a spit's worth of sympathy for her.

He finished rinsing out his cereal bowl and put it, with his coffee cup and spoon, into the dishwasher. Old habits die hard.

"Let's talk about it tonight," he said.

She ran a hand through her hair. She'd become so thin that her collarbone stood out and her small breasts sank away from their bra cups. He could hardly stand to look at her.

"You want to go to dinner tonight? I'm sorry, you know," she said. "Really sorry."

Sorry for being insane? Sorry for sucking up almost eight years of my life? Sorry for making me feel like a pissant loser? Pick one, sweetheart.

"I'll be home at six-thirty," he said.

"Thaddy still loves Alice?" she said. She'd slipped into the little-girl voice she'd often used when they were first married.

"Of course," he said. So easy. Automatic.

He wasn't one of those dentists who liked to cause people pain, even though, for most of his patients, it was their own fault that they had holes the size of the Grand Canyon in their teeth.

Madge, the best dental assistant in Hamilton County, sat on her stool across from him, irrigating the mouth of a college-age young woman who—from what he could smell, even through his mask—hadn't bathed in several days.

"Hm," he said, looking into the girl's mouth when Madge had finished. "Hey, hand me a number twenty-three explorer, would you? I want to make sure this is nice and clean in here." He paused, checking the tooth again with the mirror. "So these two nuns were talking, and the first nun says, 'I was tidying up Father Murphy's room, and, would

you believe—saints preserve us—I found a pile of dirty magazines?'
Then the second nun says, 'Oh, my. What did you do, Sister?'"

Madge rolled her eyes at him. He tried to keep his jokes fresh, but
they were together four, sometimes five, days a week, and it got tough
to remember which he'd already told. "I've told you this one?"

Madge nodded. "Go on," she said.

He continued scraping the decay out of the girl's tooth, liking the
feeling of accomplishment it gave him.

"The first nun says, 'Why, I threw them out, of course!' Then the
second one says, 'When I was cleaning out Father's room, I found a box
full of condoms.' And the first one says, 'That's terrible, Sister! Did you
throw them out?'" He glanced at the girl's face. She wore thick black
eyeliner without mascara and had a pierced eyebrow. "Have you heard
this?" he said.

The girl shook her head slightly. It didn't matter what she thought,
really. She was stuck here in this chair and had to listen.

"The second nun says, 'No, of course not, Sister. I poked holes in
them!'"

The girl in the chair groaned.

"He's in rare form today," Madge said.

Thad pushed back on his stool and pulled down his mask. "Madge,
you're the love of my life," he said. "Let's wrap it up so this young lady
can get on with her day." As Madge prepped the amalgam, he checked
the schedule taped on the wall. With any luck, and no emergencies,
they'd be finished by four o'clock.

Amber, one of his two hygienists, looked in the doorway. Her lightly
freckled face was framed by strawberry blond hair pulled back in a regulation ponytail. There was a freshness about her that never seemed to
fade no matter how long the day got to be.

"You better be careful about those priest jokes," she said. "Father
Johansen's coming in for a cleaning today."

"Father Johansen loves me," he said. "He tells the dirtiest jokes in
town. And Amber." As he took in her bright green eyes, he had to force
himself from letting them slide down her body, lithe, even with its just-

noticeable pregnancy bump beneath her penguin-dotted smock. "Tell Jennifer to order lunch for everyone from Immos. My treat. Salads, too."

"You've got it," Amber said. "Oh, and Mrs. Turner's ready in four." She smiled and turned to go back down the hall.

"There goes my diet for today," Madge said. "What's the occasion?"

"No occasion," he said.

A boy with a broken tooth from a skateboard spill was the only emergency, but it was still almost five o'clock before he got out of the office. He and Madge and Liza were the only ones left—he didn't make the others stick around, even though any one of them would have. His staff's loyalty was something he was proud of.

He found a parking space in the alley beside Wildeflowers, the florist on Victoria Square, and left the car running while he ran inside. It was a risky thing to do, he knew, but he felt like nothing could touch him today. No car-thieving punk, no nosy cop. Today was his day.

The bells on the door jingled behind him as he stood at the counter paying for the enormous bouquet of small-headed sunflowers he'd come for. The saleswoman glanced up and nodded to whoever had come in.

"Thad, buddy." Someone clapped a heavy hand on his shoulder.

Thad turned to see Jock Connery grinning above his Brooks Brothers club tie and khaki blazer. Jock's smile seemed to announce that his life just couldn't get any better.

"What's up, Jock?" he said, amused at Jock's hearty, firm handshake.

"Hey, what's up, Doc?" Jock laughed at his own joke, a joke Thad heard way too often. "We didn't get out of this hellhole once this summer. Can you believe it? What about you and Alice?"

"Every mother wants her kids at the dentist before school starts," Thad said. "It was a no-go for us, too."

"I haven't bought Del flowers in months," Jock said. "But I screwed up and forgot the anniversary of our first date. Picked up a bracelet, too." He slid a miniature Tiffany-blue box from inside a jacket pocket. "What are you in for?"

Thad signed the credit card receipt the saleswoman offered and made a mental note to shut down his credit cards and open new ones that Alice didn't have access to. It wasn't likely that she'd try to hit him there, but, really, he didn't know what to expect. He glanced at his watch. Five-thirty. She'd be getting ready for him, probably was in full makeup already.

"Independence Day," Thad said, picking up the bouquet.

Jock's eyebrows came together, giving his face a bunched, uncomfortable look. "You're a couple months late for that," he said.

Some look must've passed over Thad's face that Jock recognized. He wasn't one of the city's most aggressive divorce lawyers for nothing.

"Shit," he said. "No shit."

Thad didn't say anything. He wanted to get out of there, but he was, strangely, enjoying this moment. If someone like Jock knew, then it was really happening.

"Man, I always know," Jock said. "I mean, I'm sorry to hear it, Thad. You and Alice. You two seemed solid. We were just talking about having you two over the other night." He paused as though he might go on, but didn't.

Thad knew what he was thinking. Alice couldn't fool anyone. She looked good, even acted normal most of the time: attending luncheons, working on the occasional committee, volunteering with The Literacy League. But no one really liked to be around Alice. He had just pretended the longest.

"It happens," Thad said. He shifted the flowers into his other hand, feeling a little dopey to be standing there with them. The movement caught Jock's eye. At the full realization of what they were—Thad obviously hadn't bought them for himself—Jock's face got a shade redder.

"Listen," he said. "You call me when you want something handled. Del may fuss, but I'm your man. Right?" He waved the saleswoman over, signaling the end of their conversation. "You just let me know."

...

Although the house was in Mt. Adams, it wasn't one of the expensively renovated ones with an unobstructed view of the Ohio. Its only view of the river and the opposite shoreline was from a tiny alcove window on the third floor. But there was a frequent breeze on the hillside, even on the hottest of days, which made it pleasant.

Mt. Adams was a village within the city, with narrow, curving streets and colorful houses that crowded together as though trying to make room for everyone who wanted to live there. People walked in the evenings or sat on their porches—at least the ones who hadn't renovated their houses to the point of unfriendliness, with enclosed patios and rooftop gardens. Even though he'd been coming up here for more than a year, he hadn't dared to show his face in the village's trendy taverns, art galleries, or even a dry cleaners. Now, he didn't care.

He stood on the porch, noticing for the first time that it needed painting. He thought he might do it himself. Alice had laughed at him when he'd once suggested that he do some of the painting when they renovated the house after her father died. His suitcase rested on the boards beside him, the flowers were tucked beneath one arm, and the house key was in his hand, but he hesitated. This was a big damned deal, he knew. He'd wanted it for so long, and here he was, where he thought he'd never be. *Be careful what you wish for.*

The door opened and Amber was there, a T-shirt stretched over her baby bump. He remembered they'd bought the shirt when they'd gotten away for an overnight at the B and B she loved down near Maysville. It was there that she'd told him she was pregnant.

"Look at you," she said.

He wanted to take her in his arms right there and make love to her on the porch, not giving a damn who might see. Instead, he held out the flowers. He had wanted his decision to leave Alice to be a surprise to Amber, and he had thought of a hundred ways to tell her, but now he didn't have the words. Seeing the smile on her face, he knew he didn't have to say anything at all.

CHAPTER 6

Week 17 1/7

Del stood in the cereal aisle at Wild Oats trying to figure out the difference between the four different kinds of organic cereal bars on the shelf in front of her. One of the cereal bars had nineteen grams of sugar, which seemed excessive to her—she might as well give Wendy sugar-coated corn flakes or a Pop-Tart. Another one had seventeen grams, but also contained high fructose corn syrup. What was it doing in an organic store? The third was gluten-free, which seemed a little disgusting—who knew what was holding it together?

Wendy sat in the basket of the grocery cart playing with a sticker book.

"These are furry cats, but some cats don't have any fur," she said, holding out the book. "Daddy says cats are smelly and they make BMs in a box."

"Yes," Del said, distracted. "Cats are furry."

"Hunter has a cat," Wendy said.

"Some people do," Del said. She picked up the fourth box. It had only eleven grams of sugar. She glanced at Wendy. Fresh blueberries tended to make her stool loose and grainy, and so she didn't feed her a lot of them, but a few in a cereal bar shouldn't be so bad. She put the box in the cart.

"Let's find some fish for dinner, shall we?" she said. "Cats love to eat fish."

Wendy had taken one of the cat stickers—a Siamese whose long brown tail she'd accidentally torn off—and wrapped it around her index finger. She knelt in the cart, waving her finger in the air and making meowing noises.

"Shhhhh," Del said. "Quiet meows, please."

They had forty-five minutes before Wendy's ballet class at Miss Trefford's Dance and Deportment School. She would be cutting it close if she took the groceries home first, and Wendy got fretful if she arrived at the dance studio to find that all the other girls were wearing their leotards and she was still in her street clothes. Once she had complained to Jock that Mommy Del had "hurried upped," causing her to fall down in the parking lot and scrape her hands and knees. That had been almost a year before, and Del was sure that Jock had probably forgotten it, but Wendy mentioned it every time they were running late for dance class. But if she didn't get home first today, the dairy stuff would spoil.

She looked at her watch. They would be okay if they got in line now. She would have to think of something else for dinner.

They were about to swing into a checkout when she almost ran the cart into one belonging to another dance class mother. *What was her name?* Del just thought of her as a Donna Karan Mommy. Her clothes were always casual, yet styled in sharp, chic lines and always in black or white or denim with the occasional dash of red thrown in for whimsy.

"Why, Miss Wendy," the woman said. She beamed a natural-hued lipstick smile at Wendy and bowed forward to speak directly to Wendy's face. "All ready for dance class? Trexie's at Mom's Morning Out, but she can't wait to get there."

Wendy stopped meowing and blinked at the woman, considering.

"We just have to get our groceries home and we'll be right there," Del said. Put-together women like Trexie's mother made her feel as though she might as well be wearing a faded housedress instead of the perfectly lovely clothing she was actually wearing. Unlike Roxanne and Alice, she'd never developed a strong style of her own (of course, Alice's was newly acquired and filtered through a personal shopper). Other women's clothes often looked like better ideas to her.

"Oh, I'm so glad I ran into you," the woman said. "I'm getting a little petition together to give to Miss Julie at the school. I think that four hours for a recital is just too long for these kids, don't you? I don't see why we should have to sit through twenty or thirty other performances, even if they are each only five minutes long. Wasn't it ridiculous last spring? I have it right out in the car. I think other people would be interested, too."

"Fine," Del said. "That would be fine."

"I just knew you'd agree," the woman said. "Maybe you could ask some of the other parents to sign it? After I drop Trexie off at class, I've got to scoot on to a meeting. Then you can just give me a call when you've talked to the other parents. Or just drop it in the mail to me."

"Mail it to you?" Del wasn't sure what the woman was talking about, but she was slowly realizing that she was being asked to do something. Although "asked" wasn't quite the word.

"You're a doll," the woman said. Then she pointed at the cereal bars in the cart. "I'm so impressed you can get Wendy to eat those things. It's all homemade food for Trexie. Mommy gets tired of making oatmeal or muffins every morning, but the darlings are so worth it, aren't they?" She wheeled the cart into the next checkout lane. "I'll meet you in the parking lot!"

Del knew she should feel angry, that the woman had just dumped something on her that she didn't really have time to do. But, actually, she probably did have time. She told herself she was being too sensitive.

"Here, Wendy," she said. She picked up the box of inadequate cereal bars and handed it to Wendy. "Put this on the belt for Mommy Del."

. . .

"How was dance class today, sweetie?" Jock said, picking Wendy up from the floor. She allowed him to kiss her on the cheek, but then strained away from him. "What did you learn?"

"Put me down, Daddy," Wendy said. "I have to go see my bird." Reaching the floor, she turned and ran to the hallway. Del and Jock both listened as she made her way up the front stairs.

"It went great," Del said. "We were even on time." She didn't mention the petition in her purse. He would just tell her that she shouldn't let herself be taken advantage of. Although she knew he'd be right, she just hadn't seen a polite way to get out of it.

"Of course you were," he said, sliding his arm around her waist. "You're doing a lot better, and I'm very proud of you."

"There's just so much to do," she said. "I need more hours in the day."

He smiled. She knew he didn't actually think she had a lot to do, but that was okay. She finished snipping off the ends of the flowers he'd brought her and arranged them in a vase.

Wendy was in bed, and they sat talking over the remains of their dinner. She had found some shrimp in the freezer and put together a quick mix of tomatoes, oregano, garlic, feta cheese, and olive oil to serve on some pasta with the shrimp. Fortunately, she'd tossed a sourdough baguette into the shopping cart at the last minute before running into the Donna Karan Mommy. (She reminded herself to look up the woman's name on the dance class phone list.) But she hadn't eaten much. Jock had given her the bracelet—platinum with a diamond heart charm—before they'd finished their first glass of wine.

"I was just teasing about the anniversary of our date," she said. "I really wish you hadn't." Still, she couldn't keep her fingers off of the diamonds. She knew she didn't deserve such a gift, but Jock insisted that she have nice jewelry. There was a whole safe-deposit box full of his former wife's jewelry that would be Wendy's when she turned twenty-one, except, he'd told her, for the pearls she'd get at sixteen.

"I know. I just wanted the excuse," he said. When he took her hand and held it to his lips, she couldn't help but smile.

"Listen," he said. "I don't want to spoil our evening. Maybe you already know about this."

"What is it?" Her smile faded.

"It's about Alice," he said. "Alice and Thad."

"Did something happen to Alice?" She'd felt bad about her last conversation with Roxanne. Alice was a pain, but she was still their Alice. "Is she okay?"

"I'd say probably not," he said.

"Open it," Alice said.

"But it's not Christmas yet," Del said. It was the week before Christmas of their sophomore year and she hadn't yet bought Alice's gift. She only had about five dollars left in her Christmas envelope, and she knew Alice would expect something expensive. There was the new Janet Jackson album, but she didn't know if she could afford a CD. Maybe a cassette.

"I got it in Paris," Alice said. "I can't wait!"

"You're such a dork sometimes," Del said, embarrassed.

"I know, I know," Alice said. She was practically bouncing where she sat on Del's bed. She'd gained about five pounds on her trip, but she had a cute haircut and was wearing makeup that made her look older. Her bright coral cashmere sweater had a boat neck and extra-long sleeves that she had pushed up to her elbows. It wasn't flattering, but she was trying hard.

The box was pink, with a black velvet ribbon. Del untied the ribbon, setting it aside for her mother's gift-wrap supply box, and lifted the lid. When she laid back the finely striped tissue paper, she found a sweater just like the one Alice was wearing. She took it out and held it to her chest. The cashmere was as soft as her baby brother's curls.

"I got one for Roxanne, too," Alice said. "They had a hard time finding one small enough, but they finally did. Do you like it?"

"Thanks, Alice," she said. "It's amazing." There was no way she was going to wear it—at least not at the same time Alice was wearing hers. Still, she didn't want to hurt Alice's feelings. She was afraid that maybe Roxanne wouldn't be so nice about it.

But she was wrong.

That next Friday night, they planned a sleepover at Alice's house. Individually, they felt they were too old for sleepovers, and they weren't spending so much time together as they once had. It was Alice's idea.

She told them she wanted to drive over to the mall Cineplex to see a movie, but Roxanne insisted they go to the rep theater in Oakley to see Rear Window. *Even though she had it on VHS, she wanted to see it for real in the theater, and she told Alice that she wouldn't go along with the whole wearing-matching-sweaters thing if they went to the mall.*

Del was torn. She was uncomfortable enough about the matching sweaters—and wearing them at the mall would've been a complete disaster. So she was grateful to Roxanne for that reason. But she didn't want to see Rear Window. *It had been a couple of years since she'd last watched it with Roxanne, and she found it hard to believe that Roxanne would still want to be reminded of it.*

Alice paid for the popcorn that she shared with Del. Roxanne wasn't eating. In fact, Del hadn't seen her eat anything all day.

During the film, Alice kept whispering, commenting on what was on the screen until a woman in the row in front of them turned around and told her to be quiet. Alice made a face at her but kept quiet until they got to the part where the dog started digging in the garden.

"That's where the body is," she said in a stage whisper. It was as though she'd never seen the film before, when Del knew for certain that she had. "I bet that's where the body is."

"Be quiet, Alice," Roxanne said, loud enough for everyone around them to hear.

Afterward, Alice pouted. Even as they sat in Denny's, drinking coffee, she was bitchy, saying that she didn't understand why she wasted her time on them, why she'd even gone so far as to buy them sweaters that they probably didn't like anyway.

When she huffed off into the bathroom, Roxanne grabbed Del's wrist.

"Let's go," she said.

"What do you mean?" Del said.

"Let's just leave her here. She's acting like a brat."

"She's got the car," Del said. "That would be stupid."

But she let Roxanne lead her outside.

They stood in the parking lot, just out of the line of sight from the table where they'd been sitting. Roxanne lit a cigarette and they shared it as they watched.

Alice came out of the bathroom, still looking irritated. She paused in front of the table and looked around. When Del saw her even look beneath the table for them, she laughed smoke out of her nose, which led to a coughing fit.

Then Alice sat calmly for a few minutes. She took a compact and some lipstick from her purse and opened both. The waitress came over with the check and left it on the table.

"We should go back in," Del said. It was cold outside, and it had been warm in the restaurant.

"Probably," Roxanne said. But she didn't move.

After another minute or so, they saw a man slide out of his booth and start walking toward Alice. He was much older, maybe as old as Del's father, and wore a kind of uniform shirt with a name patch over one pocket that Del couldn't read. His dull brown hair looked oily and his jeans were a couple pounds too tight so that a tiny pooch of belly and shirt formed a kind of puffy ring around the top of his jeans. If his beard hadn't been so rough, as though he hadn't shaved for three or four days, Del would've guessed he was Joe Working Guy stopping in after his shift at the mattress plant up the road. But it was the look on his face that scared Del. He seemed to be trying very hard to act friendly, normal.

Alice looked up at him, startled, when he stopped at her table. As they talked, she fidgeted with her napkin.

Then, to Del's total surprise, Alice smiled, and indicated to the guy that he should sit down in the chair Del had vacated.

Roxanne sighed. "All right," she said. "We better go back in."

Del didn't say so, but she thought leaving Alice alone to be preyed on in the restaurant was one of the cruelest things they'd ever done to her.

...

Del lay in the triangle of light coming from the bathroom listening to Jock brushing his teeth. They had made love, just as they always did on Tuesday and Thursday nights—a habit they had quickly fallen into after the wedding. She didn't like to ask herself if that had been his schedule with his dead wife.

What was Alice doing tonight? Had she realized yet what was happening? Had there been a scene? She had probably called Roxanne. There was so much to know—and yet she didn't really want to know. Jock hadn't said it, but she knew he thought Alice had it coming. He just didn't know Alice like she did.

Jock slipped back into bed beside her and she snuggled against him. The sex with him was good—much better than it had been with any other man, though she didn't have all that many men to compare him to. Only her first husband (rough, frequent, impatient, often painful) and three or four guys back in college (repetitive, brief, vaguely ridiculous if not drunken). But tonight she knew she needed more, and it wasn't simply because she hadn't had an orgasm. The want felt serious, deep; it pressed against the tender, melting places inside her. She wasn't sure if it was desire for Jock, or the desperate fear of being in the same place that Alice was at this moment: Alone. Unwanted. Unloved.

She turned her body toward him and slid her hand up his thigh to touch him, gently, at first. But there was no response beneath her hand and she realized he was lying perfectly still and looking at her.

"What is it?" she said, pulling her hand back.

It was dark enough that she couldn't quite see the look on his face.

"You surprised me," he said. "That's all."

"I'm sorry," she said. She realized in that moment that she had almost never taken the initiative with him. Had she ever? No.

"It's okay," he said. He turned onto his side, facing her, and stroked her hair. "I'm just kind of done for the night."

"Of course," she said. "I'm sorry." But there was a small part of her that wasn't a bit sorry, that screamed, begged, pleaded, and scolded her, that told her she shouldn't have to be sorry. It felt as though she were being denied something she deserved. She knew it was foolish to think she deserved sex when she wanted it. There was no deserving about it. It had to be mutual, didn't it? It didn't matter so much if she played along sometimes when she didn't quite feel like it. She told herself it was no big deal, and tried not to be ashamed.

"I love you," he said. He kissed the tip of her nose. "Sleep well."

She would have to wait until Thursday.

CHAPTER 7

Week 17 4/7

"Roxanne, I want you to see the beaches on Jekyll Island."

"Roxanne, let's meet for lunch and talk about a piece for my place in Vail."

"Roxanne, I'm renovating a studio in Over-the-Rhine. I want your opinion on the decorator."

Sometimes, she thought she would go mad with the voices of men.

Balanced on the arm of an uncomfortable chair in a corner of the gallery, nearly encircled, she felt like a bohemian Scarlett O'Hara. Only this wasn't *Gone With the Wind,* and she wasn't pining over some wimpy Ashley Wilkes. What she was was bored. Alice had tried to talk her into blowing it off and going to dinner. But all Alice wanted to talk about was how mean Thad was, and all she could think to reply was "I told you so." The gallery was overfull—unbelievably so for some random ceramicist from Indiana—and she was getting warm. Worse, Del and Jock hadn't shown up.

"Tag, honey, would you get me a water?" she said to one of the several men standing in a semicircle around her chair. "Maybe with a twist of lime?"

Tag Murray, a real-estate developer almost twice her age, winked at her—she'd chosen him, after all, to do something special for her—and moved away toward the bar set up on the other side of the room.

She had no biblical knowledge of Tag Murray, though he was constantly hinting that he wanted to change that. His wife, Gretchen, was sweet even if she was kind of homely, and she was on the board of some foundation that had expressed serious interest in a particularly large piece of her work, so she didn't encourage him. Also, he had a moustache, and she disliked kissing men with moustaches.

The other two men, Jack Lamb and Terry—she could never remember his last name—were fairly new to her, but they were both so busy comparing stock portfolios as they tried to impress her with their wealth that she thought she might have to send them to separate corners.

She didn't bother to hide her relief when Colwyn Spenser, the gallery owner, caught her eye. Colwyn always made her smile. He was a wit and had a schoolmarmish way of holding a finger to his pursed lips when he was trying to make a decision, whether he was judging the artwork of some hopeful painter or purchasing a tie. Alarmingly tall—almost six and a half feet—Colwyn's skin was darker than she could ever have imagined skin could be, and he was always dressed with care. His round, wire-rimmed glasses sat on a nose that was prominent, patrician-thin, and he kept his white hair trimmed close. She assumed the white hair was premature, but she had no more idea of his age than she did his sexual preference. Her assumption was that if she thought a man might be gay, he probably was. But although Colwyn had a queen's fastidiousness about him, he appeared to be completely asexual.

"Excuse me, gentlemen," she said, getting up. "The master calls." She brushed Terry's arm with a light hand. No need to leave him too disappointed.

"You looked like you were about to nod off," Colwyn whispered, leading her away.

As they passed Gretchen Murray, Roxanne smiled at her. She was wearing a particularly unbecoming shade of raspberry lipstick and one of those handmade jackets covered with bits of patchwork and dangling threads that some fraud was selling for a stupid amount of money out of a Montgomery Road boutique. Roxanne knew the artist's work. She also knew that the woman had started out styling mannequins for Kmart.

"Why don't you take a little time out?" Colwyn said when they got to his office. "The wolves are certainly prowling tonight. You do look delicious."

"You're so good to me," she said, putting her hand on the door-knob.

She trusted Colwyn. Born to old-school painters—a portraitist and a landscape painter—he knew a lot about artwork as well as the art business. When she'd visited his loft to talk about him representing her, she'd seen his paintings: massive, highly textured pieces that seemed to emit their own soft, Mediterranean light. It was as if that light were a reflection of Colwyn's deep-seated goodness. He seemed almost egoless to her, and was probably the best person she knew.

Now, his brows came together in a mild scowl. "You need to take better care of yourself," he said. "You're spending too much time in that studio of yours."

It was so nice to have someone looking out for her. She lifted up on her toes and he bent down so she could kiss his cheek. He gave a damn about what happened to her, and that made her happy.

Later, much later, she wouldn't remember the moment she met him. She would hardly remember him at all. But when she opened the office door and saw him standing there, she had no thoughts of later, only that moment.

"Roxanne," he said. "I'm Varick. I've been wanting to meet the woman who created *Peace*."

He took her hand from her side and held it in both of his. Like most people, he had to bend a bit to touch her, but she hardly noticed, the move was so quick and effortless. Disarming.

She looked back to see if Colwyn was there, but he had moved back into the gallery.

For a long moment, she had nothing to say in return, and just stared. Had she seen him before? Maybe in a magazine or on the news? He spoke with an accent, perhaps central European. His chestnut silk sport coat was expensive, but slightly rumpled, as though he'd been wearing it all day. Dark black hair, as black as her own, fashionably long, but neat. Eyes that watched her, expectant. But beyond the expectancy, she couldn't read them. She didn't like that.

"Where did you see it?" she said, taking her hand away from his. But she could still feel his touch on her skin.

She'd worked on and off for almost six months on *Peace,* the first sculpture she'd done in the child/bird series. The child knelt with a red-tailed hawk perched on its knee, claws digging into the child's skin. But the child held a rope taut around the bird's neck so that the bird seemed to strain against it.

"It's in my private collection," he said.

"I don't think so," she said.

"A piece doesn't always stay in the hands of the original purchaser."

Peace had sold to Larry and Rachel Rothwell, a St. Louis couple who had a massive folk art collection; they'd bought the twelve-thousand dollar piece for their son, who obviously had sold it. She remembered the son as not particularly smart. He lived with his fiancée in a massive Upper East Side Manhattan apartment owned by his parents. It was his fiancée who had found *Peace* at a show Roxanne had had in Hell's Kitchen. She wondered if they'd sold it for drugs or debt or just out of boredom.

"Do you want to see it?" he said. "Do artists enjoy viewing their own work once it's placed, or are you like a writer who never wants to see what she has in print because she wants to fix what isn't perfected?"

"Is it here? In town?" she said. She was curious, wondering how he displayed it. Was it among other pieces or shoved into a dark room, by itself? She thought of her sculptures that way—almost worried about them. Her hands had given them life. If she didn't need the money to live, she might never let them go.

Something about this man made her defensive. She prided herself on being able to read people, to see through to their emotions, but she couldn't see anything of him at all behind his eyes. There was something disturbingly familiar about him—not his looks, or his manner, but something else. She had a feeling deep in the pit of her stomach that was like a memory.

"May I call you?" he said. "Perhaps I can convince you to come and see it in its new home. We can have dinner."

She noticed the faint scar in the shape of an arrowhead on his cheek. A childhood accident, maybe? A champagne glass flung by some angry woman?

Taking a square of notepaper from Colwyn's desk, she wrote down her cell phone number. As she held the paper out to him, she half-wanted him to touch her hand again so that she might get a better sense of him. But he took the paper by its edge and eased it into his pocket. In return, he gave her a card with his first name and a last name with a lot of consonants in it.

"Thank you for your time," he said. He was out the door of the office before she could respond.

She looked after him for a moment, then ran a finger over the back of the card. It was expensive beige stock, and engraved. Who carried engraved cards these days?

When she emerged from the office, she found Tag Murray and Jack Lamb waiting near the door. Tag smiled, holding out the water she'd asked for and looking as though he expected her to pat him on the head.

But she found herself wanting to be hurtful to this man who was so obviously desperate for her approval. There was a tension inside her that needed relief, even if it was only the small relief that minor cruelty could provide.

She rested her hand on Tag's arm and got close enough to him that, as she whispered up to him, her hair fell in a languid stream across his sleeve.

"I really don't have time to play games with you, Tag, and I don't think I want to," she said.

Not bothering to check the look on his face, she continued on across the gallery and out the door. If she expected to see this Varick person outside—and she told herself she didn't—she was disappointed. A different man stood beside a parking meter about twenty feet away. He was shorter than Varick and wore a sweatshirt with a hood draped close about his face, but he quickly turned away when he saw Roxanne looking at him. *Pervert.*

The idea of hanging around the gallery no longer appealed. She headed for her car with the thought that she might stop somewhere else on the way home and order a decent glass of wine.

CHAPTER 8

Week 17 4/7

Why did everyone in the restaurant seem to be staring at her?

Alice opened her menu, not really paying much attention to the words printed on the fragile paper inside the tired, leather-trimmed cover. She always had the same thing, anyway.

Two businessmen drinking what looked like scotch checked her out as they pretended to have a conversation. Did they think she was blind? Stupid? And the underdressed woman at the next table had her eye on the sweet ostrich handbag resting at the left of Alice's plate. Alice glared at her, resisting the urge to do something wicked like sticking out her tongue, until the woman looked away.

Les Deux Freres was an old-school restaurant, dimly lit, with cherry-paneled walls and plush appointments: velvet-covered chairs and turn-of-the-twentieth-century paintings and servers in crisp black-and-white uniforms. Her father had brought her here for every birthday since she was six. As a child, seated with him (and her mother before she died) in the main dining room, eating cake with ganache and chocolate shavings, she'd felt like a princess.

Tonight she needed to talk. She needed Roxanne, even if all she was going to hear (again!) was that Thad probably wasn't coming back and she should get it over with and call a lawyer. But Roxanne was too busy for her. Roxanne had never, ever wanted a husband. Only lovers, and the more, the better. Alice and Del had been the ones who had, long ago, made and compared notes on the men they would marry.

But now she had lost Thad. She hadn't heard from him since he hadn't come home that night. Some of his clothes, his passport, and his secret envelope of cash (of course, she knew he had it, and had thought it kind of cute) were gone, along with his shaving gear and the picture of Pilot, that stupid dog.

When another five minutes passed, and none of the waitstaff gliding through the main dining area would catch her eye, she was ready to give up and go home. The gourmet shop, where she could pick up a slice of quiche and maybe a salad and perhaps a cold split of champagne, was open until ten. Thad didn't like her to drink champagne because he said it made her act like a teenager. Yes, a little lift was what she needed after such a tiresome, lonely day. She reached for her handbag.

"I think you'll like this Sauvignon Blanc."

Alice looked up. A man—not a waiter, surely, in that sport coat— put a glass of wine down in front of her, then put a second one at the other place setting. He pulled out the opposite chair and sat down.

"I see you haven't ordered yet," he said. "Good."

Alice smiled her most polite social smile. "Pardon me?"

But in the next second, looking at his face, she had to keep herself from crying out. She felt as if the chair beneath her might collapse, or, worse, suddenly disappear. She was certain that the man in front of her couldn't be real.

"I'm afraid you've mistaken me for someone else," she said, doing her best to keep her voice from shaking. Not a mistake. She knew it wasn't a mistake. She knew *him*. What a stupid game, Roxanne had said. Why make up a lover?

He gently took the menu from where it lay in front of her and opened it.

"This lighting in here is so poor," he said, glancing up at the chandelier with its several burned out bulbs. "I'm afraid Les Deux Freres has seen better days."

She knew the curve of his cheek, the sleek texture of his black, black hair. She knew the confident set of his mouth, the slight lift of his left eyebrow as a sign of his concentration. She knew these things because she had thought them into being.

"Is this some kind of joke?" she said, trying to put a hint of indignation in her voice. She suspected that she was not really in a restaurant, but dreaming in her own bed. But if it were a dream, she would have been expecting this man, her lover. If it were a dream, the service would be better, or she would have him, alone, in one of the restaurant's discreet alcoves with the curtain drawn, and they would be making love. She would be naked, astride him on the tufted velvet chair, her hands gripping the ornate back of the thing, the gilt fracturing beneath her fingernails. She blushed to think of it.

"If you don't leave me alone, I'll have the management ask you to leave. They might even call the police. I know someone who's with the police."

"You mean the young man who calls you once a year to extort fifty dollars for a sheriff's department sticker for your Lexus?" he said. "It won't get you out of any tickets, you know. He works in a boiler room in Enid, Oklahoma." He smiled.

Hearing his voice, looking at his eyes—though she found she couldn't quite look into them, she knew they were dark, rimmed with heavy lashes that would make any woman jealous—she was suddenly afraid. But why should she be afraid if he was the product of her own imagination?

"If this is a joke, I don't think it's a very funny one," she said. Her next thought was that he was a madman, someone who knew (how?) her dreams. She told herself to just get up and walk away. Then: *He knows my name.*

"Alice," he said, and her world turned on that single word. Such tenderness in his voice. No one had ever said her name in that way before, as though it were composed of something more precious than mere letters, or simple syllables. Coming from his mouth, her name sounded special, sacred. Had Thad ever said her name in such a way? Once? No. She thought of Thad as soft, and such tenderness in his mouth would have been repulsive. This kind of tenderness could only come from a man with enormous strength, and she was suddenly sorry that she'd thought him condescending.

I am just plain Alice, she wanted to say. Not Dream-Alice.

"Do you want me to leave?" he said.

But this only confused her further. He had cut through to her heart. The most dangerous place.

She nodded.

"Don't worry," he said. He took a quick sip of wine from her glass and put it back down in front of her. "It's just wine, Alice. It's really very good." He stood and laid the open menu down in front of her. So tall! She'd never thought of him being so tall!

His lips, warm against her forehead, were real enough.

Now, practically running up the interior stairs from the garage beneath the house, she felt like a girl again, ready for her first date. Any other night, she would've come inside cautiously, double-checking the alarm, making sure nothing had been disturbed. Tonight, she left the door unlocked, feeling a small thrill in her stomach as she did so.

What about Thad?

So many feelings. So new! This was what Roxanne had talked about—the excitement, the newness. Why shouldn't she have it for herself? Her next thought was to call Roxanne. What would Roxanne have done about the man? She'd have played right along, no doubt. Probably would've ended up with her bare foot in the man's crotch, playing lap hockey. She didn't have Roxanne's chutzpah, though, or her casual ways.

Varick was the name on the card she'd found on the table after he left. She tested the word in her mouth. It was a perfect name. Could she have made up such an amazing, mysterious name? And what was his accent? Whatever it was, it was wonderfully foreign. Sexy.

She stashed the clothes she'd changed out of to go to dinner in a hamper, and hung up the damp towel from her shower in the bathroom. Her feet felt warm and sticky in her sandals and she kicked them off and put them on a shelf in the wardrobe closet just off the bedroom.

In the bathroom, she brushed her teeth and swished some mouthwash. Thad couldn't bear the taste of mouthwash, even when he kissed her. Varick wouldn't care. Mouthwash would be the last of her lover's concerns.

"Varick."

His name filled her room. There was no question that he would come. She looked around. Would he prefer some other room? Maybe the formal living room downstairs with its enormous German and English antiques, her father's passion. She could picture him there. He would be at ease anywhere, of course. So cosmopolitan!

From her lingerie armoire, she took a gold peignoir set, a silky, fluid gown with hand-tatted lace at the bosom and a matching robe whose silk was so finely woven that one could see through it. She'd bought it in San Francisco, back in May, when she and Thad had traveled there for a cousin's wedding. Thad had wanted to spend the few afternoon hours they had free sleeping, but she hadn't wanted to go shopping alone. At first he had just followed her dutifully, reading a guidebook he'd picked up somewhere, but then he'd seemed to finally relax. Giddy with the energy of the city, the crowds, the charm of the place, they'd stopped for a glass of wine just before going back to the hotel where they made love. Had that been the last time? She was sure it had. She held the peignoir to her chest, fingering its satin trim, feeling the slightest bit guilty.

Should she?

"Varick."

She lay on her bed, listening to his footsteps coming down the hall toward her room. Resolute footsteps. She felt like a virgin bride on her wedding night; her entire body shook—not with a lover's anticipation, but with an excited, guilty fear.

Out of habit she'd closed the bedroom door, and the old knob turned with noisy protest beneath her lover's hand. For the briefest of moments, she worried that it wasn't her lover, but someone else who had come in the unlocked back door. Maybe Thad? She sat up.

But when the door opened, it was her lover's face that was illuminated by the candlelight flickering on the walls of the room.

In the morning, she woke with the sun on her back and her face pressed deep into the pillow. She knew she was alone before she opened her eyes. Her shoulders ached and her wrists and elbows were stiff and her body lay heavily on the bed. She felt as though she'd been dropped from a great height.

Pushing up off the pillow, she turned over. Around the room, the candles had burned down to nothing, with the exception of the one on the nightstand, whose flame seemed to float on a tiny sea of melted wax. Her mouth was dry, but there was only the empty champagne bottle near the candle. There had been something about the champagne bottle, but she couldn't remember, and thought that maybe it was better that she didn't.

The air conditioner wasn't running and the room was already warm. Two flies seemed to have discovered her left knee and buzzed lazily above it. When she sat up to brush them away, they spiraled off, chasing toward the open window.

She looked around for the diaphanous gold robe, but didn't see it anywhere. Her nightgown lay puddled on the floor. She got out of bed slowly, not yet ready to acknowledge the blue and green bruises on her thighs. Crossing the room, she saw herself, naked, in the mirror. Despite the bruises, which she couldn't see well in the mirror, she liked what she saw there. Her body seemed more substantial to her. No longer pale and sallow, it had a kind of glow she hadn't noticed before. *Happiness!* Surely, it was from the happiness her lover had brought her.

In the mirror, she saw the reflection of the robe, as well. Only it was no longer whole, but was tied in four ragged pieces to each poster of the bed where she now recalled being tied up.

A sly kind of smile came to Alice's lips and she did something she hadn't done in months and months. She giggled.

CHAPTER 9

Week 18 6/7

"You're going to like this, baby," said Malina. Or was it Ivanka?

For a while, Dillon had a system to tell which girl was which just by looking at their faces. But now he couldn't remember the system and didn't really give a fuck anyway. They were the same. Twins. Delicious, gray-eyed fucking twins like he'd seen only in magazines up to this point in his life. Had he been here in the loft with them for three days? A week? A month? He didn't really give a fuck about that either. It was all good.

He'd spent most of the previous night on the adjacent rooftop that had been converted—nicely converted—to a sprawling patio with a hot tub surrounded by teak furniture and small potted fruit trees. He and Malina had made good use of the double chaise. Yes, it was Malina, the one with the smiley-face tattoo on her inner thigh right there where he'd had to work to discover it. It wasn't a particularly convenient way to distinguish the girls, and, once, he'd thought he was in his bedroom with Malina, but found, in the dim light from the bathroom, that he'd been with Ivanka the whole evening.

"Goody time," Malina/Ivanka said.

There were goodies and there were goodies. Malina/Ivanka was smiling. She carried the silver tea box—at least that's what she'd called it—ahead of her like it was a birthday present. He could've gone to get the thing himself from its place on the table against the wall, but he was so fucking comfortable where he was on the leather nest of the couch that he didn't want to move. But it was as though she'd read his mind. He'd awakened a couple hours earlier (there were no clocks, but he thought it might be around two in the afternoon), and after a roll around the bed with Ivanka (he'd checked), a beer, and a plateful of the jelly doughnuts he'd come to like so much, he'd had a steam shower and was feeling just fine, ready for either a nap or some powdered white fun from the box-that-never-emptied.

Malina/Ivanka settled down beside him and spooned some coke onto the tabletop. It was so fine, so loose, that it didn't need chopping at all.

"Where's my buddy Varick?" he said. It spooked him the way Varick would show up in the middle of the day, or night, never hanging around for long, and never sharing in the goodies.

"Oh, you know how he is," she said, tossing her hair back to keep it out of the coke. "He gets busy." She did a small pile and handed the glass straw to Dillon.

"Ummmm," she said, lying back. She closed her eyes.

He'd noticed that the twins always looked perfect, as though they had a standby team of makeup artists inside the first bedroom, the door of which was always closed. They'd never invited him in, and it had never occurred to him to ask. What could be inside there to interest him? He needed only the girls themselves, their centerfold bodies: each pair of breasts an identical feast; juicy red lips, lips that couldn't seem to taste enough of his skin; and legs, impossibly long and firm, that twined around him to create a playful prison when the twins joined him in his bed. Every so often he asked himself what he'd done to deserve what he was getting.

He did his own pile of blow. As the burn penetrated the membranes of his nose, and, seconds later, his throat, he thought about Amber. He should call her. But he'd misplaced his phone, and there didn't seem to be one in the apartment. What if he called and Asshole Thad answered? Fuck Asshole Thad. Asshole Thad had stolen Amber from him. Before Asshole Thad, he and Amber had been close. Even when he'd lived out of town, she would call him every day to make sure he was okay. She needed him and he needed her.

Now there was going to be a kid, too. She would be tied to Asshole Thad forever.

When he felt the rush of the coke come on him, he knew he needed to do something about Asshole Thad. It could wait, for now. But he felt strongly—very strongly—that he could improve the situation. Asshole Thad could disappear, maybe. Amber would be sad for a while, but she'd get over it.

"What's the matter, honey?"

Malina/Ivanka stroked his forehead, which was still sore from the infection that wouldn't seem to clear.

"You look so mad," she said. "Are you mad at me?" She pushed out her lower lip into a pout. Malina/Ivanka was naked, and when she leaned back, shifting her leg, he saw the smiling tattoo. He decided that Malina was his favorite.

The only answer he gave her was a smile. Fuck Asshole Thad. He licked two fingers and used them to scoop some blow out of the open tea box. Then he spread Malina's legs farther apart and rubbed the blow on the exposed, tender place between her legs. She giggled and pulled him to her.

Varick hadn't come around in a few days, and Dillon was thinking that maybe it was time to go, that maybe he needed to leave this place because it was all just too good, too fucking delicious—when he found the rig and packet of heroin next to the jelly doughnuts in the kitchen.

He knew hopheads and didn't like them. They couldn't be trusted. There was a girl he'd known in high school, whom he'd seen at a house where he'd gone to buy some weed. She sat in the middle of a laid-out sofa bed in the living room, looking like six kinds of hell. Her long blond hair that had been so beautiful when he'd seen her in the school court-yard, always laughing, was dull and thin, and she had a look on her face like she'd spent the last month scared shitless and didn't know whether to move or not. The smell coming from the paper grocery bag beside her was definitely puke. When he said "hey" to her, she stared back at him like some kind of zombie. "Why isn't there any fucking Mountain Dew?" she finally said. No one answered her, and she didn't repeat it.

"It's too early in the morning for that," Ivanka said. (At least he thought it was Ivanka. She had put on the pink robe in his bedroom that morning.)

"Let's wait until after lunch," Malina said.

"I don't want that shit," he said. And he meant it at that moment.

Malina shrugged and the girls wandered off—Ivanka to the bedroom, and Malina to the patio.

He waited until the sun went down. They'd ordered in steaks and Varick had sent a messenger by with a couple of bottles of champagne of a kind that he'd never seen before. The label looked expensive, obscure. The girls had dressed in matching white dresses that clung to them like water, and Ivanka had penciled a deep brown beauty mark on Malina's cheek, telling him that it was a better way to tell them apart than fucking them. But she said it with a sly smile to let him know it was a joke.

Was it the champagne that broke him down, finally? He didn't know, didn't care.

Malina proved to be an expert with the H and the rig, getting a look of intense concentration in her brown eyes; her manicured fingers handled the cooking tools and the syringe with calm certainty.

"Ivanka, you do it with him," she said. Ivanka nodded, solemn. "But Dillon, honey, you get to go first."

The champagne had mellowed him, but he still felt nervous, virginal. Up to now, even when he'd been offered a joint with H in it, he'd turned it down. It wasn't the needle that the luscious Malina was offering that bugged him. He was used to needles. It was the crossing of that line—a line he'd set for himself, but hadn't known he'd set.

A person could die from too much delicious.

But it wasn't just delicious. It was Love. He wanted to weep (and maybe he did) because he'd never known what Love would feel like running through his veins.

He felt the Love every day. Sometimes, they did coke in the morning, but there was always Love in the afternoon. Like one of those soap operas his mother and Amber used to watch. But he was thinking less and less of the world outside. He was happy, here with the girls.

Dillon was dreaming. As in every dream he'd had since he came here, he dreamed of being alone in the loft. It was as though he'd never been anywhere else, never lived another life outside of here.

He was counting spoons, taking them out of the cutlery drawer and laying them out on the table according to size and pattern. Every utensil in the drawer had turned into a spoon: there were tablespoons and teaspoons and long-handled spoons like the kind he'd seen people use to stir iced tea; tiny spoons for coke, and souvenir spoons like you get at amusement park gift shops. The categories were getting complicated, and he was getting anxious.

He knew he was alone, but he felt like he was being watched, judged. Maybe even by that fucking creepy statue of the kid and the bird at the other end of the room. It was his job, and he had to do it just right because he knew there was some unspoken punishment he would suffer if he did it wrong. Then there was a subtle change in the light, and he looked up to see a shadow pressing against the skylight over the couch. And while he was looking up, he felt the spoon soften in his hand. It had turned into something gel-like, still cool. As he squeezed, it melted into his hand and disappeared. Not only was it painless, it felt good! He picked up another spoon, and another, absorbing each one, pressing them against his cheek, onto his arm, even against his tongue. If the spoons were gone, he reasoned, no one could tell him he'd done his job wrong or punish him.

He couldn't remember feeling so very fucking happy before! He knew that he had to tell the twins, to share his new trick with them.

Their door was closed, as it always was. But the realization that he could've opened it any time he wanted to came over him, pleasing him.

"Malinka," he whispered, cracking the door an inch or so. Why hadn't he thought of that before? Giving them one name would have solved his problem long ago.

The air pouring through the opening was cold, much crisper than the humid air conditioning in the rest of the loft.

"Pretty, pretty Malinka."

The cold burned his cheek. There was a sound, too, an uneven, sonorous hum as from a massive hive of bees. It wasn't right. He wanted to get back to the spoons, to feel good again, because he could feel the goodness slipping from him. He tried to close the door. There was nothing in the way, but he couldn't pull it to. The handle jerked beneath his hand, and the door flew open, revealing a blackness that he couldn't have imagined when he was awake and in the world.

Something brushed against his foot and he kicked out. "Motherfucker!" Then the floor was covered with blackness, an eddying, squeaking, suffocating blackness, and something poked up out of the flood: a rat's face.

The blackness grew into such a height in front of him that he was afraid to open his mouth and scream. He felt himself falling, pulled down by the tide, and understood that he would be eaten clean to the bone, and the fear of it was unbearable in his chest and the fear finally woke him.

A sharp rectangle of light cut through the curtains and fell across the bed, stopping just short of its edge and the figure standing there. Somehow he knew that the twins were gone and that he would never see them again.

"Get up, my friend," Varick said. "It's time to go."

There were jobs he could have that would be worse than working for Varick.

But in addition to his new job, he also now had a constant jagging in his head and veins that could be soothed only by the thrill juice that was in short supply now that the twins were gone. Varick was jerking him around. Asshole. But Dillon knew it would be a mistake to call him that to his face.

But Varick certainly had his good points. For one, Varick had fixed him up with a bike for running errands. And it wasn't just any bike. The Harley Softail was a thing of beauty: its high-polish chrome and twin cam engine drew the eye of everyone who knew a damn thing about bikes and was the envy of everyone else. He didn't care much for the extended bitch seat, but Varick had told him he needed the room for packages and the occasional passenger. His first errand—a very brief one—had been to drop off a brown paper–wrapped box at the desk of a downtown hotel he'd never heard of before. What was in the box? He suspected drugs or money, but considered it wasn't any of his business. The important thing was that he'd been free the rest of the day, and he took the opportunity to show off the bike to Amber.

She looked happy, like all almost-mothers were supposed to, in her loose pink blouse and capri pants. After she gave him a beer and a sandwich, she even went outside with him so he could have a smoke on the porch. It was almost like pre–Asshole Thad times, when he could give her shit about the occasional losers she dated and the goofy clothes she had to wear at her hygienist job. But it got uncomfortable when she told him that the cops had called about the burned-out Escort.

"I couldn't get hold of you," she said. She looked worried. "They said there was no one in the car when it burned, but it still freaked me out."

"Somebody ripped it off," he told her. "I was afraid you'd be mad."

"Are you okay?" she said. "Tell me you're not doing stuff you're not supposed to be doing."

"I'm innocent, ma'am," he said, doing an imitation of some TV cowboy they'd both liked when they were kids. He took a quick drag on his cigarette because he couldn't quite look her in the eye.

"Idiot," she said, pushing at his head with the palm of her hand. "I need to know what's going on with you." But, in the end, they agreed the car hadn't been worth much, anyway.

When she asked where he'd gotten the bike, he told her he was working for a bill collector and that the company had given him a signing bonus he'd put down on the bike. She seemed to buy it.

"It's about time someone figured out that you're a smart kid," she said. Whether she meant it or not didn't matter to him. He just liked to hear her say it.

The best part of the visit was having her pull their grandfather's leather jacket from the closet and put it into his hands. It was as heavy as he remembered, and the (shamefully infrequent) conditioning he and Amber had done on it meant that it was still in pretty good shape. When he put it on, he couldn't stop smiling.

"Looks good," Amber told him.

"Hell, yeah, it looks good!" he said.

He gave her a quick kiss good-bye and was on his way out the door when she touched his arm.

"I need to tell you that the next time you come, Thad might be here."

"So?" he said.

"So he's moved in," she said. "He's left Alice."

If that wasn't the worst bullshit news he'd heard in a while, he didn't know what was. But when he saw the hopeful look in her eyes, he decided not to be an asshole about it.

CHAPTER 10

Week 20 5/7

Wendy raced ahead of Del on the scooter, only occasionally remembering to stop at each driveway to see if there were any cars coming, as she'd asked her to do.

"So, when does our entire life stop being about suicide watch?" she had asked Jock. But chasing after Wendy was one of her favorite things to do, even though it worried her sometimes that she could never love Wendy in just the right way, that she would always fall short of Jock's love for the child.

"Slow down," she called after her.

She needed to see Alice, who still wasn't answering the phone. She knew she should have checked on her much sooner. Alice had to be upset. Since Del had learned that Thad was not just living with another woman but was also having a child with her, she'd been in a low-level state of shock herself. She couldn't imagine Thad, straight-and-narrow Thad, doing something so cruel.

Leopold Avenue was almost all uphill from Victoria Park, as were most of the roads on the western side of it. Albert, Helena, Arthur, Alfred, Leopold, Beatrice, Alice, Louise, and, of course, Victoria. The city planners had probably thought themselves clever all those years ago, naming them after Queen Victoria's children to give it English snob appeal. The streets were wide and many of the houses, like Alice's house just ahead, were imposing but gracious. Victoria Square, with its natty boutiques and art galleries and quaint cafés was just a street over from the park's southern edge. It was much more fashionable now than when she had been Wendy's age. The candy shop and dry cleaners and dollar stores that had moved in in the seventies and eighties had been replaced with the more upscale businesses.

Even her parents' modest two-story off Beatrice had quadrupled in value since they'd bought it thirty years before. When Jock had asked her to marry him, she knew that part of the deal was that she'd have to come back to the part of town she'd grown up in, so Wendy wouldn't have to move out of the house she'd been born into. Wendy was even about to enter kindergarten at Our Lady of the Hills. But their house was closer to Alice's, a house considerably larger than either hers and Jock's or her parents'.

She caught up to Wendy a bit out of breath.

"Mommy Del, you're poky-slow," she said. Beneath her helmet, her face was pink with heat, and she said "slow" with a slight lisp. There was a rectangular gap where her new front teeth hadn't yet come in.

Del laughed. "Hey, I caught up."

Wendy gave a rueful shake of her blond head as if to say that she didn't know what her stepmother was talking about. "Do you want to race?" she asked.

They were almost at the top of the hill, just one house away from Alice's, a 1920s Mediterranean-style palazzo that was even larger than the brick-and-column mansions flanking it. "Let's see if my friend Alice has a glass of lemonade," she said.

She led Wendy to the newly bricked driveway below the house, which sat on a landscaped rise, high enough for the second and third stories to have a view of the park beyond the pond. She'd always loved this house, imposing as it was. When she was a child, coming here had intimidated her, but Alice's mother had always put her at ease with kind words and plates of cookies and other snacks for their play dates and sleepovers.

Wendy stared up at the house.

"Hands in pockets when we get inside," Del said. She didn't bring Wendy here often because it made her nervous to take Wendy into houses where she might break something. If Wendy was obnoxious—though she almost never was—it felt to her like she was responsible, that people would think she wasn't doing a good job. She unclipped Wendy's bicycle helmet and smoothed her hair as she ducked away. "Okay?"

It was cool in the terra-cotta shade of the front entrance, which was large enough to be an outdoor room, with sand-finished raised beds packed with flowers and towering plants. Wendy ran over and knelt beside a pond with a waterfall and terrace of creek rocks.

"Fish," she said. "Look at the big goldfish!"

"It's Saturday," Del said. "She might not be home." She rang the bell and heard the responding chimes from deep inside the house. Part of her was hoping that Alice wouldn't answer. She glanced over at Wendy. Jock didn't care much for Alice, which was another reason she rarely brought Wendy here.

"Will she let me feed the fish?" Wendy said.

She was about to tell her that it didn't matter because no one was home after all, when she saw, through the textured glass, a pale, distorted form moving toward them. The textured glass obscured whether the person was male or female, but whoever it was didn't seem to be in any hurry.

The door opened. Del's greeting died in her throat when she saw Alice's ashen face.

Alice stretched out a hand as though she would clutch onto Del. Her eyelids fluttered and she crumpled forward, falling against Del.

The only thing that Del could think was, *Shit!* She looked around, wondering if there was anyone who had seen. Alice had enough problems without passing out in front of the neighbors.

When Wendy ran over, her already wide eyes got bigger. "She's dead," she said, a tone of awe in her voice.

"I think she just fainted, honey," Del said. She didn't want her to see any more, but Wendy was too young to be sent home by herself. Jock would be angry—really angry—when he heard what she'd seen. *Thanks, Alice.*

With Wendy holding the door, she picked up Alice beneath the arms and slid her into the house's marble foyer. As she tucked a cushion from a nearby settee beneath Alice's head, the nice-girl part of her told her it would be a shame to get blood on it. But hadn't Alice brought it on herself? She shook the uncharitable thought out of her head.

"Can I call 911?" Wendy said.

Alice opened her eyes. They fixed on Wendy and it was clear that she had no idea at that moment who the child was. Wendy started to back away. Del recognized fear in her face.

"Alice," Del said. "Look at me."

Wendy was settled in the media room watching *Spongebob Square Pants* on a television screen the width of a queen-sized bed while Del tended to Alice's wound in the kitchen. Alice had refused to let her call for the EMTs or to be taken to a doctor. Del stanched the blood with a towel after seeing that the cut—long and running almost the length of Alice's forearm—was only superficial.

"Come over here," she said, leading Alice to the sink. She turned on the tap. A bone-handled steak knife with a smear of blood on its tip lay on the counter between the sink and the espresso machine.

Alice gave a muted cry when Del pulled the towel away and held her arm beneath the warm running water. They watched together as the blood swirled, almost pink, and disappeared down the drain.

"It hurts," Alice said.

"Hold still," Del said. She used the aerator to move the water up and down the length of Alice's forearm. "You want to tell me what this is all about?" she asked.

Alice had always had a self-destructive streak. Why else would she have attached herself to Roxanne, who had seemed to delight in praising her one minute and yelling at her the next? The unimpressive depth of the cut told Del that this, too, was some kind of pathetic bid for attention. She remembered how, in fourth grade, Alice had fashioned a kind of half-veil for herself when she'd had a cold sore and had worn it until lunchtime when the nuns made her take it off.

Despite the (now disheveled) stylish haircut and her socialite-slim figure, Alice looked like the sullen teenager that Del had once known her to be.

"He told me not to do it," she said. "He said I was being a coward."

"Who said? Thad?"

"Thad!" Alice repeated. Her face twisted with hate. "Thad couldn't give less of a damn." She jerked her arm away so that water sprayed over them both. Her filmy white peignoir, already streaked with blood, now clung in wet spots across her chest.

Del stared. Alice's bleeding had stopped and, frankly, she was fascinated to witness her friend's bizarre transformation.

"Thad got some slut from his office pregnant," she said.

Del glanced away.

"So you already know?" she said. "I had to hear it from a stranger. That figures."

"Alice, I'm so sorry," Del said.

"He gave *her* a baby. Not me. Not his wife! He's been fucking her for more than a year!"

Del wanted to tell her to stop the cursing because of Wendy, but, seeing the anger in Alice's face, she decided not to risk it.

"It was a stupid, mean thing for him to do," she said.

"White trash," Alice said. "Like they weren't both white trash in the first place. He used me. He's been using me since we got married. And we all know what he was using me for."

What could she say to Alice? That she was probably right? She'd never understood what any man, poor dental student or not, saw in Alice. Alice was prone to be used. Ripe to be used. It wasn't a very nice thing to think but still Del thought it. Her thoughts must have shown on her face because Alice narrowed her eyes at her.

"You're not my friend," Alice said.

"I'm sorry about Thad. But you can't do this." She pointed to Alice's arm, which now had just a few drops of blood erupting on it.

"I'm not afraid," Alice said.

"Let me call someone," Del said. She didn't know whom—911? The men in white coats? Alice didn't have any family. It should probably be Thad. She could hear Spongebob giggling in another part of the house. If only Wendy hadn't been with her. In her heart she believed that Alice wasn't dangerous, and she was angry enough now that she was probably no longer a danger to herself. In her bloody deshabille, she looked crazy, but not dangerous.

"Don't bother," Alice said.

Every muscle in her body wanted to take Alice at her word. She wanted to run down the hall and get Wendy and flee the house and pretend that she'd never dropped by at all. She wanted to continue up the hill and on to her parents' house where she could retreat into the cool of her childhood living room, letting the icy air of the window unit pour over her body, and maybe think about what kind of cocktail she might have before dinner. Her parents were into cocktails these days. Sweet and sour things in tall, frosted glasses. Rum, she thought, or maybe gin.

But no. Alice needed help.

"I'll stay here with you," she said. "Let me call my mother to come and get Wendy. We can talk."

The Alice that looked back at her was not the Alice that she'd known for so many years. It was the new Alice. The almost-pretty, hard-edged Alice. A part of her liked this Alice better than the simpering woman-child she'd been for years. This was an Alice she could deal with. Maybe.

"Just take your brat and get out," Alice said.

She fought against being indignant. What she really wanted to do was to give Alice a slap. Instead, she turned her back on Alice and hurried to the media room to collect Wendy. Wendy kept looking back over her shoulder wanting to see more of the cartoon, and Del was glad for her distraction. They left through the front door and found Wendy's scooter and helmet. She didn't even bother to put the helmet on the child, but let her start recklessly down the driveway without it.

What was it that Alice had said about being a coward? Who was giving her advice? Maybe Alice had found a real lover.

As she watched Wendy pushing the scooter up the hill, Del wondered who he was and what he wanted from poor, sick Alice.

CHAPTER 11

It was the first day back from Christmas break and the Lower School cafeteria smelled just the same as it always had: like rotten bananas and spoiled milk. Roxanne had been eating in this cafeteria since she was five years old. She'd seen a teacher almost choke to death here and had spent more hours kneeling on its floor during disaster drills than she cared to recall. Even in summer she dreamed about its painted concrete walls and narrow windows edging the ceiling. They weren't happy dreams, either. It wasn't until the next fall that she'd be allowed to eat in the new high school cafeteria upstairs, where you could actually see out of the windows and one day a week you could put in an order for pizza in the morning and get it for lunch. Nothing fun had ever happened to her in this place.

Beside her, Alice was unpacking her lunch that was full of things Roxanne was almost never allowed to have: Ho-Ho's (too expensive), a can of soda (too much sugar), roast beef from the Jewish deli on the other side of the park (also too expensive), a cloth napkin with pale blue forget-me-nots stitched on its edges (Roxanne's mother would have laughed at the idea). Alice, embarrassed, stuffed the napkin beneath her lunch bag when she saw Roxanne and Del looking.

"It's not my fault," Alice said, shoving everything into a pile in the middle of the table. "She makes me bring this stuff. Just take what you want."

Del grabbed for the package of Ho-Ho's and Roxanne took the soda.

Roxanne watched Alice. There was no trace on her face or body of what had happened in the park before Christmas, and when she had called her the next day Alice hadn't wanted to talk about it. Del had been the angry one. Del was like that—always worrying about what was right and what was wrong.

Still, something was different about Alice. She wasn't sure yet what it was. But Alice seemed less scatterbrained, more serious. She watched as Alice disassembled the sandwich and rolled the beef into short, even tubes and nibbled at their ends. Well, maybe not exactly serious. She was less whiny, anyway.

"Hey, it's Mrs. Levenger," Del said. "Hide the soda."

Roxanne lowered the soda down to her lap below the tabletop, out of the principal's view. It would be a major drag if she got detention for something Alice had brought from home. It was bad enough that her mother was always ragging her about how much it cost to send her to private school. Roxanne had argued more than once that she'd be happy to go to public school, that it didn't matter to her in the least. It was her grandparents' money that was sending her, anyway. But sending her to Catholic school was one of the few traditions Carla clung to, and was something she would never explain.

"Who's that with her?" Roxanne said. "He's cute."

"He's a priest," Del said. "You go to hell for even thinking about doing it with a priest."

Even though the priest at Mrs. Levenger's side wore the traditional black shirt, black pants, and white collar, he seemed more casual, more relaxed than the other priests Roxanne had known at Our Lady of the Hills. His thick brown hair—as dark and thick as her own—curled

*around his ears, and his eyes were dark, almost black. They'd heard the
new priest would be starting soon, replacing the math teacher who was
going on maternity leave. When he chanced to glance in Roxanne's direction, he was smiling. She held his gaze until his smile faltered just a
bit and he looked away.*

*"You're such a drama queen, Del," Roxanne said. She sat up a little
straighter and flipped her hair back over one shoulder.*

Beside her Alice began to beat at her own chest, panicked.

"What's wrong with you?" Del asked. "Alice, you're so weird."

"She's choking," Roxanne said, getting up. "Shit."

*Her use of the s-word was loud enough that it got the attention of
the other girls at their table and the room got quieter.*

*"She's choking!" Roxanne said, louder. She wasn't quite sure what
to do, and now Alice—her eyes wide and afraid—was trying to get up
from the bench. Her mouth was open, but no sound came out.*

"Mrs. Levenger!" one of the other girls called. "Alice is choking!"

*Instead, it was the priest who rushed over, making his way between
the tables as though he'd done it a thousand times before. His smile
was gone.*

*Roxanne moved out of the way. Of course, she knew that Alice
needed to be Heimliched, but she didn't want to be the one to do it.*

*When Alice saw the priest approaching, her eyes got even wider, and
she tried to back away from him.*

*"It's okay," he said. "I'm not going to hurt you." His voice revealed
a Latin accent (Roxanne soon learned he was Cuban). Alice held her
hands out as though to keep him away, even though her face was turning an alarming shade of red.*

"Alice!" Roxanne said. "Stop it!"

*Whether it was a result of being shouted at (Alice usually did what
Roxanne told her to do) or the fact that she could no longer struggle,
Alice finally stopped backing away and dropped to her knees, her
hands clutching at her throat.*

*In a second the priest was behind her, thrusting his balled fists up-
ward against her stomach. Alice's body jerked and Roxanne couldn't
help but think of the seizure Alice had had in the woods. Twice, now,*

Alice had almost died right in front of her. It made her wish, just for a moment, that she'd been kinder to Alice.

On the fourth thrust a piece of roast beef shot out of Alice's mouth and landed with a slap on the third graders' table. Del laughed and the sound of it rang out through the silent cafeteria. One of the third graders began to sob.

"Delilah O'Brien," Mrs. Levenger said, pointing to the door. She stood just a few feet away, near Roxanne, who could smell her powdery, old-lady perfume. "My office. Now."

The soda had spilled on the floor, but Mrs. Levenger stepped around the forming puddle without even glancing down at it. She took the now-crying Alice from the priest and wrapped an arm around her shoulders.

"You're fine, Alice," she said. "You're just fine."

The lunchroom monitor clapped her hands and admonished the other girls to sit back down and finish their lunches. When she saw the soda mess on the floor, she glared at Roxanne.

"Clean that up," she said.

But the principal guided Alice over to Roxanne and told her to take Alice to the nurse's office. "Someone else can take care of that," she told the monitor.

Roxanne didn't dare to look at the monitor because she knew she'd end up laughing, too. The monitor was a scrawny old bitch who worked in the lunchroom and the library, and she always had it in for Roxanne, flagging her with yellow slips if she caught her in the hall after the bell rang, screaming at her for running, inventing excuses so she could search Roxanne's locker. The woman was due for something nasty. Roxanne just hadn't decided what it would be yet. As it was, she'd done a sketch of the old bitch—naked and being devoured by demons, huge snorting beasts with horns and penises bigger than the woman's arms—and had Alice leave it on the windshield of her car.

Roxanne took Alice's hand and led her out into the hallway. Alice was still tearful, but that wasn't so unusual for Alice. Behind them, Roxanne could hear Mrs. Levenger apologizing to the priest.

"*This wasn't the welcome I planned. But I'm so, so glad you were here, Father Romero.*"

Roxanne looked back over her shoulder to see if Father Romero was watching them, but he was looking at Mrs. Levenger.

When they were on the steps, finally out of sight of the cafeteria, Del hurried back down the stairs to them.

"*Alice, are you okay?*" she said. "*I didn't mean to laugh at you. Really.*"

Alice was having a hard time speaking, but she nodded to let Del know she understood.

"*I'm so, so glad you were here, Father Romero,*" Roxanne said in a falsetto imitation of Mrs. Levenger. Then, to Alice, "*Don't worry, honey. We would've saved you. But that whole meat thing was just kind of nasty.*"

"*Quit being such a bitch,*" Del said. "*Alice could've died. Again.*"

Even though she'd had the same thought, Roxanne gave her a look that told her to shut the hell up.

"*Don't you know?*" Alice said. She stopped in the hallway at the top of the stairs. In one of the nearby rooms, the kindergarteners were singing "My Country 'Tis of Thee." "*It's him.*"

"*Who?*" Del said.

But Roxanne knew immediately whom Alice was talking about. Del had told her about the man Alice had seen in the park that night.

"*The angel,*" she said. "*He's our angel.*"

"*Jesus H. Christ,*" Del said. "*Don't start with that again.*"

"*Leave her alone,*" Roxanne said. "*She knows what she saw.*" Alice gave her a grateful look. Sometimes, she really did like Alice. But it was more interesting to her that Del sounded afraid.

Roxanne clung to the outer wall of the rectory, her heels hanging over the edge of the narrow strip of brick protruding from the side of the building.

Below her, Del whispered to Alice.

"*Go on,*" she said. "*Quit being such a wimp.*"

It was Friday night, and the lights in the parking lot between the rectory and the church had shut off at ten, minutes before they'd slipped onto the church grounds.

Alice made small grunting noises as she climbed. "It hurts my fingers," she said. Del made it up first, and edged close to Roxanne.

Roxanne turned from the darkened window and Del saw a fleeting look of . . . what? It was more irritation than anger, as though Alice were some kind of beetle or fly that was bothering her. She thought she knew in that moment what Roxanne—tiny, mysterious Roxanne with her bright violet eyes and miniature features and cloud of wavy black hair—really thought of Alice. Though it had been Roxanne who had made her their friend. But when Roxanne caught Del watching her, she smiled, blinking the look away.

On the other side of the window, a lamp came on, spilling yellow light over the priest's bedroom.

"I'm going to fall," Alice whispered, pressing against Del's side. It was only four feet down to the parking lot, and Del was tempted to push her away. It was like that with Alice—sometimes one just wanted to do some violence to her. Del knew she shouldn't feel that way, but she did. Sometimes, she prayed to be forgiven for it and she'd be gentle with Alice for a few days. But then, something about Alice's limp hair and pale face twisted into a constant whine would start to bug her and she'd be annoyed with her all over again. The fact that Alice was rich might be an attraction for Roxanne, but it cut no ice with her.

Inside the room, Father Romero was getting ready for bed.

Father Romero was a twenty-four-year-old refugee from Cuba who, at twelve, had made it to Florida in a life raft with his mother. His English was perfect, but he would tease them, pretending not to understand their directions to the cafeteria or the school office. Every girl at the school was in love with him.

No one had actually said that they were there to see Father Romero get undressed, but Del knew they weren't there to watch him pray. If they were to see something, why would it be any different from what she saw every time her older brother decided to gross her out by wandering around after a shower without a towel?

Father Romero crossed over to the dresser, removed his watch, and began to unbutton his shirt. Del giggled.

"Shut up," Roxanne said. Her words sounded cruel and grown-up, and confirmed for Del that what they were doing was not something funny, but was actually wrong.

After hanging his shirt in the closet, Father Romero turned toward the window and began to undo his belt. Could he see them? Del's body flushed with heat. She desperately wanted to be at home—doing homework, watching Grease on video, or even playing Scrabble with her mother. But there was no jumping down from the wall without the other girls. Roxanne would never let her forget it.

Alice crowded even closer. Del could hear her shallow breath and knew she was still afraid. It was easy enough to slide her foot onto the back of Alice's shoe, putting her off balance. Alice turned to her in surprise and reached out for Del's shoulder as she fell, screaming as though she were being murdered.

Alice and Del landed in a pile, while Roxanne, who seemed to have lighted on the side of the building like a butterfly, held fast.

Del rolled off of Alice, who was crying now, and got up, cursing. Blood dripped down her arm where she'd scraped it on the brick.

Father Romero threw open the window and said something in Spanish that she couldn't understand, but she thought it had the word "God" in it. Roxanne was still on the wall, her face turned to Father Romero. He looked back over at her, and Del thought she saw the hint of a smile on his lips.

Roxanne turned away and jumped down, her hair floating behind her like a silken cape. As she ran into the darkness, Del saw how Father Romero watched her until she was out of sight.

CHAPTER 12

Week 20 6/7

The bed was warm and Thad didn't want to get out of it. He drowsed, spooning against Amber. Later, he told himself that he should have known that the state of bliss he'd been in couldn't last.

"Hey, stay here," he said, when she started to get out of bed.

"Why should I?" she said.

When he pressed his erection against her, she laughed.

"Oh, now I get it," she said.

She rolled over on top of him, her hair falling over his skin and her stomach pressing against his. There was a brief moment when he thought of the child inside her and wished for a moment—just a moment—that they would have had more time to live together before a child was in the picture. But as they made a lazy kind of love in the haze of shade-filtered sunlight, all thought of the child slipped from his mind and there was just Amber—the taste and smell of her, the way she moved on top of him, slowly, a look of intense pleasure on her lovely face.

• • •

He woke to find her gone and two hours passed. The sounds from down in the kitchen—of cabinets opening and closing, silverware being taken from the drawer—brought a smile to his face. He got up and showered quickly, still pleased with the novelty of being able to do such a simple thing without worrying about getting back to Alice.

Alice. It had been almost a month. What was she doing? She hadn't called him, hadn't, apparently, tried to find him. It was unlike her. Would she do something desperate? Take too many pills or maybe drive into a tree or even set their house on fire? He thought of the Ruger and was glad he'd taken it from the house. Not that she knew how to use the thing. Alice with a gun was probably more of a danger to someone walking or driving by the house than she was to herself. Hapless was the only way to describe his wife.

He determined that he would call Jock Connery's office on Monday. There was no sense in letting Alice think there was any chance of them reuniting. Freedom felt damned good to him. He knew a lot of guys wouldn't think of leaving a wife for another, pregnant woman as freedom, but, then a lot of guys hadn't been married to Alice.

"Am I too late for breakfast?" he called down the stairs. "It's your fault I couldn't get out of bed, you know." He pulled on his pants and went down into the living room to see if she'd brought in the newspaper. "What do you say we walk down the street and get some brunch?"

"Sounds great, Sweetie Muffin Cakes!" The voice from the kitchen was a strained falsetto.

Thad stiffened. *Damn.*

"Your Honey Muffin Pie thought you'd never wakey. Her has been waiting and waiting for her Sweetie Muffin Cakes."

Dillon, Amber's younger brother, appeared in the kitchen doorway, his hand on his outthrust hip in an exaggerated, feminine stance. He made a loud, wet kissing noise.

"Where's Amber?" Thad said.

Dillon McVay was one of the few people in the world to whom he didn't give a damn about being polite. It wasn't just that his studded upper lip and crowded, gray teeth made him a dentist's worst nightmare. It wasn't even Dillon's cadaverous frame that towered a good three inches over Thad's own five feet, eleven inches. Or the black lipstick he occasionally wore, or the way Amber's carefully arranged rooms took on an air of smoky decay and hopelessness when he was in the house for more than five minutes. What defined Dillon McVay as scum was the "suggested donation" (Dillon's phrase) of about two hundred bucks every couple of weeks that Thad had been shelling out ever since Dillon arrived back in town six months earlier. For different reasons, neither of them had mentioned the arrangement to Amber.

"Grocery store," Dillon said, bored with his game. He went back to the kitchen where he continued opening and closing cabinets looking for food. "Sissy doesn't have shit here to eat. You should pay her more."

Thad followed him. "Why don't you go out and get yourself something?" As he peeled a fifty from the fold in his money clip and held it out, he tried to force a smile, but it wasn't happening.

Dillon stared down at the money as though he were being offered a three-day-old fish. The silver stud on his upper lip lifted a fraction.

"Yeah," he said. "Don't need your lousy contribution today, Asshole Thad. But thanks for playing."

"What do you mean?" Thad said. *What in the hell was going on?*

"You waste my time," Dillon said, turning to the refrigerator. He opened it and took out a soda.

"Don't tell me you've got a job," Thad said. He remembered that Amber had mentioned that Dillon had somehow replaced the stolen Escort with a brand new motorcycle. "You must be dealing, or something."

"Ha-ha," Dillon said. "The dentist made a funny."

"Then why don't you go now, before Amber gets back?" Thad didn't like seeing the two of them together, didn't like being reminded they were related. They shared both parents and there was some resemblance in their eyes and slightly rounded chins, but beyond that, he liked to think they were entirely different creatures. "I want that key that Amber gave you." He stretched out an open hand. "Now that I'm living here, you don't get to come and go like you own the place."

Dillon flipped the soda's top. "Oh, yeah. Sissy said you finally left that batshit wife of yours. I hear she's a piece of work, your little Alice in Wonderland."

"What do you know about Alice?" Thad said. Of course, the bastard had known that he was married, but his threats had always been vague. He'd never mentioned Alice by name.

"Haven't met the lady," Dillon said. "Maybe I should. She must be awfully lonesome now that you're here playing house with Sissy."

"Stay away from Alice," Thad said, taking a step toward Dillon. "You've taken enough from your sister and from me. Stay the hell away from my wife!"

"Oooh," Dillon said. "I'm scared. Won't Sissy want to know how you can't handle someone dissing the wife? You got two dicks in there, Mr. Dentist, that you can fuck two women at once?" He used the soda can to gesture toward the front of Thad's pants.

Thad started to look down, but the impact of the words finally broke through and, flushed with anger, he slapped the soda from Dillon's hand so hard that it hit the opposite wall. Soda splattered over the floor and the small white table where he and Amber often ate together.

There was a moment between them, a hesitation that couldn't have lasted more than two seconds. Thad was stunned by a sudden feral desire to beat the living hell out of the nineteen-year-old facing him. But in those seconds Dillon's face changed from that of a snide juvenile delinquent to that of a man—a frightening, dangerous man.

As though he were some kind of magician, Dillon was behind him, pressing against his back, his forearm squeezing Thad's neck, cutting off his breath. His glasses clattered to the floor as he struggled, but Dillon's grip only strengthened. Dillon grunted with the effort of holding him. Thad tried to pry away Dillon's shaved forearm with his hands, but the tendons he felt beneath his fingers were taut and inflexible. Finally, he got a solid foothold on the floor and threw himself sideways with all his strength, throwing Dillon off balance and onto the floor.

He fell on Dillon, pulling away just enough to give him a few solid punches in the stomach. He wasn't a violent man, but something about Dillon brought out the violence in him, the call to rid the world of every vile thing that might touch what he cared about: the women in his office, Amber, even Alice, whom he had tried and tried to love.

Stunned, Dillon didn't offer up much of a fight, just tried to push him away each time Thad made contact with his too-skinny gut.

Finally satisfied, Thad sat back on his heels, breathing hard. The Dillon McVays of the world were maggots, and he wasn't going to take any more crap. He'd do everything he could to keep Dillon away from Amber. He certainly didn't want their baby exposed to the poison that was Dillon McVay.

Dillon rolled over on his side. "Stupid motherfucker."

They heard the front door open. Dillon raised himself up on one elbow and wiped his mouth with his shirt.

"Can someone come help me with these bags?" Amber called from the living room.

"You're screwed, asshole," Dillon said.

"You can't let him get to you, baby," Amber said, putting a mug of hot tea in front of Thad where he sat at the kitchen table. She had wiped up the soda from the table as well as the floor.

He knew better than to ask her to ban Dillon from the house. She was blind when it came to Dillon, who was always on his best behavior when she was around, never bringing his filthy friends inside, some of whom Thad had seen slumped in the Escort like refugees from some eternal Halloween party. At least she wasn't allowing him to smoke in the house, now that she was pregnant. He took her hand. He was there to protect her, to protect the child. Somehow, he had to convince her that Dillon was dangerous.

"I want this little guy born into a happy house," he said.

"Oh, Dillon won't hang around much when the baby comes," Amber said. "He wouldn't get within fifty feet of a smelly diaper. And what makes you so sure it's a little 'guy' anyhow, Mr. Smarty-Pants?" Even though she was five months along, she'd told her doctor she didn't want to know what the sex was ahead of the baby's birth.

"Just a hunch," he said.

There hadn't been a girl born alive into the Hudson family in many generations, but he didn't want to disappoint her by telling her so. He'd watched her pore over catalogs splashed with photos of curly headed moppets in beribboned dresses and striped tights and pink hats that flopped over their ringlets. She flipped through the pages of boys' clothes just to prove to him—and to herself, he knew—that she would love a boy just as much as a girl. But he knew where her heart really lay.

"I'm sorry he ruined our morning," she said, sitting down in the chair nearest his. When she touched a bruise blossoming on his neck, he winced. "You need to keep the ice on it." But when she picked up the ice pack, he took it from her hand.

"I'm fine," he said, putting the thing down on the table. It actually hurt like hell, but there was no need for her to know it. She was upset enough.

In his mind he'd gone back and forth between Amber and Alice a thousand times. But now that he'd made the decision, he knew it was the only one. Unconsciously, he touched his fingers to his temple, which was still tender from where Alice had hit him weeks earlier. It had been a kind of pity that had kept him with Alice, and that shamed him. She was unstable, but she deserved better than to be threatened by a douchebag like Dillon McVay.

Still, he was here with Amber and, soon, their baby. He would kill anyone who tried to take away the happiness they'd found.

Looking at Amber, at the tenderness in her eyes he wanted her again. He needed to claim her, to keep her, to make her a part of himself. He wanted to spend every night in her lumpy bed with its mattress springs that groaned every time he turned over. He wanted to wake once again with her long, sandy hair stuck to the side of his cheek because he'd slept close beside her all night long.

She must have seen the want in his eyes, because the look in her own turned from gentle concern to something else, something serious and hungry that took him aback and made him question how well he knew her. She got up from her chair and indicated that he should push his own away from the table. When he did, she climbed onto his lap, straddling him, kissing his neck, gently at first, then harder, as though she wanted to make him hurt, just a little. She pressed her pelvis against him, letting him know what she wanted, what response she was looking for from his body.

When she had him in the trembling state in which she obviously wanted him, she pulled away and got off of his lap. He reached for her, but she stepped back and undid the buttons of the blouse she wore, letting it drop away from her body to reveal her stomach and breasts, which were straining against the white lace bra that he'd bought her long before she'd become pregnant. He watched as her fingers lingered for a moment on the creamy bulge of her stomach, as though caressing it, and he was flooded with desire. Before she could push her shorts down over her hips, he was against her, hurrying, desperate for her.

When he said, "Let's go upstairs," his voice was low and full. But she shook her head and pulled him down onto the floor where he shucked off his own pants. His knees were cold on the Spanish tile he'd helped her pick out the previous winter. For a second he worried for the child, and for Amber who lay with her own back on the hard floor, but when she reached out for him, all thoughts of anyone's discomfort abandoned him.

He tried to hold back and wait for her, but seeing her beneath him on the floor, her eyes closed and her lips parted in pleasure, with her hair spread over the tile onto which he'd almost collapsed an hour before, he couldn't help himself. The anger that had filled him earlier was replaced with an intense certainty, a powerful sense that what he was doing was right, that this woman was *his*. The child, who was curled safe inside her even as he thrust himself against her womb, was his as well. He would have them both for as long as he wanted, and he wanted them forever, despite crazy Alice and the fuck that was Amber's brother.

When he came, he squeezed his eyes closed and cried out. The release was fast and sweet, and when it was over he felt an inexpressible surge of happiness. Sweat dripped from his forehead and down onto Amber, who laughed and wiped it away with the back of her hand. He kissed her.

God, he loved this woman!

They lay together—embracing, kissing, whispering, laughing at the fact that they were on the kitchen floor—until their sweat began to cool. Finally, Thad sat back and reached for his pants. Out of the corner of his eye, he caught a movement at the window. His smile faded when he saw—outlined by the noon-bright sun—Dillon's face pressed against the glass. As Dillon turned away, his aspect filled with hate, a shot of sunlight pricked a facet of the diamond stud decorating his nostril and flashed a shower of color through the window and onto his sister's face.

CHAPTER 13

Week 21 2/7

"Mommy Del! Mommy Del!"

She heard the words but missed the urgency, the fear in the child's voice from behind the door. All that mattered was the man's breath on her neck, in her hair, the warm meniscus of sweat between the curves of his body and hers.

The hotel bedroom was so thick with yellow light that she could almost feel it between her fingertips. Its texture was like the air in dreams she'd had of flying, dreams in which she could move through the sky, her arms curving in a wide breast stroke, far above her house, higher even than the trees.

"Please, Mommy Del." The little girl was sobbing now. "I need you."

The man turned his head toward the door, staring at it, hard, as though he would make the child go away just by doing so, but Del made a quiet shushing noise and anchored her fingers in his hair, pulling his head back to her chest.

They were on the floor now, having wrested all the covers from the bed so that the stained and threadbare mattress pad lay exposed. If she was in any pain from the carpet abrasions on her back, she gave no sign. The only thing that mattered was that this man, this beautiful, beautiful man was deep inside her. A low, satisfied moan welled up from her gut and through her parted lips. She didn't want to think beyond this room, beyond this moment. She had never felt so alive, so conscious of every breath, every small movement, as though she were living in slow motion.

"Let me in," Wendy said. But her voice was muffled now, as though she had pressed herself—her face, her very lips—against the door to get closer to her stepmother.

Del's memory of how she'd come to this room was distant, like a film she'd seen years earlier. She and Wendy had come downtown to return an evening bag she had bought at Saks. Now it lay on a nearby chair, its delicate chain slipped from its miniature shopping bag to sparkle in the sunlight like a frozen silver stream. She had first seen the man watching her through the window of the ice-cream shop where they'd stopped for an after-school treat for Wendy. Being watched so carefully unnerved her at first. She'd never been the kind of woman to turn heads: her figure was more athletic than voluptuous or stylish, her thighs and even her waist tended to be muscular. Men had never flocked to her as they had to Roxanne. And even though, thanks to Jock, she had plenty of money for clothes, she never felt as though she'd quite developed a style of her own. But she forgot all of that as she felt the man's eyes on her. There was something almost too familiar about him, as though they were already lovers who were merely playing a game, a game in which they were pretending not to know each other. She'd heard of couples playing those games before to keep their relationships fresh. She wasn't the game player: Alice played games, pretend games, with herself. Poor Alice's whole life had been pretend. She pitied Alice, now.

Her body felt primed, as though she were strung through and through with fine tensile wire. If it were a game, what would come next? She exaggerated her interactions with Wendy, dabbing at the child's ice cream smeared lips with a napkin, laughing at some school anecdote about a boy and the guinea pig he'd brought for show-and-tell, knowing all the time that the man was watching. Waiting for her.

When Wendy finished her ice cream, Del gathered their things together: Wendy's sweet new backpack with the yellow daisies, her purse, and the bag from Saks. The ice cream shop was empty, and there was no one to say good-bye to.

The man outside the window adjusted his sunglasses with one hand and looked off, briefly, down the street, before turning back to Del.

"Come on, honey," she said to Wendy, who was dawdling at the water fountain. Wendy turned, water glistening on her lips and chin, and wiped the back of her hand across her mouth.

"I was thirsty," she said, running to Del in that curious, flat-footed way of small children.

"When you're thirsty, it's good to get a drink," Del said.

Of course, once she stepped outside, it should have ended. He should have melted away into the early rush hour crowd on its way home to dinner or the gym or cocktails. Jock himself might even have walked by, hurrying home to Wendy and her.

But the man gave no indication of leaving.

Once there had been a hypnotist at a carnival—not at their Catholic school, of course, but at a nearby public high school—and Roxanne had talked Alice into paying for all of them to be hypnotized. Roxanne and Alice, even Del, herself, had laughed, saying that she—Del—was not the kind of person who could be hypnotized. That she was too practical, too sensible, and could never relax enough. But it had been she who had been the first to go under, doing all the silly things that the hypnotist suggested: crying on command, distributing invisible flowers to the others, pretending to rock a baby to sleep. The truth was that she remembered doing all of those things, and that they had simply felt right to her.

This was not right at all, she knew. But it felt right. She was hesitant as she took the man's arm, and still held on to Wendy with her other hand. But once she felt the solid presence of the man's flesh, the musculature underneath his sleeve, she gripped it firmly.

Wendy was her witness. If Wendy was seeing it, it was real. If Wendy was there, there was no turning back. She followed Del and him without question until they reached the brass-framed glass doors of the Summit Hotel, four blocks away.

"Is Daddy here, Mommy Del?" she said. Even though she got no answer, she stood quietly by while Del requested a suite and slid her credit card across the counter to the disinterested clerk. Fifteen minutes before, there would have been a hundred considerations—a thousand! Down even to what the pasty-faced, unshaven clerk would think of her standing here with a handsome man and a worried little girl asking if her father would be here. But with this man beside her, she felt a surge of strength, a kind of bravado. Why should she care what a peon hotel clerk would think?

The clerk handed back the credit card with a paper slip to sign. More evidence. But she wasn't worried about being found out. Already she was prepared to confess, as she always did. Though, really, what in her life had she ever done that was as worthy of confessing as this? In her mind, she had already been with the man beside her, trashed her marriage vows. All that was left was to follow through.

She remembered holding the firm green stems of the roses, which had never existed, between her fingertips—how cold and smooth they felt. But the hypnotist had warned her of the thorns, and, sure enough, she had pricked herself when she almost dropped one of them. She had cried out, believing she'd been hurt.

"You've been waiting for me," the man whispered when he had closed the bedroom door on Wendy, who sat obediently on an ottoman in front of the television. His voice was accented, maybe European? It didn't matter to her at all.

In fact, she realized that she *had* been waiting for him. Wasn't this the sort of thing Roxanne had been encouraging her to do her whole life? To not worry so much? To lighten up? With this man, she was laying her burdens down. Years and years of burdens. But that was not her foremost thought. Now, she just wanted the fact of him.

She breathed in his musky scent—a scent so overwhelming that it forced Jock's name out of her mind. Though the man's torso and arms and legs were completely devoid of hair—the skin of his back was almost as soft as a child's—he smelled of earth and animal, and she had the sense that if she were to scratch the surface of that perfect skin it would fall away to reveal that he was not a man at all. Because the idea thrilled her, she tightened her legs around him as he eased himself out of her and moved down her body, to her waist and to her groin. His tongue was rough, further abrading her skin, this time in the tender fold between her upper thigh and groin, then the most tender place of all.

It seemed a natural progression, the heat that was building inside her, the desire to have this man, but she felt the desire for her own pleasure slipping away from her. Now her need was something else. There was something she wanted to do—indeed, had to do.

When he was inside her once again, his chest heavy on her back, her cheek pressed against the thin carpet that smelled of cigarettes and mold, she was finally satisfied. There was only that exquisite moment, with him. And when he came, the molten fluid that shot into her seemed to scorch the recesses of her body, flaying the meat from her delicate bones. But she didn't scream.

The scream—loud and pained and prolonged—erupted from the little girl in the other room.

"Hurry," the man whispered. He helped her up from the floor.

If he noticed that she was trembling with pain and anticipation, he didn't tell her so. She stood, her face uplifted to his. When he kissed her on the forehead as one might a child, she felt the knowledge of herself, the identity of Del, the person she had been for thirty years, shrink away like an ebbing tide.

But the rightness, indeed the mercifulness of his action swelled her heart.

Del—though in that place she was only Del to the little girl who was now strangely quiet on the other side of the door—went to the window and, with the help of the man, stepped up onto the rattling wall heater that he had, inexplicably in the summer heat, turned on full blast when she'd first taken off her clothes. She stood, framed in the sunlight, struggling with the broken window lock. Finally, its parts crumbled into her hand and slipped through her spreading fingers onto the floor and the wide sill beneath her feet.

Wendy began to throw herself against the door. The quiet thuds beat out a steady rhythm as though she were playing a sad accompaniment.

The woman who used to be Del slid the narrow window open, pushing it to the side on its rusty track. A hot, pavement-borne breeze caught at her hair and caused the plastic pull for the curtains to sway gently near her shoulder. The man caressed her calf for a moment before letting go. She turned, smiled down at him.

As she took a step backward, she blew him a kiss and he smiled back at her.

Time stretched into something slow and elastic as she fell, her arms and legs loose as a doll's as she dropped through the air. She felt cold. Above her she could see the man watching out the window after her. But he didn't look the same to her—tangled hair fell about his shoulders and his face was no longer even that of a man, but something so fierce and gnarled and repellent that she had to look away. It was only in the fraction of the second before her body hit the Plexiglas roof of the delivery van backed into the hotel's loading dock that she remembered who she was and was afraid.

PART II

You Can Die from Too Much Delicious

CHAPTER 14

It took several tries to get the Buick wagon started. As the junior staff member, it was Romero's job to make sure both the parish cars were in good working order and always filled with gasoline. But what did he know about cars? He wasn't a chauffeur, and he wasn't a mechanic. If one morning it didn't start at all, he'd just have to call the garage. Before backing out of the lot behind the rectory, he flipped the air on full blast and ran a finger around the edge of his collar. Now that he'd received full orders, he didn't mind the uniform so much—he had earned it, after all—but the bishop was a stickler for appearances and he didn't like his priests wearing short-sleeved shirts, even on an unseasonably warm April day.

He had come to enjoy Saturday mornings. At any other parish, it would have been his job to practice with the altar boys and girls. But Father Frankl, his superior, wanted complete control over them, which was fine with Romero. He knew it was vain to crave those few hours away from the church and his duties, but he couldn't help himself. Ac-

celerating the car so that the church and school buildings were quickly behind him, he felt like he was off on a holiday.

"Where are we going?"

Glancing in the rearview mirror, he was stunned to see Roxanne climbing over the middle seat on her way to the front. Her soft black curls fell into her face, blending into her low-cut brown T-shirt. But even in that glance he couldn't miss those violet eyes—Elizabeth Taylor eyes. She was thirteen, but he forgot that when he looked into them.

Was anyone else watching? There was a Jeep in the next lane over, but the driver wasn't paying any attention. Romero was alone in the Buick with one of his students for no official reason. Certainly he would be censured if anyone saw them. Frankl would see to it.

"Never mind," she said, slinging a sandaled foot over the middle of the wagon's front bench seat. "I already know."

"This isn't funny, Roxanne," he said. "Does anyone know where you are?"

"Who? Like my mother?" Roxanne gave an unpretty snort. "Let's see," she said. She settled onto the seat and ticked off his plans on her small, olive-tinged fingers. "First, you take the recycling to the recycling station—and by the way, it really, really stinks back there. You shouldn't leave it in the car all night. And then you go pick up stuff at the dry cleaners, where I hear they do everything free for you guys. Just like you're cops or something. Right?" She paused for a moment and pressed the wagon's radio On button so that U2's "Two Hearts Beat as One" came screaming out of the speakers.

When he reached over to turn it down (though, if he'd been alone, he probably would've left it up), his fingertips brushed hers; he pulled his hand back as though he'd been burned.

Roxanne turned the music down herself.

"Then you go and get coffee at that 7–Eleven right before the parkway, and after that you go across town to that botanica shop where they sell all those candles with saints and stuff on them. Santeria stuff," she said. She sat back, relaxing against the seat as though she were just along for the ride.

He sighed, hating that she'd been right about every one of his plans.

But what could she know about his trips to the botanica? Surely, she didn't know their purpose.

He was a believer, but his personal ties to Santeria, the folk religion with its orishas—the saints—and its santeros, who were the guides to the spirit world for its practitioners, weren't too deep. But when the few believers in his parish had learned that he was Cuban, one was dispatched to find out if he was sympathetic to them. He was, of course, but it was endangering his position in the Church. Both the bishop and Father Frankl referred to Santeria as "savagery." While he knew his disobedience was wrong, he couldn't help but enjoy his small subversion. He didn't take such a narrow view of God's rules of worship.

"Will you get me a soda at the 7–Eleven? It was so hot back there." Roxanne leaned forward to gather her thick hair into a single twist and let it drop onto her shoulder. He tried—and only God knew how hard he tried—not to notice how her shirt gaped at the neck to reveal the tops of her breasts.

"I should drop you off on the next corner," he said. But the truth was that he liked having Roxanne around. Roxanne was a breath of something fresh, something very real. She was a work of art in the making. And good art came from above, right? At the same time, he knew that even thinking of her as anything other than just another hormone-driven teenage soul needing guidance and a firm hand that her mother wasn't providing was simply temptation waiting to bring him down. God could lead him into temptation, but, as a priest, he was expected to be better than average at staying the hell away from it.

"Get me a soda first. Please?" she said. "You at least owe me that. Plus, you have to let me come with you." She cut her eyes to him, looking through her thick lashes. She seemed to believe she was entitled to be there.

This time it was his turn to scoff.

"I should have spoken to Father Frankl back when you and your peanut gallery were hanging around outside my window. Alice—or any one of you—could have been seriously hurt."

"Alice is a crybaby," she said.

"Cruelty is never flattering," he said.

"*You just don't understand how we talk about one another. It doesn't mean I don't care about her,*" she said, turning to look out the side window.

What was so wrong with having one of his younger parishioners along to help him with his Saturday errands? He tried to compose his face to look relaxed, nonchalant, just in case anyone was watching. But he couldn't exactly take her inside the dry cleaners with him. Recycling, maybe. A youth group sort of thing. Without the group.

"*You're going to have to stay in the car,*" he said. "*And if anyone says anything to you, just say you're doing service hours.*"

"*Do I still get a soda?*" she said, and smiled.

Romero pulled into an angled space in front of Monetta's Gift Shop. He'd been surprised to find Santeria so alive in middle-class Cincinnati. After he'd been approached at the church, he'd noticed a healing bracelet on the wrist of a woman on the altar guild, then he'd seen a less-than-discreet shrine in the kitchen of Bryant Carter, a male parishioner who was dying of cancer. Father Frankl had already given him oblique warnings against "indulging" the parishioners, but Romero figured that a dying man deserved all the help he could get.

To Romero, Santeria was more than a simple syncretization of the African Yoruban and Roman Catholic faiths; it was a deepened expression of Christianity, a faith that he knew seemed cold and distant and (oddly, given its origins) European to so many people in the world. Santeria was vibrant, its traditions born in the womb of civilization itself. It brought the souls and the sweat of the faithful into immediate contact with the Living God. He suspected it was this immediacy that threatened the Church that he loved and respected: the occasional animal sacrifices were messy reminders of the unenlightened days before Christ's sacrifice, the dancing and music and trancelike states of worshippers an affront to the now-antiseptic mass. Although he and his mother were both initiates, neither of them relied on the ceremonies or cowrie shell readings to guide them on a regular basis. But he understood the people who did.

Monetta sat outside at a café-style table drinking iced tea with a woman he didn't know. She shaded her eyes to get a better look at who was in the car.

"Stay here," he told Roxanne.

Before the words were out of his mouth, she had already set her giant cup of Mountain Dew on the floor mat and gotten out of the car. He watched as she paused at the table and exchanged a few words with Monetta. Then she bent and wrapped one arm around Monetta's shoulders and kissed her on the cheek. The impulsiveness of the act didn't surprise him, but Monetta's smiling reaction did. They obviously knew each other already. He felt a little ridiculous. Fooled. How well did Roxanne know Monetta?

Monetta was a comfortable-looking woman with dark, expressive eyes and just the slightest hint of a moustache lining her upper lip, and, beside her, Roxanne looked like a kind of young nymph. But there was nothing naive about Roxanne's manner. Ever flirtatious, she tilted her head as she talked, and directed a quick, playful glance at him as Monetta waved her inside. He felt his skin warm when Monetta also looked his way. But Monetta's calm expression never changed.

What would he say about Roxanne? Worse, what would Monetta say? He never should have brought the girl here. Monetta was too smart, too perceptive.

He got out of the car and greeted Monetta in Spanish. All is well, he told himself. Nothing was wrong. But if nothing was wrong, why was he perspiring?

"A beautiful day for being outside," he said, worried that he sounded as idiotic as he felt.

"Father," the other woman said, grabbing at his arm. "I am ill for more than three weeks with this—¿cómo se dice?—this rash on my skin." She twisted her forearm so that he could see the red, flaking skin covering the inside of it. "The doctor tells me it's all up here." She tapped at the side of her head with an index finger.

Sometimes, he actually enjoyed the rock star status that wearing the collar afforded him: he was a priest, doctor, babysitter, psychiatrist, marriage counselor—one parishioner had even asked his decorating advice. Maybe she'd thought he was gay, believing the stereotype that gay men were supposed to know about decorating.

But here he was on Monetta's territory. "Perhaps Señora Monetta . . . ," he looked to her.

"¡Basta!" Monetta said, waving a hand at the woman. "You don't do the things I tell you. You haven't even been to mass for a month. How will the saints hear you when you pray if you won't even take communion?"

Dolores stood up and jerked the sleeve of the blouse down over the angry rash.

"Hechándome insultos a me no te ve dar negocío," she said.

"Then you need to listen to me," Monetta said, replying in English. "Put me out of business if I'm so insulting. If you had listened to me as well as the doctor, you'd be better by now. But don't bother the priest."

Dolores looked from him to Monetta. He knew he should say something comforting to her, but what he really wanted to do was laugh.

"Buenos días, Father," she said. "I'm sorry to give offense." She started off down the sidewalk, her overlarge purse thumping against her side.

"But I want to help you if I can," he said.

If she heard him, she didn't give any indication. Her legs were so thin, he wondered how she could keep from wobbling on her patterned high heels. He thought that, once, she might have been an attractive woman, but something inside had obviously soured.

"Don't worry about her," Monetta said. "She'll be back tomorrow. I'm the only one who will put up with her." She gave her fingers a light snap. "Now, where's your list?"

Inside, Roxanne was bent over several large trays of beads.

"What's this?" she asked, holding up a large, yellowish bead.

"Goat bone," Monetta said. "Those are all new from Africa."

"You're allowed to import goat bone?" Romero said.

Monetta shrugged. "The hippies like them," she said. "Earrings, bracelets. They think they're recycling nature."

"These would make great offerings for an orisha." Roxanne held up a pair of glass orbs with delicate waves of amber and flecks of green buried deep inside. *"Chango would like them, I think."* She smiled.

Monetta shook her head, obviously amused. *"Ah, you come to four, five ceremonies when you were nothing but a baby girl and you think you know everything."*

"Oh, I know plenty of things," Roxanne said. She picked up a necklace and held it to the light in the window.

Romero almost laughed out loud at her teenage confidence.

"Follow me," Monetta said, gesturing him toward the back hallway. Just outside the large room where she performed ceremonies and consulted with her clients, or her many godchildren, stood a rattling white refrigerator; she reached inside and pulled out a bundle of green herbs.

"I've already told Bryant what to do with these," she said, putting them in the canvas bag he'd brought along. Bryant had also done mission work in Africa. It was throat cancer that was killing him.

"I would bring him down here, but I can't risk it," Romero said. *"Maybe Paulette, his wife. He's not doing well."*

"Poor Paulette. She tries to understand, but she cannot bring herself to think beyond what her childhood faith has taught her. Still, she is a good woman to give Bryant what he needs. When the time comes, I will go to him," Monetta said. *"No one is asking you to risk your position in the Church, Father Romero. Only you could make that choice."*

His road to the priesthood had been a complicated one. The priests he had known in Cuba were brave men. They weren't afraid of anything—not the waffling bishops who tried to appease both the government and the cowardly Vatican, and certainly not of Castro himself. It had been a clear case of hero worship. As a boy, he'd thought often of becoming a priest and wondered if God would send him a true calling. But the night he and his mother had escaped Cuba, everything changed for him. His desire to be like those men had transformed him that night. His call had come and his vocation became a blood promise.

Out in the storefront, Roxanne was at a mirror, trying on a pair of earrings.

"We are all Roxanne's playthings," Monetta said quietly. "I saw it in her the first time her mother, Carla, brought her here. She will cause somebody harm someday."

Roxanne said, "Are you talking about me?"

"Ah, niña," she said, "someone is always talking about you, aren't they?"

"I hope so," Roxanne said. "How much are these?" she held up a pair of bright enameled earrings and a handful of black and gold feathers.

Monetta shook her head again, but it was with a kind of resignation. After he paid for the items he'd bought, Romero motioned to Roxanne that it was time to go.

"Wait a minute," she said. "Do you have more things back here?" She disappeared down the hallway.

"They don't know what they want, these children," Monetta said. "I would tell you to be careful, but I do not need to say that to you."

She was probing, and he tried hard to hold her gaze. He didn't want to look away, lest she think he was trying to hide something. He pressed his mouth closed, but nodded. It struck him as ridiculous that she would talk to a grown man this way about a thirteen-year-old—particularly a priest. But standing in this shop, with its ropes of shells and garish beads and candles plastered with glittering images of saints and jewelry and plastic flowers, and the residual prayers of the hundreds if not thousands of restless souls who had passed through its door, he knew things were too complicated already. He would keep his mouth shut. He was as lost as the day he'd killed a man during his escape from Cuba. At least that man had died, and his death had been final. But this hell that he was entering threatened to be a fresh hell every day that he saw Roxanne.

"Here I am!" Roxanne said, almost running from the back room. She had pushed her hair behind her ears to show the earrings to their best effect. He saw that she was carrying the feathers and something else—were they turtle shells? She was like a child. Sweet Lord, she was a child.

He knew he was damned.

CHAPTER 15

It was too cold for the dunking booth. Romero knew they should've canceled it when they learned that it was going down into the fifties that night, but there was a line jutting out into the Spring Carnival's makeshift midway in the parking lot and they would've missed out on a lot of donation money if they had. A quarterback from St. John the Divine sat on deck, dry as a stone and shouting that no one could take him down. Romero didn't like the boy's attitude, his smug grin and bold catcalls into the crowd. He was showing off for the girls, the ones who stood off to the side, giggling, admiring.

"Will you have a go, Father?"

Romero turned at the synthesized voice. He looked down to see Bryant Carter in his wheelchair.

"That kid's a cheeky bastard," Bryant said.

Bryant looked like hell; even in the uneven glow of the portable lights the carnival people had set up his skin had a dirty yellow tinge to it. Only fifty, he looked eighty, and if he weighed ninety pounds,

Romero would've been surprised. He saw the bracelet that Monetta had sent on Bryant's wrist and there was a telltale bump underneath his shirt that was surely some kind of amulet. But what had these things done for him? Like a sacrament, they were outward signs of some grace that was (it was to be hoped) working within him. He'd heard Bryant's confession. The man was not ready to die. He needed all the grace he could get.

Romero rested a hand on Bryant's shoulder and gave it a gentle squeeze. "There's a season for everything, my friend. I think this kid's enjoying his." With his words a great shout went up. Ahead of them some other hulking young man had just narrowly missed the mark.

Bryant held out an unsteady fist to Romero.

"Go get 'em," Bryant said, dropping a wrinkled five into Romero's hand.

After Bryant's wife, Paulette, went up to speak to the carnival committee member running the booth, she moved Bryant to the head of the line, and Romero, with a slightly embarrassed reluctance, followed.

"I'm in trouble now," the boy in the cage shouted. "God's after me!"

The crowd laughed.

Romero stepped up to the line with the same wave of happy anticipation he'd always experienced when he stepped up to pitch as a boy in Cuba. Then, of course, he'd worn a well-oiled glove on his left hand and always had a wad of gum in his mouth. Fresh gum, dripping with sugar. Funny how his school equipment and books had always been crap, but the baseball team's equipment was always the best. If he'd waited and gotten a little older, he might have made it out of Cuba by playing baseball. He knew he'd been that good. But God had had other plans.

He let the first one fly and felt, more than heard, the thud of its hitting the wall. The crowd murmured its disappointment. The quarterback teased him that he should've warmed up.

A chant came from among the girls standing to one side.

"Dunk him! Dunk him! Dunk him!" It went on growing louder. He saw that Roxanne and Del led it, Roxanne the loudest. She was wear-

ing makeup, which wasn't allowed during school hours. He had heard rumors about her mother, how she never came to church, how she was always leaving Roxanne alone. No wonder the girl seemed so independent. It amused him, the way she tried to look older. She was successful at it, too. She didn't look like she was playing dress-up like some of the other girls did. She looked seductive. He looked away. He hadn't purposely avoided her at the carnival. In fact, she'd recently been absent from school and he'd succeeded in not thinking of her for almost a day. But there she was, and suddenly he was twelve, standing on the mound, hoping to impress a girl who was watching.

He swallowed, trying to force down the emotion that came into his throat. He closed his eyes, and in his mind, he prayed, "Holy Father, take the burden of this sin. Holy Father, take the burden of this sin. Holy Father, take the burden of this sin." But instead of feeling relieved of the sin, he could only see Roxanne's face behind his closed eyes. So be it.

Turning the second ball to just the right place in his hand, he opened his eyes and threw without aim.

Before the quarterback could look surprised, he was in the water and some of the men of the crowd were stepping around Bryant's wheelchair to clap Romero on the back. When they cleared, he saw Paulette wheeling Bryant away and almost went after them. He looked around to see the quarterback scrambling back onto the deck, as though to prove he was unbeatable once again. There was already someone else stepping up to the line.

Could he fault himself for scanning the crowd of girls for Roxanne? Looking for her pleasure? Her approbation? Yes. That was the only answer there could be. But she was gone. He thought he recognized the back of Del as she walked away. He wasn't sure. Maybe Roxanne hadn't been there at all. He felt sick. Angry with himself. He hoped that no one had seen him looking.

He didn't see her the rest of the night. Shortly before ten, when things were winding down, he was cornered by two members of the hospitality committee who wanted to talk about making Doughnut Sunday a weekly event. As they spoke, he felt as though he were living in some sort of alternate reality. Was this the stuff the adult world was made of? He listened, perhaps even nodded a few times, but he never really cared about what they were saying.

He remembered lying with his cheek against the stone floor at the foot of the crucifix in St. Margaret-Mary, the Spanish-built church in St. Augustine that had helped settle him and his mother after their arrival. The stone was rough, wonderfully solid, and cold against his skin. It had been only a month since he'd had to kill the fisherman who had attacked his mother. Lying there on the church floor, knowing he was safe, that his mother was safe, that he was never going to be found out, he felt the love of God reach down for him. He knew his decision to become a priest was the right one.

But it had brought him here, where he was afflicted with temptation born of the flesh and the mind, and not to some quiet monastery where he could reflect and reform his soul.

The head counselor at the seminary had been kind, but firm.

"You're not a contemplative, Romero. The Lord wants your prayers and your faith," he said. "But he also wants your youth and your talents. He wants you apart from the world, but in it."

So he was being tested.

There was room in the rectory for four priests, but Our Lady of the Hills hadn't needed so many since the early sixties. It was only he and Rudolph Frankl, now. Frankl watched him, he knew. Frankl didn't trust him, and he suspected it wasn't just because of his ties to Santeria. But Frankl couldn't watch him every moment, and because the chief priest's bedroom was at the opposite end of the rectory from his own, there was no worry that he would awaken as he opened the kitchen door.

He hadn't slept. He'd thought about going over to the church to say mass, which was always his privilege. But he knew that, with his soul in such a state of sin, he would defile the sacrament. To whom could he confess? Not to Frankl. The seal was inviolate, of course, but Frankl would spur him on to some public repentance, would, perhaps, even drive him from the parish. Wouldn't that be the best thing? He thought of his mother down in Florida, comfortable with her sister's family.

"Aí, Romero," she would say, with shame in her voice. "Me dío tu promesa." He was repenting for both of them.

A light frost had crept over the ground, and the sky was at least two hours away from a bright, mid-April dawn. Shoeless and wearing only a T-shirt and gym shorts, he made his way to the rosebushes planted beneath the rectory's dining room windows. He'd thought about getting some clippers from the garden shed, but didn't want to cross the driveway where he might be seen. His pocketknife would do.

Unmindful of the thorns that pricked at his hands, he swiftly cut five long switches from the bushes and secured them into a small bundle with a piece of twine.

Back in his room, the shades were already pulled down. He'd learned his lesson. But weeks earlier, in that moment when he'd held her gaze from the window—it was then that he had realized how much he wanted her. He turned away from the mirror to strip off his shirt. He couldn't bear to see himself, couldn't bear to look at the face that was the mask for every unclean thought he'd ever had, the eyes, the lips that betrayed him again and again.

Already, his fingers and palm were spotted with tiny pinpricks of blood, but he didn't yet feel any pain. He wrapped his hand around the bundle of switches and prayed:

Holy Father, let my sin be struck from your sight. Let your blood wash over me, cleansing me from all offense. Let me be chastened like a child. Let me know the purity of your love and forgiveness. Let my sacrifice be pleasing to you, O Lord.

He fixed Roxanne's body in his mind—her soft pink lips, the curves of her cheeks and of her slight shoulders, the jewel-like intensity of her eyes—focusing on each bewitching part of her as he raised the bundle of switches over his shoulder and beat them into his skin. With each stroke he felt an exquisite pain that intensified when he dragged the thorny switches up his back to begin again.

CHAPTER 16

Week 25 2/7

As the man from the delivery service brought in her grocery order, Alice pressed herself against the open kitchen door, standing as far back from him as she could.

"Warm for November," he said, flashing her a smile as he passed. He didn't wait for any kind of response. "This is a great old house. You live here all alone?"

Alice held her robe tighter against her body.

"I need to see the list," she said. "Last time, they forgot the anchovies I asked for."

He squinted a bit and looked up at the ceiling as though he were trying to remember something. She didn't trust his clean-cut look: the neatly pressed khaki pants, trimmed chestnut hair, and polo shirt with the delivery service's logo stitched over one breast. He reminded her too much of Thad.

"Store must've been out. I just do deliveries, you know?" he said. He gave a diffident shrug and set the delivery box on the counter to unload the bags. When he was finished, he held out a clipboard so she could sign for the order.

As she took it, her robe fell open and she saw his gaze slip down to her breasts. She signed quickly and pushed the clipboard back into his hands. She didn't bother closing the robe again. Did he like what he saw? She stared back up at him. But instead of a look of embarrassment, or lust, she saw only laughing derision in his eyes.

"Get out," she said.

He grinned and jogged down the stairs to his still-running car, bumping the empty box against his leg.

Alice slammed the door behind him. She thought of calling the delivery service and reporting the bastard, but the truth was that she didn't care to take the time. Plus, she'd already had one service refuse her further business after she'd had to scream at them for overcharging her. There just weren't that many delivery services that would deal with groceries.

It had been more than a month since she'd left the house. Not long after Del's funeral, she simply decided that she wanted to stay inside. Her highlights were grown out and her nails looked like hell, but the only person she wanted to see was Varick, and he always came to her. In fact, she hadn't even wanted to go to the funeral, but Roxanne had made her.

When Roxanne had come over to tell her about Del's suicide, her face had been puffy, her olive skin splotched with red. At first, Alice had thought something horrible had happened to Roxanne. Roxanne never cried. This was a new Roxanne—a transformed Roxanne. She found herself holding Roxanne as she told her how Del had signed into a cheap downtown hotel with her stepdaughter, Wendy, and had locked the child into another room before plunging, naked, out the window.

Why hadn't she been surprised at what Del had done? A part of her, a part of her she could barely hear but whose voice was getting stronger, told her that what Del had done was right and necessary. But what she couldn't find the words to say to Roxanne was that—while she remembered Del, remembered their friendship, remembered that she should care about what happened to her—at that moment she didn't really give a damn.

She put the groceries away, taking her time. She had nothing else to do. It had been twelve days since Varick had come. She didn't mean to count (Of course she did! She counted every minute that he was away from her!), but it was an old habit from when she and Thad had tried to become pregnant. She always knew when the first day of her last period had been. The last had begun eleven days before and had only lasted a couple of days. Even though her period was always irregular, Varick never came to her while she was menstruating. Given the things they had done, it surprised her that he would care about such a thing. But this time he'd been away so long. She was worried.

Beneath the grocery bags she found the latest envelope of papers from Jock's office. Another bastard. Del would've hated Jock for taking Thad on for a client. She took the envelope, stuffed it into the garbage disposal in the sink, turned on the water and flipped the disposal's switch. But instead of shredding the thick wedge of paper, the disposal hiccoughed and ground to a slow halt.

She fell asleep in the media room with the glow of the television on her face and began to dream within a few seconds of closing her eyes. There was music in the dream, piano music that came from another room, not the one in which she stood looking down at a baby on a changing table. It was the palest baby she had ever seen, its skin whiter than her wedding veil. She stroked its belly and it laughed and she laughed, and so she did it again. She knew nothing about the baby except that it was lovely. When had it last been fed? Did it need its diaper changed? Opening the diaper, she found that the baby was a girl child, but the diaper wasn't wet at all, so she closed it up again, suddenly afraid that someone had seen her, would want to know what she was doing. But the child itself was content, and seemed to be humming along with the music, some sort of waltz. Mozart, she thought, in the part of her brain that remembered such things. She held the baby close and stepped away from the table. They were in a hospital room, its walls the same icy white as the baby's skin. She felt like a stain in this white room with this paper-white child, unworthy of even touching its copper-colored curls. But the baby didn't mind her, only continued its quiet humming and from time to time pushed its tiny tongue between its lips, making her laugh.

Looking at the child, she felt her breasts tighten in the way she'd heard young mothers describe—a numbness came over them, a numbness that filled them and made them feel heavy, pendulous. They knew only one relief.

Dream-Alice took the child to the chair by the room's single window and sat down. The child was suddenly ravenous, its tiny mouth working, searching for the breast. Its face closed in frustration and it waved its fists, striking Alice more than once as she struggled to unbutton her blouse.

When the release finally came and she felt the milk draining from her, she began to weep with happiness. A gift! It felt like a gift she'd been given, this child, this moment. The milk flowed fast, out of both breasts at once, so that the one the child wasn't nursing on began to soak her blouse and sweater. The extra milk leaked onto the child, making it kick, angry, against her. The child nursed harder. The child, not toothless as she had thought, began to bite her.

"No!" Dream-Alice shouted at the child. She tried to pull the child from her breast, but it wouldn't give up.

"No!"

She put her hands beneath the child, but its skin was slick with milk. The pain was nothing like she'd ever felt before and the whiteness of the room itself pulsed with it. But as she tried to pull the child away, it only bit harder.

Finally, its body pink with anger, the child drew its head away for a breath. Dream-Alice pitched the child to the floor, where it shuddered to stillness, its eyes open in surprise. But the pain didn't stop, and seemed, in fact, to increase. It traveled from her breast to her limbs, her brain, her gut. She was pain itself. Dream-Alice and Alice both cried out. Alice opened her eyes to see Varick lying beside her on the deep sofa, his whisker-rough face buried in her neck. It was his hand on her left breast, frozen in a tight squeeze around the tender flesh.

. . .

When she next awoke, the sun was in the sky again and she was in her own bed.

She rose and showered, rinsing the smears of blood from her body. It stung some, and she cringed when she moved her left arm. But she knew that, if he saw her moving slowly, he would think her weak and tiresome. Was she weak? Had she been too weak to even keep Thad? Drying off in the mirror, seeing what her lover had done to her body, she knew that Thad was the one who was weak, not she.

"Darling?"

When she got no answer from Varick, she panicked. Now that he had returned, she didn't want to be apart from him. He couldn't have left the house already!

She heard voices downstairs—talking, laughing voices. After tying yet another silk robe around her, and putting on a little makeup, she followed them to the kitchen, where Varick stood, in his bare feet, cooking eggs on the Viking range. His hair was damp and he wore his shirt untucked; the loose silk couldn't quite disguise the sensuous bulk of his upper back and shoulders. She realized that she hadn't ever really heard him laugh before. But of course, his laugh was deep and genuine and he looked so easy and comfortable there in her kitchen. But she couldn't picture him there in the distant future. There was only darkness, an opaque wall that kept her from seeing anything beyond this moment.

She'd understood from the beginning that there would be no winning Varick, no fairy-tale relationship or long-term romance. Varick was here, now. Later he would be gone. And what would she be left with, then? Nothing. She'd be alone, as she'd never been before in her life. He was the one man who wanted her for herself, and herself only—and he would be gone.

The eggs smelled terrible. She wondered how long they had been in the refrigerator. Even less appealing than the smell of the eggs was the sight of the young man sitting on the granite-topped kitchen island.

"My Looking Glass girl arises," Varick said. He gave the eggs a final push around the pan and set them on a cool burner. Then he wrapped a hand around her upper arm (it hurt and she started to pout, then caught herself) and guided her over to the young man, who slid off the counter to stand before them.

A young man who looked like this one would once have frightened her: pale, pale skin (nearly as pale as the child in the dream) and color-less lips, black-dyed, unruly hair cut in a vaguely feminine, layered style, like a singer from a metal band from her childhood, tattoos around his neck and across his forehead—were they inverted tears? No, they were fangs, and not very well-done fangs at that—and silver studs on the crest of one ear, and several more on his upper lip and at his brows. Was it Varick who had changed her, made her bold and less afraid of the strange things in the world, things that were beyond her understanding? The person standing in front of her made her want to laugh, he looked so stupid.

"My Heart, this is Dillon," Varick said.

"How nice to meet you," Alice said, arranging a smile. She held out her hand, half hoping he wouldn't take it.

"Now, where to put you," Alice said. She glanced down at the over-stuffed duffel bag at Dillon's feet. "I know. Come with me." At least this was something she knew how to do—to settle a guest. But he wasn't really a guest. Not according to Varick.

Varick had devoured the vile eggs before declaring that Dillon was to be her new assistant, her majordomo. He would run errands for her, take care of security, keep her from being too lonely when Varick couldn't be with her. She'd wanted to tell him that she didn't need any-one else, that she had friends to keep her from being lonely—well, Rox-anne, anyway. But she wouldn't need anyone. She only needed him!

But then he'd gone upstairs to finish dressing and had said his good-byes before she could tell him so.

From the front hallway, they went up the main staircase. Alice trailed her fingertips over the hand-carved Italianate railing. Her father had loved European things.

"Sweet digs," Dillon said. "You've always lived here?"

"I went away to school for a while, but it didn't work out," she said.

That hideous, long semester in a roach-infested dorm suite with a girl she couldn't stand, a girl who'd had the nerve to screw her boyfriend in the next bed while Alice was supposed to pretend she didn't notice. She'd spent more than one night on the couch in the common room, waking to find people staring at her.

"Yeah, I hear you," Dillon said.

She hadn't decided yet if he was dangerous. He didn't seem to be aggressive and he followed her dutifully. If Varick trusted him, then she supposed she could. She didn't care much to look at him because he looked haunted to her, like he'd seen unpleasant things that he couldn't forget. She wondered if he'd ever killed anyone. The notion sent a thrill of electricity up her spine.

Steering away from the primary upstairs hallway, she led him to the back of the house. Would he attack her in her bed? No, Varick would kill him if he laid a hand on her, she was certain. Still, she reminded herself to lock her door when she went to her room.

The back hallway was narrower than the front, and darker. The doorways were all a little shorter than the ones in the rest of the house, as though the rooms beyond housed small people, or children.

"Is this where they kept the slaves?" Dillon said.

"Don't be an ass," Alice said. Somehow the profanity came naturally between them. "This house wasn't built until the twentieth century. There weren't slaves around here, anyway." Really, she had no idea if slaves had been kept in the area, and didn't much care.

"Take a joke," Dillon said.

She showed him to the room closest to the back kitchen stairs, imagining that that would be how he would come and go. Varick had told him to move his motorcycle into the garage, and he'd done it right away. It was clear that he would do anything Varick told him to do.

She felt herself flush at the memory of what he'd had *her* do only that morning. When she looked again at Dillon, she felt like she'd been caught and she waved her hand in the air as if she would dispel the image. But Dillon was smiling at her. *He knew.* It wasn't just that he'd witnessed the passionate kiss she'd shared with Varick before he left the house. He knew what Varick did to her, what she did for him.

"This will be the best place for you," she said, turning away to push open the door ahead of him. He had to duck his head slightly to enter the room, which was done in neutral greens and beige. It was a masculine room. Still, he looked all wrong for it, like a sideshow freak who'd wandered by mistake into a fine hotel.

"My husband didn't like having guests," she said. "So we put them in this part of the house." Mentioning Thad flustered her. When would it stop?

Dillon used his foot to slide the duffel a few feet closer to the closet. She watched as he made his way around the room, checking into bureau drawers, glancing under the bed. He even stood in front of the window to check out the view, as though he were a potential boarder trying to make up his mind. Apparently satisfied, he came over to her.

"But Asshole Thad isn't coming home, is he?" he said.

"I don't think that's any of your business," she said. She didn't like the way his eyes were narrowed, the studs along one brow dropping with his scowl.

"It's my sister he's fucking," Dillon said. "It's definitely my business."

CHAPTER 17

"He belongs to all of us, not just you, Roxanne," Alice said.

She leaned back to pull a section from the cinnamon coffee cake her mother had bought for breakfast; she did it without lifting her feet from the water of the hot tub, where Del and Roxanne were immersed to their chins. Built directly into the floor of the basement, the hot tub could seat at least twenty people. For Del and Roxanne, it was one of the highlights of sleeping over at Alice's house. The other was the food Alice's mother fed them: snacks of filet mignon, homemade pizza for dinner, pies and cakes from Busken bakery for dessert. There were always M&Ms in the candy jar in the kitchen and root beer in the refrigerator. Alice, though, only picked at the food, while the other two stuffed themselves—but she was the only one who ever gained any weight.

"I don't want him," Del said. She hadn't wanted to be a part of Roxanne's ceremony in the first place. "He's too old. And what are you going to do with him, anyway? Before you go to hell, I mean."

Roxanne ignored her. She scooted down the step to position her lower back in front of a water jet.

"I didn't say we wouldn't share him, Alice," Roxanne said.

"That's gross," Del said. She'd seen the pictures from the magazine that Roxanne had stolen from her mother's current boyfriend, the pictures of the man and two naked women outside on a picnic blanket. All she could think of when she saw the picture was how much she hated getting chigger bites from the grass and how much worse it would be not to have any underwear on at all.

Alice giggled.

"I still don't believe that's where he came from," Del said. "We knew the school was getting a new priest anyway."

"You just don't get it," Roxanne said. "It all came together at once. It was cosmic serendipity. One couldn't have happened without the other."

"Whatever," Del said.

"He could be like a man sandwich," Alice said. "And we could be the bread!" Her laugh was high, giddy.

Del had had enough and she got out of the hot tub. "You two are disgusting," she said. "Why can't we just talk about boys—actual boys like the ones we actually know, the ones who can take us to dances and movies and concerts. Why does everything have to be so gross?" She stood dripping on the tiled floor.

Roxanne looked up. Her dark curls were pulled back and clipped to the top of her head so that only a few damp tendrils hung about her face. She was the only one who'd gotten into the hot tub naked, not caring if either of Alice's parents would accidentally see her. Del knew Roxanne thought of herself as sexy, like the girls in the magazine. Then she saw the irritation drain from Roxanne's eyes, and Roxanne gave her a smile.

"Oh, Del," she said, lifting her hand from the water to wave Del back to the hot tub. "Get back in. Don't you know by now when I'm teasing you? Nobody's going to do anything. And nobody's going to hell. It's just a game."

Alice looked confused. "What do you mean?" she said. "Somebody should have told me that."

"He's real enough. We brought him here," Roxanne said. "But we're not going to do anything. Not really."

"I thought we were going to—" Alice stumbled over her words. "You know."

"Don't be ridiculous, Alice," she said. "We're only thirteen." She rolled her eyes at Del. "Come on, silly. Get back in the water. We've got all afternoon."

Del didn't believe her, but she wanted to.

"But, Roxanne, you said we wouldn't be virgins anymore. You said it would be better than with stupid boys our own age," Alice said. "That's what you said."

"Come and sit by me," Roxanne said. "Don't freak out. You're not going to be a virgin forever. Even Jesus's mother wasn't a virgin forever. We can try the spell again if you want, and get you someone more our age."

"Could we not?" Del said. "Can't we just go meet boys at a basketball game, or something?"

When Alice got back into the hot tub to sit beside Roxanne, resting her head on Roxanne's shoulder, Del sat down where Alice had been.

"Sure," Roxanne said, giving Del another smile. "Basketball it is." She shifted where she sat.

"Alice, honey, your big old elbow's poking me," she said. "And move. Your mom's going to come down here and think we're queer or something."

Alice pouted, but moved over.

As if on cue, Alice's mother opened the door. "Sandwiches!" she said.

Roxanne watched from the slivered opening between the cupboard doors as Romero took off his shirt. She felt her own breath, warm against her face. She was afraid, but only a little. The only men she had ever seen naked were statues at the museum or photos in magazines, their bodies firm and almost perfect. She saw that Romero's body was like that, his chest and arms and face browner than her own, and smooth. She thought of Michelangelo's statue of David, which she had seen in an art book. David, almost girl-like in his slender pose, but naked, with nothing hidden.

Romero hung his shirt and pants on the valet and disappeared into the bathroom for a few minutes, closing the door behind him. She heard water running and the toilet flush. She worried some about getting pregnant, but was certain that it couldn't happen the first time she had sex. Surely, he would know what to do. She asked God to let her do this, just this once.

She was naked beneath the lacy white gown that she had brought from home. Carla would never miss it, buried as it was in the third dresser drawer down for at least a year. Her new favorites were turquoise, bright red, and purple negligees and teddys that, she said, made her feel young again. The gown had smelled vaguely of her mother's Obsession perfume until she aired it out and sprayed her favorite lemony scent on it to freshen it. The stiff lace rubbed against her nipples, making them sore. But she wasn't thinking about that. She was thinking about what she would do once she was in Romero's bed.

When he came out of the bathroom, he shut off the bedroom lights and opened the curtains overlooking the parking lot. He stood looking out and she wondered what he was thinking about. Did priests think only about God? She knew it wasn't true for him—she had seen the way he looked at her. Would he go to hell if he touched her? Del could be right. They might all be going to hell.

He turned to his bed and knelt down beside it. She could hear the whisper of his prayers but not the words.

Then he was in bed.

It was hard to wait, to be silent. He turned and sighed many times before settling on his side, facing the windows. The lights in the parking lot were out, and so there was only moonlight falling across the lower half of the bed. She thought about her bicycle—the one she hated—leaning against the garden shed, and tried to remember if it was out of sight.

Listening to his breathing, she thought he might be asleep, and pushed open the cupboard door. But when she stepped out, it all began to go wrong.

He sat up to look at her, the moonlight carving out the features of his face. He didn't look quite real. Could he see her in the darkness?

She started to take a step toward him, but found she couldn't. Then he was out of bed and shaking her by the shoulders.

"What are you doing? What are you doing, Roxanne?" His voice was a gruff whisper. He was angry. But there was something else. Something frightening. She told herself not to be afraid, that he would not hurt her. But the realization that she was alone in this room with a man—a man she knew she should want, should, right then in fact, be touching as she had planned, the way she had read about in the sex book—paralyzed her.

"Madre de Dios, what do you want from me?"

But she could not speak. Her lips parted, and his mouth was on hers, crushing it, and he was pushing his tongue into her mouth, crushing her to him, and he tasted of toothpaste and garlic and sleep. His end-of-day beard was rough against her face and her eyes were open, but his were closed, pressed tightly shut with the force, the effort of kissing her. She liked it, that kiss, and kissed him back, trying to snake her small tongue around his. Still kissing her, he held her with one arm and swept the other down her back to her legs and he lifted her from the floor and carried her over to the bed.

He dropped her onto it. "This is what you want?" he said.

She tried to remember what she was supposed to do, but she could only lie there, her mouth open, puzzled over the sudden absence of the kiss.

"You're trying to kill me, aren't you? You, a child!"

"I'm not a child," she said.

He sat down on the bed near her and put his face in his hands.

Watching him, she no longer felt at all afraid. The fear had been replaced by something else—a kind of hunger that had nothing to do with food. She reached out to touch his arm.

"I'm not," she said.

He let her hand rest there for a moment, and it was as though she could feel him deciding what he should do. She almost felt sorry for him. But this new feeling inside her pushed her pity away.

"I could hurt you, Roxanne," he said, turning to her.

"You won't hurt me. I know you won't," she said. "And I'm not afraid."

He pushed her arm away and rested his hand on her chest. She could feel the heat from his hand through the thin nightgown as it moved up her body. Before she could speak, his fingers tightened around her neck. He didn't squeeze hard enough to cut off her breath, just hard enough to grip her so that he could raise her up off the pillow to look into his face. She knew that only a little more pressure would kill her. She didn't struggle. She knew he wouldn't let her die.

"You're not going to do this to me, puta," he said. "I don't know how you got in here, but you're going to get out of my room. I don't want to see you again. Here. In school. In church. Anywhere."

He pushed her back to the bed and she lay gasping for breath.

"Where are your clothes?"

When she didn't answer, he went to the cupboard and felt around for her things. She sat up. What she had been feeling was transformed. Was she angry? No. But neither will she do what he's told her to do. No one told her what to do.

He tossed her clothes onto the bed.

"You can dress in the bathroom," he said.

"I won't," she said. "I'll put on my clothes in here. If you don't let me, I'll scream for Father Frankl."

"I'm not going to be blackmailed by a child," he said. His face was ugly to her now, twisted and mean. He didn't move.

Roxanne crossed her arms in front of her and, with him watching, raised the gown up, over her hips, her waist, her breasts, all the time looking back at him. She slipped it over her head and let it drop to the floor. She shook out her hair and stood, unmoving and naked before him, knowing she had won.

CHAPTER 18

Week 27 4/7

Thad brought the car around to the front of the office to pick up Amber for her OB appointment. As she came out the door, she turned back to wave good-bye to Patty, the new receptionist.

He had held an office meeting a few weeks earlier to let the staff know about both his divorce and his relationship with Amber. Their reaction was more generous than he'd anticipated. He'd thought that maybe the older women in the office would be the ones to condemn him, but he'd only lost Jennifer, the twenty-five-year-old receptionist. She'd quit outright before the meeting was over, telling him and Amber and everyone in the room that she'd suspected what was going on since Amber had started showing and thought they were both disgusting. Amber cried in his arms that night, but she had kept her composure in the face of Jennifer's cruelty. When Jennifer left the room, he told the remaining women that if they wanted to go as well he'd release them with severance pay and good recommendations, but no one took him up on the offer.

It had been one of those times he was grateful for the smallness of the office, and the loyalty of the women who worked for him. He knew that he probably deserved worse, and was damn glad for what he got. Then again, they all knew Alice. And they all knew Amber. They'd been careful around Amber for a while afterward, but now the tone in the office was once again light and familiar.

"Ready?" he said, as Amber got in. She sank heavily into the passenger seat and pulled the seat belt, snug, over her belly.

"You bet," she said. She leaned over to kiss him on the cheek.

Amber had picked a doctor on the west side of town, close to where she'd grown up, but, more important, far away from any of the gynecologists and fertility specialists that he and Alice had frequented. But this waiting room, filled with bored pregnant women, had the same lilac-colored, generic femininity about it as all the others. Once again, he was the only man in sight.

When had his life been taken over by women? He'd grown up with two older brothers and all the attendant noise and sports and fights and he'd held his own. There had been the frat brothers and other guys to hang around with in college. But not so much in dental school, which had been filled with women. And then, the practice. Again, women. Not only was his staff female, but many of his patients were women and children. Amber had told him how the women in the practice had all begun to menstruate at the same time, like they were girls in a college dormitory. She thought it was funny, but he just didn't want to think about it. He needed to call Jock and set up a golf game or something. It would be a relief to get away for a few hours, to be in the company of other men and just not have to give a damn. With a couple of other guys in the foursome, he wouldn't have to spend all morning talking with Jock about Alice.

Finally, after sitting in two different waiting rooms for half an hour each and reading far more of a food magazine than he cared to, they went in for the ultrasound.

"Dad, you sit right on that stool, there," the woman seated in front of the ultrasound machine said. She was like a large, friendly cat at home in the middle of her own dim little cave. "That way you can see the screen and hold Momma's hand at the same time."

From her own stool she looked at Amber over her reading glasses, which sat far down on her nose, almost folded into her fleshy, unlined face. "And you, Momma, you hop up there and tug your pants down and your shirt up and we'll see what baby's up to today."

He and Amber took their places, Amber winking at him as she shimmied the maternity jeans she'd changed into down over her hips.

As the technician readied the machine, she prattled on about the weather and how poor the Reds' season had been and how the Bengals weren't looking much better. "You a football fan, Dad?" she said.

Thad allowed as how he was, but that he didn't get to games very often.

"With the price of tickets," she said, "who can go?" She glanced over Amber's paperwork.

"All right, Momma," she said. "I'm going to squirt some of this heated-up jelly on your tummy and see what's what."

"That feels good," Amber said, as the woman spread the jelly with the ultrasound wand.

The technician laughed. "Oh, let's leave the feeling good stuff to Dad, right Dad?"

Thad laughed easily.

"Now, you told me last time you didn't want to know what sex Baby is," the woman said.

Amber looked at Thad and smiled. "I think we changed our minds," she said.

He didn't know whether to discourage her or not. Would it be worse for her to find out it was a boy when it was born? He knew how badly she wanted a girl, but he also knew his family's history pretty much ensured it would be a boy. Did he care as well? As surrounded as he was by women, the thought of having a girl child appealed to him— a girl with Amber's kind demeanor and hazel eyes, which would brighten whenever he came into a room.

"It's up to you," he said.

"They almost always change their minds," the technician said. "I wanted to know with all four of mine. It's easier to say when one's a boy, you know. But there aren't any money-back guarantees."

"I'm not worried about that," Amber said.

The image grew clearer on the screen. Thad could see it was definitely a baby. It was twenty-seven weeks along, and he could make out the shape of its face, the rounded tip of its nose, the arm that seemed to be folded against its chest in sleep. The picture was clear, but strange, almost like a transmission from some alien world. One of the child's feet seemed to press against the screen, pulsing, as though trying to push its way out. He wondered if Amber could feel it.

Amber squeezed his hand as she stared at the screen. Boy or girl, he knew he had competition, already. He could see by the look on her face that she was in love.

The baby stretched.

"Pretty good visual for twenty-seven weeks and four days," the technician said, freezing the image. "There's not a lot of wiggle room." She pointed to the screen. "I'd say that's our money shot right there."

"What do you mean?" he said.

"Look right there," she said. "What do you see?"

"I can't tell," Amber said, squinting. "I can't see anything."

"My point, exactly," the technician said.

Amber was quiet all through dinner and at the maternity store in the mall where she'd wanted to pick up a couple new pairs of pants. She'd told him she was just tired, but he knew it was more than that. It was bad enough that she had to deal with him and his divorce from Alice, but now, the doctor had frightened her. He regretted telling the doctor his family's history in front of her, how the female babies almost never made it to term, usually miscarrying before the eighth month. But he also knew it was better this way. They had to be prepared.

"Sixty years," the doctor had said. She shook her head. "Of course, we'll keep a sharp eye on things, but those are some serious odds, Amber."

As they left the mall's parking area and drove toward the highway, Amber leaned her head back and closed her eyes. If she was angry that he hadn't warned her, she didn't say. It was just as well that they drove in silence. He couldn't think of anything to say that might help. While, technically, he hadn't lied to her, he knew he hadn't been honest enough.

His father made him leave his new knights book—a gift his grandmother had brought him when she'd come to stay while his mother was in the hospital—in the car. He looked back as the door of the car slammed shut, feeling the unfairness of it. His mother held tight to his hand as she pulled him across the wet grass. He was wearing a new shirt and pants, nicer even than the ones he usually wore to church, and black leather shoes with short laces that had belonged to his brother, Rick. He longed to squat down and touch the grass they walked over: it was thick, like fuzzy green carpet, like the grass at his friend Evan's house. But his mother wouldn't slow, and his shoes skidded on the slick leaves of grass. She looked angry, like she did when he'd done something wrong.

Behind them came his brothers and their father. No one spoke. Even in church, when he'd tried to show them the pictures of the armor and horses in his book, they'd shushed him.

Ahead was the same white box covered in flowers that had been in church. He'd never seen so many flowers except when he went with his mother to the florist shop. Inside the box was his sister, Rose, they'd told him. And she was dead. But he'd never seen her. His brothers had seen her and had told him she looked like a baby that was sleeping—only she was dead.

He wanted a sister. He liked the girls in his kindergarten class and didn't mind when they begged him to be the dad when they played "house" at school. He liked being the dad and telling the other kids what to do.

Would there be another sister? What was this one like? He imagined the baby inside the box looking like a doll, with curly blond hair and painted blue eyes and wearing black plastic shoes like the doll from the toy shelf at school that someone had named Africa. Someone had stolen Africa the week before, though, and everyone's cubby and backpacks had been searched, and Miss Roberts had sat them in the circle and told them why stealing was a sin.

He sat beside his mother in a folding chair like the ones at home she got out for Tuesday bridge.

He tugged on her arm. When she inclined her head, he whispered, "Will we get another one?" He wasn't sure, but it only seemed right to whisper, even though they were outside.

"Another what?" his mother said. Her face didn't look so angry anymore.

"Another sister?"

But she only stared back at him. Her nose was red and her hair was messier than it had been at church and he could tell she was sad. Finally, she shook her head and turned away. She let go of his hand and began to dig in her purse for something. After a moment, she pulled out a package of wintergreen LifeSavers and gave him one. He hesitated before taking it.

"It's okay," she whispered, handing him the roll. "You can have them all." Now there were tears in her eyes.

Unsure how to comfort her, he sucked on the mint and looked away. He stuffed the rest of the roll in his jacket pocket before his brothers could see what he had.

There was a green cloth spread out in front of them, but he could see there was a hole beneath it. No one had told him, but he knew they were going to put his sister in the hole, just like they'd buried Jason's dead guinea pig in the backyard.

The priest talked, but only for a few minutes. Then they all stood up again. He watched as his mother and father went to the coffin. Jason came over and put a hand on his shoulder.

"Get off!" Thad said, shrugging the hand away.

"Be quiet," Jason said, his voice a whisper. "Just shut up."

"What are we doing?"

"We're going home."

A minute later, his mother and father walked away from the box. His mother clutched a white rose she'd taken from the spray on the box's lid.

"Why are we going?" he asked her. "When are they going to put the box in the ground?"

"After we leave, son," his dad said, picking him up.

He knew he was really too big to be carried, but he didn't struggle. As they walked toward the car, he looked back at the cloth-covered hole and his sister's box, which was there by itself with no one to watch it. Even the priest was walking away, talking with his grandmother. His sister was in a box, and they were leaving her there.

Back at home, he slept. The next day was another school day, but they had let him stay up and watch Andy Griffith on the all-night channel until someone said it was midnight and he should go brush his teeth and get in bed.

He dreamed. There were birds flying above the car as he drove with his mother; he was in the front seat, where he almost never got to sit because Rick always called it first. They were on their way to the grocery store, and his mother was singing the "Down by the Bay Where the Watermelons Grow" song and she tried to get him to sing along, but he told her that no, he didn't want to. She sang on as he watched out the window. They passed the grocery store and the post office. Then he saw a park that he didn't know—it had swings taller than any he'd seen before, tall enough for giants, and monkey bars as well. Two men in suits of armor guarding the gates of the park held lances high up into the air as though they would pierce the sky. But beyond the swings, in a corner of the park beneath the picnic shelter, he saw two people. One was a woman, but she was so pale, her skin almost glowed white. There was a man, too, a horrible-looking man whose teeth glinted and flashed like metal, and who Dream-Thad thought was wearing a heavily-patterned shirt. But as the man and woman walked toward him he saw the man's arms flex with the weight of the white box he carried, and Thad realized the man was covered in elaborate flower tattoos. His sister was in the box. His sister was being stolen!

He screamed for his mother to stop the car, but she only sang louder, and he couldn't get her attention. He rolled down the window and yelled for the pair to stop, but the woman only waved and smiled, her lips stretched thin over her yellowed teeth. The man and woman started out the gates of the park, and the men in armor let them pass. Thad screamed again, and awoke, alone in his room, the vibrations of

the scream still pulsing in the air around him. He waited in his bed for
his mother or father to come and hold him, but no one came.

In the passenger seat beside him, Amber sat up.

"Did I fall asleep?" she said. "I'm sorry. Where are we?"

"You did," Thad said.

Amber looked out the window. "Thad, why are we here?" There
was a note of panic in her voice. Night had fallen, and streetlamps were
on. The windows of the houses around them were lighted as well.

He knew what he'd done. Out of habit and distraction, he'd driven
to the house he'd shared with Alice for so many years. What a stupid
thing to do! They had just passed Beatrice Avenue and were on their
way down the hill; the house was coming up on the left. The road was
crowded with parked cars, which was unusual every day of the year except during June's Festival in the Park. Now it was the end of November.

"I don't know," Thad said. "I—I'm sorry. I don't know, baby. I was
just driving."

He slowed as they came down the hill, and their eyes were drawn to
the house, which was blazing with light. Cars of all kinds overflowed
the driveway. Two young women not older than sixteen or seventeen
started across the road in front of them.

"Thad!" Amber said.

He braked the car, and one of the girls flipped him off, then walked
past slowly, her black or purple fingernail polish and heavily made up
eyes dark against her skin, stark and overexposed in the headlights.
The other girl kept her head down, hurrying in a pair of stiletto heels.

"Who the hell are these people?" Thad said. "How did this happen?"

He told himself that he should have paid more attention to what
was going on with Alice. Jock had told him that some "creepy-looking
guy" had answered Alice's door when one of the servers went by, but
Thad had let it go. Because Alice wasn't messing with their assets or
opening accounts in his name, he'd thought he was as good as free.
He'd walked away from her, and had thought she could just go to hell

her own way. This, though, he could hardly ignore. From the look of the cars and the two girls and the shadows and burning points of cigarettes he saw in the driveway, he knew Alice was somehow in over her head. She was occasionally flaky and unpredictable, but this party hinted at darker things.

"You think we should do something?" Amber said. "You think she's okay?"

They were the same questions he asked himself. Amber was generous when it came to Alice, even encouraging him to check on her because Alice had been so dependent on him. He could have told her things that would have made her less sympathetic, but he didn't.

"I don't think there's anything to do about it now," he said. Two police cars came up the hill ahead of them, their flashing lights strobing off the nearby trees. He tried to remember if he'd ever seen police cars doing anything but passing through on their street.

Thad drove slowly down the hill, offering the police a polite wave as he passed.

CHAPTER 19

When Father Frankl turned the Buick into Bryant's long driveway, Romero saw the last thing he wanted to see among all the vehicles parked there: Monetta's small Honda, with its bright yellow Jesus=Peace sticker on its bumper. He said a silent prayer to ask that the house not be filled with incense and drumming and Monetta's godchildren. Bryant was about to meet God face-to-face. He didn't need the condemnation of Father Frankl to hurry him along.

But when they walked in the open front door, there was Bryant, lying on the hospital bed in the living room with his eyes closed, surrounded by his family, with Monetta near his head, rubbing something aromatic on his forehead and chanting softly. He also saw several of Bryant's friends from church—at least two of whom, he knew, were sympathetic to Monetta's ministrations. The only sounds in the room were Monetta's soothing voice and the regular ticking of Bryant's oxygen machine. Frankl turned back to give Romero a look that said, This is all your fault. ·

The windows in the house were all open. Paulette, Bryant's wife, was weeping. When she saw Father Frankl, she began to weep harder.

"You can leave now," Frankl said, gesturing toward Monetta.

"Father," Romero said. "There's no need."

Frankl ignored him and pushed past the other visitors to get to Paulette.

"Paulette," he said, taking her hand. "You called me. You know it's time to end all this foolishness."

Paulette nodded, but her children made it clear they thought she was wrong.

"You have to let her stay," the oldest son said. "Dad asked you." The daughter agreed. Romero knew that neither of them were initiates, but they obviously respected Bryant's wishes.

It was Monetta who silenced them.

"You should honor Father Frankl as you honor your own father," she said. "His sacraments are our sacraments. The orishas would not stand in the way of Our Señor, as you should not."

"Don't try to flatter me," Frankl said. "Paulette wants you to leave."

"Does she have to go?" Paulette said. "Why is everyone being so ugly? Bryant can hear you. He shouldn't have to suffer that, too."

Romero couldn't bear to see the pain on Paulette's face. The past year had aged her seven—he could hardly see the young woman she had been in the family and wedding pictures hung all over the house. There were new creases of sadness in her face that hadn't been there even a month before.

"Monetta, shall we go outside?" Romero said.

Monetta nodded and leaned to kiss Bryant's head, which had only just begun to regrow the hair he'd lost during chemo. Then she took Paulette's hand and pressed it gently to her cheek.

Outside, there was a chill breeze, cold for late April, and the sunshine was bright and stark. Romero thought that it was a shame that Bryant would die on such a day, that he would probably never open his eyes again to see the beauty of it.

"You should go back in," Monetta said. "Father Frankl may need you. He won't like you talking to me."

"*Father Frankl is misguided,*" *he said.*

Monetta shook her head.

"*You are too young,*" *she said.* "*You don't know what his burdens have been.*"

"*He's robbing Bryant of his right to die the way he wants to.*"

Monetta smiled. "*Bryant is on his way. Nothing Father Frankl can do will touch him now.*"

Was she saying that the last rites, the healing unction and the Eucharist that Father Frankl was probably already administering would do nothing for him? For his soul? Why didn't his own faith step in and close that gap, that tiny sliver of unbelief that always seemed to slip in, so quietly, so assuredly, when he least expected it? No matter how many times he'd been told at seminary that such a thing was normal, that he wouldn't be human if Satan couldn't work in that glimmer of doubt, he couldn't bear the fact that he was susceptible. Ever since he'd come to this city, he'd felt the tangible presence of evil around him. He was plagued with desire. Plagued with doubt.

He knew it would have crushed him if he hadn't found some relief. He had acknowledged the desire, and, with Roxanne's help, had given himself completely over to it. There was a kind of purity in the awfulness of what he had done to her. With her. That night, those hours he'd spent with her had seemed to hold a lifetime of relief. But she hadn't come back, and now wouldn't look him in the eye. He felt himself imprisoned all over again. He envied Bryant his coming death.

When they finally went back inside, Monetta sat in a chair just inside the door, watchful, but wearing a look of peaceful confidence on her face.

Father Frankl indicated that he should act as his server, and he watched as Frankl administered communion to Bryant in his shallow sleep by placing a drop of wine on his lips as though he were an infant.

The rest of the family had all stepped back. Only Paulette and Father Frankl and Romero were near Bryant. Father Frankl had done what he'd come to do, and they all stood watching, waiting with Bryant in this quiet pause. The breeze from the open windows made soft billows of the curtains and played over their skin. Did Father

Frankl know that Monetta had opened the windows to ensure the safe transport of Bryant's soul? Romero doubted it.

Bryant's daughter began to sob. Paulette watched her across the bed, helpless. He knew she was afraid to let go of Bryant's hand.

He took the small chalice containing the wine from Father Frankl and set it on the table next to the bed. As he touched the silver paten, Bryant grabbed his arm. Paulette cried out.

Bryant's eyes were open and fixed on him.

"Bryant," Paulette said, trying to push Romero away. "Bryant."

But Bryant's grip on Romero's arm was strong and wouldn't be broken. Neither would he look away, at his wife.

Her voice was pitiful. "It's me, Bryant. Please."

Romero put a hand over Bryant's.

Bryant's eyes were sad, full of pity, as he looked at Romero. He moved his lips as if he were trying to speak. Paulette fumbled for the voice box and held it to his throat, her hand shaking.

"Lost," he said, the mechanical sound of it like a message from another world.

Paulette and Father Frankl looked at Romero, and both missed seeing Bryant's eyes close as he slipped back into his coma.

CHAPTER 20

Week 27 6/7

"I miss her," Jock said. "And Wendy—she doesn't like me to leave her alone at all. I'm impressed that you got her to bed."

Roxanne shrugged. "We just had a little girl-talk. She told me she knows that Del and her mommy are both in heaven and that they like to have lunch together. Daisy sandwiches, hummingbird nectar, that kind of thing. They wear Disney Princess ball gowns, too."

"She has *some* imagination," Jock said. He lifted the bottle of Syrah from its place on the table. "More?"

Roxanne held out her glass. Jock looked much thinner than when she'd seen him at the funeral. She tried to remember how old he was. Forty? Forty-three? He was still muscular, but she guessed he'd been spending less time at the gym and more time with Wendy. She was aware of him sexually, as she was with almost every man she was close to. (With the exception of Colwyn, of course. Colwyn was just Colwyn.) She suspected Jock wouldn't want to be with anyone for a good long time.

The conversation stalled. It was strange to be in Del's house with Del gone. When she'd walked past the first floor master suite, she saw that one of Del's robes was still hanging on the back of an open closet door. There were signs of Del everywhere: photographs; the drawing that she herself had done of Del more than ten years earlier, now in a frame that was much grander than the sketch itself; Del's car out in the garage. The tidy Mercedes had been Jock's second anniversary gift to her.

"I still can't get it out of my head, Roxanne. Who do you think he was?" Jock said.

He'd asked her this before, and she still didn't have an answer. Del would've told her if she'd been having an affair. Maybe she wouldn't have told Alice, but she would've told *her*. The whole thing was just too freakish.

"You just said yourself that Wendy has an amazing imagination," she told him. "Maybe she doesn't want to believe that Del would've done that to herself."

"We're not talking about a fucking daisy sandwich," Jock said. Then, "I'm sorry." He ran a hand through his hair. "The police dropped it so fast after the cretin at the hotel desk told them she was alone with Wendy when she took the room, and then when the autopsy didn't show any evidence she'd . . . you know . . . been with anyone else—it's just been killing me. I don't want to believe Wendy. I don't want to believe Del locked herself in a room with some creep while our daughter—*my daughter*—waited outside the door and heard God knows what. It makes me sick."

"Jock." Roxanne didn't know what to say.

"So you believe Wendy?" Jock said. "How can you think that of Del? She wasn't like you, Roxanne. She didn't sleep around."

Roxanne stared back at him. She saw now that he wasn't doing well, that what Del had done was eating at him from the inside.

"I'll go now," she said, standing up. He hadn't hurt her feelings. She just didn't want to see where this would go.

"Wait," Jock said. "Don't go, Roxanne. Please."

Roxanne pictured the bedroom he'd shared with Del, the enormous four-poster bed that she'd helped Del find at auction, and the delicate slipper chair that Del had loved even though Roxanne told her it didn't suit the scale of the room. Del had loved her, but not in the silly, slavish way that Alice and so many men had. Del was—of anyone in the world—the person she could trust the most. She thought she was done crying over the stupid thing that Del had done to herself, but, as Jock moved closer to her, she felt her throat tighten.

"Really, Jock, it's okay." She reached for her purse and looked around for her cloak.

"Wait there," Jock said. He'd stepped so close to her that she thought he might try to kiss her, but he suddenly turned away, headed for the front of the house.

Roxanne sighed. She had only come because she wanted to be close to Del and Del's things for a while. But now she was tangled up with poor Jock. Men were so tragic.

As large as he was, Jock moved quickly, and he was back in the family room in a moment, carrying a checkbook binder.

"What are you working on?" he said, his demeanor had changed. He was almost the man he appeared to be when Wendy was around: serious, but confident.

"What do you mean?" she said.

"I mean, are you working on any commissions now? Or on a show?"

Roxanne laid her purse back down on the side table. "I'm planning a show in early January," she said. "It's almost ready. I'll probably do two more pieces." There was one started already, back in her studio. It was coming to her, what she would find in the clay. It would be a girl this time, she thought, a girl on the back of a golden eagle, the girl leaning forward, diving with the bird, bloodlust in her movement, if not in her eyes.

Jock lay open the binder on the coffee table and flipped to the blank checks.

"I want you to do something for me," he said. "Forget about the last two pieces if you want. I'll make up the income to you. I want you to do something special for me. For Wendy and me."

She was so taken by surprise that she had no idea of what he was going to say next.

"Listen," he said. "You can put it in the show if you want. I don't mind. Then we'll make a place for it here. Wendy will love it." His voice was excited. "You're the best person I can think of to create a memorial to Del."

She glanced over at the sketch on the wall, which she'd done the summer after her junior year in college. She'd arrived at the apartment to find her mother deep into some program that required her to sell enormous quantities of cleaning supplies. The living room, dining room—even Roxanne's bedroom—were filled with stacks of heavy cardboard boxes. There was a new boyfriend, too, a guy named Daryl who didn't seem too awful, but she didn't like the meaty warmth of his hand when he rested it on her shoulder as he talked. Her whole life she'd managed to keep her mother's boyfriends at a fairly comfortable distance, and she wanted to keep it that way.

Del didn't take much convincing to drive down to Herrington Lake with her, but Alice wouldn't go because she hated to camp. Their cabin was rough, but they spent their days on a rented boat on the lake. Del's fiancé had come down for a day in the middle of the week as well. Roxanne hadn't liked him from the first, but she couldn't talk Del out of marrying him, then or later.

On their last day, they packed a lunch and Roxanne took her sketchpad with her onto the boat. They found a remote cove on the eastern side of the lake and dropped anchor. It was peaceful there, but the area beyond the trees was dark and intimidating and something in its hidden recesses called to the secretiveness inside Roxanne. *Why was she always drawn to darkness?* But Del had been so beautiful that day, laughing and freckled and carefree. There wasn't an ounce of secretiveness in Del; she was somehow the antithesis of what lay beneath the trees. It had been as though she'd never seen Del before. Del had always just been there: someone to listen to her, to help her get what she wanted, to help her get away from the things she didn't want. The sketch came to her quickly, but it was as detailed as if she'd labored over it for weeks. She had loved Del that day, and even she could see it in the sketch.

"I wouldn't know what to do, Jock," she said. "You have to tell me what you want. Do you want a sculpture? Do you want her likeness? There are people out there—expensive people, sure—who do stunning portraits. You just have to tell them a little bit about her. Give them photographs."

"I don't want that," he said. "You. You, Roxanne, knew her better than anyone. Do a sculpture of her. That's what you like to do best, isn't it?"

But this was Del. She didn't know if she could capture Del again. She didn't know if she wanted to try.

Jock filled in one of the checks and held it out to her. It was made out for ten thousand dollars.

"That's a down payment," he said. "You tell me when you need more and it's yours."

She took the check. The money would be more than enough. "I don't know if I can," she said. "You need to remember her the way she's in your head. So does Wendy. I can't bring her back to you."

"Please," he said. "Try."

CHAPTER 21

Del knocked softly on the door of Father Frankl's office, not really knowing what to expect. Roxanne had left her a note in her locker after lunch: Just trust me this afternoon, okay? R. She had the sick feeling that it had something to do with Father Romero and the way Roxanne had stopped talking about him but still stared hard at him in math class, never speaking to him unless he made her answer a math question. There was something wrong. She'd spent the previous afternoon at Roxanne's house, and even though they had drunk most of three beers and watched Rear Window, *their favorite, Roxanne still wouldn't tell her what was going on.*

What was it about Roxanne that she had to make a big deal out of everything? Nothing was ever normal with her.

Father Frankl opened the door. He wasn't smiling.

"Sit there, Del," he said, indicating an empty chair in front of his desk. She'd been in the dim, paneled office only a few times—and only when she was being disciplined. Its walls were lined with Father Frankl's

degrees and certificates, and painted portraits of the priests who had run the school for the past seventy years. Their stern faces looked down on them like so many judges in a courtroom. Roxanne and Alice sat in the other two chairs. Alice's face was splotched and wet with tears.

As Father Frankl went around to his chair, Del whispered to Alice. "What's wrong? Where were you today?" But Alice wouldn't look at her.

"Del," Father Frankl said. "Where were you yesterday afternoon?"

Del glanced over at Roxanne, who was looking out the window.

"Am I in trouble?" Del said.

"Right after school. Were you where you were supposed to be?"

"I was supposed to be tutoring with Father Romero," she said. "But I forgot."

"Forgot?"

Roxanne had asked her to come to the house while her mother was at work, but Del really had forgotten about the tutoring session until they were almost at the house. Had Father Romero called her mother?

"I walked home, through the park. He only tutors me every couple weeks," she said. "It's not like it's a big deal or anything." Did he believe her? She couldn't tell.

"Are you uncomfortable being around Father Romero?" Father Frankl said. He held a pen in his hand, but wasn't writing anything down.

"I don't know," she said. "What do you mean?"

Father Frankl looked uncomfortable himself. "Has Father Romero ever been inappropriate with you?"

"Tell him, Del," Roxanne said, leaning forward. "Tell him how he touched you in the hallway that day."

Del felt lost, unsure of what to say. She knew she was playing some kind of role here, or a game, but she wasn't sure what it was.

But it was Alice who spoke.

"Yesterday I went to try to find you during your lesson and you weren't there. But Father Romero was in the room and he kissed me. Then he took down his pants and made me—" She got suddenly quiet and put her hand over her mouth.

"It's okay, Alice," Roxanne said. She came over to put her arm around Alice's shoulders. "You don't have to say anything else."

"No, he couldn't have done that," Del said. "Father Romero wouldn't do that." For all their fantasizing and daydreaming about Father Romero, she couldn't see the kind man she'd gotten to know doing something like that. Of the three of them, she felt like she knew him best. He had never even hinted at anything like that with her. She looked over at Roxanne, whose face didn't give her any hint that Alice might be lying.

"This isn't happening," Del said.

"Why would Alice lie about something like that?" Father Frankl said. "Do you know why she might lie?"

"He tried to rape me!" Alice said. "I can't believe you're defending him!"

"You should have seen her when I got there, when she came out of the room," Roxanne said. "You didn't see her. Did you?"

Neither did you, Del wanted to say. She knew where Roxanne had been. Roxanne was lying, but was Alice? Why?

"These are allegations," Father Frankl said.

"Tell him, Del. Tell Father Frankl what he did to you," Roxanne said.

"You should have brought Alice to me," Father Frankl said. "Or one of the other teachers."

"He told me not to," Alice said, looking up. "He said he would hurt me." She began to cry again. Del had seen her upset before, but never like this. Still, she couldn't believe it of Father Romero. He'd been nothing but kind to all of them. But the way she'd seen him look at Roxanne—she knew he'd thought about Roxanne in that way. There was no missing it. Alice, though. Who would want Alice?

"I don't want my parents to know," Alice said. "Please don't tell my parents."

"No one has to know," Roxanne said. "Do they?" She looked over at Father Frankl, whose eyes shifted away from her to Del.

"Really. I don't remember," Del said, her voice almost a whisper. "He might have touched me in the hallway. It was a long time ago."

She tried to picture it, Father Romero pushing against her in the crowded hallway, feeling something firm cupping her breast. This was when they were talking about him every day, wondering what he was like, wanting him to pay attention to them. Had she imagined it, or had he really touched her on purpose?

"He never said anything to me," she said.

"But he did touch you?"

"Something touched me," Del said. "But I can't be sure."

Father Frankl looked vaguely disappointed with her, as though he'd expected her to say more, as though it were her fault they were sitting here.

"It's okay, Del," Roxanne said, stroking Alice's hair.

Del wanted to tell Roxanne to stop but she couldn't do it. She hated how wrong this felt. Was Roxanne really capable of being so cruel? Was Alice?

"What's going to happen?" Alice said. "Do I have to see him again?"

"It will be taken care of," Father Frankl said. "But it's my duty to talk to your parents." He looked at Del and Roxanne. "I want all of you to know it would be a mistake to gossip about this. I see how this has affected you, and we have to be careful that it doesn't affect the whole school."

"Please, Father," Alice said. "I just want it all to go away. I don't want anyone to know. Please? Nothing happened. Nothing really bad. What if I don't have to see him? Maybe you could put me in a different math class."

"Don't you see how awful this is for her, Father Frankl?" Roxanne said. "How could you make her tell someone else?"

"That's a decision for her parents," Father Frankl said.

"But they'll make a big deal about it. All she wants is to forget about it."

"It's not her decision anymore," Father Frankl said. "You girls need to go home. You're excused from school tomorrow, Alice. I'll inform your teachers that you continue to be ill."

They were dismissed. Del held Alice's damp hand as she led her out.

No matter if Alice was lying or not—and she was sure she was—she felt sorry for her. Alice was sick.

But when they reached the hallway, she turned to see Roxanne still in Father Frankl's office. She was closing the door, leaving them on the other side of it.

"What are you doing?" Del said. The only answer was the clicking sound of the door shutting.

"Leave her alone," Alice said. "She knows what she's doing."

It was late enough that all the students were gone and only the kindergarten teacher was left to hurry past the church on her way to the parking lot.

"Alice. Oh, my God, what is going on?" Del said. "I don't understand. What happened? Did something really happen?"

"We shouldn't be talking about this here," Alice said.

"I want to talk about it," Del said. "I don't understand."

Alice took a tissue from her skirt pocket and blew her nose.

"You're so funny," she said.

"What's that supposed to mean?"

"It means that you almost screwed it all up," Alice said. "He almost didn't believe you. But it's going to be okay."

She'd been right. Alice had lied; they were going to ruin Father Romero—and she was a part of it.

She grabbed Alice's arm.

"This is psycho-bullshit," Del said. "We can't do this to him. He didn't do anything to us. Any of us!"

"You don't know anything," Alice said, still walking. "You always act like you're so smart. You're such a goody-two-shoes."

"You mean I'm not a liar like you two."

They reached the street, close to the concrete steps of the church.

"She didn't tell you because she knew you'd be a baby about it," Alice said. "Someone needed to be like a witness. They wouldn't believe her if she just told them what he did to her."

"What are you talking about? You're not making any sense."

"Father Romero didn't do anything to me, but he raped Roxanne. Weeks ago. And she didn't tell you, she told me!"

Del had never before seen such an ugly look of triumph on anyone's face. Alice did look sick—or crazy. What about Roxanne? What was she supposed to believe? It was impossible to imagine Father Romero so driven by lust that he'd attack someone. Especially a thirteen-year-old. Even Roxanne.

"She went just to talk to him and it happened. But she knew nobody would believe her because she went to his room alone. So we had to do this."

Wasn't it what Roxanne had really wanted? Wasn't it what Roxanne had been after all along?

"He's evil," Alice said. "Just plain evil."

It was only later, behind the closed and locked door of her own bedroom, hearing Roxanne say the words herself that she could believe it.

"I thought he was what I wanted," Roxanne said. "But I didn't want it that way." Her eyes filled with tears. "It wasn't like I thought it would be. I was wrong, Del. I was so wrong."

Del held Roxanne in her arms. She seemed smaller, even younger than usual. She didn't know what it was about Roxanne that made her want to protect her, even though she was (more than) capable of taking care of herself. It had been that way ever since they were young.

She remembered how the art teacher in fourth grade had been cruel about a picture that Roxanne had done: they were working in pastels, and while everyone else's pictures were bleary and smudged, their subjects unrecognizable, Roxanne's had been of a chestnut mare with a beautiful foal with dark, gentle eyes. The teacher had said Roxanne was showing off, that she had no modesty and was only trying to make the other students look incompetent. Roxanne had been hurt, embarrassed.

Whose idea had it been? Hers? Or had it been Roxanne's own idea to use an X-Acto knife to slash the painting the teacher had done of the church? It hung in the front entry of the school, and it had been noth-

ing to sneak out of Wednesday chapel and slice three neat cuts through the canvas and sneak back into church again.

There was no longer a question of believing her. She loved Roxanne more than she loved her brother or her parents, even if—or maybe especially because—Roxanne frightened her sometimes.

Del wrapped her arms around Roxanne and held her close. "Don't worry," she said. "He can't hurt you anymore."

CHAPTER 22

Father Frankl folded up his newspaper and tossed it idly onto the yard of starched white tablecloth between his bowl of bran cereal and Romero's plate of toast.

"There's a piece in Section B about how judges are sending sex offenders to rehabilitation camps instead of jail." He all but sneered, and would not look at Romero.

"Why didn't you go to the police?" Romero said in a quiet voice.

Mrs. Kemper, the housekeeper, was nearby in the kitchen. She and the rest of the school's staff had been told that he had been called to live as a contemplative in an Iowa monastery. Only Father Frankl and the bishop knew the real reason he was going, and the bishop's office had made all the arrangements. He was to travel by bus, stopping in fifteen small towns in Indiana and Illinois and changing buses in St. Louis before arriving in Keokuk, where someone from the monastery would pick him up. The monastery specialized in marketing greeting cards and jellies.

"I don't want you at the school today before catching your bus this evening," Frankl said, ignoring Romero's question about the police. He got up and left the room, leaving his dishes for Mrs. Kemper.

Romero pushed down the urge to go after the bastard and give him a serious beating. He knew how to fight and he was feeling antagonistic now instead of remorseful. Roxanne had brought him to this.

He went to the window, his own breakfast untouched. The clear morning air carried the laughter of girls crossing the courtyard on their way to mass. A supply priest was already executing what had been his church duties. The bishop had thought of everything. One of the girls noticed him in the window and waved. Her name was Christie. She was fifteen and one of the innocents. It sickened him that they weren't all innocents.

He saw Del and Alice coming onto campus from the street, inclining their heads together, talking as they passed between the church and the administration building. He'd thought about confronting them, asking them why they hated him so. But he knew it wasn't that they hated him. It was that they loved Roxanne.

Where was she? Alice had come back to school after three or four days, but had been removed from his class. Roxanne hadn't been in school for more than a week.

Why wouldn't she come back to him? It was after midnight, and he had been lying there for hours watching the ceiling, listening for her footsteps in the hall. He waited for her to cross the shadowed bedroom like some benevolent spirit, her lips curved in a teasing smile. He thought of how she once challenged him on an algebra answer, and she had been right, which gave him secret pleasure. Artists were often strangely good at math. He liked that she was smart and beautiful. He knew that she would grow into an extraordinary woman. He had tried to push her away for her own sake, but she had seen through him. That was the way of women like Roxanne.

He imagined being rougher with her than he had been the first time. He would be sorry, though, and ask her forgiveness. She would give it to him with a kiss.

The single night they were together, he kept having to tell her to be quiet because she had begun to talk and to tease him. She was, for all her surprising and pleasing skill, still just a girl, and he was grateful that Father Frankl was half deaf. When she left him, he went to the window in the hallway to watch as she wheeled her bike from behind the garden shed. But she hadn't looked up. Had she even known he was there?

A few days later, she suddenly stopped speaking to him except when she was in the presence of others, and only about insignificant things. He was afraid to call her house, though he picked up the telephone a hundred times to do it.

Then there was Alice, who had showed up in his classroom when he was expecting Del. She'd been nervous, making some excuse about looking for Del.

Then there were Father Frankl's accusations, the details about his anatomy that Frankl said that Alice gave him. But it wasn't Alice who knew those things firsthand.

He slept an hour before dawn and woke thinking of her again.

Two suitcases and a box of books sat waiting back at the rectory. But a few hours before the bus was supposed to leave, Romero stood in the doorway of Monetta's shop.

She looked up from the counter where she was turning the pages of a catalog and waved him inside.

"I missed your party, amigo," she said. "I felt so bad, but Robert is still in bed with the flu." She shook her head. "¡Que niño es ese muchacho! To suffer well is not in his nature."

But as he got closer to her, her face changed. "Romero, what is wrong?"

He'd imagined that he could come here and wish her a fond goodbye, that he might tell her some story about how he needed some quiet in his life, that God had shown him a new direction. He wished that God had been silent over the past weeks. God was the pounding in his head. God's voice wasn't still and small, but he'd almost been able to contain it, to separate it from the trappings of his job and his prayers for his parishioners and his mother. He told himself that God had nothing to do with Roxanne—even though God had been watching. God had seen every kiss, every touch, had felt every sigh. Was God ashamed of him? Jesus had faced down the demons plaguing his followers; Monetta, too, refused to suborn the manifestations of the more dangerous spirits that her godchildren or others who attended the ceremonies experienced. She was fierce in the face of them. Unafraid. She had seen it all.

Monetta went to the front door and slid the BACK IN AN HOUR sign into position. Then she led him to the back room.

This was where she practiced. It was a bright room—the chairs were hard plastic and the floor tiled because Santeria, though a rich and beautiful and loving religion, could be messy. Several vessels sat about the edges of the room, some empty, some with their layers of stones and offerings inside. Shelves and shelves of tureens almost hidden by thin lace curtains lined the walls. A terraced array of candles decorated with Jesus and the saints burned at one end. But even with so many candles burning, the room smelled of pine-scented disinfectant. Monetta kept the place scrupulously clean.

"I will read for you," she said. "Sit down." She took a rough linen bag from a cane étagère in the corner and put a wooden tray between them. She emptied the bag of its small collection of cowrie shells.

Romero looked but could make nothing of them. He had no training, no gift. It was as though he were a young child again, uninitiated into the knowledge of the mass. Was this what he'd come for?

She studied the shells for several minutes. Then she studied him. Gradually, her eyes, usually so kind, seemed to pierce him. Even the gentleness of her mouth and full cheeks, dark with masses of freckles she'd acquired from picking soybeans as a child back in Cuba, couldn't disguise the fact that she didn't like what the shells were telling her, what her eyes saw in him.

"When you go from here, don't come back," she said.

"What do you mean?"

"There's nothing here for you anymore. You're meant to pass

through here. I don't know why the shells didn't tell me before." She looked away. "Go, now, Romero."

He hung his head. How had he gotten here? What was he supposed to do?

"You don't understand," he said, his voice almost a whisper. "I need your help."

"You are beyond my help," she said with resignation. "I have never said that to a person in my life."

"What if I love her?" he said.

"Yo tengo una tía que toca la guitarra." I have an aunt who plays the guitar.

He almost laughed at the saying he'd heard his mother say all his life. But he could see in her face that it wasn't a joke.

Monetta shook her head. She gathered the shells and put them back into the bag.

"You hurt her, didn't you?" she said. "And now you are feeling the pain. I don't want to know this."

"But you can help me," he said, grabbing her arm. "The orishas. We can drive this from me. Make me pure again."

"Maybe the orishas can help you," she said, pushing his hand away. "But I will not."

"Aren't you sworn to help me? You want to hear my confession? What I did to her? How I took her? How I kissed her in my bed?"

Monetta raised her hand and slapped him, hard, on the side of his face.

"I am not one of your gringo therapists to whom you can spill tu tripa and go on your way. You had a great stain on your soul already that was washed clean, no? And now you've done this thing. You've let the snake of lust into your bed, and although a woman brought it, she was a woman who was also a child. You will pay for being weak. I and twenty of my godchildren could spend a week praying and begging the saints and painting you blue, but I don't know that it would do any good. I have misread you, and for that only I beg your pardon."

He lifted his hand to his stinging cheek. He knew he deserved it. She knew about the man he had killed for his mother, but he wasn't surprised. Monetta was more powerful than he had realized, but she wasn't going to absolve him. He'd already made an anonymous confession to a priest in a downtown church. Cowardice had driven him to slip in among the old women waiting in line with their petty grievances and sorrows—cheating at cards and haranguing their elderly husbands, bad-mouthing their daughters-in-law—and not mention that he was a priest as well as a fornicator. It had been a stupid, empty attempt to fool both himself and God.

To see the scorn on Monetta's face—a face he'd come to like so well, to trust—felt worse even than being sent to be a jam and bookmark-peddling monk. He'd hoped for absolution from her, but when he looked away from her face and around the room, he no longer saw a refuge where someone who was hurting could find relief and succor, but only a set of scarred plastic chairs, cheap, shredding tapestry, and childish images of made-up saints.

When his hands began to shake, he knew he had to get out of the shop and away from Monetta. Without looking back at her he hurried out, stopping just long enough to knock a laughing pair of day-of-the-dead skeletons in wedding clothes to the floor and crush them beneath his foot.

Romero leaned back against the worn upholstery of the bus seat. There had been days over the past months when he couldn't have stood it, when the slightest touch of his own shirt made him want to scream with pain. It had been worse when he added the weight of his cassock or an alb. But now his back and shoulders were nearly healed. When had he stopped the flagellation? It hadn't been a conscious choice. Or had it? He closed his eyes, trying to ignore the tinny stream of unintelligible music coming from the headphones worn by the teenage boy in the next seat.

"What's that?"

Roxanne touched his shoulder. He tried not to flinch. He was surprised she could see the wounds in the darkness. They had been together two hours and already he hated to think of her leaving.

"Don't," he said. "Just let me hold you." He tried to kiss her, but she ducked her head away so that only her hair brushed his lips.

"Did a cat scratch you or something?" she said. She ran her fingers lightly across his back and over his shoulder blades. "You don't even have a cat."

"No," he said, wanting her to stop. But when she did, he regretted it. He couldn't bear to have her near him and not touching him. There were times, in class, when he was tempted—God, he was tempted!—to make some excuse to lead her from the room and steal into a closet or a shed with her. Anyplace. It was madness, what he felt. Surely, no one had ever been tortured like this before. What had he done to deserve this suffering? If it was a test from God, he was certainly failing it.

She fell back onto the pillow, narrowly missing the headboard, and looked up at him. Some of the mascara she'd put on before she came to his room was smudged around her lower lashes.

"Why would you do that? It's like those monks, isn't it, those ones in Greece who used to hit themselves. But they did it for Jesus."

"They did it because they sinned," he said. "But I guess it was for Jesus. For his forgiveness."

"What a creepy bunch of bullshit," she said. "Like Jesus is actually paying attention to us." She leaned her head back a little more to get an upside-down look at the crucifix hanging above his bed. "No way." When she turned back to him, her lips were shaped into a mischievous smile.

Though twenty admonitions came to his mind, he kept silent and lowered his face to hers to kiss her, and this time she didn't turn away.

In St. Louis he got off the bus and picked up his two bags. The bus for Keokuk didn't leave for another six hours and wasn't yet even listed on the departure board. He went to find the men's room. The station was unlike any other he'd been in before, clean and bright and as large as a small airport terminal. The music coming from the overhead speakers was light jazz, maybe Spyro Gyra. In the bathroom, a man in a gray suit with an overcoat hanging over his arm was at one of the basins *washing up. When he crossed Romero's path, shaking water from his hands, he said, "Excuse me, Father."*

When the man was gone, he looked at himself in the mirror. He'd lost about fifteen pounds since Christmas. The white collar peeking out of his serviceable charcoal sweater gaped around his neck. Beneath his eyes, the skin sagged in weary half circles. Father! Priests were supposed to help others with the most important matters of all: those of the soul. He couldn't help himself out of a paper bag.

The last letter he'd gotten from his mother sat folded in his pocket. She still hated telephones, even though she now lived in a country where they were unfailingly reliable. She wanted answers about why he was leaving a prosperous Cincinnati parish for a monastery in Iowa. But what could he tell her that wouldn't kill her? He missed what they had had before: his Spartan, dusty childhood, the way they had faced their poverty together. He knew now that it was a kind of greed that had brought them here, and not some idyllic quest for freedom and opportunity. He wanted, needed to see her. But he couldn't lie to her face.

In one of the larger stalls, he removed his pants and sweater, as well as the shirt with its priest's collar, and changed into a pair of jeans and a work shirt from his bag. Then he took all of his priest's garb, his missal, and his Bible, and put them in one bag; his toiletries, furnishings, and a few civilian clothes went into the other. Coming out of the stall, he saw a different man in the mirror.

It didn't take him long to find the hallway with the lockers in it. When he left the station, he was still wearing the plain coat he'd arrived in, but carrying only a single bag.

PART III

Flight

CHAPTER 23

Week 29 5/7

"I can't think of a single reason you should see Alice," Jock said.

They were in the country club's tavern room, having just finished a long eighteen holes. Outside, a sharp wind was scouring the last few leaves off the trees, and Thad found that even the neat Maker's Mark he was drinking wasn't warming him up. The morning had started out clear, but Amber had almost had to push him out the door to play golf with Jock. After their visit to the doctor, he was reluctant to leave her alone, but she had insisted.

"Alice has just been too damned quiet about this whole thing," he said. "It's not like her."

"So what if she's misplaced a couple of the things we sent over? She hasn't contested anything so far. That lawyer of hers—Javits—could make plenty of it if she wanted him to. Why he hasn't dragged your girlfriend into it surprises the hell out of me. It's the women who get really pissed about the infidelity stuff."

"She's got plenty of money from her folks," Thad said. "What else could she want from me?"

"Some women send their asshole exes dead flowers, some spray paint their Lamborghinis, some try to hire hit men. Of course, most of the prospective hit men they find are Feds anyway. You'd be surprised what will make a woman feel better."

Thad decided to ignore the "asshole ex" comment. Looking at it objectively, he knew he fit the category. But Jock hadn't been the one to watch Alice become more and more self-possessed, more focused on transforming herself into something brittle and untouchable, once they'd gotten the final verdict about her being unable to conceive and carry a child. And, by that time, he knew that he didn't want to have children with her, that she was hardly fit to be a wife, let alone a parent. Sometimes, he thought he was being harsh, but then he would think of Amber and how blessedly normal she was.

"You should meet Amber," Thad said. "Alice liked her."

"Oh, that's ugly," Jock said.

"Really. You'd like her, too. She's different." Thad leaned forward, wanting to convince him. "She doesn't care about money and status and all that crap."

The look Jock gave him told him that he'd heard those words plenty of times before. Sometimes, it wasn't so great having a divorce lawyer for a friend.

By the time he was back in his own car, ready to head back to Amber, Thad was feeling mellow and finally warmed by the whiskey. He thought that maybe Jock was being too nervous, too much of a lawyer. It wouldn't hurt to drive by the old house, to see if it was still standing after the party he and Amber had witnessed.

There were times when he missed the house on Leopold Avenue, with its long hallways of overdecorated rooms, and the media room that had been his private domain, his place of refuge when he couldn't risk spending too much time with Amber. Alice talked about how much she loved the house, but he suspected that, for her, it was too full of memories of her parents. Although he hadn't known her mother, he'd heard other people besides Alice talk about her and had deduced that the woman's relentless cheerfulness had been a little hard on Alice, who had been plain, and frequently moody—far more like her father than her mother.

Maybe it was the baby that Amber was carrying that made him want to be clear of Alice, to make sure she wasn't a part of his life or his thoughts any longer. Alice was poisonous. He was more certain of that every minute he spent with Amber.

Sitting in the driveway, he debated whether to use the house key that was still on his key ring. He and Alice were officially separated, and if he used it there might be legal questions. Worse, Alice might think he was coming back to her. That was a scene he didn't want to even imagine. He put his keys in his pocket.

The stairs up to the back door were littered with cigarette butts and crumpled wrappers and other debris. Several beer and soda cans lay in the landscaping; someone had upended a Red Bull can and had stuck it onto the tall, tubelike remains of a summer plant. His foot made contact with a lipstick case so that it shot into an overgrown holly bush. Where the hell were the yard maintenance people? It was almost December, and the beds should have been re-mulched, the plants settled for the winter. He wondered if Alice had canceled the contract.

A nagging sense of responsibility came over him, but he fought it off. This stuff was Alice's problem, now. Not his.

Forgetting his earlier resolve, he took out his keys and slipped his house key as quietly as he could into the keyhole. It wouldn't turn. So, she had changed the locks after all. For the first time, it occurred to him that Alice might be seeing someone, that some other man might have a key that worked in the new lock. He didn't like the thought—not because of Alice, but because he still felt proprietary about the house.

Just as he was returning his keys to his pocket, the door opened.

Was this Alice?

Her hair was cut short—shorter than he'd ever seen it. The uneven bob hanging about her chin gave her the look of a waif, and her cheekbones and collarbones stood out in sharp relief against her jaundiced skin. Her virgin-white dress—or was it a nightgown?—was badly soiled in places, as though it hadn't been washed in several wearings. But if her cruelly thin body and peculiar clothes gave an impression of vulnerability and weakness, her sharp, bright eyes contradicted it all. They arrested any feelings of tenderness or sympathy that had begun to form before he'd gotten a good look at her.

In an instant, the fierceness in her eyes was gone.

"Thad, dear," she said, "come in." The shift she wore was so transparent that he could see the shape of her (or rather lack of shape) beneath it. Once upon a time—it felt like a hundred years ago to him, now—he'd have wanted to put his hands on her waist to pull her to him. But he knew that if he were to do that now, it would only be out of a desire to harm her in some way.

The kitchen shades had been closed to block out the afternoon light. As he followed her inside the soles of his shoes made sucking sounds against the filthy floor, and he put his hand to his mouth as some defense against the foul odors in the air: old food, spilled wine and beer, cigarettes and pot. Opened and presumably empty Chinese carryout cartons and pizza boxes covered most of the countertops. The house was oppressively warm, making the smell worse. Had she dumped the housecleaning service as well?

"Would you like some tea?" she asked, stopping to turn back to him.

"No," he said. "I just came by to see how you're doing." He fingered his keys in his pocket.

"I'll make some for myself, then," she said, moving toward the teakettle on the range. She lighted the flame beneath it, her motions as slow and deliberate as a sleepwalker's. "Tell me if you change your mind." She gave him her hostess's smile, one he'd seen a thousand times when they were entertaining people. It was not a flattering smile—her teeth had become stained and damaged—and now that she was even thinner than she'd been even two months before, it gave her face the appearance of a grinning death mask. "Why don't you sit down?"

He glanced at the chairs and table at the other end of the room; they, too, were covered with debris. "We haven't talked in a while," he said, but made no move to sit.

"I've just been so busy with this and that. We should probably get together and have dinner or something like civilized people." She turned away to pull a mug out of the overflowing sink. "We could pretend, anyway." Her laugh sounded shallow, forced.

"I'm serious, Alice," he said. This couldn't be his wife—he'd pictured her a hundred times on her ass in the media room, her face a snarl of lipstick and powder and the smell of wine and White Shoulders coming off of her as though she'd bathed in both. She'd been a shrew, like someone's too-pampered pet in a tantrum. This barefaced woman in the soiled gown was a different creature.

"Do you need something?" Thad said.

"Need something?" she said. "I haven't needed so little in my whole life. And what I do need, I just have delivered. I don't know why I didn't think of it before." She shrugged.

In the shadowed light, he could make out an irregular purple mark on her neck. A hickey, maybe? What the hell had happened to her? He wondered if the cigarette smoke he smelled was hers. He knew she'd smoked as a teenager, but she hadn't since they'd met. She might have gotten hold of some prescription drugs. He'd always thought her doctor was too loose with her sleeping pills and the pain pills for the endometriosis. But he suspected something worse than drugs. Alice had lost some connection to reality. He wanted to hold a mirror to her face, to make her see what was happening to her. She wouldn't see it, though. She never would. Self-reflection had never been one of her strengths.

When Del had called him about Alice's pathetic suicide attempt, she'd made it sound like it had just been an angry bid for attention, that Del herself didn't really take it seriously and neither should he. He'd been all too ready to accept the theory, to push it to the back of his mind. Then Del was dead, and he'd been all too happy to try to forget their conversation. *If Alice were to die, wouldn't everything be easier?*

"So, why are you here, Thad?" she said. "Doesn't Jock have everything he needs from me? I think Mr. Javits has taken care of all the paperwork. Then again, maybe you want more of your things?"

Why, indeed?

"I drove by here the other night, and there was some kind of party going on," he said. "People in the street. They didn't look like the sort of people we know."

Between them, the water in the kettle began a low rumble.

"So who's the snob now?" she said. "I didn't think you were so choosy these days." Her lip lifted in a delicate sneer.

He could see that her facade was fragile. Jock had been right about his coming here. Next, Amber would be the issue, and he'd never wanted Amber to be spoken of between them.

"What kind of pills are you taking?" he said. "What is your doctor giving you?"

"If you're not going to have tea, why don't you just take what you want and go?" she said.

"Believe it or not, I do care what happens to you, Alice, and I don't want to see this"—he indicated the mess in the room with a wave of his arm—"happen to you."

"Please take your things, Thad," she said, her voice almost tender. "I can't do anything with them. I've put a bunch of stuff in boxes down in the garage."

Why hadn't it occurred to him that she would move his things? He had imagined that everything would be right where he had left it that morning, so many months earlier. The house had been frozen in his memory, with Alice, half-naked on the stairs, asking him if they could meet for dinner.

He knew he wasn't going to get anywhere with her. She didn't want help—didn't even know she needed it. He should just have gone home to Amber. She was waiting, lovely and uncomplicated, and he had chosen this.

"Go on," Alice said. "You're done here, Thad. Alice can take care of herself." She crossed her arms over her chest, looking, with her roughly chopped hair and plain dress, like a defiant novitiate.

He knew better. He also knew that she had no family beyond him. With Del dead and Roxanne—well, who knew anything about what Roxanne was up to—Alice was alone. Jock would know what to do about her. He couldn't, in good conscience, leave her to disappear into the mess she was creating for herself, let her drift in this state of waking madness.

"Sure," he said. "Whatever you want."

It seemed to satisfy her. Moving quickly now, she came around the island and went to open the door that led downstairs to the basement and garage.

"Everything should be there," she said, once again the cheerful hostess. "You can just back the Audi up to the garage and pile it in!"

So he was dismissed.

He'd never liked the basement, even though it was finished to be just another wing of the house, only underground. With the giant, step-down Jacuzzi pool that Alice's parents had put in, pool tables (two), regulation shuffleboard table and antique dart boards, outdated gym equipment, and an authentically replicated English pub room that could host thirty people, it was more like the forgotten recreation section of an abandoned resort hotel than someone's basement. In truth, he'd almost never spent any time down here. To get to the garage, he didn't have to see much of it (what he did see was as littered as the upstairs), but, still, he hurried. The place seemed to echo with the voices of the people who'd partied down here even years before he'd been born.

Reaching inside the rotting interior garage door, he felt for the old-fashioned button light switches. Alice had loved them since her child-hood and hadn't wanted them replaced. Finally finding them, he pressed one, and then the other, flooding the low-ceilinged interior with light.

Alice's Lexus sedan was parked in its space. He had thought of buying something similar for Amber to replace the sensible Subaru wagon she'd been driving for the past five years, but had decided that it wouldn't suit her. Maybe a minivan, now that she would be driving the baby around, or one of the bigger Toyota hybrids. He loved how sensitive she was about things like the environment.

There were, indeed, eight or nine boxes piled against the wall, neatly labeled in Alice's cultivated Catholic-school hand: Trophies,

Sports Equipment, Summer Clothes, and Winter Clothes. The rest said Books. Those were really the only things he wanted, but there was no way he was going to get them all into the A4.

He dragged one of the boxes away from the wall. It was filled with textbooks from dental school, mostly, and some World War II histories. He wasn't one to read fiction. As he started to drag it back to its place, he chanced to catch something out of the corner of his eye—nothing moving, but a shadow of some kind just on the other side of the Lexus.

Leaving the box where it was, he went around the car. It wasn't a shadow, but something much more substantial. It was a motorcycle. A motorcycle that was way too big for Alice to handle.

But he didn't get a chance to inspect it because something heavy and fast-moving hit him on his back, just at the base of the neck. And for the briefest of moments, the air in front of him exploded with light, and he fell to the oil-spotted floor, unconscious.

"Why did you hit him? You didn't have to hit him," Alice said. "What if you killed him?"

Dillon nudged Thad with the tip of his boot. He liked seeing Asshole Thad on the ground. It would've been fine with him if he'd killed the bastard. Easier.

"He's not dead," he said. "Go ahead and check."

The woman was a mess. She hadn't changed that dress in three days. And he didn't know what she'd been doing in the media room with Varick and the other people she had in there the night of the party, but from the smell of her, he didn't think she'd showered since. What Varick wanted with her, he couldn't imagine. Then, what did Varick want with either of them?

Alice knelt beside Thad and held her hand in front of his mouth and nose.

"I think he's breathing," she said. She touched his hair, then pulled her hand away, as though remembering he wasn't hers anymore. They belonged together, these two—Alice in Wonderland and the Asshole. But he could see why Asshole Thad preferred Amber to the thing at his feet. "What are we going to do?"

He really hadn't thought beyond this moment. Whacking Asshole Thad had been a gut reaction. He'd been upstairs when he saw the Audi pull into the driveway, and moved to listen at the top of the back stairs when he heard Asshole Thad's voice. Wasn't his sister enough for the son of a bitch? But, no, he'd only come to gloat, to pretend some husbandly concern for the ex. Standing there with the piece of scrap pipe in his hand, Dillon was at a bit of a loss. If Alice hadn't been there, he would've gone ahead and just turned Asshole Thad into fucking sausage. But there she was. And she had a big mouth.

"What will Varick say?" She looked up at him.

Shit. Varick didn't like him taking what he called *personal initiative*. He'd also promised that Asshole Thad would be taken care of if—and the if was implied, not spoken—Dillon did what he was told and only what he was told. So far, that had meant babysitting Alice in Wonderland and delivering a few after-school-type snacks of both the male and female sort (He'd pegged him that first night—the guy went either way, but so far hadn't tried to fuck with him.) for Varick to enjoy at the loft or local hotels at his leisure.

"Screw Varick," he said.

Alice looked around as though Varick might be there. Listening.

"Don't say that," she whispered. "I'll have to tell him if you say that."

"I don't think you will," he said, giving her a gentle but solid kick on the leg with the same foot he'd used on Asshole Thad. He wasn't ready for her when she sprang up at him, clawing at his face. One of her ragged nails caught on a lip stud, nearly ripping it out, skin and all. He ducked away in pain, holding his hand to his mouth; he could only think of smashing her face against the concrete floor of the garage. But when he turned back, his desire for self-preservation overcame the desire to make a pile of her the way he'd made a pile of her almost ex-husband. He didn't like to think what Varick would do to him if he hurt his little Alice in Wonderland.

"You bitch," he said. "He's almost through with you, you know."

"Liar," Alice said.

"Look at yourself," he said. He touched his lip. *Fucking great.* Blood.

Despite the fact that she was shaking with anger and, no doubt, cold, she did what he told her to do and looked down at her gown.

"There's nothing wrong with me," she said. "Why do you say that?" But when she looked back up at him, he could tell that there was a part of her that knew, a part that was aware just how far she'd fallen in the past couple of months.

He was getting the itch. He'd been stupid to screw with Asshole Thad. Varick wouldn't like it, but he could blame it on the itch when Varick got there with the H that he needed so badly. He'd been greedy with what was left after the party. Then again, Varick hadn't asked him to do anything since then. Then again, maybe he could take care of the itch himself; maybe he didn't have to wait for Varick this time.

"I'm out of here," he said. "You deal with it." He dropped the piece of pipe on the floor and hit the button that controlled the door behind the bike. He thought of going by Amber's house. He hadn't seen her in more than a month and he missed her. But the itch was too strong, and now that he had some spending cash courtesy of Alice in Wonderland, he could afford to supplement what Varick gave him. This, too, Varick wouldn't like. But it wasn't like the son of a bitch owned him.

"Where are you going?" Alice asked. She sounded desperate, a sad little kid.

"I'll be back later," he said. "Just don't fucking go anywhere."

Alice watched him back the bike out of the garage. When he started it, she covered her ears as the roar of the engine echoed off the garage walls. She wanted to run after him to make him come back. She didn't like to be alone. But looking down at Thad, she realized she wasn't quite alone.

She sat down on the floor beside him, unmindful of the cold concrete and the fact that she wasn't wearing any panties. She wasn't concerned so much anymore about being cold. Varick had shown her that it was the intensity of the experience that counted, that there was no such thing as suffering. When had she begun to understand? She couldn't remember. There had been so many long nights, so many painful mornings. He'd been a thorough teacher, and had touched her in ways that this man in front of her never had. Thad had never cared enough.

Where was the girl? The pregnant slut? Maybe she would come looking for him.

She put her hand to her hair. It felt strange to her. Greasy and thick. She'd cut it herself one afternoon, frustrated with waiting for Varick. He'd been pleased—had even smiled. She had so many lovely clothes upstairs. She was so much prettier than the slutty girl. She had so much more to offer. Except, of course, a baby.

She sat up on her knees. She wasn't as strong as she had been, so it took some effort for her to turn Thad, who looked as though he were sleeping, onto his side. Sadness welled up in her. Did she miss him so much? *Not really*. Life was different now. She didn't want him back, and had been truthful about it.

His glasses had fallen off, giving him a vulnerable look. She picked them up and moved them to where he would see them when he woke up. Then, she slipped her hand into his front pocket and felt around for his keys. She could feel his leg through the pocket fabric—the leg he would sometimes throw over her in the night as they spooned together. But she wouldn't think about that.

"What are you doing there, Princess?"

She reddened and pulled her hand from Thad's pocket. Turning, she saw Varick standing in the doorway.

"I've missed a little fun here today, have I?"

Alice jumped up.

"I didn't do it," she said.

"Of course you didn't," he said. "You're not a violent person, are you, my Alice?"

"No."

He came over to her and pulled her so close to him that she was standing tiptoe on the concrete.

"No, you're not. You love him, still?"

"I don't love him," she said, her voice muffled against his jacket. There was a longing inside her that she remembered, though. There was regret.

"What was he doing those nights when you were waiting for him like a good little wife? Was he out with the boys, talking dirty about the sexy wife he couldn't wait to get home to?"

"I don't know," she said.

Varick let her down. She saw the concern in his eyes, the way that he cared for her. No one had ever cared for her this way. He was a miracle. A flush of vanity came over her, and she ran her hands down the front of her shift. Was she pretty to him at this moment?

"You do know," he said, resting his hands on her shoulders. "He was fucking her. Amber. He fucks her every day now."

Why did he insist on reminding her of such an ugly thing? "Let's go upstairs, please," she said. She was trying not to beg.

"Why do you think he came here today? Do you think he was really interested in you, Alice?"

"It doesn't matter."

"What did he give her, Alice?"

"I want to go upstairs," she said. "I don't want to be here." She twisted her hands together. Why did he have to remind her? She'd been so happy. Her life was complete, now. She didn't need anything. Only him.

"Don't you know it was her? She's the one who took what belonged to you, my darling."

She turned her head to see Thad still lying on the floor. He hadn't moved.

"She was his Eve. She tempted him. And he was weak."

She had tried not to think too much about the girl. About the child. That was the part that hurt.

Varick was looking closely at her. So concerned! So much compassion in his eyes! What had she done to deserve it? He truly knew her heart. He knew what was in her mind, every minute.

"I know what they did to you," he said.

Alice nodded as the tears flooded into her eyes. How long had it been since she'd cried? Del's funeral, certainly. That little girl, Wendy, so precious with her golden curls and troubled eyes. Motherless, again! She'd longed to take her in her arms, but hadn't wanted to go near

Jock, the traitor. How her heart had longed for the comfort those tiny hands might hold.

"Precious Alice," he said, pulling her close again. "We'll make it all better. I'll help you. You'll see."

And she believed him.

CHAPTER 24

Week 30

It wouldn't come. Roxanne had been sitting at her worktable with the clay-covered armature in front of her for most of the day. The light in the studio was barely bright enough for shadows, the perfect companion for the emptiness she felt inside. After several false starts, she was disgusted with herself. Her larger pieces always grew from sketches, but this bust of Del—someone she'd known almost her whole life—should've come easily without a picture or sketch. Del's image was clear in her mind. Her fingers had often touched Del's face, her hair; they should be able to find that face within the clay. The truth was that she didn't much enjoy doing likenesses, and she knew—no matter if he said otherwise—that was what Jock was looking for. It had been only obligation or, more likely, pity that had made her even consider taking the commission on. She didn't even like to do commissions. But this was for Del.

Jock wanted a kind of memorial, something little Wendy could look at, could even touch if she felt so bold. She wondered if that was something Wendy really wanted.

Roxanne hadn't lied when she'd told Jock how Wendy had prattled on about her mother's tea parties, but she'd left out the other part, the part in which Wendy described seeing the faces of "bad" people watching her two mothers from the windows of their cottage, how the bad people scratched at the glass, trying to get in, how it was only Wendy's special powers that kept them out and kept her mothers safe. It wasn't the kind of story that normal little girls were supposed to tell. Something had changed Wendy—and she was certain it wasn't just losing two mothers in her young life.

What in God's name had she seen in that hotel room?

Roxanne half believed that there had been a man involved. What else could've made Del trash her life in such a bizarre, dramatic way? She knew Del. Del was sensible, Del didn't really believe in magic, Del didn't make stuff up, Del didn't put up with bullshit. She wouldn't have jumped out of a window on a whim. The autopsy would have indicated drugs if they'd been in her system.

Del hadn't been an angel by any means. Whenever Roxanne had needed her, she'd been there, going along with pretty much whatever Roxanne asked of her. The things they'd done—the witchcraft, the occasional lies—were mostly harmless. But Del had been the one with the conscience. What they'd done—what *she* had done—to Romero, the priest, hadn't been harmless, had it?

Funny how the thought of him was no longer so painful, though she could still remember his face and the feel of his faint beard on her skin. Who had been the victim there?

She'd known as soon as she saw him at school a few days after she'd gone to his room that she would never go back. There had been something in his eyes as he returned her math paper, folding it slightly so that her hand would have to come in contact with his. Their secret. It was a look that Alice sometimes had: a soft, needy look. He was desperate for her. She already understood that she was saddled forever with Alice. She couldn't stand the thought of having Father Romero to deal with as well. So she got him out of her life the best way she knew how. In the end, of course, it had gotten too complicated—life-shatteringly complicated. But at least, by then, he was gone.

What little sunlight there was began to slip away. But she didn't need to see the clay so much as to feel it. Across the room was the piece she'd just finished: a boy kneeling on the back of a great horned owl in flight. Clutched in the boy's hand was a steel-headed spear she'd found in a downtown junk shop. She couldn't get away from the birds—birds and children. In her mind was a world populated by the two, a world of intense innocence, but not a perfect world. She wasn't the only person who recognized the violence inherent in innocence. Her work was popular enough, though the reviewers were often harsh. It was the violence of the natural world: the untaught, the unmolded, the unrestrained. Maybe she missed that part of herself.

The bust of Del wouldn't quite fit in the upcoming show, but she would put it in anyway. She knew it would mean a lot to Jock. Why that mattered to her, she wasn't sure. It had to be Wendy she cared about.

When her phone rang, she didn't recognize the number on the caller ID. There wasn't anyone she wanted to talk to, but, grateful for the interruption and ready to give up on the bust for the day, she answered it.

Roxanne knew the building. Most of the upper floors were artists' studios of some kind, but she'd never been in the penthouse. Coming up on the rattling elevator, she began to regret having agreed to meet Varick (such a strange name) at his place. She wasn't looking for a date and surely he must imagine this to be some kind of date. Whatever it was, she was going to get to see *Peace* again, and that was something.

Seven, she remembered, was supposed to be some kind of a holy number. She didn't know why this thought occurred to her as the elevator door opened and she saw the number on the wall, but there it was. Realizing she was still clutching the scrap of paper with Varick's name and address, she tucked it into the pocket on the inside of her slim silk handbag.

She'd dressed quickly, but with care, in a short turquoise and black skirt with black jet beads sewn into it, and a black cashmere sweater whose neck framed the delicacy of her face. A thick row of black and silver bracelets jangled on her left forearm, and her legs were covered in lacy black tights; her black ballet-style shoes were glove-soft leather. If this visit was going to turn into something serious, she wanted to look her best.

The front door was scarred steel and as unprepossessing as its neighbors. She knocked, rather than ringing the buzzer. When there was no immediate response, she felt a sense of relief. It had begun to rain outside, and she wouldn't have minded going home and working a little longer. She was about to turn away when she heard the lock slide back.

"Roxanne," Varick said. "I'm sorry. I was sautéing mushrooms and I'd just put the wine in. Come in."

"You're cooking?" she said. It was the last thing she expected. He took her rain cape, shook it gently, and hung it on the empty row of brushed stainless steel hooks near the door.

"Don't worry, I'm not going to poison you." When he smiled, she was taken aback. He looked younger and much more relaxed than he'd seemed at the gallery. "Make yourself to home," he said. "Isn't that how the country people say it?"

She laughed. "I haven't heard that one."

Was he blushing? He headed for the open kitchen at the other side of the room. "Can I get you some wine? You smell lovely, like the rain, by the way."

Inside the loft, she was surprised to see all was white and glass and chrome, a room of texture rather than color. She asked herself what she'd expected. Medieval swords, Moroccan leather, ball-and-claw chairs? Or bachelor ratty?

"Look where you've put it," she said. As she crossed the room, she let her hand drift over the buttery suede of one of the couches.

"The window glass is treated," he said from the kitchen. "It won't be damaged."

Peace sat on a twenty-four-inch pedestal, framed in the window by the lights of the city. The building wasn't tall, but situated as it was on the side of the hill, the view of the city and the river beyond it was stunning. But it was *Peace* that took her attention.

It was four feet at its highest—the head of the boy—and she had to raise her arm to stroke the top of it. She'd forgotten the energy in it, the tension in the boy's hand that held the tether, the way the bird quietly resisted the boy's restraint. There wasn't one thing about it that she would change.

"Perfect," she whispered. She leaned into it, feeling the natural cool of the clay against her skin.

"It is," Varick said, suddenly there beside her.

"I meant where you've put it," she said, embarrassed. The sculpture was the focal point of the room.

"Here," he said, handing her a glass.

The wine was a deep, jewel red and tasted of old oak barrels and currants.

"They seem happy here," she said. "Thank you."

"It was my dearest wish."

Roxanne laughed again. He was teasing her, but she didn't know why. She'd been prepared not to like him, but found she was no longer put off by his European shtick. In fact, she found it kind of appealing.

"I need a few more minutes in the kitchen," he said. "Will you join me?"

"So what is it you do?" Roxanne said. She ran her index finger around the inside edge of the cup that had held the crème caramel. She touched the tip of her tongue to her finger, flicking the caramel off with a deft, catlike motion. It was the penultimate course of five, including the salad, which had come—in true gourmet fashion—after the salmon fillets. A plate of sliced persimmon and Stilton cheese sat on the counter, waiting. Everything had been executed perfectly. Only the mushrooms in the salad were unpleasantly bitter, but she'd washed them down with the white Bordeaux he'd served with the fish.

"I'm a collector," he said.

She glanced around the room. *Peace* was the only artwork in evidence.

"Art, yes," he said. "I'm selective about what I display."

"What else?" The meal had been filling and Roxanne felt her body warming.

"I collect people," Varick said.

"Somehow you don't seem the type," Roxanne said. "Not a party-goer. You're not a Republican, are you? But no, you're European. That would be weird."

Varick smiled.

"So, where are they?" Roxanne said.

"Maybe I was speaking metaphorically. Or maybe I keep them in the spare bedroom."

"And that scar on your face. Where did that come from?"

He smiled. "My secret," he said.

She wasn't just warm, now. Her body was flushed with heat. She put out her hand to steady herself in her chair, but the table seemed to move far away from her, and Varick with it.

"Maybe you did poison me," she said. Her own voice seemed distant.

"No," he said. "I would never do that."

"No, you wouldn't, would you?" she said. What would be the point? She was a consenting adult, she'd come here of her own volition. Of course, there were some guys who got off on doping and raping women. But how did he know she hadn't told several people where she'd be?

"Maybe some coffee," she said.

As he made his way toward the kitchen, he stopped and touched her shoulder. "Are you all right?" he said.

And if, later, she'd been able to remember—had even tried to remember—it was at that moment that things started to change.

"I want to sit on that delicious couch," she said, getting up. "Or maybe look out at the city. People bitch about this town, but I wouldn't live anywhere else."

She stood at the window, pressing her forehead and a hand against the glass. There were so many people out there, people she would never know, and, frankly, didn't care to know. It was enough that they were out there. Unlike Alice, she didn't mind being alone. It was strange that Alice wouldn't answer her door or return her calls anymore. It had been weeks and weeks since they'd talked, since just after Del's funeral. The truth was that she hadn't tried too hard to connect with Alice. She didn't need Alice's pain.

Was it some reflex, some unspoken need of her own that made her reach her hand out to touch the sculpted arm of the boy? Her fingers curved around his forearm and rested there. Her fingertips, though callused, were sensitive; there was warmth there in the boy's arm, the warmth of a real body. But she didn't draw her hand away. Was it strange? Yes. Was she afraid? Not for a moment. She turned away from the window to look at the boy, but there was no sign in his frozen face, no clue to the warmth—surely there was life inside—below the surface of his skin.

She put her other hand on the arm. Yes! There! She could feel something coursing beneath the surface, some palpable presence of life.

Glancing back over her shoulder, she saw that Varick was no longer in the kitchen and she was alone.

She didn't want to take her hands away. This was what she'd missed with every thing that she'd ever created. No matter what she discovered in the clay, it had never been life. Until now.

The thought filled her with an unreasonable happiness. The whole damned evening had made her happy. It wasn't anything like the minor thrill she got from sex or good food. This was visceral, substantial. She smiled at her reflection in the glass, superimposed over the shapes and lights of the city beyond.

Isn't this what she'd always wanted—even going back to that stupid ritual she'd done with Alice and Del to bring them a boyfriend? To put life, actual life into something that she created?

Taking her hands off *Peace,* she called Varick's name, but he didn't answer. A movement near the ceiling drew her attention, and she looked up to see a snow-white owl sitting atop a cylindrical pendant light. It seemed to be watching her, but without interest. That was the way with birds—their eyes held no expression. Waiting, silent, she wondered if it were actually alive, or if it were some kind of robot or decoration. Though her host didn't seem to have that sort of sense of humor.

"Hello?" she said. As she looked on, it twisted its head in that easy way owls had. And so it was alive. She followed the movement to see that other owls, maybe twenty or thirty of them, were settled along the freestanding wall to her left, like some avian art installation.

She walked toward them, fascinated. A few of the owls seemed to regard her, to wonder what she was, what she was doing. It didn't occur to her to be afraid. She had sculpted a few owls, and had borrowed a couple of taxidermy specimens for her work, but she'd only seen them live in zoos, never in the wild.

It was only in that moment that she realized there was music playing somewhere in the room, some chamber music with violins.

Where was Varick? She called his name again.

In answer, there was only the restless settling of the owls.

Sensing movement behind her, she turned to see the white owl swoop down at her. Its attack was silent, but Roxanne's scream filled the room. She stumbled away, falling against a chair, but the owl stayed with her, its wings open in full sail and beating at her shoulder, its claws clutching at her hair. Then it was gone, headed back toward the ceiling.

Huddled on the floor, she looked up to see that it had settled once again on the fixture. She felt small. Around her, the room was darker, softening the stark outlines of the furniture and the watching birds. The room felt smaller, too, as though it were shrinking in size.

Above her, the owls along the wall were excited, hooting softly to one another, stretching their wings, moving an inch or so at a time from side to side. She couldn't look away. They seemed agitated, ready for some change; did she dare to think that they might be preparing for something? A voice inside her head told her that she needed to get out of the room, but she felt like she was part of a scene, some performance that couldn't be carried on without her. Heavy as her body felt, she pushed up from the floor to stand.

Varick had abandoned her. Perhaps she was somewhere else altogether. Maybe when she had touched *Peace* she had been transported to another, more dangerous place. Or was she dreaming? Although she felt as though she were living a nightmare, she knew she was awake.

Peace. A sound from that end of the room, the sound of something breaking, cracking. A restive sound. The owls quieted.

Before she turned toward it, she understood what she would see.

The owls came for her first: feathers, claws, the force of air stirred in a hundred directions. They dove at her in predatory silence, coming close, brushing her face, her lips, tugging at her hair. She tried not to scream, to keep her mouth closed. Would they have her eyes? They jabbed at her hands as she pressed them against her face, and she could hear the delicate black beads from her skirt snapping in their murderous beaks.

Surrounded, buffeted by their strength—and where was hers? Where was her control at this moment? She could feel her clothes being tugged at, pulled from her body.

She was on the floor again, her skirt and tights shredded, her sweater unraveled, the yarn of it twisted around her arms and neck. If she could only open her eyes! It was a nightmare, wasn't it? But if she opened her eyes, they would be pecked out in an instant. She had to keep them closed. But if she'd been able to open them, she would've seen that some of the owls were also attacking one another in the frenzy, slamming against the windows to get to the darkness that lay beyond. They were desperate to fly, solitary and sane to better ground—anywhere but this four-walled corner of hell.

Though her fighting was blind and her mouth was rimmed with fine down feathers and flecks of blood, she fought for long seconds after the owls dropped away in ones and twos. Some, wounded by her flailing hands or their own brothers and sisters, collapsed onto the floor, their hearts stopped. Others managed to alight to the wall perch, spent, their bodies listing.

Once she realized the attack had stopped, Roxanne lay still, wanting to open her eyes, but afraid. She could still feel the birds' presence, hear it, even, over the thudding of her own pulse in her ears. In pain, yet unable to cry, she wrapped her arms around herself. When she finally opened her eyes, the first thing she saw was the white owl, staring from its perch on the light fixture above her head. But it wasn't staring at her.

Later, she will not remember what just happened to her. She will not remember what is about to happen. She will not, that is, remember with that part of her brain that enables her to function every day of her life—the part that talks to clients, to Colwyn, the part that balances her checkbook or orders food in a restaurant or drives a car. It will live in the darkest part, the part where the child inside her still lives, where the memories of the women whose blood runs through her veins live on.

It was the red-tailed hawk that hung over her now, circling the upper reaches of the loft, shed of its clay prison. Its cry was distant, mournful. Its cry was her own. She had created it, had endowed it with a crude, unknowing soul. She was hypnotized despite her pain and the cold of the floor beneath her. She was hypnotized and didn't see the boy ease down from the pedestal, flexing and stretching in his newfound skin. She didn't see him move with the silent, easy grace of an athlete from chair to tabletop to couch, or see him kneel on a broad, upholstered arm to watch, though his eyes were stone blind, as the hawk circled lower, lower, to enfold her in the shadow of its open wings.

CHAPTER 25

Romero sat on a bench near the sea lion exhibit eating a chocolate- and nut-covered ice cream bar. It was his forty-second birthday: thirty years since he and his mother had made it out of Cuba, eighteen years since he'd received his master of divinity degree, seventeen years since his life had ended at the hands of three preteen sluts.

Schoolchildren swarmed nearby, standing on the concrete picnic tables and benches to get a better look at the animals. They wore khaki and navy uniforms, similar to but less formal than the ones the girls had worn back at Our Lady of the Hills. He didn't need the reminder. He'd left the house to get the hell away from his lives—past and present.

He wore the uniform of the older, but not old, academic: blue jeans and a white cotton shirt, worn brown belt, and a hurriedly shaved face. His belly was more taut than those of his colleagues, and his eyes had acquired a sharpness that appealed to a certain kind of female student—the kind who didn't require a lot of explanations or caregiving and didn't expect a relationship. He was irritated with the circumstances that had surrounded him for more than a decade. He'd had enough of the shitty apartment, the faculty meetings, the liberal whining of his office suite-mates, the laziness of one-half of his students, the smug confidence of the rest.

There was a birthday card from his mother on the kitchen counter. Inside, there was no note, just the words HAPPY BIRTHDAY! underlined twice in pen, the greeting signed, "Mama." When he'd opened the card, a check for five hundred dollars had fallen out. She sent one every year. He put it aside to deposit it in the account that held the money from the last nine she'd sent.

After breakfast, he'd checked his e-mail. For the first time in several months there was a new Google Alert for Roxanne. She had donated a small sculpture to a Cincinnati AIDS foundation, but there was no picture of her on the page, which told him the foundation didn't know anything about marketing. Roxanne was the product, not the beautifully formed pair of embracing male nudes the photographer had posed on an ugly yellow Formica tabletop.

Before the Internet, he'd had to scour the Cincinnati papers at the library, read art journals (where he'd seen only two mentions of her in all the years he'd searched), and his subscription to the Our Lady of the Hills newsletter (falsely requested in the name of Mrs. Matthew C. Curtis. It was how he'd learned about her graduation from art school and her debut show).

Seeing that first picture of her in the newsletter had unnerved him. She'd pulled her hair back off of her face (to look older, he was certain), and her features were sharper, but her lips were still full, perhaps even more sensuous. He had bitten those lips, nipped at them, playing with her, and she had laughed. Her eyes looked out at him from the picture with mocking tenderness. She had been twenty-three. After that, he'd been able to find her online and in the newspaper more often: art openings, society parties, professional associations. Every time he saw her image, he felt something acid in his gut, a burning that made him want to strike out at everything around him. Her life—and Del's and Alice's—had continued, had grown and changed and developed some

kind of substance. This was his: eating ice cream on his birthday at the
zoo like some lonely freak.

Christ was all about forgiveness, kindness, and compassion. In fact,
at the seminary, one student said he'd boiled down Christ's command-
ments to a single pithy statement. "Jesus says, 'Don't be an asshole.'"
Now that he'd left that part of his life behind, the commandment didn't
apply. He was free to be as much of an asshole as he wanted. Christ's
opinions had ceased to be an issue.

But later, he wondered if it hadn't been that joker—Mr.-Everything-
Happens-for-a-Reason—God who had made sure he was at the zoo
that day.

"You didn't really think I was in there," the woman said. "That's so
silly!" She pushed playfully at Romero's forearm with her manicured
fingertips. Her smile was Hollywood bright.

Romero had seen her—had definitely seen her—in the baboons'
Plexiglas enclosure, beckoning to the pair of olive baboons sitting side
by side on a rock. But now he guessed it was some trick of the harsh
lights of the Primate House, lights that seemed to be focused carefully
on the exhibits. He was embarrassed that he had called to her to get out,
to get away. Fortunately, there had been no one else around to hear.

"But thanks, anyway," she said.

Now that he was close to her, he saw that her artfully applied
makeup couldn't hide the fact that she was only nineteen or twenty. A
girl, really, despite her full breasts and overprocessed blond hair.

"It was so bright outside," Romero said. "And then walking in
here." He didn't bother to finish the sentence.

"Oh, I love your accent," she said. "You sound just like Antonio
Banderas. I love Antonio Banderas. He's the cutest old guy ever."

Romero smiled, flattered, despite her clumsy guile. The white-bread
girls at the community college often said similar things, and they liked
him to talk during sex. He wondered if it was the Spaniard, Banderas,
of whom they were thinking when they closed their eyes.

"They're weird, aren't they?" the girl said, turning back to the baboons. "Almost like people. They look like they're thinking really

hard." She furrowed her own fair brow as if to copy them. The baboons didn't look directly at them: one stared off at a point above their heads, the other seemed to be busy digging something out of its ear.

"They live in families," Romero said. "They pick lice off of one another. And that is the extent of my baboon knowledge."

As they watched, the baboon that had been staring got up and started toward the back of the exhibit, but the other one stuck an arm out as if to stop it from going. The first one wouldn't stop, though, and after seeming to consider for a moment, the second baboon went after it, jumping on its back and tugging, hard, at the fur at the back of its neck.

"You think they want to be alone?" the girl said, giggling.

The baboons began to wrestle, rolling from one ledge and down onto another, then sprang suddenly apart, screaming. Even though their bodies were covered in fur, Romero could see the immense strength in them, and knew that if he were in that enclosure, a single one of them would be capable of killing him.

The girl laughed again, but she sounded nervous this time.

"Maybe they'll stop if we go away," Romero said, gently taking her elbow to lead her toward the capuchin monkey exhibit on the other side of the room. But just then a young man, maybe twenty-five, entered the building. In one hand he held an expensive digital video camera, its strap secured around the back of his fingers as though he might begin filming any moment. When he caught sight of the girl, he called her by name—Malina—and told her she needed to get her "butt back to the aviary."

"This is my friend," she said, touching Romero again. "He saved me from the baboons."

She smiled and turned her gray eyes back to Romero. He'd never seen a girl with gray eyes before.

"What's your name, hero?" she said.

"Let's go," the other man said, ignoring Romero.

"We're shooting a little movie," she said. She put her finger to her lips. "Shhh. We're not supposed to be here, really. It's about a girl who works at a zoo. But we're doing most of the filming at the hotel."

It was then that Romero realized that her beige silk blouse had epaulets and buttoned pockets that—if the definition were very stretched—almost suggested a safari-style shirt. But the dark green, thigh-skimming shorts and high-heeled sandals she wore weren't convincing at all.

"There's always a party when we get done," she said. "It's at the Shelley, in the suite on the fourth floor."

"Jesus," the younger man said. "You can talk to her later, buddy." He grabbed at Malina's hand and pulled her away so that she almost stumbled in her teetering heels.

When they were out of sight, he heard her call back, "See you, Mr. Baboon Man!"

The door to the hotel suite was propped open, and Romero went inside, keeping an eye out for Malina.

It was a homelier crowd than he'd expected, and calmer. Somehow, he'd imagined that the party following a porno shoot would be a straightforward orgy—an Hieronymus Bosch scene with writhing bodies and lots of pot and cocaine and booze (not that he didn't see plenty of plastic cups and bottles in people's hands). But if a stag film orgy had been what he had expected, what in the hell did that say about what he was doing here?

Around him were several men in their mid–late thirties, looking tired and bored. One played a handheld video game, his entire body swaying and dipping as he manipulated the buttons. The noisiest group was around the television in the corner watching a baseball game. (The Cardinals at Philadelphia. He'd thought about staying home to watch it himself.) The girls lounged in another corner, dressed simply in layered tank tops and shorts that weren't any different from the clothes his students wore every day. He didn't see Malina among them, and was about to wander over to the group around the television when one of the girls broke away and approached him.

"You're the baboon guy," she said. "Malina said she'd be out in a couple minutes. She's always meeting people in weird places." One of *the girl's false eyelashes had been carelessly applied and Romero kept thinking she was trying to wink at him. She had a bad case of acne that showed pink through her powder and foundation.*

"St. Louis sucks," she said.

"Not making any new friends?" Romero said. Maybe she was sixteen. She definitely wasn't old enough to be drinking the tequila he could smell in the cup she held in front of her. "Been to the zoo?"

"I haven't been anywhere except this stupid fucking hotel," she said. "Get it? Fucking hotel? God, I crack myself up sometimes."

The Shelley had been one of the Central West End's carriage-trade hotels in the 1950s, and had been restored four decades later. But little had been done since. He wasn't surprised that the management turned a blind eye to "little movies" being filmed in their rooms.

"There's the Science Center not far from here," Romero said. "You could go on your lunch hour." From the look of derision on her face, he knew she didn't understand that he was joking. But he decided to let it go.

"Lunch hour," she said. "Lunch hour, lunch hour, lunch hour. You are pretty funny. You should talk to Danny over there by the keg. He's all for getting us into a union. Aren't you, Danny?" She shouted this last bit so that another girl told her to be quiet.

Danny looked up to nod at her, but then went back to filling his cup. Romero recognized him as the guy with the camera at the Primate House.

Looking back at the girl and her full, pouting mouth and bad skin, he felt a strong urge to upset her. "Does your mother know what you do for a living?" he said.

"Fuck you," she said. The flush of acne beneath her makeup was suddenly more pronounced. She pointed to one of the closed doors. "Malina's in there, asshole, probably blowing her boyfriend right now. You can go watch." She stalked back over to the group of girls. Turning back to see that he was still watching her, she flipped him off.

He was a little turned on by the girl's vehemence, her confidence. He liked the contrast to her not-quite-formed but desirable body and the pathetic dabs of acne medicine that he knew were supposed to be invisible on her face. Given her combative attitude, she probably liked to be roughed up by the men she had sex with. He could see himself causing her some pain, making her beg him to stop.

No. He didn't need to go there.

He'd almost made it to the door when he heard Malina's voice calling after him.

"Hey, Mr. Baboon Man! Don't leave," she said.

"You should bite his dick off!" the other girl said from across the room. The other girls giggled.

Malina stood with the door of the other room open behind her. The lights beyond were dim enough that he couldn't see inside.

"Seychelle is such a bitch," she said, rushing over to him. "And so freaking embarrassing. I'm sorry."

"Sure," Romero said. "I've got to go, anyway." He couldn't help but see that Malina was different from the other girls. She seemed fresher, her skin and makeup perfect. She was smiling, too. She seemed happy.

"Please don't go," she said. "I'll be sad if she's ruined everything. She's just a fluffer, but she thinks she should be on camera." She gestured toward the open door. "At least come inside and meet my friend. That's where the real party is anyway."

A pleasant fug of sweet smoke hung in the air. Malina offered him a water-filled glass tube that looked something like a vase, but had a tiny bowl attached to its side with a chunk of burning hashish in it. He shook his head.

"Not a player? Smart," Varick said. "I like to keep my head clear myself."

He sat in a comfortable leather chair that looked much more valuable than most of the other furniture Romero had seen in the hotel. In fact, the entire room in which they sat was more like a bishop's private study, the windows hung with thick velvet blackout curtains and more chairs and small sofas scattered around. The other people in the room were paired up, smoking and drinking wine, talking earnestly. One couple was making out in an oversized chair in the corner, the girl, blond, with the same build as Malina, seated on the man's lap. He couldn't see her face. There was no bed in the room.

"How cute is he?" Malina said. Her eyes had reddened from the hash, and her smile was less theatrical, but she was happy, still. "I think you should hire him, Varick. Look at those cheekbones, and he has such a sweet butt, too."

Romero laughed.

"I don't think a job in the movies is on your friend's career path," Varick said.

"Afraid not," Romero said. "I'm what you'd call camera shy."

Malina pouted. "That's no fun."

"Malina likes her job so much that she can't imagine everybody else wouldn't want to do it, too."

"She must be very good at it," Romero said.

This time it was Malina's turn to laugh. But it was a hesitant laugh. Self-conscious. He was suddenly reminded of Alice and the way she'd laughed only at jokes that other people thought were funny. She'd laughed nervously that late afternoon, the last afternoon. She'd known what she was supposed to be doing, only she never quite got it right. She'd been a terrible actress. He wondered what Malina was hiding.

"Both Malina and her sister are excellent at their jobs," Varick said. "Employees most could only dream of, with a kind of loyalty that money can't buy."

Malina, who was sitting on a low hassock near Varick, leaned her head down on his lap, and he stroked her hair with tenderness. Romero heard a sound that he thought might be Malina purring in her throat, but he decided it was coming from the stereo. So Varick was the boyfriend. More than a boyfriend.

Desperate to break the moment, he cleared his throat. "So," he said. "Are you, like, a producer or something?"

Varick gave Malina a light tap on the cheek, her signal to get up.

"Varick grants wishes," Malina said. "He's like a fairy godfather. But sometimes he's a little expensive."

Varick gave her an indulgent smile that lifted the scar on his cheek a fraction.

"I've been a lot of things," he said to Romero, suddenly serious. "I was in real estate for a while. My terms back then were cheap—and still are, I think—but there are some people you can't give stuff away to. Also in the produce supply business. Good stuff. It was organic and fresh, a flavor that would really wake you up in the morning." He leaned forward a little so that a lock of his wavy dark hair hung down almost into one eye. "I stay out of politics, though. And I'd never be a barrister. You have to lie too often."

The blond woman from the chair in the corner came to sit beside Malina on the hassock. Their clothes were different, but their faces, their hair, even the swell of their breasts were exactly the same. Identical twins.

Varick snapped his fingers to draw Romero's attention back. Or had he? The girls had unsettled Romero. Malina put her arm around the other's waist.

"I was even a boat captain once," Varick said. "Far, far south of here. Maybe you know it? Out of Isabela de Sagua?"

Romero hadn't thought of Isabela de Sagua in a long, long time. It was part of the story of his life, but it was that part he'd learned very early to leave out.

Smiling at Romero, the second twin put a hand on Malina's right leg and began to stroke her thigh, up and down, from the knee to just at the V of her crotch.

"I got out of the business because of an injury," Varick said. "Ungrateful passengers." He smiled. "But I'm very forgiving."

Malina nuzzled the neck of her sister and Romero heard the purring sound again.

Ungrateful passengers.

But Varick looked nothing like the bastard Romero had pulled off of his mother on the boat. Varick wasn't the one who had to be clubbed with the fish billy until they were certain he wouldn't hurt her again. Varick wasn't the one they struggled to throw over the side of the decrepit fishing boat to disappear into the water. It had been al-

most thirty years earlier, and he had watched that man's weighted body sink beneath the black waves with his mother standing by his side.

He knew he should stand up and leave the room, get the hell out of the hotel. But he was fascinated, drawn to whatever Varick might say next. He had the sense that what Varick was saying was important.

The second twin unzipped Malina's sweater a few inches and slipped her hand inside.

It was Varick, though, who had most of his attention.

"You've been unhappy," Varick said. "It's a shame how unhappy your life has been."

Romero listened.

"We can't really say, though, that you're completely blameless, can we? I mean, while I find your taste in sexual partners delightfully titillating and historically nonproblematic, current culture and laws take a rather dim view of the subject."

"It was just her," Romero said. It seemed right, somehow, that Varick knew. "There weren't others. Not like her."

"Not like her," Varick echoed. "Special."

"Not a good word," Romero said.

"You love her, you hate her, you love her, you hate her," Varick said. "Very Shakespearean. I love Taming of the Shrew."

Malina's sweater was half off her body. The other twin was kissing her neck.

"And her friends? What about them? Where would you like to see them in, say, a few months?" Varick said.

Romero looked back at him. He knew he didn't have to answer. Hate was easy. Hating was easy.

"You have to choose with your special one, though," Varick said. "The other two are easy. But your project, your violet-eyed one. You will have to decide."

When Varick stood up, Romero was surprised at how tall he was. His smile was benign and Romero had the distinct feeling that Varick might pat him on the head. Instead, he rested a hand on the head of one of the twins, the one who still wore her shirt, and bent to kiss her shoulder. At Varick's kiss, the twin distractedly reached for his arm and, as he walked away, let her hand fall back to her sister's waist.

Watching him leave the room, Romero wondered when the couples who had been there as well had gone.

What would it cost him? But even as he asked himself the question, he knew.

As if he'd heard the question, Varick paused at the door and said, "We'll talk tomorrow." Then he closed the door, leaving Romero alone with the twins.

CHAPTER 26

Week 30

Romero put his ear to the door to listen. Outside the bedroom, Roxanne was laughing.

He was overcome with the memory of her: the shape of her lips, the wetness of that delicate mouth that had so frantically searched for his in the darkness. He had heard that laugh down hallways, outside on shining days, low and disturbingly confident that long-ago night when he had tried to help her dress before she left his bedroom. He had almost stifled that laugh forever that night, grabbing her by her pretty neck, wanting to frighten her, wanting to frighten himself into staying the hell away from her. But he couldn't do it, just as he couldn't bring himself to stop what he'd now put into motion.

Varick. He was out there playing his role, doing what he was meant to do. Before Roxanne had arrived, Varick had told him to wait in the bedroom until it was time, as though he were a child or a moron. But he didn't want to wait. The waiting was killing him. This was killing him.

In the bathroom, he washed his hands again. These days he felt like he'd never be clean again. Of course, the harder he scrubbed himself, the thinner he could feel his skin becoming. His body was disintegrating, bit by bit, eaten away by the sins he had committed as well as the ones being committed by Varick in his name. It had begun with his hair and fingernails—even now the last three nails were hanging off and kept getting caught on his clothing. His skin felt as though it were melting from his body, detaching from the flesh and muscle beneath it. But it was going to get much worse, he knew.

There is no health in me, Father.

Prayers had begun to invade his thoughts. For how many years had he left that part of his soul (that endangered thing) empty? He'd stopped that conversation, quit the habit like a three-pack-a-day smoker. He and God were no longer on speaking terms. Still, the prayers came, despite the fact that there was no absolution for him.

"You want to talk now, or do you want me to wait until you get yourself cleaned up, Father Romero?"

The bus door closed behind Romero and he was face-to-face with one of the least likely detectives he could imagine. But was she police, or was she private? Given that they were in south St. Louis and that she spoke to him in Spanish, he figured she was probably private. Not local. He could tell she was trying to look professional, collected; but even at 5:30 in the evening the temperature was over ninety degrees, and she was heavyset and wearing a binding black poly suit with a black-and-white polka-dot blouse that didn't look like it was breathing well either.

He was filthy himself from his job working landscape maintenance for a service out of nearby Clayton, though his sweat had cooled on the bus. Yes, he wanted to get cleaned up.

She waited in the living room of his duplex rental while he showered and put on fresh clothes. What the upstairs neighbors—a retired couple who kept way too many cats—would make of her, he didn't know. He usually kept women as far away from the place as possible.

When he came out again, she asked him for a glass of water. He was embarrassed that he hadn't offered her anything. His mother had taught him better. As she reached for the glass, he noticed the shoulder holster inside her jacket.

"First thing most people want to know is how I found them," she said. She was suspicious of him, already.

"I would think the diocese would be glad to see me go," he said. He didn't know how much they'd told her. He thought about the deposit he'd put on the apartment. If he were dragged back to Cincinnati, there would be lawyers, trouble. Four months he'd been gone. There'd be no protection from the Church. Not the kind he needed.

"I wouldn't know about that," the woman said. As she took a drink of water, beaded sweat from the glass dripped onto her shirtfront and she brushed it away with a self-conscious flick of her hand. "I came up here from Florida."

The brief letter he'd written to his mother had explained that he needed to be away on his own for a while. His whole life had been spent as a dependent—first with his mother, then with the Church. It had seemed a good enough excuse. But the son of a bitch from the shelter whom he'd trusted to mail the letter from Texas had obviously never sent it. It sickened him to think that his mother probably thought he was missing. Surely, the Church had told her what he had done.

"Have you told her you found me?"

He'd never been one to like to watch, but that's what he was reduced to. Because his body was failing him, it had been months since he'd even been able to have an erection; no drugs, no seductive young woman affected him.

When Roxanne's and Varick's voices became fainter, he cracked open the bedroom door to see that they were seated at dinner. He could see the back of Roxanne's head, the way she tilted it with coy attention when Varick said something witty. And who was wittier than the devil himself?

Those first years after he left Cincinnati he had missed her, even after what she'd done to him. Even now, seeing her—hell, seeing just the back of her—there was a part of him that wanted to go to her, to take her face in his hands, to touch her one more time before some harm came to her. But even if he wanted to, he couldn't stop what was coming. He'd purchased that harm himself, and there was nothing he could return to buy it back.

He called in sick to work. It was a first for him and the owner had been surprised but didn't ask any questions, just as he hadn't when Romero had signed on. Romero had pretended not to know English so well, and the owner assumed he was just another unskilled illegal and so paid him in cash, which worked out just fine. The Mexicans on the crew suspected otherwise and kept a respectful distance from him. But he knew that the owner depended on him, and that he would still have a job when he went back.

A bright green taxicab stopped in front of the duplex and his mother got out. She carried no luggage, only a capacious leather shoulder bag that she clutched close to her body. Not yet fifty years old, she was as beautiful as ever. Romero recalled the friends he'd made after coming to the States wanting to come to the house to look at her, to hear her speak her hesitant, softly accented English.

A part of him wanted to rush out to her before she made it up the porch steps, but he held back. How much did she know? He waited until she rang the bell.

"Tu pelo se ve demasiado largo," she said. He was twelve years old once more, and he knew that he would kill for her again if he had to.

He held the door wider so she could come in.

She stood in front of him, a good five inches shorter than he, but her size had little to do with her power over him. He'd had to stay away from her, to stay out of her reach in order to keep his resolve to leave the Church. One word on the telephone from her, and he would've been at the monastery with a story about just having needed some time to think. Now, he wanted only to sink into her arms, to hear her tell him that everything was going to be all right again, as though he really were a twelve-year-old kid.

When she did put her arms around him, he felt the distance between them—the distance he had created.

"I thought you were dead," she said against his chest. "Why would you let me think you were dead?"

"Mama," he said.

She pulled away and walked around, taking in the apartment's tiny living room and shabby, stained furnishings. She tugged at the edge of the couch's rumpled slipcover before sitting down.

"What did you think? That I would believe some lying child puta over you? Am I such a stranger to you?"

"Don't, Mama," he said.

"You knew I wouldn't let you break your promise to God. That's why you wouldn't call me, why you let me think you were dead in some alley. And then the priests. They said they would find you, but they didn't. They said that you had gone away in shame," she said. "They didn't even look. I know they didn't even look."

"I didn't want you to see me here," he said.

"I know your heart, my dearest," she said. "And I know that your life belongs to God, and not to you." She sounded so certain that he almost believed her. "Me promestiste."

"It was wrong," Romero said. He'd wrestled with the angel of his commitment to the Church and the Church had come out the loser. "The way I went there—what if it wasn't for the right reasons? What if I didn't really belong there?"

"It was the only thing that would save your soul," she said. "What you did. What we did."

"I'm not going back."

She didn't answer right away. She was so much older than she'd been when they'd left Cuba, but her mien was younger, less burdened. Her clothes were expensive now. Her new husband was good to her—he gave her tasteful gold jewelry that flashed against her sun-soaked skin, jewelry that was appropriate for the wife of an owner of a chain of tire stores. She was happy in Florida. She had her sisters there, and a hundred friends through her Church parish. She was on the altar guild and the Martha guild. Her guilt and suffering were buried deep in her eyes. Perhaps he was the only one to see it, but it was there.

"You have to," she said, twisting a sapphire and ruby ring around one finger.

"Isn't it supposedly God's grace that will absolve us, Mama? Isn't that what you ask for in your prayers?" he said. "Trying to sell me to the Church didn't buy anyone's salvation or forgiveness."

"But it was a promise," she said.

"Didn't a couple of naked people once promise not to eat a certain fruit?"

"You're being ridiculous."

"Don't you want to know if that girl was really lying?" Romero said. He knelt down on one knee in front of her. When he tried to take her hand, she lifted it to his face and caressed him.

"I know she was lying," she said.

"There was another girl, Mama," he said. "A very beautiful girl." The color drained from her face and she pulled her hand away.

"I loved her, Mama," he said. "But she did this to me. She made the other girls lie. And I loved her." The words came out, unbidden. He'd killed a man in front of her. For her. Now he was telling her that he was something worse than a murderer, and he could see her struggling with the knowledge. She wanted to love him, but she was revulsed as well. "If all love comes from God, how can any love be wrong?"

He wanted to tell her that it had been Roxanne who had pursued him. That, at thirteen, she knew exactly what she'd been doing in seducing him, at manipulating his heart until he'd nearly been driven mad. She had never told him that she loved him. She didn't have to. Looking at his mother, he understood that there was no explaining. It had been a kind of sickness that had possessed him. Roxanne had possessed him.

"But you're sorry," she said. Her voice was strained, pleading. "And the Church will take you back. They are waiting for you to come back."

When she saw in his face that he wasn't going to do what she wanted, her tone changed.

"What if the girl's parents press charges?" she said. "What if you end up in prison? If you're in the Church they'll be lenient. Or the Church will pay. You need to go back. For both of us, you need to go."

She stood up so that he had to stand, too, to talk to her. She was angry now. Hurt.

"Mama, please," he said. "Please." He held his arms open.

She took a step forward, but then pushed him and hit at his chest like a petulant lover.

"Al demonio," she said. "Nos vamos al demonio, Romero."

Dinner was finished. Varick left the room as though he would go into the kitchen, but then he veered toward the doorway from which Romero was watching. He slowed, smiling at Romero (a smile that once would've frozen the blood in his veins, but now elicited nothing but a kind of thudding acceptance) as he walked on past, disappearing into the rear of the loft. Out in the living room area, Roxanne was moving cautiously, as though she'd had too much to drink.

So lovely even from so far away. He had a memory of desire that almost—almost—translated into a response from his body. But that was gone now. What an irony it was that he'd lived all those years as a celibate, alternately castigating himself for his sinful desire and, later, slaking that desire with the woman who now stood across the room. It was in moments like this that he knew that God had a twisted sense of humor.

Roxanne put her hands on the sculpture. He'd recognized it as one of hers when he first walked into the loft, and the spiteful twinge it had caused reminded him again why he was there. What had he been able to produce in all those wasted years? A few trees planted early on. Years worth of grade books emblazoned with JOSEPH P. DUNSMORE COMMUNITY COLLEGE, full of the useless data of immigrants looking to learn English and bored housewives amusing themselves with him and a semester or two of conversational Spanish. Varick had taught him that revenge wasn't just the province of God. He could have it for himself. He'd just been slow to take it.

What if he walked out into the room, revealing himself? Would Roxanne recognize him? Would she be afraid?

Romero touched the skin on his jaw. Whiskers no longer grew there, and the skin around his nose and mouth was tender and bruised-looking. Since Varick had brought him here a few weeks before he hadn't gone outside much. The day when he would have to bandage his face in order to go out at all was coming rapidly.

Roxanne looked around her as though someone might be watching. She touched the sculpture, running her hands over the boy's arm; it seemed to give her pleasure. After a few moments, she spun around, calling for Varick. Romero expected Varick to answer, but there was only the music coming from the stereo in answer.

What had her attention? She looked toward the ceiling, rapt, then at the open wall separating the living room from the unfinished part of the loft. He could see nothing unusual, but the look of dismayed concentration on Roxanne's face told him that she was seeing something that he couldn't.

Some men paid to see sex, but he was paying for something much more important, and although Varick wasn't there to tell him, he knew that he was witnessing the beginnings of the hell he had purchased especially for Roxanne.

Roxanne began to hit at the air, crying out at nothing. She was like a sleepwalker living a vivid dream. Whatever she was imagining seemed to be attacking her, and she flailed her arms and kicked out at it.

When she threw herself to the floor, Romero came out of the room so he could see better. But he caught himself and stepped back. Later he would see her and she would see him. Now was not the time. He knelt down (such pain in his knees!) to see her through the legs of the furniture. She thrashed and cried, pounding her fist against the floor. He heard fabric rip and saw bits of it slide across the floor. He remembered watching her play volleyball in school. She'd been small but tough, attacking the ball with all her strength, grunting with the effort of a serve. The other girls had been careful to stay out of her way. Would she die tonight? He didn't think so.

Finally, she lay still, and Romero could hear the music again. Vivaldi. He waited, thinking that Varick would emerge. He could hear Roxanne breathing hard across the room, and the two of them waited, though neither knew what for.

A loud cracking noise from the far end of the room drew the attention of them both.

He saw Varick standing over Roxanne. But was it actually Varick? Romero closed his eyes for a long moment, thinking the moisture would change what he was seeing.

This was not a Varick he'd ever seen. This Varick's face was bulbous-cheeked and his mouth opened on a crowd of jumbled, yellow teeth. Naked, his skin was the color of a decaying plum—grayed, but suffused underneath with a kind of red glow. There was a sense of awesome, endless power about his body. This Varick was the physical world: all that was real and alive and intensely human. The opposite of sublime. Romero closed his eyes, feeling weaker but also triumphant. He had made Varick powerful.

Because his eyes were closed in that moment, he missed the unfolding of Varick's massive wings. It was only when he heard Roxanne cry out—a pitiful mewl unworthy of the being in front of her—that he opened them to see Varick lower himself onto her body. He knew then that it was safe to come out and watch.

CHAPTER 27

Week 30 1/7

Roxanne was tipping the driver of the van from the art supply store when her cell phone rang. She'd thought she'd lost it the preceding evening—she was certain she'd been away from the house, but where?—but there was the driver holding it when she'd opened the door. He had found it on the front step, and asked if it was hers.

Seeing that the number was Alice's, she waved the van driver off.

"I thought you weren't speaking to me. You never answer when I call," Roxanne said.

"Can I come over?" Alice said. "I need you to fix something for me."

Roxanne ran a hand over the materials the driver had left behind. The bust of Del that she'd begun the day before sat on the studio table. *So inadequate.* Finally, she had a picture in her mind and knew what she was doing. And although she was logy from the nightmares that had left her exhausted and aching when she finally woke up in her bed, she knew she should at least ask Alice how she was.

"Have you gotten yourself out of that depressing house?" she said. "Or are you turning into some kind of vampire? Nobody's seen you in forever, Alice."

"You don't need to pretend," Alice said.

Roxanne knew she was supposed to respond with some platitude that would make Alice feel better, but she resisted. Pity-me was Alice's standard mode. What a boring game. But Alice jumped into the void.

"Just cut the bullshit," she said.

Ah, something new from Alice. And not a pleasant something new.

"What is *up* with you, Alice?" she said.

"I'm almost there," Alice said. "Five minutes."

"Wait," Roxanne said. But when she looked at the screen, it said, Call Ended.

She was in the studio when Alice let herself in the front door. It was with a deep sense of regret that she turned away from the unpacking of the media, the setup of her workspace, and the sketch she'd been working on all morning. She'd been thinking that it would've been nice to have Del's actual measurements, but decided she could work just as well without them. It wasn't true realism she was in search of—just enough would do.

Hearing Alice coming down the hallway, Roxanne turned to greet her. But when she saw how changed Alice was, she found she couldn't speak.

"Nice to see you, too," Alice said.

When she shrugged her black shearling coat from her shoulders, it dropped to the floor as though slipping from a too-small hanger. Roxanne marveled at how gracefully Alice moved as she bent to pick it up; her skeletal frame seemed too fragile, too brittle to bear any sort of movement at all. Never before a blonde, Alice's hair was a solid peroxide white, and looked like it had been trimmed with dull kitchen shears. The powder coating her face was surely meant to be translucent, but instead was layered on so that it appeared opaque, theatrical. A smear of bubblegum pink gloss across her lips did little to hide the chapped, bitten lips underneath.

"Take off your glasses," Roxanne said.

"So, what are you working on?" Alice said. She didn't move to take off the glasses, but went straight to the abandoned bust.

"Alice, honey," Roxanne said.

Alice sighed. She took off the impenetrable black sunglasses and turned to Roxanne. "Happy now? You're not going to try to make me drink tea or something, are you?"

"Of course not," Roxanne said. "I just want to know what's going on with you. You get that you're not all right, don't you?"

The skin beneath Alice's eyes was a transparent, rosy blue, and the eyes themselves were empty of any emotion except anger, and maybe disdain, if that was an emotion. With her hollowed cheeks and too-prominent bone structure, she looked scary as hell.

"Fine, I'll drink some tea, then. If I eat any food, I'll puke."

Small talk felt ridiculous to Roxanne, and Alice wasn't offering much, so they went to the kitchen where she made their tea in silence. She didn't eat sweet things herself anymore, but she found a tin of un-opened chocolate cookies some supplier had sent her as an early Christmas gift and arranged a few on a plate.

"So you're trying to make me sick?" Alice said.

"Does Thad know you're doing this to yourself?" Roxanne said. As distant as they'd become, she could hardly bear to look at Alice's face. Alice was killing herself.

"That's pretty harsh," Alice said. But Roxanne detected a feint in her manner, a chink in whatever freaky armor she had put on. Alice had turned aggressive, but it was the aggression of a frightened dog— tentative, then foolishly sudden, intense.

"You have to stop mourning this relationship," Roxanne said. "He's not worth it. He's proved that a hundred times over. But he's got to give a damn about what he's done to you."

Alice's laugh was derisive. "What are you? A fucking therapist? What he did was betray me, Roxanne. If there's anyone who should know about both sides of the betrayal thing, it's you."

"I hate that he's done this to you," Roxanne said. Talking to this

Alice was like talking to a stranger. It was as though someone else were inside Alice's (almost unrecognizable) body. She couldn't help but think of another part of her life, a time when she might have believed that someone had cursed Alice, or put some kind of spell on her. But she pushed the thought away as just too freaking ridiculous. She was way beyond that stuff now.

"It's this," Alice said. Her thin voice was suddenly confiding. "It's payback, Roxanne. Some horrible payback for every bad thing I've ever done. And I can tell you that this minute, but in another ten I don't know if I'll remember what I've said. It's like that now. But I need you to help me because Thad took everything from me. I need you to make sure he pays. I want him dead or sick or out of his fucking mind—whatever that stupid magic of yours can do. I want him to pay."

"What you need to do is to stay away from Thad," Roxanne said. She couldn't believe what Alice was asking. They weren't thirteen anymore.

"I don't need to get close to him," Alice said. "I don't even want to see him."

"You know that was just a bunch of bullshit, honey," Roxanne said. "Tell me you understand that."

"It wasn't bullshit to you back then. I was there every time. Except for Mr. Schottly."

How long had it been since Roxanne had heard that name? One of her regrets.

They were in the public library to do homework. Del grabbed at the doll the second that Roxanne pulled it out of her backpack. Though it looked less like a doll than a bundle of rags with bits of tea-dyed linen for hands and a head. She tugged on the thick lanyard wound around its limp body, but Roxanne had wrapped it tightly enough that it wouldn't move.

Del turned the doll over in her hands. "What the heck is this?" she said. But before Roxanne could answer, she spoke again. "This is Mr. Schottly's. The thing from his keys."

"*Of course it is,*" Roxanne said, *taking it back from her. They'd just come off a two-day, in-school suspension because Schottly had caught the two of them smoking in the bathroom. Alice's mother had died, and she was out for a semester-long trip to Europe with her father.*

"*Why do you have to be such a freak?*" Del said. "*I thought you were over that witchcraft stuff.*"

And, really, she was. But she hadn't been able to resist. Schottly had it in for her, letting other girls get away with smoking in the bathroom or ditching class by sneaking out the emergency exit in the janitor's room, but never giving her so much as a warning before turning her in.

"*I did it myself already,*" she said.

She hadn't wanted help from Del or Alice, anyway. It had been a meditative, solitary thing. She'd done the research and learned how to do a ritual dedication of the doll to Schottly so that the two were connected, and then it was all about visualizing Schottly's higher being to find out what his weakness was. Finally, the message had come to her that it was his gut. Schottly was fat, for sure, always swigging Mylanta or Pepto-Bismol. She had seen his ravaged stomach in her mind. If she concentrated enough, she could reach out with her fingers and pull at it, twist it in her hand to put the man in agony. She used the seven colored pins, starting with the white one, putting it in the doll's head. But it was the wait afterward, the week of removing a single pin every day, that had been the hard part. It was a kind of voodoo, a kind of dark magic—not Santeria, which was not magic at all, though everybody, including priests like Father Frankl, thought it was. Ever since everything that had happened with Father Romero, she could barely think about Santeria.

"*I just thought you'd want to see it,*" she told Del.

Del shook her head in disgust. "Let's just do the stupid math. I don't want to be here all night."

Mr. Schottly was absent from school the next day. Del didn't mention it, but Roxanne knew she had noticed. Then he was gone for a week, and at mass the girls were told to pray for him.

"*It's a coincidence,*" Del said. "*He has really bad ulcers. One of them ruptured or something.*" She pushed at Roxanne. "*It wasn't you!*"

"Sure," Roxanne said, truly surprised that Schottly had been out for so long. It wasn't as if she wanted him dead. There were rumors that his screams were so loud in the night that his neighbors had called the police.

Del insisted that they take get well flowers to him, but the school secretary wouldn't give them his address.

"It's sweet of you girls," she said. "But it's a matter of privacy. You could make him a card." She smiled.

"What does she think?" Del said. "We're not in kindergarten."

The second week, a second ulcer ruptured and he developed peritonitis. By Thursday, he was in a coma.

Roxanne—for the first time in her young life—prayed hard for another person.

The funeral was on a Tuesday. She watched Mrs. Schottly, surprisingly trim and fashionable in a brown faux fur coat and a large black bow holding back her blond hair, follow the big oak casket down the aisle of the church. She looked like she could be one of the students' mothers and not the wife of a fat janitor who liked to snitch. Roxanne wondered for a minute if she were glad that her husband was dead. But she felt bad about thinking such a thing and, in her head, asked for God's forgiveness. Mostly, she believed in God. You couldn't believe in the dark stuff without acknowledging the good.

As they bowed their heads to pray for Mr. Schottly's soul to go from strength to strength, Del elbowed her.

"You have to stop," she whispered.

"What?"

"You know," Del said. "It's wrong."

The words that came out of Roxanne's mouth surprised even her. "I know," she whispered.

Del reached over and squeezed her hand.

"Coincidence," Roxanne said, almost believing it. Now that Del was gone, everything they'd done seemed even more childish to her. Worthless. But terrible, grown-up things had come of that stuff. A good person she wasn't, but at least now she could take herself seriously.

"That's what Del wanted to think. But I never believed it," Alice said. "I was in the park, remember? And I was there for Father Romero's big exit." It was a clear accusation.

One thing that Alice had never really been was mean-spirited. She'd always been a follower, always done what Roxanne had asked her to do.

"I wouldn't even know where to start," Roxanne said, finally sitting down close to Alice, who smelled of unwashed clothes. "And I wouldn't if I could." She reached out to touch Alice's hand, but Alice pulled away. "This is about you."

"Varick said you wouldn't want to help me."

"What did you say? Who?"

"He's mine," Alice said, turning to her. She bared her teeth like an aggressive animal.

Varick. Why was she overcome with a sudden wave of revulsion? She had dreamed of him—now she was certain. But the images were all shadows to her, like so many shades of black imposed on one another.

"He bought *Peace*," Roxanne said, almost to herself. "He wanted me to see it."

"Why would he want to have anything to do with a slut like you?" Alice said.

Another woman might have slapped Alice, or thrown her out. But Alice was one of the few people in the world she could pity without any sense of irony or amusement. Del was gone, leaving Alice as her oldest friend. But she saw now that she would have to let her go.

"Don't worry," she said. "I met him once and he's not my type," she said. But she had, of course, once thought about sleeping with him, hadn't she? Again, the revulsion.

She reached over to smooth her hand through Alice's trashed hair. "Is this what he likes, Alice? Is this what you want?"

"You don't know anything," she said, jerking her head away.

"Of course, I know something," Roxanne said. "I know that you're really messed up and that you should let me help you."

"So do what I want you to do, then," Alice said. "Take care of Thad for me. And that little cunt, too."

"Jock can help. He can speed up the divorce so you can move on."

Alice screamed, sweeping the porcelain mug and the plate of cookies onto the floor. "I don't want to go to fucking court! I want him dead again and again for giving that bitch a baby when he couldn't—or wouldn't—do it for me!" She got close to Roxanne's face. "You don't care what happens to me. You've never cared what happens to me. You think I don't know it! I worshipped you, you stupid bitch, and this is how you pay me back. You kill people, you ruin their lives to get your own way, but you can't do anything for me!"

"Stop it!" Roxanne said. She tried to grab Alice by the shoulders, but Alice was too tall, too strong in her anger and pulled away.

"It's coming for you, Roxanne," she said, her voice hoarse. "Worse is coming for you, and you don't even know it yet. You're sitting here in your hip little slutty artist life thinking everything's so great, but it's all coming down. And you're going to come down with it. Because this"—she grabbed at her loose shirt and wasted body—"is your fault, Roxanne. I don't know why, yet, and I may be dead before I figure it out. But because you won't help me, Varick will. And you're going to be the one who ends up paying!"

Watching Alice, Roxanne understood what true madness was. She'd read about it in books, had seen it on film, had heard people talk about it. She remembered seeing a picture once of Charles Manson. She remembered the jolly, half-sly look in his eyes. Alice didn't look jolly, but she had the half-sly part down—the rest was pure anger. Alice was lost, and she couldn't do anything about it.

Finally, Alice tired of staring at her and swept out of the room, knocking a stool on its side as she went.

Roxanne heard the front door open and bang against the wall. She followed, watching, as Alice got into the Lexus (its right front headlight cracked and bumper dented) and backed out of the driveway, just missing the mailbox. Why did she have a sudden urge to laugh? Surely, it was just the release of tension. Alice was suffering.

Was it really all her fault?

Still preoccupied with Alice, she went back to work, setting the bust on a shelf with other unfinished projects. She looked around for a sketchpad.

So, Alice had found herself an actual lover. This Varick was obviously a cruel lover; perhaps even some kind of psychopath, and he had somehow found them both. But, no, she would never contact him herself. She didn't need to let someone like that into her life, into her head. Even as she thought it, something told her it was too late. The best she could do was to forget the dream and get on with her work.

She asked herself just how much she actually owed to Alice. She, Roxanne, was the one who had paid: aborting Romero's child had been her only choice. All those other things—the small violences, even Mr. Schottly—hadn't meant anything. Del and Alice hadn't had to endure anything but a few questions, and Romero was out of her life. She had no regrets.

Alice had shaken her. But only for a while. That morning, in the torpid wake of the dream, she'd discovered the shape of the piece that she would do for Jock and Wendy. Taking her sketchbook in hand, she began to draw. She worked until the pale sunlight crept away from the windows, taking every thought of Alice away with it.

CHAPTER 28

Week 31 2/7

Dillon was exhausted and his joints hurt like he was getting the flu. He put a couple scoops of what Amber called "high-test coffee"—some silly name she'd picked up from their grandfather—into the coffeemaker. He wondered how she was, how big she was getting with Asshole Thad's kid. She had sounded good when he'd called her a week earlier and had even asked if he needed some cash. Funny how cash wasn't such an issue for him anymore. How fucking strange was that? But he couldn't chance going to see her. After Alice had taken herself on a random trip in the car, even wrecking the front of it, Varick had been all over him. He couldn't leave the house for five minutes. And he didn't want to get too far from his new love, the sweet brown stuff that Varick had shown up with last time, stuff that was potent enough to snort so that he didn't have to mess with a rig, and that was cool. But Alice wasn't getting any easier to handle.

His hand shook as he opened the dishwasher to empty it. When had he become a fucking butler? Truth was that he had a lower tolerance for filth than his hostess. Another weirdness.

He heard a crash from the front hallway.

"Shit." He knew what he'd find even before he got out of the kitchen.

Alice was sprawled at the bottom of the stairs, naked. She lay on her back, legs spread, exposing a V of bruises on her inner thighs; her pubic hair had been shaved or waxed away, and the area directly below it was a raw mass of red and purple. There were teeth marks on her left breast and a jagged pattern of half-healed sores across her abdomen. Her eyes were closed. A pristine, pale blue blanket lay on the steps just above her. When he picked it up, he found it was soft—the softest stuff he'd ever laid his hands on. It was the kind of soft he imagined Amber liking. He wondered if she would have more things like this blanket now that she was with Asshole Thad.

He didn't like to touch Alice. He'd had to deal with some skanks in his life, but she was something different. In another life, of course, she would have sneered at him if he'd so much as looked at her on the street. But now she seemed contaminated to him, full of whatever Varick was. *And just what was Varick?* He had thoughts about that, but he never let them get too far. Letting her die, though, seemed problematic to him. Varick wouldn't want her dead. Would he? And if she were, what would be next for him?

"Come on," he said. He knelt to put an arm behind her and raised her to a sitting position. She opened her eyes with a low, pained moan. With his other arm, he tried to shake the blanket out over her.

"Can you get up?" he said.

Suddenly, she seemed to come to herself, but she didn't freak out to be sitting there, naked and broken in front of him. He remembered seeing her that first day in the kitchen; she hadn't been bad-looking—he'd thought she was kind of hot—and she had even been vain, worried about her makeup and what she was wearing. Now, she didn't even have the dignity to be embarrassed. Or was it that she didn't understand anymore what she looked like? She pulled away from him and wrapped the blanket around her shoulders.

"I'm hungry," she said.

"Yeah, we'll have to go into the kitchen for that," he said.

So, she was talking again. Sometimes, after Varick left she didn't talk for a day or two, which was usually fine for him. But there were times it was just too damned quiet in her freak show of a house. The one party they'd had was Varick's deal. His own friends weren't welcome and he had spent most of the night playing pool with some asshole with a Eurotrash accent like Varick's. But he'd won a couple hundred bucks off the bastard.

In the kitchen, Alice sat down at the table while he searched in the refrigerator for something to feed her. He found some bagels and an unopened package of cream cheese. He didn't bother to toast the bagel, but smeared the cream cheese as thick as he could without being stupid about it. He wanted her to eat—it wasn't just that he was afraid of what Varick would do if she died under his care. There was something when he looked at her. She was like a little kid, or a retarded person. Right now, she seemed helpless, but when she eventually came back to herself, she would get to be a handful all over again. No wonder he was so fucking tired.

When he set the plate down in front of her with a mug of coffee, she had a thumb and two fingers far back in her mouth.

"Uck," she said, dropping something on the table in front of her. It was a tooth, a molar, broken off and hollow. "Stupid crown."

He'd never seen a crown before, but it looked nasty and he didn't want to touch it.

"Thad put it on. Bastard."

"Eat your breakfast," Dillon said. Asshole Thad. So he was a crappy dentist, too. Fucking figured.

"You have to take me over there," she said. She took a napkin and pushed it back where the hole in her mouth was and moved it around. He was surprised to see that it came out without any blood on it.

"Where?"

"I want to go on your motorcycle. To your sister's house. He said you have to take me." She said it with a stubborn tone, like she was a seven-year-old demanding a treat.

"I don't get it," Dillon said. But didn't he want to go there himself? Amber was the best part of his life. The thing in front of him was all bones and skin. He was tired of all the ugliness around him. Being in Amber's house, even if she wouldn't actually be there, held a certain appeal.

"He left something for you," Alice said. She smiled, and it was a gruesome smile. "You get it when we come back."

They parked the bike one street over from his sister's house. Beside him, Alice was wearing a black down parka and a black cap and sunglasses. He'd talked her into a bath before they left the house, though she had argued that there wasn't any reason. Afterward, she'd doused herself in that damned perfume she liked so much, and he didn't know which was worse—Alice with B.O. or Alice disguised as a fucking flower. She'd also put on a little makeup and tucked her shaggy hair up into the hat. On her shoulder hung a big black purse that looked like it was stuffed full. With the addition of blue jeans and a pair of spike-heel boots, she looked almost human. It was weird to be out with her.

"Stay behind me," he said.

"That would look stupid," she said. "Like I'm your bitch or something."

"Yeah. Or something," he said. He felt like shit. The joint he'd smoked before leaving the house hadn't done much to make him feel better. Now, despite the pot, he felt like he was going to throw up.

They went to the back door. His key still worked.

Inside, the house was warm and smelled of the vanilla candles Amber liked so much. Alice pulled off her sunglasses, squinting in the light-flooded kitchen. Seeing her pinched, pale face, he felt a stab of regret at bringing her here.

"They had sex in here, didn't they?" she said. "I bet they do it everywhere."

"What'd you want to come here for, anyway?" Dillon said. Almost as a reflex, he went to the refrigerator and pulled out a cold soda. He had wanted to bust the back door down when he saw Asshole Thad take off his pants. And Amber—he was ashamed, but he couldn't look away, even though he knew he shouldn't be seeing her there, half-naked on the floor, with that look on her face.

"Research," Alice said.

It freaked him out how she had changed since he'd found her sprawled on the front stairs that morning. Not so helpless.

"Whatever," he said.

They walked through the tiny house, slowly, almost reverently. There were photographs of Amber and Thad everywhere, but not of anyone else. No, he saw the one of him with Amber and their mother when he was twelve in its place at the end of the mantel. They'd gone to Disney World that summer, while Amber was still doing her hygienist program. She had her arm crooked around his neck and was pulling him down to laugh into the camera. He'd hated to have his picture taken then, and always. But she could get him to do anything she wanted.

Alice stopped at a table that was covered with photographs in their frames. Amber and Thad at the races. Amber and Thad at a winery. Amber and Thad, kissing in silhouette, in some tropical beach bar. She picked one up, smoothing her fingers over the glass.

"Must be love," she said. Her cold and uninflected voice gave him the creeps.

There was more of Asshole Thad around the house now: a putter and one of those stupid putting machines by the coffee table, a sweatshirt, a pair of running shoes. He pulled a cigarette out of the pack in his jacket and lit it. It felt good to smoke in here, to light up in the love nest. He wondered what else he might leave behind. Take a dump somewhere? Puke in Asshole Thad's underwear drawer? Much as it amused him, he didn't want to do that to Amber.

"What's upstairs?" Alice said.

"Stuff I've seen before," Dillon said. He wasn't as pleased to be here as he thought he would be. Plus, he felt like shit and the infected stud was starting to hurt again. Varick had given him something that he said was an antibiotic, but who the hell knew what it actually was. He put the soda on the coffee table and kicked the putting machine so it skidded across the floor and slapped against the wall.

Alice was already up the stairs.

He sank down on the couch and picked up the television remote. They'd upgraded the cable since the boyfriend had moved in—yes, Amber and her baby would have plenty of good things now that Asshole Thad was permanently on the scene. Finding the game show channel he'd started watching since he moved in with Alice, he tuned in to a *The Price Is Right* marathon that he'd started watching the night before.

There was something about the Barker guy that reminded him of his father, the way he smiled every time he got done saying something. Of course, his father hadn't held a skinny microphone on a stage with big-titted women crawling all over him. But he had sold refrigerators for a time, and mattresses and televisions, so maybe he had something in common with the Barker guy after all.

Amber kept the house warm, and, crappy as he felt, after about ten minutes of the show and no sounds from upstairs, he eased into a comfortable sleep.

What woke him? It had been a dreamless sleep, but good. He'd forgotten how well he slept here at Amber's.

"Dillon." Alice whispered his name down the stairs.

"What the fuck?" he said, shutting down the television. "Where are you?"

"Up here," she said.

Above his head he heard the floor creak as she ran across the boards.

What a whack job she was. It was a shame, what with her fucking house being such a decent place to crash—gothic as hell, but with steady groceries. He was certain she'd eventually end up dead or in the loony bin. Sooner or later, someone would decide they gave a shit about her, or she'd have to show up in court for the divorce or something. He didn't think Asshole Thad would be the one to try to fix her. It sure as shit wasn't going to be Varick.

Like Teflon, that Varick. Perfect. Seamless. Nothing touched him. Nothing moved him.

The previous Thursday (or Friday—the days were all the same, now), Dillon had opened the door to one of the guest rooms to look for some soap, and he had found Varick with Alice in Wonderland instead. There was a single row of candles burning on the dresser, but there was plenty of light for him to get a look at what Varick was doing to Alice, the impossible, inhuman shape into which he'd caused her to contort for his own—and there was no doubt about this because of the easy, conspiring smile he wore when he turned his head toward Dillon—pleasure. He felt the bile rise in his throat but was able to turn away and shut the door behind him without puking right there on the Oriental rug in the hallway. Taking the bike—another blessing from Varick—he rode downtown the long way to blow some of the crap out of his head.

The Smoking Duck had a bartender named Josie who had once let him feel her up while she was on a break. But what he liked best about her was her deep cigarette laugh, and how she pretended to like his jokes. The place was empty, though, and Josie was on vacation and he drank three or four beers standing at the bar. There were no women there. After what he'd seen, he wasn't so sure that he'd ever want to fuck a woman again.

But at the end of the day he did go back to the house. In the kitchen he found the small package that Varick had left behind for him. He took it up to his room, happy to forget where he was for as long as its contents would let him.

"I'm not playing fucking hide-and-seek with you, Alice," he said, getting up from the couch. He heard her giggle, then more light footsteps above his head. "Let's go."

He found her lying on Amber's bed, wearing a swath of filmy pink gauze that looked like it might be one of Amber's nighties. Her bruised and scarred body was like a stain on the vast white spread. Spikes of her butchered hair jutted across the ruffled pillow shams he remembered Amber fussing about paying so much for at J.C. Penney.

"What the hell?" he said. "Where are your clothes?"

She pouted. "Let's play that you're Thad, and I'm your sister," she said. "Look, I'll even stick my belly out like I'm pregnant. See?" She pushed out her stomach, even bringing her hands up behind her to lift herself off the bed. But she collapsed, laughing, after just a few seconds.

She couldn't mean she wanted him to fuck her, could she? This was wrong, *so wrong,* on so many levels. He glanced behind him. What if Varick showed up? It was like Varick to show up at weird times. What was she doing? She wasn't just sick. She was hell itself, this woman, and he knew she was trying to drive him mad.

"Get dressed," he said. "Quit it!" Inside, he was shaking.

She stopped laughing, and held out her arms to him. "Pretty please," she said, pouting. "Don't you want your Sissy?"

Later, he remembered hitting her. (She hadn't even cried when he hit her—another accomplishment of Varick's no doubt.) Later, after he was back at the house and he'd gotten her to give up what Varick had left for him, after he'd gotten his payment for whatever fucking sick game Varick had decided they'd needed to play. He knew that it hadn't all come from this twisted, pathetic woman he found himself inexplicably bound to.

Later, he let himself think about what he'd found when he'd finally gone in search of her clothes. Later, he asked himself where she'd gotten all the blood she'd spattered across the walls and furniture and pink blankets and stuffed animals and diapers up in the room at the top of the house, the one that Amber had told him would be the baby's nursery. That was later.

CHAPTER 29

Week 31 2/7

"Don't touch me!" Amber cried out in her sleep, then fell quiet again. She was finally resting, despite the voices and frenzied activity around them and the ever-burning lights above the curtained emergency room cubby they'd been in for the past four hours. A nurse stepped inside the curtain to cast a questioning glance at Thad, who whispered that Amber was talking in her sleep.

"Sure," the nurse said. He went to Amber's bedside and peered at the display of the machine that recorded her pulse. "Still elevated. We'd really like to see it come down."

"Did the drugs knock her out?" Thad said.

"Mostly exhaustion," the nurse said. "Stress. Now that she's stable, and the baby's pulse is down, she needs the sleep. We'll get her into a room as soon as possible. It will be awhile, if you want to go grab a cup of coffee or something." He left the cubby.

Thad let his head and chin lower to his chest. So much blood all over the nursery, then the stricken look on Amber's face as she sank to the floor in pain beside the bassinet with its sodden, ruined eyelet. The thighs and back of her bright white uniform pants were soaked with blood. Yet, even through the panicked realization that the blood on her clothes was Amber's own, he recognized the smell of Alice's perfume in the air.

"I can't get a restraining order on the basis of smell," Jock said. "Did you call the police?"

"Amber's asleep," Thad said. "I need to get back to her in case she wakes up. The ambulance showed up fast and there wasn't time to do anything else. What if she dies, Jock?"

There was a beat of silence and Thad realized that, of course, Jock was still very much dealing with Del's death.

"Shit, I'm sorry," Thad said.

"It sounds like the doctors have everything under control," Jock said. "I don't know what else to tell you. Was anything stolen?"

The first thing they'd seen on coming home was food and soda out on the counter and in the living room. Amber had laughed and said Dillon's name with more affection than Thad liked. The idea that Dillon was around again had pissed him off—he'd gotten used to the son of a bitch being out of the picture. Then there was the second mess in their bedroom: the rumpled bedspread and the torn pink teddy hanging off the edge of the bed, the contents of Amber's pajama and underwear drawers strewn over the floor in random piles.

"What if it wasn't just Alice?" Thad said. Alice didn't have that kind of initiative. She was a follower, not a leader. There was something in the back of his mind that told him she hadn't been alone. That afternoon, in their garage—now Alice's garage—there had been that shining motorcycle. And it couldn't have been Alice who knocked him out.

"Sounds like vandalism, pure and simple," Jock said. "Were any windows busted, locks broken? Anything?"

"The police won't do anything, will they?" Thad said.

"They'll take a report. Look at the damage. If we're lucky, they'll have a talk with the neighbors, but I wouldn't count on it."

"The nursery is trashed," Thad said. "I'm telling you she's lost her mind."

"I'll give her lawyer a shout and see if he knows anything." But Jock sounded skeptical. "Seriously, Thad, I think you're probably looking at some neighborhood punks who knew you two were away at work. File a report if it makes you feel better."

Feel better.

After hanging up, he hurried to the cafeteria and grabbed a cup of coffee and a stale-looking bagel. But when he got back to the emergency area, Amber was gone.

"Upstairs." The nurse gave him the room number.

Amber opened her eyes when he pulled a chair close to her bedside.

"Stupid dreams," she said, shaking her head. Then her eyes opened wider and she tried to sit up, one hand grasping at her belly. "The baby. What about the baby?"

Thad pushed her back gently. God, if she wasn't the most beautiful woman he'd ever seen. Every time he looked at her, he couldn't believe he'd worked beside her for two years before realizing how beautiful she was. He found himself wondering how long it would be before it would be safe for them to have sex again. Would they have to wait for the baby to come? Noticing where his thoughts were heading, and asking himself what kind of jerk thinks about sex when the woman he loves is suffering and their child is in mortal danger, he gave himself a mental kick in the ass.

"She's hanging in there," Thad said. "But you need to lie down. Rest."

"You can't be serious," Amber said. "What's wrong with you? Where's the doctor?" She felt around for the call button.

"Amber. Stop," he said. "They're worried about the placenta separating. Throwing yourself around isn't going to help it any."

She laid her hands on her belly and, feeling the plastic-coated wires attached there, she looked up at Thad. "Oh, God," she said. Her eyes filled with tears that quickly spilled over onto her cheeks. "He can't take our baby. Please don't let God take our baby."

"Amber, please," he said. He wasn't a crier himself. Seeing Amber so desperate made him want to do something—anything—to replace the fear on her face with the sincere calm he was used to. He reached out to stroke her hair, but she pushed him away.

"You stop it," she said. "You didn't think this baby was going to live in the first place. You and the doctor. You don't love this baby."

He knew it was the fear talking and that arguing with her would be pointless. They just stared at each other, both helpless in the face of things they couldn't control. But in that moment of confused pain, he had a sudden, clear understanding—a picture in his mind—that it was Dillon who had been in the garage at Alice's, and that it was Dillon who was behind it all.

CHAPTER 30

Week 31 4/7

"Aren't you a darling to help out our poor Jock? Del would've been so, so pleased, I know."

Bitty Schulz gave Roxanne a polished grin as she piled her coyote-trimmed coat into Roxanne's arms, then drifted off into the noisy living room, leaving Roxanne with the coat and no one to answer. As she hung up the coat (a hideous, jewel-studded Christmas tree stuck to its front) in the generous closet tucked beneath the front stairs, she wondered how in the hell a grown woman—forty, if she was a day—could let herself be called Bitty. Bitty Schulz was just another reminder of why she disliked most other women so much. *Bitch.* Bitty Schulz hadn't been there to hold Del's hair back so it wouldn't fall into the toilet the first time she drank too much beer, or to share a hundred late-night tear- or laughter-filled phone calls with her. Roxanne knew there might have been times when she'd treated Del badly, but they had been more than friends. Bitty Schulz was nothing to Del.

"Come see the presents I got!" Wendy came running out of the living room to tug at Roxanne's hand.

Roxanne had tried to fashion Wendy's curly hair into long ringlets, the way Del had for special occasions, but had only succeeded with about half so that Wendy's head had an uneven, slightly lopsided look. Trailing after the child, she found herself giving people smiles that she knew weren't any more genuine than Bitty Schulz's, and wondered how Del had managed to bear it.

In her own work and life, she tried to be nice to people. She knew abusive artists, artists who would charge clients ten or twenty thousand dollars for artwork and the privilege of being jerked around, but it wasn't the way she worked. This just wasn't quite her crowd. These lawyers and judges and their lacquered wives/concubines weren't hip enough to appreciate her pieces, let alone buy them.

Wendy led her to a corner near the Christmas tree. It was eleven feet tall, trimmed by the same decorators Del had hired the previous year. This year, it was covered in peach and gold ribbon and hung with glittering faux fruit. A Renaissance angel sat at its top, head bowed, its feather wings spread wider than its silk-dressed shoulders. She thought back to the spindly artificial tree she'd grown up with and the cheap glass ornaments mingled with ones she had made at school over the years. Did Wendy make ornaments at school? What did she do with them?

She knelt beside Wendy, the slim burgundy satin skirt she wore—not burgundy, really, but a deeper color, oxblood—threatening to split a seam. It was a skirt for standing in, and not much else. She'd wanted to wear her black cashmere sweater with it, but couldn't find it anywhere in her closet or drawers. A pair of her black tights was missing, too, tights that would've been just right for this particular skirt. The loss of these things bothered her. She rarely lost things and never in her own house.

"Wait," Wendy said. She ran over to a side table, grabbed a piece of chocolate candy, and stuffed it into her pretty mouth.

She came back and pushed the half-opened gifts at Roxanne. There were tiny, tiny dolls with plastic clothes, a bead set, and a velvet-etched color-by-number kit with the face of Jesus on it.

"These are great, honey," Roxanne said, helping her to unwrap the rest of them.

Wendy tried to talk, but her mouth was full of caramel and chocolate.

"I don't like this," she said, making a face. She started to spit the candy out onto the floor.

Roxanne tore off a piece of wrapping paper and held it out so Wendy could spit the candy into it. Kids were so gross. The lump of candy was warm through the paper. It could only have been worse if Wendy had thrown up on her.

"Yuck," Wendy said.

"Go brush your teeth," Roxanne said. "Or get something to drink."

Wendy ran off.

What was she doing here? She got up, the candy in her hand. As a sculptor, she was used to unusual textures—but still. Yuck. Thank God she had no children of her own. What would she do with Wendy if she were hers? It was okay to be some kind of pretend aunt who could bring presents and things. But a parent? A mother? Her own mother had finally given it up and moved to Texas with a boyfriend when Roxanne graduated from college. It was in Roxanne's blood to be hopeless at the nurturing thing.

She saw Jock near the caterer's bar, talking to a group of men, none of whom she knew. But when he caught her eye, he gave her a quick smile and a wink.

For weeks she hadn't left the studio except to go to the grocery store and had only checked in with Colwyn over the phone. It was just the figure of Del and her, in the studio, alone. She felt like she was getting to know Del all over again. Hers would be a happy Del, a beautiful Del, a free Del, a Del she couldn't wait to reveal at the gallery in a few weeks. There had been no fits or starts after she'd rejected the idea of doing a traditional bust. She was in a kind of groove now, one that didn't need hypnotic music or hours spent at a museum or gallery or inspiration from photographs or books. She knew her subject and found everything she needed in her memories of Del.

But then Jock's call had come and she'd looked at the careless pile of unopened Christmas cards and catalogs on her dining room table and remembered that it was Christmastime and how much Del had loved Christmas and Jock and Wendy. It felt like an opportunity to her. An opportunity to be nearer to Del, even while being away from her work. It would be a change too, from the long days in the studio, and the longer nights, the sun setting winter-early around her, and the dreamless hours of heavy sleep that dogged her until ten or eleven in the morning. Yes, change. A break. An opportunity.

Also. Closer to Del. The things Del loved. The people Del loved. She thought about Jock. She'd never slept with the same man Del had. What would it be like? Would she feel the same things as Del? Would he touch her in the same way he'd touched Del?

First, though, she had to get through the party. And just to make that chore more bearable, instead of dropping the ruined caramel onto a waiter's tray or into the kitchen garbage, she went to the front closet and stuck it in the satin-lined left pocket of Bitty Schulz's fur coat.

As Jock saw the catering staff out the side door, Roxanne opened the silver chest to put away the small pile of demitasse spoons they'd used for the party. She wondered if it had bothered Del that the chest still bore the initials of her predecessor. Del had been quiet and uncomplaining about things like that—even about living in the woman's house.

"You don't have to stay," Jock said. "Wendy and I can put all this stuff away tomorrow." He stood at the entrance to the kitchen, his face flushed from the heat in the house and the several cocktails he'd had. But he was smiling. She could tell he was glad she'd stayed.

"Here, help me with this monster," Roxanne said. She picked up the walnut chest and held it out unsteadily for Jock to take.

"This will be Wendy's, I guess," he said, hefting it into his arms. Roxanne followed him into the dining room. "The silver belonged to her great-grandmother. I don't know if she'll ever use it, though. Del almost never did."

In the dining room, all the chairs had been moved toward the walls in discreet groups to make room for the dinner buffet on the table.

When Jock settled the silver chest onto its matching stand, he and Roxanne began to move them back to the table. At one point their hands brushed as they situated two chairs side by side. It had been happening all evening.

"Wendy seemed to have a good time," Roxanne said. "She smiled a lot."

"Yeah, she's pretty excited about Christmas. Finally, she's excited about something."

They finished the chairs and Jock gathered the long tablecloth into a loose ball. "What do I do with this?" he said.

Roxanne laughed. "I'm the wrong person to ask," she said. "My mother owned one tablecloth, and it was plastic. Maybe the dry cleaners? Don't they do that kind of thing?"

Jock wrapped it into a tighter ball and dropped it onto a nearby chair. "I can handle that," he said. "Later."

He flicked the light switch and the chandelier blinked out. Suddenly, they could see out of the enormous set of bay windows that looked out on the front yard. The mellow glow from the three gas-lighted lanterns near the walk and driveway illuminated a scene of fast-falling, brilliant snowflakes.

"Damn," Roxanne said. "How long has it been snowing? I had no idea."

It wasn't the first time she'd stayed at Jock and Del's house because of snow. Her front-wheel-drive car wasn't much better than a skateboard when the roads were slick. Her mother had tried to teach her in their battered sedan one snowy afternoon years before, but it hadn't gone well and they had ended up in the ditch outside the Pizza Hut. She remembered being self-conscious, wondering if any of her friends were inside, watching. Funny, that—she remembered being self-conscious about so few things. Alice had been the self-conscious one.

Alice.

In the guest bedroom, Roxanne reached behind her back and undid the row of buttons on her skirt so that it slid to the floor in a soft puddle. She let her panties fall to the floor as well.

She hadn't seen or heard from Alice since Alice had run out of her house. She couldn't think about Alice. She told herself she wasn't responsible for her. Alice was going to die because Alice wanted to die. And she'd obviously found someone to help her.

There was a muted knock on the door.

"Just a minute," she said. She shimmied the stretchy lace top she was wearing over her head and slipped into the terry robe she'd found in the closet. Glancing in the mirror, she arranged her hair over her shoulders and scrunched her fingers through it to give it some life.

"Ready?" Jock said. He had changed into sweatpants and a zippered fleece with just enough of his chest exposed for her to see that the hair peeking out was thick and almost black. She wondered about the first time Del had seen Jock naked. Del hadn't told her if they'd slept together that first night they went out. Had it been in this house?

"The bartender wasn't shy about his pours," he said. "But a cognac sounds pretty good."

"How about by the Christmas tree?" Roxanne said. They kept their voices low even though Wendy's room was far down the hallway. There wasn't any sign of desire in his face. He was just affectionate, open Jock, a little high, but obviously secure in her approval and friendship.

There was a single, dim lamp in the upstairs hallway. Roxanne blinked as they made their way downstairs into the brilliant light of the foyer's chandelier. As they crossed to the living room, Roxanne's bare feet were cold on the marble. She began to tiptoe, hurrying to the living room rug.

"Cold?" Jock said.

"Just my feet," Roxanne said.

"We can take care of that."

She followed him to the master suite.

"You'd probably be better off with a pair of Wendy's," he said, handing her a pair of white athletic socks he'd pulled from his dresser drawer. "They'd fit you better."

Roxanne laughed and sat down on the upholstered bench at the end of the bed. She was conscious of him watching as she let the bottom of the robe fall open to put on the first sock. She was conscious, too, of the air in the room, the faint presence of Del: of the perfume she had put on at the antique dressing table in the corner, the breath she had exhaled sleeping beside her husband, her laughter at Jock's jokes and Wendy's little stories.

"There," Roxanne said, getting up when she was finished. "I don't think I have a single pair of socks at home that are this warm."

She hadn't known it would happen here in Del's bedroom. But could she have asked for a better place? Jock put his hands on either side of her face and kissed her, not gently.

She loved the pressure of a man's body against hers, particularly if it was a body as substantial as Jock's. By the time his arms were around her, she found herself responding just as aggressively. Del had been much taller. Would it feel different if she were taller?

He stopped kissing her mouth and moved to the tender place just below her right ear, to her neck, and to the base of her throat. The touch of his tongue and wet lips on her skin sent a shot of intense warmth through her body and there was no question of having to talk or think herself into making love with him that very minute. She tried to imagine herself as Del, to imagine what Del might think or feel, but found she didn't want to anymore. There was no time. His hand was in her robe, rubbing hard against her breast, squeezing, kneading it as though he had to convince himself that she was real. Then it was between her legs, his fingers sliding into her like a teenage boy's might, testing, exploring.

How long had it been since her body had answered a man's like this? But when he picked her up and laid her on the bed onto the inches-thick down comforter, the one that Del had ordered from France, she thought of the other man who had laid her down on a bed so roughly. She'd been so young. *A child,* he'd called her. But how she'd wanted to please him! And she found she wanted to please Jock. Only now she had no question about how to do it.

Jock stood close beside the bed. Roxanne rolled onto her side and took his hand and kissed it, letting the tip of her tongue leave the slightest tickle of wetness at the base of his palm. Then she pulled it onto her body, somehow shed of its robe, and moved her own hand beneath

Jock's shirt, searching with her fingers to find the waistband of his sweatpants.

But Jock stepped away.

"Don't," Roxanne said.

They hadn't stopped to turn off any lights, and Roxanne could see a fine sheen of perspiration across his brow. His face was a terrible sight to her, his eyes filled with pain, but desire, too. His lips pressed tightly together, hands now held in fists at his sides. There was nothing soft or weak about him, but he was obviously gripped by powerful suffering. It might have been the first time in her life that she recognized suffering in another human being's face. *No. Not the first time.* What about Alice? What about Romero, those days in school after everything had fallen apart? His eyes watching her from the front of the room. Keeping sight of her as she tried to lose herself in the crowded hallways.

But what the hell good did suffering do anyone?

Jock bent to pick up her robe from the floor and laid it across her legs. Now, he wouldn't meet her eyes. He turned from her and left the room.

The snow was still falling when she went back up to the guest room, intending to get her clothes and leave. Somewhere in another part of the house, she could hear a television.

She could only think to get out of the house, leaving Jock with both messes. She hadn't seduced him, she hadn't done anything except say she would stay the night. But when she got back to the room, she was colder than she could ever remember being before and wanted only to crawl into the perfectly made-up bed. Her body was still confused, ready for something that was obviously never going to happen.

Keeping the robe tightly around herself, she shut off the light and got beneath the comforter.

Feathers. They were in her mouth, in the corners of her eyes so that even blinking was painful. And the smell. Her nostrils were filled with the smell of dead, rotting things.

Jock was there, kneeling over her. His hand was between her legs and it felt good. But the feathers flew into her mouth as she tried to cry out her pleasure. His eyes watched her with cold detachment as he worked. She couldn't thank him, couldn't reach out for him, couldn't even ask him to stop if she wanted to.

The walls around them were glass, sparkling with the lights from a thousand surrounding buildings.

"Watch," Jock said.

And he was no longer Jock, but the Renaissance angel from the Christmas tree, a beautiful, sexless being, its face full of compassion for her. It pursed its lips, which were the color of a faded rose, and blew the feathers from her eyes and mouth.

But when the angel entered her, her body was engulfed in a whole new kind of pain—searing, gut-melting pain, and hot tears squeezed from her eyes. Her tears even escaped her dream, wetting her face and streaming down her temples and into her hair.

"Look!" the angel commanded. The angel's face became the face of hell itself, and she tried to twist away, but found she was soldered to the angel at her groin. Melted.

"¿Te deule?" It was another voice. A familiar voice. The face leaning over her was human, but ruined. A face she knew. Romero's face.

She woke, her body and the robe soaked with sweat, her groin and gut and heart all throbbing.

Across the room, the door opened, revealing a wedge of dim light from the hallway. Was it that which had wakened her? Or had it been the dream? She knew she couldn't handle Jock at that moment.

But the footsteps across the room were hurried and faint. Not Jock.

Wendy ran to the bed, and, seeing Roxanne there, she scrambled up beside her.

"You woke me up," she said, snuggling close. "I have bad dreams, too."

CHAPTER 31

Week 32 4 / 7

Romero shut the door of the loft behind him, not bothering to be quiet about it. Varick was out, as he usually was. Where? He didn't know. Surely, doing more collecting. Too, he'd never known Varick to sleep. Some mornings, when Romero came out of his room, Varick would be standing in front of the stove making one of his hideous omelets or downing some of whatever slop it was that he kept in a pitcher in the refrigerator. Romero had taken the plastic off it once when he was alone and held the pitcher to his nose. His sense of smell had deteriorated sharply, but he could make out anise and something peat-like and foul that made his stomach churn. He couldn't imagine what Varick's insides looked like—if he even had any. There were nights, too, when Romero awoke to sounds from the living room that he couldn't imagine being made by any human. And come daybreak, there was often some remnant left behind: a woman's handbag, eyeglasses, a cosmetic blond pony tail, a book by William Vollmann, one by Janet Evanovich, a set of false teeth, a prosthetic foot, a tennis ball.

Sometimes, he suspected Varick of having a glorified body as Christ was supposed to have when he was raised from the dead, a body that was as substantial as flesh, but could be many places at once, could appear and disappear at its owner's will. It seemed to him that, as his own body deteriorated (this morning he looked in the mirror to see that his eyebrows were reduced to nine or ten stiff, curled hairs), Varick seemed to become more attractive, more vibrant. He was a handsome bastard, and was only getting better-looking and more jovial than the day they'd first met. Romero himself was slowly dying, his body the food on which Varick's and Romero's own sins feasted.

Theirs had been a simple enough agreement: Romero's life for the promise of the ruin of Del, Alice, and Roxanne.

Ruin. He hadn't wanted to say the word *death* out loud. But he thought that Varick had understood him well enough, and he'd extracted Varick's promise that he would live to see what his own life had purchased.

Long before he met Varick, he might have gone to a santero, of course. He knew about Palo Mayombe, whose dark rituals were supposed to be akin to Santeria, rituals that would've helped him take his revenge on the girls. But there was a heart to Santeria that he was unwilling to exploit—even though he no longer believed in the God at its center. No, it wasn't that he didn't believe. He simply refused to acknowledge God. Maybe he was being sentimental. The religion had been too close to him, and he to it. It was the religion of his aunts and his mother's friends—even his mother, on occasion. It was Monetta and Bryant and a handful of people who had once cared about him. He didn't need sentiment getting in his way. There was never a whiff of sentiment about Varick's methods. Varick was unholy. Varick was evil. Varick was darkness itself. Certainly, there had been nothing sentimental about Del's death. And he'd seen Alice from a distance. She was a walking corpse. It wouldn't be long.

It was the process of their suffering that mattered most to him. His own suffering hadn't been too painful. Yet. In fact, he wondered if he wasn't already in hell, if hell were simply the mediocre existence of humanity.

...

Standing just inside the crop of woods behind Roxanne's house, Romero felt the cold finger its way up his pants legs. He was cold all the time now, so it was all the same to him. In the next house over, a dog yelped to be let outside. He leaned against a smooth-barked beech tree to get more comfortable as he watched Roxanne move around in her studio. Unlike many of her neighbors, she didn't bother to light her backyard, so he was nearly invisible to anyone looking toward the woods.

The studio window was a rectangle of honeyed warmth in the surrounding black: Roxanne safe and untouchable behind the glass, he in the outer dark. It was that smug comfort he wanted to take from her, as well as the unflinching confidence that he'd seen in her from the very beginning. Without it, he knew she never could have affected him. His relationship with God had been too strong. As he watched, she stopped her work and, taking the clip from her hair, slipped off the oversized sweatshirt she wore. She tossed the sweatshirt out of his sight and adjusted the spaghetti-thin straps of the white camisole riding an inch or two above her jeans. If he had had any semblance of sexual feeling left in his body, he would've been aroused by the way her fingers brushed against her own skin, or the way she flipped her hair forward to once again twist it into a careless, tendriled knot. Those physical responses were gone, having reached some kind of frantic, aching peak during the nights he'd spent with Malina and Ivanka. Only now did he realize that his congress with them had been the thing that had started the process of his own approaching death.

He moved closer to the house, keeping to the yard's ragged shadows, so he could get a better look at what Roxanne was working on. Varick had hinted that he knew what it was. But he was always teasing, rarely giving Romero a straight answer. Because it was turned at an angle, he could see only that it was a long figure, perhaps reclining. Roxanne pressed close to it, one hand wielding a small, sharpened stick from which she frequently wiped bits of clay. He saw that her face— when he got a glimpse of it—wore a look of intense concentration, composed and mature. She was serious about her work. It was something he'd never expected of her, of the Roxanne that had grown up in his imagination. There she would always be the same manipulative, cruel child.

He pushed any other thought of her far back into that dead space in his mind, the space where he kept the things he didn't really want to know.

She was so close to being finished with the figure of Del that Roxanne could hardly bear it. Her fingers trembled as she etched the final details of the delicate pattern of flowers into the clay dress flowing gracefully over Del's long legs. Years before, they'd laughed over the busy Laura Ashley print, the dress bought by Del's mother for her on sale at the mall. But Del had packed it because it was light and sleeveless and cool and they knew it would be hot at the lake. There, for just that afternoon, Del had looked like the girl she'd been at seven, barefoot, even, as Roxanne remembered her often being when they'd played in the summers. The figure was the image of that day: a calm, happy Del, a person for whom only good things should happen.

It wasn't long before the gallery show. Colwyn was calling her daily for arrangements, but tonight she had turned off her phone. Such a massive work needed time to dry, and while the individual sections she had done—the arms, legs, the torso and head, which weighed rather more than she thought it should—were well-dried, the layer of clay that held them all together would take a while, and she needed to finish the detail. She reminded herself to turn the heat up in the studio again before she went to bed.

Even as she created this lovely version of Del, what Del had done to herself still plagued her. Nothing had ever come of Jock's investigation into the desk clerk at the hotel where she'd died, and she thought that his throwing the Christmas party was a final acceptance that Del had chosen to take her own life. Still, for both of them, the mystery of *why* was left. She was trying to live with it. Mystery wasn't so bad. In fact, the religion into which she'd been born was rooted in it.

But once the piece was unveiled at the gallery, she hoped that it would bring closure for them all, that she would have brought Del's essence back to them and they could all move on with their lives. Jock, particularly, needed some peace.

At first, she'd been angry about what had happened between them. But Wendy had redeemed the whole evening. Roxanne recalled how Wendy, cuddled against her, had fallen back asleep almost immediately, her faint breath soft against her skin. In the morning Jock had made them all pancakes, but the breakfast had been strained. He had kissed her at the door, but it had been a brusque brushing of his lips near her cheek that she'd hardly felt. He wouldn't meet her eyes.

She'd come to the decision, though, that she should be with Jock. And Wendy. It wasn't necessarily love that she felt for them, but obligation. In her own heart, she felt like she was making something up to Del.

Outside, she heard the neighbor's dog—a friendly boxer mix named Gretel—barking furiously. It was a terrified, whining bark that alarmed her, and it sounded like Gretel was near the house. The neighborhood was usually quiet, and although she never particularly worried about her safety there, she felt compelled to see what was going on.

She left the studio and opened the front door in time to see the dog knock a man to the ground at the end of her sidewalk. Gretel growled as she sandwiched the man's arm in her teeth, and the man cried out, trying to push the dog away. But his pushing was ineffectual, and Roxanne had the sense that he wasn't very strong. Heedless of the fact that he didn't belong in her driveway, and may even have meant her—or someone else nearby—harm, she ran outside.

"Gretel!" Roxanne shouted. "Back, Gretel!"

But the dog would not even look at her and continued to tug on the man's arm. The man cursed, trying to shake the dog off. He beat at it with his free arm.

Where had she heard that accented voice before?

Madre de Dios, what do you want from me?

She was frozen for a moment, but then kicked out at the dog, which lost her grip for just a second so that her teeth had hold of only part of the sleeve.

The man twisted away, putting the dog off balance, and he started to get up.

Beyond them Gretel's owner, Daniel, began shouting for Gretel. She whined as the man she'd attacked finally kicked her away.

"Hey, that's enough," Daniel yelled.

Roxanne's eyes were frozen on the fallen man's face. It had been his voice—*I could hurt you, Roxanne*—but was this his face? This ruin? In the streetlamp, his skin, once a creamy caramel color (a mix of indigenous Central American, he had told her, but mostly Spanish from long ago), sagged, sallow, against his cheekbones and across his forehead.

She tried to say his name, but the word wouldn't leave her mouth. He stared back at her for the briefest of moments, and in that time she recognized a torrent of emotion in his eyes: rage, fear, pain, maybe even a hint of tenderness.

Then he was gone, running off down the sidewalk and disappearing around the corner.

Daniel called Gretel again to keep her from running off after him. She stayed behind but kept barking.

"Are you okay?" Daniel said. "Did he hurt you?"

"You shouldn't let Gretel out like that," she said, her voice condemning. "She could hurt somebody. I should call the police."

"She probably saved your ass," Daniel said. He'd asked her out several times, but Roxanne had never had any interest. Plus, she didn't like that his friends sometimes pitched their beer cans back into the woods when they were playing horseshoes and drinking in his backyard.

"Gretel doesn't know any better," she said. "You do."

Roxanne hardly knew what she was saying. The words just came out in a rush while her mind was moving in another direction. What was Romero doing at her house? Surely, it couldn't be any sort of coincidence. She wanted to tell Alice and Del, to find out what they would make of it, to find out if they'd seen him in town after so many years. It was impossible to think about him without thinking about the two of them as well. They were of a piece, like some medieval tableau, a triptych, with herself and Romero in the center, and Del and Alice looking on, but still a part of it all.

Now, Del was gone. Alice was as good as gone. Would Alice even remember who he was? *Of course.* Alice's words came back to her. "It's payback, Roxanne."

So lost was she in the past that she didn't notice when her neighbor walked away, calling her a "flake" under his breath. Gretel followed, looking back once or twice at Roxanne, puzzled, as though she was confused at the response she'd gotten for doing what she knew was right.

Romero made it back to the loft, but by the time he let himself in the door he was dizzy and had left behind a trail of blood from the car, onto the elevator, and into the front hallway.

"Man, you look like shit."

Dillon lay stretched out on one of the sofas. Another young man, maybe two or three years older than Dillon, sat in a chair, his hands pressed between his knees. A shock of his thick black hair hung over one eye and his ruffled white shirt, tight, pinstriped pants, and pointed boots were almost dainty. Dillon looked pleased with himself. His companion was no doubt some kind of midnight amusement for Varick. The presumed victim wore a rhinestone-studded ankh about four inches long on a chain around his neck. Varick would get a kick out of that. Romero was sure he'd be seeing that in the morning, like some bit of bone or gristle left undigested by a finicky owl.

Romero peeled his jacket off, unmindful of the other two, and found he could barely move his left arm. The sturdy leather jacket (a gift from Varick, who had pronounced his worn red St. Louis Cardinals jacket "sad") should've protected him, but his skin was so fragile that the pressure from the dog's teeth had ripped the flesh. The sleeve of his shirt was soaked with blood.

"Nasty," Dillon said.

"Aren't you supposed to be somewhere else?" Romero said. He knew Varick didn't like Alice left on her own.

"She's got company," he said, coming over to get a closer look at Romero's arm.

Romero didn't need to have the tender mercies that Alice was receiving from Varick described to him. He knew that his imagination was inferior to the reality of Varick himself.

"Will you get the bandages from my bathroom?" Romero said. He and Dillon had come to a kind of understanding over the past few months, and had even smoked a little dope together. Now, of course, the stuff had no effect on him.

Dillon shuffled off in the direction of Romero's room.

When Dillon was gone the other man jumped up from the chair and hurried across the living room, his boots tapping lightly on the floor. He leaned against the table that separated him from Romero.

"*Esté Varick,*" he said. "*¿Me va pagar?*"

His voice was breathless. Romero thought he was laying it on a little thick.

"*Mejor,*" Romero said. "*Te va comerá.*"

The man laughed nervously.

"You are a kid-der," he said, in English. "Nobody eats peo-ple." He leered. Romero couldn't imagine that anyone would find this pathetic fop desirable. He shrugged. The movement pained him.

"If you want to live, you'll haul your stupid ass out of this place and never look back," he said. "Because if you don't, you're going to spend the next few hours before you die wishing you were dead already."

The smile on the man's face melted away.

Romero really thought that the guy would need more convincing. In the end, he found he really didn't give a damn about whether Varick played Parcheesi with the guy or served him up in a mole sauce. But he hated that he had seen him, met him. He also blamed this small flare of compassion on the throbbing tear in his arm.

"*Di le a Díllon que tengo negocio,*" the man said, moving quickly to take his white leather duster from the hook by the door.

"Hey, man," Dillon said, coming out of the bedroom. "It's early, man. Don't go."

Romero wondered if the man heard the tight note of panic in Dillon's voice.

But before Dillon could protest further, the door slammed.

"Shit," Dillon said, tossing the bandages and the ointment on the table. "Fuck."

"Can't be the first time one got away," Romero said.

Dillon eyed him, but Romero looked steadily back.

"What?" Romero said. "Come on, I'm bleeding. Help me out here."

"You told him to go, didn't you?"

Dillon looked menacing enough with the fangs across his forehead, and now he had a festering sore where one of his eyebrow studs had been. But Romero knew he had no room to comment, there. His entire body was a festering sore.

"I'm so screwed," Dillon said, shaking his head. "If you want help with this, man, hurry the fuck up. I'm definitely not going to be here when Varick gets back." He tore open the paper-wrapped roll of bandages. Romero thought to tell him to wash his hands, but he realized it was a stupid concern and didn't say anything.

"You think I like this shit?" Dillon said. "It's just my life, man. Just my life. It's like a fucking job—only a job with honey on it."

Romero knew he meant the heroin.

"Lives can be changed," Romero said. He flinched just a bit as Dillon shifted his arm gently so he could apply the ointment. He wondered how Dillon had turned into such a careful nursemaid.

"Sure. Tell me you think it's not too late for the two of us," Dillon said.

"Maybe," Romero said. He thought about Roxanne's face as she bent over him. It was the face of a woman who gave a shit about a man—someone she thought was a stranger—lying in her driveway. But that flicker of compassion was nothing in the face of the years of his life she'd stolen.

"I don't know what your deal is with Varick," Dillon said. "But I would put the chances of him changing any plans at a big fat zero percent. Very unfuckinglikely."

CHAPTER 32

Week 33

"The police want to keep it informal, but they said it's okay if you're there," Jock said. "Well, what they really said was that they couldn't keep you away because you're technically still half owner of the house. But if she doesn't let you inside while they question her, just back off, okay?"

"I don't want anything to do with that house," Thad said into the phone. After what had happened to him the last time he was there, just thinking about being near Alice made him tense.

Amber gave him a questioning look from their bed where she'd been ensconced since the previous day. She wasn't on total bed rest, but the doctor had warned her not to use the stairs or leave the house unless it was to go to her office or the hospital. They'd turned the tiny den off the living room into a temporary bedroom because the upstairs was off limits. He was just as happy to keep her downstairs. He'd had a service in to clean up the mess and quickly repaint the nursery, but hadn't yet had a chance to replace everything that had been ruined. Alice had been damned thorough.

"Do I need to be there?" Jock said. "Keep an eye on your ass?"

Thad almost made a joke about Jock looking at his ass, but decided that he wasn't in the mood.

"I'll let you know what happens," Thad said, hanging up.

Amber reached for his hand as he laid the phone down. She was looking a lot better than she had in the hospital. Even though the doctor had said that the bleeding had nothing to do with the shock of what they'd found in the nursery, Thad still didn't believe it was a coincidence.

"Please just stay here," she said. "Nothing good can happen over there."

"There's some stuff we need to know," Thad said. "Like if Dillon is really living there."

Amber shook her head. "I don't think he is."

"I saw a motorcycle there," Thad said. "And you said he had one now."

She pulled her hand away. "That's just the dumbest thing I've ever heard," she said. "Why would he have anything to do with her? Or she with him? She wouldn't be caught dead talking to Dillon."

"Then how did she get in here?" Thad said.

"I don't know," Amber said. "We don't even know it was her."

"Of course, it was Alice," Thad said. "Dillon's hooking up with her makes a weird kind of sense to me."

"You've had a key to this place for more than a year," Amber said. "Maybe she copied it."

Thad shook his head. She just didn't want to believe anything bad about Dillon.

"I'm not blaming you for it, but you've got a blind spot when it comes to your brother, Amber. The guy is dangerous."

Amber's eyes narrowed and he knew he'd upset her, but he couldn't stop himself.

"He tried to kill me. He's dealt drugs out of our—*your*—house. He looks like someone's version of a twenty-first-century Dracula, and, besides that, he smells like he hasn't bathed since he was twelve. There's something just basically bad about him, Amber. Sometimes, I can't believe the two of you are related."

He almost mentioned the afternoon that he'd caught Dillon watching through the kitchen window as they made love, but this time he did stop himself. Amber's face was flushed, and he realized that her blood pressure was probably going through the roof.

"I'm sorry," he said.

"Of course, you're sorry," she said. She kept her voice in check, but it was full of anger. "First of all, you told me you hit him first. Second, you're the one who doesn't know anything about growing up with an asshole father who showed up only to beat the crap out of you and make fun of the way you didn't read so well. You don't know anything about having a mother who thought it was a really fun game to go off of her antipsychotics for a few days to see what would happen. You wouldn't know anything about that, Thad, and you don't know anything about Dillon, and obviously less about me, if that's the way you look at him. I see a scared little kid, and you see a monster. You're just like every other schoolteacher or doctor or social worker he ever had to deal with in his life."

She stopped, almost breathless.

"Amber, please," he said. What the hell had he been thinking? He just wanted her to see the truth. But now wasn't the time to deal with it.

"Nobody ever treated you like shit for no reason at all—except maybe for Alice, and who's to say that you weren't lying about that the whole time just so I'd feel sorry for you? Maybe she was perfectly nice to you at home and you just thought you'd make your life a little more interesting by slumming with me."

"That's insane, and you know it," Thad said.

"Go back to work," she said. "Then go to your precious Alice's house, just like you used to."

There had been a few times when they'd come close to arguing about Alice, but he'd never seen Amber as she was now. He knew that she was just talking from her hurt, but no matter how fragile she was, he didn't want to hear it.

He left the room and she didn't call after him.

...

He got to the house on Leopold fifteen minutes before the police had said they would arrive, thinking that he might catch Dillon leaving. He was tempted to go around to the garage door and look inside, but he told himself to be patient. Dillon was a screwup, and he'd eventually make a mistake and show himself.

There was no question in his mind that Dillon had been the one to hit him from behind down in the garage. He hadn't told Amber what had happened because he was, for whatever reason, slightly embarrassed about it and knew he should've been more careful around Alice. This time there would be police around, and, even if Dillon wasn't there, Alice was her own worst advertisement. If he could get her locked up somewhere that she could get the care she obviously needed, Dillon couldn't exploit her, and she'd leave them alone.

It was after five o'clock and already fairly dark. Inside the house, there were lights on, but he couldn't see Alice moving around. The last time he'd seen her she'd been disheveled, even slovenly, and hadn't made much sense when she spoke. Could she have gotten worse? He wanted to get this meeting over with and was relieved when he saw the unmarked Chevy police cruiser pull into the driveway. But as he got out of his car, he was stunned to see thousands of tiny white Christmas lights blink on all over the yard. They were strung over the landscaping, on bushes and the smaller trees, most of which seemed to have every single branch outlined. It gave the impression of a blissful fairyland. As strange and disturbing as Thad found it (Alice had always told him she thought Christmas lights were tacky), he was distressed even more by what he overheard the male policeman tell his female partner as they made their way to the front door: "Would my wife and kids ever be crazy about this!"

"Please, won't you let me get you a cup of coffee or something?" Alice sounded desperate to be hospitable.

They sat in an awkward group in the formal living room, the room that Thad most despised in the whole house with its dark, intricately carved European antiques and massive fireplace that one could almost step into. This had been the room in which Alice's father had grilled him about his plans to marry Alice. How he wished he'd failed to make a good impression that afternoon.

"No, thank you very much," the female officer said. She'd introduced herself as Detective Pattisapu and her partner as Detective Simms. "Maybe we could get some more lights on in here? I want to make sure our notes are clear."

Alice gave her a smile that could only be called charming. "Of course," she said, hopping up to turn the chandeliers on.

Thad hadn't yet gotten his bearings. He felt like he had walked into the middle of some play for which he had no script. This couldn't be Alice: her hair was still short, and now bleached a shocking white, but was styled to look pixieish, like a 1960s fashion model. She was dressed in a pair of dark, skinny blue jeans tucked into high-heeled suede boots; her pale pink cashmere sweater hung loose over her torso, but the effect was relaxed and casual. The dark circles beneath her eyes were gone and her usually thin lips were softly pink and looked full and healthy. Though still alarmingly thin, she was nothing like the bruised and shattered thing that he had seen weeks before.

The house was spotless and smelled of vanilla and cinnamon. Candles burned here and there, and there was a plate of homemade cookies on the nearby coffee table. He thought he could hear Christmas carols playing in another part of the house, and half expected Mrs. Claus to come wandering through with cups of hot cocoa.

"What the hell is going on here, Alice?" he said.

The two detectives tensed and Alice looked at him with a calm that couldn't, by any stretch of the imagination, be called cynical.

Alice gave him a sheepish smile. "I don't know what you mean," she said. "I'm just trying to move on with my life, Thad. Are things so different? Am *I* so different?"

"Move on?" Thad said. "I couldn't give a crap about what you're doing here, Alice. I just want to know what you were doing at . . ." Here he stumbled for a moment. His house? His girlfriend's house? He came up with: " . . . the house in Mount Adams."

"Mr. Hudson," Detective Simms said.

"He prefers Doctor," Alice said, quietly.

"What is that supposed to mean?" Thad said. "I've never objected to Mister."

"Dr. Hudson," Detective Pattisapu said. "Maybe you'd like to wait outside for us? Mrs. Hudson has agreed to let you be here while we ask a few questions, but none of us wants this to become unproductive."

"It's all right," Alice said, her voice still low. "Thad has every right to be angry."

Suddenly, he was the bad guy here and he didn't like it. Alice was playing some kind of game and he was going to have to keep his shit together if he wanted this to go anywhere. He sat back in his chair.

"I just lost my head," Alice said. "I don't know what I was thinking, going over there. I knew it was wrong, but I couldn't help myself."

She began to get tearful. Thad kept himself quiet in his chair, though what he really wanted to do was laugh at her audacity. He'd been right. She had been the one in the house, the one who had ruined the nursery. Was she capable of such an evil? Yes. He glanced at the detectives. So far, they seemed unmoved by her tears.

"I got a phone call from Amber's brother, Dillon," she said. "He was angry about Thad, but I told him I couldn't stand to hear about them. It's been very, very difficult since my husband left. He and Amber McVay are having a child together."

Detective Pattisapu wrote in her notebook.

"I've tried to move on with my life," Alice said. "But it was such a temptation when he said he would let me into the house while they were away. It was the kind of closure I was looking for, you know, to see for myself where Thad had gone. I don't expect anyone else to understand." She looked directly at him. "Especially you, Thad. I know it was such a—I don't know how to say it—it was such a violation. I'm so sorry about that."

Thad wanted to jump across the table and rip her lying throat out. Had she always been this manipulative? The answer was, of course, yes. But he couldn't believe that he'd put up with her for so long.

"So this Mr. McVay let you into the house?" Detective Simms said. Of the two of them, Simms seemed to him to be the one less likely to buy into the story Alice was spinning. A black man about Thad's own age, he exuded a professional confidence that the smaller and much younger Pattisapu seemed to lack. He turned to Thad. "Were you aware that Mr. McVay had a key?"

"It wasn't my choice to give him a key," Thad said.

"And Miss McVay owns the house?" Pattisapu said.

Thad noticed the wedding ring on Pattisapu's finger. Now he was the philandering husband. There was no way to get out of it. He nodded.

"I just wanted to see," Alice said.

"Dillon was there with you, wasn't he? You and Dillon planned this whole thing together," Thad said.

"No!" she said. "I'd never met him before. He was just at the house when I got there."

"This is all bullshit," he said.

"Dr. Hudson," Pattisapu said.

"What about the blood?"

"Do you mind if we ask the questions?" Pattisapu said. He knew she was getting impatient with him, but he wanted to get to the truth.

"What about the blood, Alice?" he said, again.

This time, both of the detectives looked at Alice. She put her face in her hands.

"There was considerable destruction of property, Mrs. Hudson," Detective Simms said. "Would you be more comfortable with your lawyer here? We can continue asking the questions later."

"Do you know how long we tried to have a baby?" she said. Now, her face was flushed and her voice was choked. Her eyes rested on Thad. They weren't accusing, but pleading. He had to look away.

"It was killing me," she said. "I couldn't stand to see all those little things. Those were things that Thad should've been buying with me." She put a hand to her chest. "But he was with her, and not me. It just wasn't fair."

Pattisapu shook her head.

"I just wanted to hurt them," Alice said.

"Are you sure you don't want your lawyer?" Pattisapu said.

Alice shook her head. "It was animal blood," she said. "I went to the farmer's market downtown—to one of the butchers' stalls—and told them I needed it for cooking."

"You're sick," Thad said.

"I know it was a horrible, horrible thing I did. I just want you to forgive me."

She was crying again, her shoulders hunched protectively.

"Please say you'll forgive me, Thad?" she said.

Detective Simms exhaled loudly, as though he'd been holding his breath. Everyone in the room looked at Thad.

"We can charge her with criminal trespass," Pattisapu said. "If you think it's necessary."

They stood in the driveway, surrounded by the twinkling Christmas lights.

"You believed all that?" Thad said. "That act?"

"Don't worry, Dr. Hudson. This was just a first pass," Detective Simms said. "We're not going to let this go away."

"A first pass? This wasn't some kind of impulsive thing my wife—I mean my soon-to-be ex-wife—did," Thad said. "You should have seen her a few weeks ago. She's a mental case. She needs to be locked up before she hurts someone else."

"Our department deals with a hundred domestic disputes a day, Dr. Hudson," Pattisapu said. "When people's emotions run high, they do things they regret later. There might be those who think your wife has good reason to be upset."

"She poured blood all over a baby's room!" He couldn't control his voice any longer and took a step toward Pattisapu. "That's not like keying my car or slashing my tires. It's fucking psychotic!"

Pattisapu put a hand out in front of her. "Dr. Hudson, you need to take a step back from where you are, right now."

Suddenly, realizing he was facing down a cop, Thad did take a step back. But he didn't look away from Pattisapu, who looked both angry and uncomfortable and had put a hand to her back, presumably ready to draw her weapon.

Simms held both his hands in the air. "Let's all take a deep breath here, Dr. Hudson. I agree that these look like the actions of a disturbed individual. You have an excellent case for a restraining order, and if you follow us downtown we can get the ball rolling on that. The next step is pressing charges, but that's going to take additional time. Although it's up to both you and Miss McVay, I would recommend that you pursue that option."

"Damn right I'm going to pursue that option," he said.

"We have our notes. We'll need any evidence you might have saved. It would be helpful for us to have Dillon McVay's contact information. Can you help us with that?" Simms said.

Thad knew that there was no way that Amber was going to let him involve her brother. Although he could easily get Dillon's number from her phone, she would know he'd done it, she would know he'd gone behind her back. Yes, Alice was crazy, but Amber seemed inclined to just let it go. Plus, she was already angry with him.

"No. I can't," he said. "If you want to talk to Dillon, I suggest you just hang out here a few hours."

Pattisapu brightened. "Like Detective Simms said, Dr. Hudson, we have our notes." She turned and walked to the car.

Detective Simms stood for a moment longer, watching Thad.

"Seriously, man," he said, taking out a business card. "I'm not supposed to comment on this kind of thing, but your wife has some definite issues. You need to get that restraining order. If you don't come down tonight, you should get it done tomorrow." He held out the card to Thad. "Call us if anything else happens."

Thad slipped the business card into his coat pocket without looking at it. As the detectives drove away, he stood in the driveway and looked back at the house and the thousands of lights surrounding it. It didn't feel even remotely like Christmastime to him.

CHAPTER 33

Week 33

Dillon stood in the doorway of the study watching his sister sleep. Back when he was still only seven or eight, and she was already in high school, she had liked to sleep until noon on the weekends. But something in him never could resist waking her. She was one of the few people in his life who never yelled at him or told him he was stupid, and he had just wanted to be around her. The best moments were when he could snuggle against her as she slept so that she would put her arm over him as though he were one of her stuffed animals. There was no question of doing that now, even though he didn't feel much different inside than he did back then.

When they'd visited their grandfather years before, they had camped out in this den together, sleeping on the floor in his musty sleeping bags. It was a safe place, a comfortable place, even though the air inside the house always smelled of onions and cigar smoke. The television was always on in the front room, as well: wrestling and basketball and cable news. Even with the door closed, they could hear him talk back to the television, arguing politics.

"Hey, Amber Dawn," he whispered. He was worried that there was something seriously wrong with her for them to have moved the bed downstairs.

She didn't stir.

"Amber," he said, a little louder. "Wakey-wakey, eggs and bakey."

When she still didn't move, he went to sit on the edge of the bed. A dim lamp glowed on the TV table set up next to the bed. He wondered if she had some of the same fears of the dark that he did. No. He doubted it. He knew that there were things to be afraid of and that the only way to avoid them was to get a good, hard shot of H. He wouldn't wish those fears on anyone except Asshole Thad.

Amber opened her eyes, but didn't seem surprised to see him there. "Hey, you think those fangs will scare the baby?" she said. She looked over at the clock. "All I want to do is sleep these days."

"Not your kid," Dillon said. "I'll just be wacky old Uncle Dillon. If your boyfriend lets me even see it."

"*It* is a *she*," she said, struggling to sit up. "And of course, you're going to see her. She's my baby, too." She gestured toward the table. "Hand me that water."

He watched as she drank. She didn't look any older than a lot of girls his own age. But she looked tired, maybe a little sad. Asshole Thad obviously wasn't doing her any favors.

"Is Thad home?" she said. "Or did you use your key?"

"I made sure my buddy's car was gone," he said. He knew, of course, exactly where Asshole Thad was. Varick had told him to stay clear of the house for a couple of days and he had no desire to hang out with the cops. The truth was that he was happy for the break from Alice in Wonderland. Though Romero at the loft wasn't much better company.

"We have to work on that," Amber said.

Not fucking likely, he thought.

"You want anything to eat? Where are you staying?"

"I got a place," he said.

"You always do," she said. "You know, Mom threatened to come up when I told her what was going on with the baby."

"Is it going to be okay?"

"The baby?" Amber said. She laughed. "Probably not if Maureen the Grandma from Hell really does show up. You remember when she decided to start doing day care?"

"Hey, that had to be some kind of record," he said. "Getting shut down by the county after two weeks."

Amber made a face. "I'm not too worried. Even if she did come here—which she won't—Thad would put her in a hotel or something. There's just no room for her."

"So, you're going to stay here?" Dillon said. "Seems pretty small for Dr. Moneybags."

"I don't know that we'll be here forever," she said. "Maybe when the baby's a year or two old we'll get something with a yard. How great would that be?"

"Sure," Dillon said.

Amber smoothed the covers over her enormous baby bump. It freaked him out to see it—to see her that way.

"So, what is it?" she said.

Dillon was quiet. He looked away, out into the dark living room. He liked this house. He remembered how—as screwed up as their life usually was—it was almost normal when they came here. His head hurt. He was going to need another hit in a couple hours. He could feel himself sliding.

"I didn't have anything to do with it," he said, pointing to the ceiling, upstairs where the nursery was.

"I know," Amber said. "You told me that on the phone."

"I mean, that's some fucked-up shit," he said. "I wouldn't do anything like that." He gave her a slight smile. "Well, not to you anyway."

She pushed at his arm. "You wouldn't do that to anyone."

He liked that she thought that about him. Unfortunately, he couldn't trust Alice not to open her mouth. Still, Amber would eventually forgive him.

"Do you know who did it?" he said.

Amber shook her head. "I don't want to think it was Alice. But I don't know who else would even have thought of it, who else would be so mean. What I don't understand is that she's been so, well, she hasn't exactly been cooperative about the divorce, but she hasn't been a pain in the butt either." She hugged her arms to her. "It just gives me the creeps knowing someone was in here," she said.

"She sounds like a whack-job," he said, thinking, *I wish I could tell you the half of it, Sis.*

Before he left, she made him fix peanut butter and jelly sandwiches for both of them. He ate with her, even though the last thing he wanted was food and he thought he would vomit up the milk before he got half the glass down. Being with her was worth it, though, like the old times before she'd gotten serious with Asshole Thad, way before he'd moved into the house. Before he left, she made him promise to come by the house on Christmas Day, but he didn't know that it was a promise he would keep.

If he could have anything in the world, it would be to get Asshole Thad out of his sister's life. Baby or no baby. Asshole Thad had made his sister's life unsafe. It was ironic that even though Asshole Thad was the one living with his sister, he was the one with his thumb on Alice. He was the one keeping Amber safe.

Now, though, with Varick on the job with Alice, he could go back to the loft and make himself feel better.

CHAPTER 34

Week 35 2/7

"It means a lot that you shut down the gallery for me," Roxanne said, taking Colwyn's hand. A features reporter from the *Enquirer* and her photographer had just left the gallery and she and Colwyn were alone. She was feeling anxious, the way she always felt just before a show. Most of the work she'd done over the past two years was in this room. Many pieces had already been sold. But now she had to think about what she would do next, and, for the first time in a long time, she didn't know what it would be.

"What's this, darling?" Colwyn said, looking down at her over his glasses. "Bald-faced gratitude? Please, oh, please. Are those prescription drugs you're on?"

"Don't be mean," she said. "I know that after the holidays is a down time for you, but it's just nice not to have to spend all night setting things up." It stung her that Colwyn would ever have thought her ungrateful. He was one of the few people she genuinely gave a damn about. They both knew she could've shown in New York or San Francisco, but she was happy to do it here. It had worked out particularly well given that *Delilah* needed to stay in town.

"Well, if you've finished playing Pollyanna, then let's talk about what to do with that," he said. He pointed to the stork, which they'd centered in the display space in the gallery's western window.

"Does it fit?" he said. "I mean, is it emblematic of the entire show?"

"Too late," Roxanne said. "It's already first in the catalog."

"But is a stork really a bird of prey?" he said. "While it does have a baby in its beak—and, by the way, I like the way its tiny fists are all balled up. It looks scared to death. Do you think it's in pain?"

"It's not *eating* the baby, Colwyn," she said.

"Stunning," he said. "Just stunning. But I just don't know if it's in the right place."

"Everything will look different when we get *Delilah* in here," she said.

As she walked toward her car from the gallery, she saw two men near her parking meter, and she suddenly remembered the night of the Indiana potter's show and the man who had been hanging around. *Why remember that particular night?*

The man had been wearing a hood, which had seemed an odd choice for a warm September evening. And there had been something familiar in the way he moved as he hurried away. She'd been too preoccupied to think about it any further right then. Now, she was certain that it had been Romero, just as it had been Romero in her driveway.

Was he stalking her? For weeks now, ever since that lost night back in November, she'd felt a shadow over her.

She nodded to the two men as she went around them to get into her car, but they ignored her and kept talking. Neither one looked familiar, and they were both too young to be Romero. One of them dropped a cigarette butt on the sidewalk and ground it out with his foot.

She was tired and a little freaked out. Colwyn had pressed and pressed her about *Delilah*. But she'd been adamant about not having it delivered until the morning of the show, which gave her at least another day. Her plan was to get home quickly and finish wrapping the foam and plastic around the extending parts so they wouldn't be risked during the transfer. The movers Colwyn used were generally dependable, but she didn't want to take any chances.

On the way home, she stopped to pick up a bottle of wine and a few groceries. Her pantry and refrigerator had suffered over the past few weeks. She didn't eat much when she was working a lot, and her clothes were even feeling a little loose. That would change when she took a break—a break she knew she needed. She thought back to the summer, recalling that someone had told her about his place on Jekyll Island. But she was thinking about somewhere more remote. Maybe Bali, or Argentina. Or Turkey. Plus, she hated staying at the homes of her clients and other so-called rich people. Knowing rich people didn't do you any good. They rarely shared, and usually only wanted to show off their toys. But she also knew that if she were better at sucking up to the ones she knew, and was willing to put up with their petty prejudices and tiresome opinions, she'd already have sold every single piece in the show and could give herself a hell of a vacation.

Turning the corner of her street, she could see her bright little house, the house that belonged to her and no one else. But now, there was someone parked in the driveway, and, as she got closer, she had the shock of seeing that it was Del's car. Pulling in behind it (of course, it was Jock driving it, though she hadn't been expecting him), she waved at Wendy, who was climbing out. Jock held her back until Roxanne shut off her own car's engine. But then Wendy came running over to tap on her driver's-side window. The glass between them muffled her small voice.

"We came to see you!" she said.

Jock looked as though he hadn't been sleeping much. His face was puffy, and there were fleshy pouches beneath his eyes. He sat at the kitchen table, but seemed so agitated that Roxanne was surprised he was staying in his chair.

"You think Wendy will be all right out in the living room by herself?" Roxanne said. "I don't think there's anything out there that could hurt her."

He took the glass of wine she held out to him. "We got her some of those plastic ponies with all the hair on the way over. Plus, she's got plenty of junk in that flowered backpack Del got her. She never lets it out of her sight now."

They were both quiet at the mention of Del's name. Roxanne wondered if it would always be that way. Del had been gone almost four months, but in the weeks since she had started *Delilah,* she'd felt as though she were living in a protected stretch of time that might never end. Looking at Jock, she knew that time was over and that she was going to have to decide what was (or wasn't) going to happen between them.

"I didn't expect to see you until the show," she said. "In fact, I didn't know if you would even bother to come."

He surprised her by shaking his head. "I don't know if I can," he said. "I've picked up the phone to call you—I don't know how many times."

It wasn't the answer she was expecting.

"Then I'll get your check," she said, getting up. She felt the knot of tension in her chest tighten further. "I don't want the money. I haven't deposited it yet."

He grabbed her hand, stopping her.

"I know I owe you some kind of an apology, Roxanne," he said.

"It's bad enough that you brought Wendy with you today," she said. "Just let me go get the money."

"Damn it," he said. "Please let me talk."

"I'm too tired to deal with this right now," Roxanne said. She tried to keep her voice low enough that Wendy wouldn't hear.

"It wasn't like things were perfect with Del," he said.

What the hell did that mean?

"I really don't want to hear this," she said. "Please don't tell me that she didn't understand you."

He stood up and grasped her arms. She hated how miserable he looked, hated that she didn't know whether she felt anything for him or not. It was all mixed up in her head: the need to be nearer to Del, the need for sex, the adoring, probably screwed-up little girl a couple of rooms away, the darkness she felt closing in on her.

"She didn't tell me why, Roxanne," he said. "You have to tell me if you know why she did it. I feel like if I could just get inside you, inside your head, you might have an answer for me. You knew her better than anyone else. Better than I did."

"Funny," she said. "I thought you wanted *me*." Given her own feelings, it was an unfair thing to say, she knew. But she didn't care about fair.

"You think it was easy to be around you when you came by the house, sitting across from me at a table, or swimming in our pool? You think I didn't want you a hundred different times? But I loved Del. And she left me. She's gone."

"Am I supposed to be flattered?" she said, pulling away.

"You were in our bed," he said.

"I didn't get there all by myself," she said. Of course, she might as well have put herself there, she knew.

"Oh God."

She could see how he was struggling, that the combination of guilt and desire was killing him. *I could hurt you, Roxanne.* He needed saving from himself. It would be so easy. All she needed to do was to put her hand to his face, to touch him, to let him know it was all right to pull her to him. She could make it happen if she wanted to. But she wasn't thirteen anymore. She wasn't desperate for someone, anyone, to want her, to touch her. What would it cost her this time?

His beard was rough against her hand.

As he kissed her, she felt as though she were falling back, back to a place that was at once familiar and thrilling and frightening as hell. She knew it was wrong, but it was a comfortable kind of wrong, and she remembered hearing someone say once that the definition of sin was the attempt to recapture past pleasures.

CHAPTER 35

Week 35 2/7

At first Alice was angry when she saw Roxanne's sculpture at the loft. It only confirmed what she had suspected—that Roxanne was trying to steal Varick from her.

"What do you mean, *steal me*?" Varick said. He stood in the kitchen chopping up fruit for a salad. She was grateful that he hadn't gotten out the eggs. The rancid taste of the omelet he'd made her two days earlier was still on the back of her tongue.

"My whole relationship with Roxanne is based on a lie," she said.

"There are lies and there are lies, as you well know," Varick said.

"She told me I was her best friend. She must have told me that a thousand times, and I believed her every time. But it was a lie. It was always Del," she said. "It was Del who she really loved, and not me. I was the pity friend."

"Don't pout," Varick said. "It seems that Del has ceased to be a threat to your relationship."

She stood looking out the window and down onto the street. They were just one floor higher than Del had been when she jumped.

"Why do you think she did it?" she said.

"Maybe someone made her," he said. He popped a strawberry into his mouth.

"You could make me do that," she said, turning back to look at him. "You know I'd do anything for you." She smiled. "I *have* done anything for you."

Later, when they were in bed and the pain (the familiar pain, the expected pain, the desired pain) that he had caused her was finally subsiding, she snuggled down against his chest, rubbing her cheek against his skin. She felt like a dull shadow beside him. He was vibrant, filled with light and goodness. The scar on his face had faded so that she could hardly see its shape anymore. Even though she felt only as substantial as a shadow, she was grateful to be there.

"I'm thinking that I never want this to end," she said.

"It's going to end," he said.

He'd told her from the beginning that he wouldn't always be around. But she didn't want him to go.

How would she function without him? She was still exhausted from the effort she'd had to make when those stupid police had come by the house. If he hadn't told her what she needed to do, she would've been lost. She had some vague memory of being different, of not being so dependent on him. But she didn't like thinking about that time.

"I didn't like having Thad around me," Alice said.

"Wouldn't having him back be better than being alone?" Varick said.

"But I'm not going to be alone! You're not going anywhere. And I doubt Dillon can get his act together long enough to find another job. I think he's on drugs," she said. "I saw him with a needle in his room once, but he didn't even know I was standing there watching."

"Yes, Dillon," he said. "What to do about Dillon?"

"That sounds like a song," Alice said. She put the words to an aimless tune. "Whaaat to do about Dil-lon, Dil-lon."

"You're very funny, dearest Alice," he said. He kissed her on top of the head.

"Will you wait a little while?" she said. "Don't leave me just yet."

"I'll wait as long as I can," he said.

She was glad to hear it. By the time he took her back to her house, an idea had formed in her head. She had finally thought of a way to please him, a way to make him stay.

A gift. A gift to please them both.

CHAPTER 36

Week 35 4/7

Varick told Romero to be at the gallery by 7:00.

"And try some of this on your face. You look like hell," he said, tossing him a jar. Romero held his hands out, but didn't catch it.

His reactions had slowed. He felt as though he were moving through thick, brackish water, and if he had to run now he knew he couldn't do it. As recently as four or five months earlier he was playing pickup basketball games at his neighborhood park back in St. Louis. But he tried not to remember things like that. They smacked of regret, and he'd sworn off regret.

The jar—thick, blue glass—rolled up against the wall, but didn't break. When he got to it, he saw it was makeup.

"Extra-moisturizing," Varick said. He grinned, showing his crowded, unappealing teeth, his only visible flaw. The rest of his body was perfect. Even the scar on his cheek had disappeared. He had turned the heat up in the loft again so he could walk around naked, and Romero was compelled to look. He needed to see Varick's perfection almost as much as he couldn't bear to look at his own deformities. "You don't want to scare the kiddies."

Romero unscrewed the jar's lid and held the jar to his useless nose.

"It's got a girly smell," Varick said. "But it's not cheap stuff. I got it from our Alice. You could benefit from a little freshening up."

"Corpses smell," Romero said.

"Don't be so hard on yourself," Varick said. "You should be rejoicing today. It's judgment day for your friends. Even I might be surprised."

Romero might have taken offense at Varick's suggestion that he smelled, but it was more than a suggestion, he knew. It was a fact. How long would it be before he was truly dead, instead of just a festering ghoul? From the amount of hair he'd lost and the number of teeth (six, all in the back of his mouth), and the sores, the deepening holes in the most tender parts of his body, he thought it wouldn't be long.

"How did you know?" Romero said. It was a question he'd wanted to ask for a very long time. "Back in St. Louis?"

"Ah, we're feeling sentimental here at the end, are we?" Varick said. "Anxious for the trade secrets?" He shook his head as though he were reluctant to go on.

But Romero doubted that Varick would pass up an opportunity to show off. Wasn't that what the insignificant trophies left behind in the living room were all about, as well as Alice's and his own grisly deterioration? The most dramatic demonstration of all had been Del's messy fall from that hotel window. *Look at me! Look what I can command!* The ultimate celebration of vanity.

"You're a smart man, Padre, but I don't know if you'll be able to wrap your head around it," he said.

Romero almost said that it was his right to know, but knew that wouldn't have compelled Varick. Still, he felt a sudden, desperate need to understand how Varick had known so much about him, how he had come to this place. How did the Varicks of the world always know what they needed to know?

"Does that matter?" Romero said.

"Think of it this way," Varick said, leaning forward some. Sunlight melted over his skin, caressing it like closely fitted armor. It was only in that moment that Romero realized that the only hair on Varick's body was his beard and the tousled crop of thick black hair on his head.

"It's all about pain. Pain cries out to pain: call and answer, call and answer. It forms a kind of chain." He paused. "No, not a chain, exactly. More like a web. And when there's a quiver in that web—a particularly strong or poignant call—I can rush to it, bringing comfort and relief. Don't you feel comforted? Haven't I done well for you?" He looked concerned now.

"Comforted?" Romero said.

"Maybe relieved is a better word," Varick said.

Romero imagined Varick as an enormous spider, bulbous with whatever hideous relief he was offering, skittering over a web of writhing humans, their limbs interlaced and fused together. Macabre as the image was, he felt the corners of his mouth begin to twitch into a smile.

"What is it?" Varick said. The condescension was gone, replaced by the closest thing to worry that Romero had ever heard in his voice.

"Don't you know?" Romero said, tempted to toy with Varick. He had nothing to lose.

Varick stared back at him. Never before had Romero felt Varick peeking into his mind. Varick had just seemed to know what he was thinking. Now, he had the sensation of whispered movement in his head, like a feather drifting through.

If Romero hadn't known Dillon, hadn't seen what Varick had done to Alice, hadn't witnessed Varick's rape of Roxanne—that nightmarish transformation from man to whatever-the-hell he was—he would have been tempted to believe that he had made Varick up. Or at least had, in his own madness, convinced himself that the guy had imaginary superpowers.

"Who would have guessed that you were possessed of such a sense of humor, Padre?" Varick said. "So literal-minded. Now, you're like Little Miss Muffett. Time for you to be frightened away." He smiled, showing his repulsive teeth again. "Boo!"

Any sense of amusement Romero had felt withered. He moved past Varick and continued down the hallway, leaving Varick standing in the living room in his full, naked, and joyful glory.

. . .

Monetta's shop wasn't where he remembered it to be. He drove up and down several city blocks searching for it until he realized that the tiny strip mall that housed it had been completely renovated and expanded. Most of the cars in the parking lot were either new models or not very old. The neighborhood had gentrified, and though many of the faces he saw were still Mexican or Cuban or Guatemalan, there was a distinct change in the atmosphere.

He went inside the gift shop, which smelled of fresh paint and new polyester carpet. All around were shelves filled with glassware and Day of the Dead figures, and racks hung with colorful woven goods: scarves and handbags and chic Peruvian wool wraps and sweaters.

"Can I help you?" A thirty-something man behind the counter looked up from a piece of jewelry he was beading. He wore a tight red satin shirt and several gold necklaces that seemed to have been carefully selected to complement the gold hoop at the edge of his right nostril. Was it Romero's imagination, or did a brief look of disgust cross the man's face when he looked at him? The makeup had looked fine in the bathroom mirror, but Romero knew he wasn't seeing so well these days.

When he first tried to speak, nothing came out but a hoarse croak. He cleared his throat.

"Monetta," he said. "Is she here?"

The man looked back down at his work and slipped a bead onto the needle. "Nobody does that stuff here, anymore. You'll have to get your voodoo fix somewhere else. You people should pass the word."

"Do you know where she is?"

"Yes," he said. "But she's a nice lady and she's sick and she doesn't need you people hanging around."

Romero came closer to the counter. The man leaned back on his stool, narrowing his eyes.

"I need to see her."

"Not my problem," the man said. "If you don't want to buy something, then have a nice day and go away." He gave a backhanded wave toward the door and pressed his lips together beneath his sparse, overgroomed moustache.

"Do you know what leprosy is?" Romero said, starting to peel off a glove. Though he knew that the boils and sores erupting on his skin weren't actually leprosy. Leprosy was treatable. What was happening to him had only one, nonmedical, cure.

The man sighed. "My older brother died riddled with Kaposi's sarcoma," he said. "Don't even think you're going to scare me. I mean, you're wearing a zip-up sweater. You're not exactly the bogey man."

"I just need to see her," Romero said. He wasn't sure what he was looking for from Monetta, but he knew that, whatever it was, he had to have it today. Today was his last chance.

The man shook his head. "You know that saint shit's all made up," he said. "There's only Jesus." He put down the bracelet he was working on and pushed up his sleeve to reveal an eight-inch long crucifix inked on his inner forearm. Christ's head was bowed forward, his body slumped in pain. Total capitulation. The words, *Tout Est Accompli,* were inked in a speech balloon near the cross. *It Is Finished.*

"Sure," Romero said. He didn't bother to ask why the tattoo was in French.

The man tugged his sleeve down again. "There's just no getting through to you people, is there?" he said.

The houses on Monetta's street had so far escaped the notice of the accountants and stockbrokers looking for an edgy address. Her brick two-story stood alone on one side of a double lot, right next to a large rectangle of dirt that must have once been a vegetable garden. The front porch was swept clean, and a bright blue porch swing creaked on its chains in the winter wind.

Monetta answered the door.

Romero tried to smile when he saw her, but when he looked at her eyes, he saw they were blank and unseeing.

"Yes?" she said. "Whoever you are, welcome."

A thick-bodied white cat rubbed affectionately at her ankles and ran past Romero and into the yard. *What would he find here? Forgiveness?* He had to fight the urge to run away himself.

"It's Romero," he said. They stood in silence for a moment until recognition registered on her face.

"Come in," she said, stepping back from the door. But she did not smile.

She made them a pot of strong tea, which she prepared without fault. He waited for her to have a misstep, but the only thing for which she asked assistance was carrying the tray to the front room.

"The cats get in my way sometimes," she said. "*No tienen corazón.*"

They sat drinking their tea in a long silence.

Finally, Romero spoke.

"I don't know where to begin." He hadn't expected to find her suffering. Now, despite that suffering, she took the weight of the afternoon from him and put it on herself.

"Then I will speak," Monetta said. "Because if I were a person to be afraid of things, I would fear your sitting here in my house when I told you to go away and never to come back."

He started to interrupt, but she held up her hand.

"One day I took out the shells and I could read nothing there. Only silence," she said. "God's silence. And the next morning, I opened my eyes to total darkness. Do you know what it's like to open your eyes and see nothing? It was as though I needed to peel layers and layers of cataracts away, but I put my hands to them and found nothing was different. But the doctors, the brilliant doctors, they tell me that they can find nothing wrong, that the blindness is all in my head. I've had every test that they can think of, and this is what they come up with: that I am as pitiful and crazy as Dolores, God rest her soul."

"You could never be pitiful," Romero said.

"*Sepulcro abierto es su garganta; Con su lengua hablan lisonjas,*" she said.

He felt his entire body go cold. *Their throat is an open tomb. They flatter with their tongue.* The way she sat there, with her expressionless eyes, pronouncing him to be faithless and evil, chilled him more than any unholy thing he'd seen since he'd met Varick.

"What do you want, Romero? It's not goodness that brought you back here."

Had he really expected forgiveness? Absolution? She was no priest.

"I need you to tell me what you saw in the shells," Romero said.

"I should have reported you to the police."

"If you had told me, maybe I wouldn't be here today," he said.

Monetta bowed her head and closed her eyes. Her lips moved, but he could hear no sound. She was praying, certainly. It was a strange thing for her to do if God wasn't listening, or speaking back to her. How strange that it was true for both of them now.

Finally, she raised her head.

"Perhaps you're right," she said. "Perhaps we would both be redeemed today if I had tried to help you. But there are some things, Romero, that one shouldn't have to bear. Later, when the child came to me, I couldn't turn her away."

"Why would she come to you?" he said. "What did she tell you?"

He imagined Roxanne pleading with Monetta to tell her where he'd gone. Had she missed him in the end, even after her deception? The idea that—by leaving—he'd denied her the forgiveness she might have sought, had never occurred to him.

"Can't you guess?" she said. "I was the only one she could turn to. Her mother?" She shook her head. "Carla was in need of a mother herself. I knew that the first day she came around the shop looking for what she called true spirituality. She was more lost than her own daughter. Roxanne needed someone who could help her, to treat her as a cherished child, not like some object of lustful desire."

At this, Romero's face colored with heat. *It hadn't been like that!*

"You can't guess what she could possibly want from me, Romero?"

Romero shook his head, but then remembered her blindness. "She wanted to find me," he said.

"I thought you were a humble man when I first met you," Monetta said. "And I think that you *were* humble, or else you wouldn't have been so good to people like Bryant and the others who were suffering and could get no solace from the Church. But the years have not been kind to you," she said. "Now, you have both the stink of death about you and the vile smell of arrogance."

"I'm dying," he said.

"Of course, you are dying," she said. But now, at least, her voice held a bit of sadness. "What I did for Roxanne went against everything I have ever believed in, against my faith in God, against my responsibilities as a santera. And I have to ask myself if maybe I am paying for what I did with this." She touched two fingers to the outer corner of one eye. "But I don't think you deserve to die any more than that child deserved to have her life damaged by you."

"Deserve? I'm not concerned about deserving it."

"Oh, but I think now you might be concerned," she said. "What I did, women like me—the women whom people call witches—have been doing for centuries, and I'm perfectly willing to go before God when it's my time and justify what I did for Roxanne. I just pray that I have so little time left on this earth that I won't ever have to make that decision again."

Romero was silent. Thinking.

"Are you so dense?" she said. "I gave the child an abortofacient. A child, Romero. You impregnated a child with a child. Then you ran away."

A child. *His child.*

The knowledge bled through him, spreading pain like poison. How could he not have known? Like some vain, stupid teenager he had been so consumed with desire that he hadn't given a moment's real thought to that particular consequence. He'd been too worried about their souls! He pulled at his shirt, desperate to tear it off. Monetta had used the word *vile*. He was so far beyond that.

"Why didn't you tell me?" he said. "Why did you let me leave?"

"She didn't know about it until after you'd gone. It was almost too late when she came to me," she said. "She was too ashamed to even try to find you. But I think she was angry, as well. How is a child supposed to know how to react when a man of God seduces and impregnates her? It was better that you were gone. As it was, she did you a kindness."

CHAPTER 37

Week 35 4/7

When his private phone line rang, Thad picked it up immediately thinking it might be Amber. He was in his office, late, doing neglected paperwork, and had hesitated to call her. Things had been tense at the house since their fight about Dillon just before Christmas, and Christmas itself had been a sad affair. They hadn't even bothered with a tree. He had picked up a prepared meal at a gourmet grocery and given her the store-wrapped sapphire earrings he'd picked out before she'd gone on bed rest. She was still convinced that he didn't care about the baby, that he was certain it would die. He couldn't tell her that he just didn't want to hope too much.

"Hello?" he said.

There was nothing but the distant sound of a television in the background—some afternoon celebrity gossip show.

"Amber?" he said. He glanced over at the caller ID. Not Amber.

"God, Alice, what do you want? I thought you understood that the restraining order means you can't call here."

"I just wanted to talk to you for a minute," she said. "Did you have a happy New Year?"

"My New Year's was fine," he said. "I'm hanging up now. Good-bye."

"Wait! Please wait," she said. " I really need to talk to you. Listen. Will you come over to the house?"

"You and I have nothing to say to each other that can't be said through our lawyers."

But then an idea came to him.

"Unless you want to tell me the truth about what you and Dillon were doing at Amber's. Is that why you're calling me?"

"Why can't you just come over to talk?" she said. "We used to talk all the time. Remember when we went to Paris? How we sat in the *Jardin des Tuileries* and talked all afternoon?"

"I'm hanging up," he said.

"Maybe I know more about that Dillon person," she said.

Thad shifted in his chair. He wanted to be very careful about what he would say next. He knew she wanted something from him and Dillon was the bait.

"I have to go by the gallery first," he said. "You're not going to be at Roxanne's opening, are you?"

She laughed again. "Roxanne and I aren't exactly close these days," she said. "You can come over afterward, can't you?"

As soon as the call was over, he gave in to his need to hear Amber's voice and dialed the house. When he told her that he would be later than he'd thought, she told him to drive safely and hung up the phone.

Alice's call had been so distracting that it took him another forty-five minutes to finish up his work. He didn't know if he could get any kind of confession from her, but the police and the prosecutor weren't moving fast enough for his taste. Even if he did get a confession, what would he do with it? She'd deny it later, of course. She was at least that predictable.

He found a parking space about a block away from the gallery. A light snow had begun to fall, bright flakes flickering in the glow of the streetlamp. Back at the house Amber would be getting herself some dinner about now, maybe settling onto the couch in front of the television. The almost eight months of the pregnancy had begun to wear on her, and her confinement had made it worse. He thought things might improve once the baby arrived. If it arrived safely.

"Thad, honey," Roxanne said, taking his hand and bringing it to her cheek. "I can't believe you came."

"Roxanne," he said. He leaned down to kiss her.

"Of course he's here," Jock said.

He hadn't wanted to come. In fact, he didn't know any man who actually wanted to attend an art opening. And although he hadn't minded Roxanne's early work, her most recent stuff was disturbing, its tableaux of children and birds grotesque. Alice had bought one of the child/bird sculptures the previous spring, but he had insisted that they install it in an outdoor portico leading to the dining room so that he didn't have to see it every day. The girl-child it portrayed, a sad little thing with a parakeet on her shoulder, seemed soulless to him, empty of all joy. Now, he could only connect that piece to Alice. It seemed to suit her.

"You didn't bring your friend," Roxanne said. "Amber, is it?"

She was looking as fuckable as ever. Her cabernet velvet dress was cut low on her chest and her dark hair spilled over her shoulders. A lustrous white pearl the size of a dime nestled between her breasts, the gold of its delicate chain a subtle contrast to her skin.

"Amber wasn't feeling well," he said. "She sends her regrets." He couldn't imagine Amber in this place. She was nothing like the shallow, expensively dressed women scattered about the room, and never would be if he could help it.

He glanced at Jock, who stood at Roxanne's side, obviously keyed up. Jock also couldn't take his eyes off Roxanne. Thad told himself that he should've seen it coming. Roxanne was convenient. Available. Definitely desirable. Thad could hardly blame him. She had come on to him in their kitchen at a party once, but he'd been too surprised to respond with anything but a polite rejection. Now that he had Amber, he could see that Roxanne had never been what he was looking for. He did take a closer look at the necklace Roxanne was wearing and wondered if it hadn't come from Jock. It looked far too conservative for Roxanne's taste. How ironic it was that they were surrounded by Jock's and Del's friends. From the looks that Roxanne was getting from many of the women in the room, Thad didn't think she'd be welcomed to any of their book clubs or ladies' luncheons anytime soon.

For most of the next hour, he also had to endure the blatant stares of most of those same women. He had, after all, abandoned one of their own—crazy as she was—for the help. But he nursed a Maker's Mark that took the edge off the evening, and spent his time talking with their more sympathetic husbands. How much would he rather have been sitting with Amber on the couch rubbing her feet or helping her practice her breathing exercises? (She was still harboring the hope that the birth would be natural. She was so young and fit, he asked himself through the gentle mist of the bourbon why she shouldn't be hopeful.)

The show's main attraction, the piece that Jock had commissioned from Roxanne, sat beneath a drape in the center of the room. It was like Roxanne to make a big deal out of her own work. She loved drama. He could see it now in her wide, superficial smile, and the way she leaned forward to the man who was speaking to her, as though he were saying something fascinating. Thad knew better. The guy, a city politician, was a first-class bore.

One of Alice's friends, Patsy something, a social skeleton with an uncorrected overbite, spied him from the caterer's bar and tried to wave him over. No doubt she'd heard about the restraining order and wanted to find out the details without actually having to talk to Alice. And when Alice was eventually prosecuted for what she'd done in the baby's nursery, he would have to go into hiding to avoid people like Patsy. He thought he was going to have to duck into the bathroom or something, but his phone buzzed in his jacket pocket and he took it out, grateful to be able to put her off.

Seeing that the number was Amber's cell phone, he was even more grateful. As he moved toward the door, away from the noisy crowd, he was jostled by a haggard-looking man who was just coming in. Noticing the man's thick, uneven coat of facial makeup, he wondered what sort of people Roxanne was surrounding herself with these days. Once outside, he put the phone to his ear, the man forgotten.

"Hey, are you doing okay?" he said.

There was a sound like someone was fumbling with the phone.

"Amber, is everything all right?" Thad felt his heart beating harder in his chest.

Finally, Amber spoke, her voice a hoarse whisper.

"Alice."

CHAPTER 38

Week 35 4/7

If there was one thing that Alice was good at, it was dressing appropriately for every occasion. This evening—from her ribbed turtleneck, fitted pants, and fleece jacket, to her most comfortable soft-soled shoes and roomy backpack with its elastic cording on the outside that was perfect for tucking in soft goods, like towels or small blankets—she was dressed entirely in black. Black was not only slimming, but it could hide many sins.

Her new life lay before her, just on the other side of Amber McVay's kitchen door. Varick would be so pleased. He wouldn't think twice about staying with her now!

Pushing the door open, she stepped over the small pile of glass on the other side. Years ago, Thad had given her the emergency car hammer, and she'd used it to break the window. She smiled at the symmetry of it all. Grateful for the sound of the television in the next room, she closed the door behind her as quietly as she could and slipped the backpack off her shoulder and onto the floor. She had rehearsed in her head what she would say to Amber; she would be reasonable, and not hold a grudge. Thad had hurt her feelings with the silly restraining order, but she could be very forgiving if given the chance.

Taking a deep breath, she slid an unsteady hand into her jacket pocket to feel for the handcuffs. Just because she knew she would succeed—she *had* to succeed—it didn't mean that what she was about to do wasn't frightening.

She was even more shaken when the overhead light came on to reveal Amber—looking frightened and very young—standing in the opposite doorway.

She wasn't prepared for how enormous Amber's belly was. If Amber had been a friend, she would have wanted to touch that belly, giggle over the roundness of it, and find the little bumps that were the baby's hands or feet. She wasn't heartless, no matter what ugly names Thad called her. She even felt a little sorry for Amber. Every Christmas, she had shopped for just the right thing for every girl in Thad's office, and she knew that Amber was fond of pink things, flavored coffees, and vanilla-scented candles. Like Alice, she was a girly-girl.

But then she noticed that the zip-up workout hoodie that she'd bought for Thad the previous spring hung down on either side of Amber's belly, and that she wore SpongeBob bedroom slippers. *What was she? Eleven?*

They stood there, speechless, for another three or four seconds, while Alice considered that she didn't have to do this. No one was making her do it. Varick didn't even know what she was doing. And it was really all for him.

Amber turned to run. The house wasn't deep, so it was only a matter of seconds before she was out of the kitchen and almost to the front door, with Alice nearly on top of her. Chasing Amber felt beneath her dignity. She'd thought Amber might be resting, that it would all be easier than it was turning out to be. But then she got close enough to push Amber down over the coffee table, so that magazines and food and a cell phone and a couple of remotes scattered across the floor. It felt damned good to have Amber writhing there on her side, even though it had been a kind of accident. *Such a rush!* Amber didn't have any choice about what was going to happen to her. Now Alice herself knew the power that Varick felt each time they were together in her bed—and she liked it.

But as she fumbled again in her pocket for the handcuffs, Amber rolled off the table and onto the floor, emitting a startled cry. She scrambled to her feet with a speed that belied her ungainly body, and was halfway up the stairs before Alice could grab her by the hood of the jacket. She pulled, as hard as she could, grabbing a good handful of Amber's strawberry blond hair with it, and Amber started to tip backward. Alice leaned back against the wall, trying to get out of the way as Amber fell, but Amber reached out, pulling Alice down on top of her. They slid down the stairs on Amber's back, Alice draped over her great, protruding belly.

When they reached the bottom, they rested there for the briefest of moments, and Alice felt frozen, uncertain. Beneath her, Amber began to moan. Alice pushed away and tried to stand, but found that her left ankle was twisted or badly bruised, and she stumbled.

Now she was angry. Amber had the baby that belonged to her. She hadn't wanted to kill Amber in the process of taking it, but if Amber was going to be uncooperative, then she had no choice.

She spotted the X-Acto knife that had been in her pocket with the handcuffs on the floor nearby. She bent down and closed her hand around it. As she did, Amber surprised her again by grabbing at her weak ankle and pulling her off her feet. She went down again, this time hitting her head on the coffee table.

She opened her eyes to see the ceiling. How long had she been out? It felt as though she were waking up from a long, long sleep, and her heart sank when she realized where she was and that she had failed. Varick would be so disappointed in her when she told him what she'd tried to do for him.

But then she saw Amber kneeling not very far away from her. It wasn't too late! Amber had the phone in her hand and Alice heard the beep of dialing numbers. Still clutching the X-Acto, she tore off the cap.

Amber croaked Alice's name into the phone.

Alice jabbed the X-Acto into Amber's shoulder, causing Amber to make a sound that wasn't quite a scream, ending whatever she might have said next. The phone fell to the floor and Alice grabbed the telephone and hit the Off button. Thad's cell number disappeared from the screen.

Where was Thad? Alice shook her head to try to clear it. Thad was probably still at the gallery, which wasn't more than fifteen minutes away. She had to decide.

"Alice, please," Amber said, lying on the floor, her voice full of tears. "Just leave. Just get out, now. You have time."

The phone began to ring again.

"Shut up," Alice said. "You did me a favor by taking Thad away from me. I found someone better. But now you have to shut up and let me think."

"He's coming," Amber said.

Alice knew that she had to choose. She looked from Amber's flushed face to her belly. It was there. So close! She could be so fast!

When Amber saw where she was looking, her eyes got wider and she tried to push up to crab-walk away. But her shoulder collapsed, and Alice was on her in a second, rolling her onto her side and clicking the handcuffs onto her wrist. Then Alice let her go and she flopped onto her back again. This time, she began to scream.

"Shut up!" Alice said. How had it come to this? She knew she just should have killed her when she'd had the chance and now she'd lost her nerve.

The cell phone had stopped, and now she heard another phone, maybe a landline, ringing in the bedroom.

"Shut up, shut up, shut up!" she said again. She saw some paper towels on the floor that Amber had been using for napkins—of course, she would use paper towels instead of lovely cloth napkins—and balled them up and shoved them into Amber's mouth, pulling her fingers out again quickly so Amber couldn't bite her.

She ran into the kitchen and brought the backpack into the living room and settled beside Amber to dump out the contents. She could feel herself calming now that Amber was under control. The gag and her difficulty breathing were scaring the hell out of Amber; her chest heaved up and down. Alice took the tie-down cords she'd found in the garage at home and tried to wrap them around Amber's ankles.

"Stop kicking," she said. "Or I will kill you and don't think I won't. You think I'm some kind of pushover because I'm letting Thad divorce me, but I'm not. Stop it, Amber!"

Something in her voice must have gotten through to Amber because she did stop kicking, even though she was still breathing hard. Tears fell down the sides of her face. Alice secured the cords.

"This is going to hurt some," Alice said. She lifted Amber's T-shirt, exposing the white, veined mound that held the baby safely inside. She ran her hand over it lovingly, feeling the lumps and bumps that were the baby's unknown parts. "But I'll be fast, so don't worry." She settled herself on Amber's knees and leaned over to pluck a utility knife from the pile of things she'd brought with her.

Amber began to make panicked noises in her throat and thrashed her head from side to side.

Alice pulled down Amber's sweatpants and was vaguely disgusted by the sight of her pubic hair. It made her think of Thad, who probably saw it every day, now. She worked hard to quell that little bit of useless anger and got to work with the sound of the constantly ringing phone competing with the television. That Thad. So persistent when it came to his girlfriend. His baby.

Amber gave one final whimper and went limp. Alice hoped that she hadn't died. But whatever had happened to Amber, it was going to make what she was doing that much easier.

CHAPTER 39

Week 35 4/7

When Romero saw the panic on Thad Hudson's face as he rushed from the art gallery, a feeling of pity welled up inside him. He knew that whatever he had begun with Varick was coming to its unbearable end. The husband and his girlfriend were sad collateral. It wasn't Thad's fault that he'd been manipulated into marriage by a lying bitch. (And from what he'd witnessed of Alice, she had grown from a dull, manipulative child to a dull and dangerous woman.) He almost reached out to take the man's arm to say a quick blessing over him, but he knew he couldn't. The words would be empty of meaning for them both.

As Thad passed him to go outside, the wind caught the door, flinging it open, but Thad kept moving. The blast of cold air made the roomful of well-dressed people turn, almost as one, toward Romero. He stood frozen for a moment in their irritated gaze, then turned back himself and shut the door.

He didn't like art galleries. One of his colleagues at the community college had tried to get him interested in her work (or, more likely, her), and had dragged him to a couple, but he never saw the kinds of things he'd read about in seminary or had seen in museums. The various pots and giant canvases covered in shades of white paint, or blue, or glued-together bits of glass and wire didn't speak to him of anything transcendent, not in the way artwork inspired by the Church did. He knew it was probably considered an unenlightened view.

Still, Roxanne's work reached him. Each angry piece seemed to scream: this is inside me, this is the taste of the sin into which I was born.

He shook his head briskly at the teenage girl who asked him if she could take his coat and saw relief in her eyes as she smiled and moved on. He wasn't sure what kind of shape his clothes were in beneath the coat. His pants were too big, and the belt he wore was at its smallest possible size, and he couldn't be certain that the injuries he'd suffered weren't weeping again as they had been, on and off. His breath was short and wheezed in his chest. The fact that he hadn't even taken a second glance at the coat girl in her tight mesh shirt and skintight black jeans was an even more telling comment how he was feeling.

On the way to the bar set up in the corner, he saw the silk-draped form that seemed about the size and shape of the sculpture he'd seen through the window of Roxanne's studio. He could tell nothing from the lumps in the drape, but he knew it was some kind of tribute to Del.

Del had been as much of a disappointment as Alice. Alice hadn't been very bright or interesting, but he had seen something better in Del. He had trusted her.

At the bar he asked for a whiskey, knowing it would scorch his throat. It would probably be his last drink. Ever. If it burned a hole in his stomach lining, it would be just another hole. When the bartender handed it over, he gave a nod toward Romero's gloves.

"You must be cold," he said.

Before Romero could answer, he felt someone move in very close beside him. Roxanne looked up at him for a moment before she spoke. Her eyes looked glazed—maybe from excitement, maybe from the glass of wine she was holding. She didn't seem repulsed when she looked at him, not the way the others in the room did. Of course, she'd seen him in her driveway. And did she remember him from that night in the loft, how he'd looked down into her face as Varick—whatever or whoever he was at that moment—was about to rape her? Somehow, he thought (but at the same time could hardly believe) that she didn't remember that night. There was more to come, he was sure, but he didn't know what it would be.

"Father Romero?" she asked, almost in a whisper. The look on her face was a confusion of pain, wonder. No sign of pleasure. But could he have expected that?

"Roxanne," he said. Dear God, she was beautiful.

"It was you the other night," she said. "I don't understand. Why are you here?" There was an edge to her voice. Fear?

In her eyes he could see the girl-child who had looked on from the crowd when he'd sunk the kid in the carnival booth. The girl who had made him feel like he was twelve again, the time before his own life had changed. Before he'd made that first promise to God. Before he'd broken it irrevocably. How could he have thought that she'd changed so much?

"I stopped being a priest a long time ago," he said. "Please just call me Romero." Hadn't he asked her to call him by his name once before, long ago?

"You must have heard about Del," she said.

He could tell she was trying to collect herself, to stop being surprised at seeing him. It wasn't working very well. "Is that why you're here?"

"That would be part of the reason." Gesturing toward a nearby sculpture, he said, "You've done very well with your artwork."

But Roxanne wouldn't be distracted. As she folded her arms protectively across her chest, his eyes were drawn to the low V of her dress, and the iridescent sheen of the necklace and the skin there. He looked away.

He tried to clear his throat to speak, but something caught and he began to cough. Several people turned to look their way. His cough was deep and sounded painful even to his own ears. When he was done, he swallowed hard, forcing whatever had been caught—probably a large chunk of his throat or perhaps even his epiglottis—down into his esophagus.

"Are you okay?" Roxanne said. She turned to the bartender. "Michael, a glass of water, please? Quickly."

Romero took the water from her and drank.

"Thank you," he said, when he was finished.

"You're sick," she said. "Is that why you've come back here?"

The irony was that he was sick precisely *because* he had come back, but he couldn't tell her that.

"Did you want me to come back?" he said. Time seemed to collapse back into that moment he'd watched her leaving the rectory in the early dawn. *What had he done?*

She put her hand on his wrist, the one holding the glass. "You have to know that I didn't understand that it meant anything," she said. "*We* didn't know. Any of us."

He knew this, of course. He had known it all along. They had all been children.

"I saw Monetta today," he said.

There was a change in her eyes, a subtle shift, a split second of understanding, and he knew she was about to break down. They were more connected to each other in that moment than when they had lain together in his bed, their bodies joined together in skin and sweat and desire. Joined together in beautiful sin.

She pulled back her hand and slipped away, the crowd closing behind her.

Roxanne moved through the crowd, numb to the people around her. Why had she sought out their company? Their money? Their admiration? She saw now that they were worthless animals, every one. She might as well have just made them all up, like demon bit players in a medieval play. They were beasts: beautiful bodies and beautiful clothes and beautiful smiles, but with the heads of animals. A donkey here, a pig-snouted woman there, a drooling dog. Even Jock was different. What was he? A pit bull, of course, his head cocked to one side, listening, even smiling.

She smiled and nodded, feeling the full force of the last seventeen or eighteen years bearing down on her so powerfully that she wanted to turn around to see what it looked like. But she knew what it looked like: Romero. Not an animal, but a man who seemed to be wearing a wax death's-head mask of himself. *Her fault. All of it, hers.*

She hadn't conjured him all those years ago—and never for a moment thought she had. It was Alice's fantasy that he'd actually appeared that night in the park. Roxanne had just used that fantasy to amuse herself, to tease Del and Alice. But she had used Romero as though she had conjured him, as though he had belonged only to her, like some kind of grown-up toy.

Now she saw what she had done for what it was, and it was a sick kind of knowledge. Yes, Father Frankl had used ugly words for him, but it had been her choice all along. Romero had wanted her to leave his room that night, but she wouldn't. Instead, she had stood naked before him. That was the last trick she'd had in her bag. The trick she'd known would work.

Then she had killed his baby.

Where was Del? Where was Alice? She wanted to scream for them, but knew that if she opened her mouth, not one person in the gallery would understand. Del was gone. Del had tried to tell her. Del had been the one who got it right from the first, who had told her that it was a stupid game.

She had wanted to know that she could reach out and take what she wanted. She had wanted something special, someone who belonged to her, and her only. Alice had understood that part.

"Roxanne, are you ready?" Colwyn touched her elbow. "The natives are getting restless, dear heart. Bitty Schulz is on her third martini and I fear she's going to start nibbling the bartender."

He took her chin gently in his hand. "What's this?" he said. "Tears?"

"The big reveal," she said. "You know how I am."

"No, I don't know this," he said, pushing her hair out of her face. "Where's my ball-breaking little bitch? Do you want me to do the unveiling for you? Can I get you a Valium?"

"Maybe a do-over," she said. "Did you ever have do-overs when you were a kid?"

"You should know by now that I was never a kid," he said. "I was born with a Gardner's in one hand, a Cuban cigar in the other, and wearing a regimental tie around Mr. Willy."

She couldn't help but smile.

"Look over there," he said. "There's your *patrono* looking very pleased with himself. See how happy you've made him? This is all for your darling Del, precious. Del wouldn't want any tears. She knew they would spoil your makeup."

"Screw makeup," Roxanne said, running a finger beneath one eye.

"That's my girl," Colwyn said. He gave her a gentle push in Jock's direction.

Seeing Jock, she couldn't get the pit bull image out of her mind. When he caught sight of her he smiled, then excused himself from the woman he was talking to.

But as he neared she saw she'd been wrong. Jock wasn't a beast. He was human, just as Romero was human. It was she who was toxic. A danger to others. She wanted to tell him to stay the hell away from her for his own good. And Wendy. Wendy was already attached to her. She loved Wendy, didn't she? She could never hurt Wendy.

She looked around to see where Romero was. He stood near a wall, making himself as inconspicuous as possible. She could still see the old Romero beneath the makeup and behind the halting, painful walk. What else could she possibly say to him?

"Are you ready?" Jock was anxious, too wound up to have let the several drinks he'd had even touch him.

"Hey," she said. "I was thinking that maybe we should have just brought it to your house," Roxanne said. "What if you hate it?"

"Did you love Del?" Jock said.

Probably not enough, she wanted to say. You didn't love her enough, either. Or we would know why she walked out of a seventh-story window on a sunny weekday afternoon.

"You don't need to ask me that," she said.

"Then anything you do that's for Del is going to be fine with me," he said. He made a move toward her as though he would hold her, or kiss her, or perform some other intimacy. But he checked himself, suddenly aware of where they were.

"Sorry," he whispered. He looked so happy, though, that it worried her. Despite the fact that a part of the evening's purpose was to honor Del, she knew that he considered their kiss in her kitchen as the beginning of something. And even though she'd known all along that it was a something she didn't want, she knew that she had led him on and that she owed it to him, and Del, and Wendy not to let it continue.

At least she was going to be able to give Jock and Wendy something real, something true: a happy image of Del that might wipe away, at least for a while, their painful imaginings of her last few moments.

She made eye contact with Colwyn to let him know it was time to begin.

Romero could see that Del's husband was in love with Roxanne. He didn't doubt that most of the other straight men in the room were as well, and not a few of the women. All these years he'd thought that it was Roxanne's fault, that she had coerced or manipulated or seduced the people around her into thinking her desirable. But it had just been some strange gift she'd been given, just as some people were athletic, some were good at math, some were musicians.

He thought of his mother. Her gift was survivability. Now, she was thriving. He'd hated her for it for a while, but now he saw that she couldn't help herself. She was living the life that a single mother—educated, but shunned by her community—in Cuba could only dream of back in the 1970s. When he'd let her down, she eventually let him go, no doubt making her own new deal with God.

"Penny for your thoughts, *Padre*," Varick said. "What's the matter? Feeling puny, are we? You should be celebrating. How's that whiskey?"

Of course, he hadn't seen Varick come in the door. He'd probably squeezed himself in through some sewer pipe or in a basket of fruit like any other rodent. His face was flush with health and his dark eyes shone with happiness. Even his hair was glossy. He looked delighted, as though he'd been showered with sunshine and wrapped in rainbows.

"It tastes like antifreeze," Romero said. "But so does everything else."

"It's just the excitement," Varick said. "You've worked so hard for this." He looked at his watch. "Our dear Alice has done her part, but I'm not quite sure what she's up to next. Free will is a funny thing. Such a fine experiment, but hardly reliable."

"Yes, we're sadly unreliable," Romero said. He watched the women nearby stealing looks at Varick. Idiots. He was torn between shouting at them to get the hell away and pushing them into Varick's arms.

The tall black man who Romero guessed was the gallery's owner rang a tiny bell that could barely be heard above the din. After a few rings, the room was mostly quiet, except for a few people finishing up their conversations. Then they all turned in what he imagined was happy anticipation toward the gallery owner, Del's husband, and Roxanne, who stood between the two men.

He couldn't bear it. Varick was too pleased.

There had been one birthday, back in Cuba, when his mother had announced that they were driving into Havana for the day to go to a movie house in the old part of the city. He'd been there only once. Originally opened in the 1930s, its walls were carved with scenes from local folk stories. Some of the theater's original red velvet seats were still in use. There were VIP boxes above the loge as well. Before each film's showing, the magnificent pipe organ that had been used for silent films rose from the floor, yet remained silent as a kind of stately, bitter reproach to the noisy screen glimmering above it. The theater was more beautiful to him than any church. Even before they left the house, the thought of going there filled him with such excitement that his whole body tensed, and he had to go throw up in the sink.

He excused himself from Varick and found the restroom down a short hallway. When he was done, he wiped his mouth with a paper towel and saw that it was covered with the disgusting makeup Varick had pressed on him. He didn't bother to look in the mirror.

Back in the gallery, he avoided Varick and went to stand close to the front.

Roxanne barely heard what Jock was saying. At any other show she would have been worried about who might buy what piece and what she was wearing. Marketability was so important. Tonight, she wore a dress that she remembered Jock had particularly admired, but now she felt a vague sense of shame at her motivation. She was missing the elation, the thrill that presenting a major new piece of work usually gave her. And yet she couldn't shake the feeling that she'd stood here before, feeling this very same apprehension. Her comfort was in having done justice to Del. It was the one thing of which she was completely confident.

Jock stopped speaking and turned to her wearing a broad smile. People were applauding. Colwyn kissed her on the cheek before moving out of her way so she could pull the drape's cord. But at the last second she asked Jock if he would do it for her. When she saw how pleased he was, she knew she'd done the right thing.

He stepped forward and took the cord from Roxanne. Responding to his gentle tug, the cord held taut for a second before the red silk began to course like bloodied water over the piece and fall to the floor.

There was a silence, a collective holding of breath in the room, and Romero struggled to make sense of what he was seeing.

A sort of frame had been built behind the horizontal figure, uprights of varying heights that seemed to suggest a piece of furniture, or maybe a window. The figure itself was female, and nude, her legs and arms splayed in the air, and her body suspended at an angle, her head lower than her feet. She seemed to be falling.

Aside from the bizarre attitude of the figure, it was the look of fear and utter hopelessness on her face that shocked Romero. Here was Del, her eyes fixed on a sight too terrifying for words, too paralyzing to allow even a scream to escape her throat. He knew what she had seen. But Roxanne had seen it, too. He knew she had because he had been there with her in the loft. Only it hadn't killed her then. This is what had happened to Roxanne. Varick had planted it inside her.

Roxanne covered her open mouth with her hand. In that first second, she thought that someone had replaced the sculpture with this hideous thing. But the longer she looked at it, the clearer it was to her that it was her own work. She knew her hands remembered forming every detail, every awkward curve of her best friend's body—they had even cut those steel uprights that made up the background. She had spent several days etching what she'd thought were flowers into Del's flowing skirt—but now she saw that what she had done was to cover Del—*Oh God! It really was Del!*—with thousands of tiny, striated feathers. This was Del in flight. Del in death.

Worse than the realization that she had been fooled—had fooled herself—was the knowledge that Del's suffering was inside her. Now, she, too, was paralyzed.

She could only watch as Jock fell to his knees in front of Del's tortured figure. He touched it, moaning, running his fingers over the pattern of feathers hugging its shoulder as though it were the most tender skin of his beloved.

She could only watch as he stood up and stumbled toward her, his eyes filled with hate.

She couldn't respond when he tackled her, slamming her head against Colwyn's shining mahogany floor, his hands crushing her throat.

One of the things Romero had been praised for as a child was his quickness. Like everyone else in the room, for the first few seconds in which Del's husband was attacking Roxanne, he stood unable to move. Did the others think that, perhaps, Roxanne deserved it? She had taunted Jock, fooled everyone there into thinking she was virtuous, but then had revealed herself to be unspeakably cruel.

He alone knew the truth. The real joker was Varick, the man who was quietly slipping through the frozen crowd to get to the door.

Romero had noticed the spear attached to one of the nearby sculptures—it was clutched in the hand of a child kneeling on the back of a great horned owl in flight. The shaft was made of wood, but the wood was old and soft, and he had no trouble breaking it off.

As he moved toward Jock and Roxanne, a woman lunged for him, grabbing his leg as she fell. Her fingernails dug into his pants, and, through them, into his fragile flesh, so that he screamed in pain. But he kicked her away, making solid contact with her chest. When he glanced back at her, he saw it was Malina, one of the twins. Wimpering, she drew back into the crowd.

Romero could hear the cries of horror and fear erupting behind him. But no one else tried to stop him, and—despite the pain in his leg—he was able to throw himself on the larger man. But Jock didn't loosen his grip on Roxanne (she was expressionless now, her head thumping against the floor, loose on her shoulders) until Romero sank the metal point of the spear into his neck, just at the tender, vulnerable place beneath his right ear.

CHAPTER 40

Week 35 4/7

Even before his phone started ringing, Dillon was awake. But he didn't want to open his eyes. For the first time since he'd moved in with Alice in Wonderland, he was comfortable in the back-hall guest room. He knew it had something to do with the woman, Josie, who was stirring beside him.

"Your phone," Josie mumbled. She drew one of the extra pillows over her head to block out the ringing.

He remembered needing to get out of the house and going to The Smoking Duck to grab an early lunch and a beer. He remembered seeing Josie come in the bar's front door to pick up her paycheck, the loose shape of her long red hair framed in the sudden glare of sunlight, the way she'd brought out his lunch to him when she saw it was waiting back in the kitchen. She had sat down at his table, even eating a few of his French fries. When she complained about the cold outside, he told her about the Jacuzzi pool at the house where he was staying.

They had spent the afternoon fucking in the pool and smoking the truly decent weed she had stashed in her purse. With her B-cup tits, bony hips, and plain, makeup free face, she wasn't nearly as fine as Ivanka or Malina, but then she wasn't scary as hell, either. And she hadn't asked too many questions, even when she saw all the pictures of Alice and Asshole Thad around the house. He liked her.

Alice herself was nowhere to be seen, and he couldn't believe his luck. Knowing he was pushing it, they ate one of the frozen gourmet pizzas Alice kept in the freezer, then fucked upstairs in his bedroom until they passed out.

He didn't want to answer the phone, but it kept on ringing. It had to be Alice, or maybe Varick wanting to know where Alice was. It was always his fucking day to watch Alice.

Finally, it stopped. But he was fully awake now. If it had been Varick on the phone, there would be a problem. He really didn't know where Alice was.

Josie pulled the pillow from her face. "What time is it?" she asked. She raised up and looked at the digital clock glowing beside the bed. "Eight-thirty? Wait. I'm off tonight." She settled back on the pillow. "Hey, I'm hungry."

"There's food," Dillon said. "There's always food here."

"Like a magic castle," Josie said.

Dillon didn't want to tell her exactly how much the house was like something out of a creepy fairy tale, complete with a wicked witch.

"Let's get the hell out of here," he said. He didn't like how dark the house was around them. If Varick wasn't downstairs already, he would be soon. Alice, too. He'd made a mistake bringing Josie to the house. What had made him do it, he didn't know. But it had definitely been a mistake.

"Whatever," she said.

Before he was out of bed, the phone rang again. He picked it up to see Amber's number on the screen.

He answered it. "Am, what's up?" he said.

"Where's Alice?" Asshole Thad said, sounding even more pissed off than usual. "Your sister—the baby," he said. "The EMTs have got her in the ambulance."

"Why the fuck are you on Amber's phone?" Dillon said, trying to sit up. "Alice is in an ambulance?" Varick would kill him deader than a hammer if anything happened to Alice. *Shit.*

"Not Alice. Your sister is bleeding to death because someone—*God*—someone cut her. They tried to kill her and take the baby," Thad said. "They've got the baby and we don't know if it's dead or alive. And you better tell me that Alice is there with you. Are you at the house with Alice? Because I don't give a shit if you're living there. I just want to know where Alice is."

"Where is Amber? What hospital?"

"You have to see if Alice is there!" Thad was screaming into the phone now, not bothering to hold back anymore.

"She's my fucking sister," Dillon said, standing up. "And if it weren't for you, she wouldn't be bleeding to death."

Josie sat up, pulling the sheet to her chest.

"Listen, Dillon," Thad said. "I know it was Alice. I'm sending the police out there, but, please, you've got to tell me now if she's there."

Before Thad was finished speaking, Dillon was moving fast down the back hallway on his way to Alice's room. He couldn't keep the picture of Amber out of his head: Amber bleeding, dying. He imagined her on her living room floor, her life seeping out of her. Had he dreamed it? Had he seen it? He was the one who had brought Alice into her house. What a stupid, fucked-up thing to do *that* had been.

He'd listened to her bitch and moan for hours on end about how badly she wanted a kid, how Thad was messed up, that it wasn't really her fault they couldn't have a baby. It had meant nothing to him one way or the other—and he'd never argued with her. Asshole Thad obviously hadn't had any baby problems with Amber.

Amber. Alice. Varick. Now it all made a stupid kind of sense.

The bedroom was dark and empty, as he'd known it would be. He flicked on the overhead light. The sheets of the bed were exposed as usual, and the room smelled close and nasty. It reeked of perfume and that other foul odor that was now so familiar to him: wet, rotting fur, like a dead animal. *Varick's smell.*

"She's not here," Dillon said.

"What about the car?" Thad said. "Go look in the garage."

He didn't like taking orders from Asshole Thad. But the thought of Alice knifing Amber made him sick.

Josie, a sheet wrapped around her, followed him downstairs without speaking.

Alice's car was gone, as he knew it would be.

After backing the bike out of the empty garage, Dillon left the overhead door open, not caring fuck-all if the whole neighborhood came inside. He knew it was pretty shitty of him to abandon Josie at the house without any way to get back to her car at The Smoking Duck, especially since the police were probably on their way, trying to find Alice. But when he told her that his sister had been attacked, she seemed cool about it and said she'd be out and dressed before the police got there. Something about the way she wouldn't look at him when he was leaving, though, told him he shouldn't bother looking her up again. That kind of sucked.

In the pocket of his jeans, the phone was ringing again. But once the bike was started he couldn't hear it anymore.

CHAPTER 41

Week 35 4/7

It was a bad night to be out on the bike. The roads were slick with patches of black ice, and, despite the thick leather of his grandfather's bomber jacket, he was freezing his ass off. Until today, there was only one person in the world who could get him out on the bike on a night like this. Now, there were maybe two.

A nagging in his brain told Dillon that he should call his mother. Amber had put her off for the whole bed rest thing, but if Amber was dying, she probably needed to be told. Asshole Thad wasn't any kind of family. It was *his* place to be at the hospital with Amber—not Asshole Thad's.

He knew he hadn't been the best kind of brother. Back when he'd spent a couple months in juvie, Amber had come to visit him every week, always bringing him brownies or cookies she'd baked. She'd looked so happy the day she finally signed him out of that hellhole. He was supposed to live in the house with her, but he'd only stayed there a week, forcing her to lie to the social worker. She'd lied for him so many times, and always gave him cash when he needed it. And when he'd pawned those antique maps she'd found in their grandfather's house when she moved in, she never said a thing about it. Why she was so good to him, he didn't know.

He'd taken people to University Hospital before, and knew right where they would have Amber, trying to put her back together again. Asshole Thad had told him that the EMTs had done what they could there in her living room and then loaded her into the ambulance. They had to restart her heart once. Dillon couldn't get the picture out of his head of Amber bleeding to death right there on the same floor where they'd played *Sorry!* when they were kids.

Fucking Alice!

A quieter, more hesitant voice in his head echoed: *Fucking Varick.*

Varick had played him. Oh, he'd known what the deal was with Varick. It had been a pretty sweet deal. Varick was magical, as far as he was concerned. No one on the fucking planet was able to get better drugs, better service at a restaurant, or to get women (or men) to do things that sane, reasonable people wouldn't even consider. Truly admirable.

But he couldn't deny that there was something very, very wrong with the guy. What about those ten or eleven people he'd brought to the loft for him? He'd seen one of them back on the street, but the woman had grabbed his sleeve and started talking in some made-up, crazy language, and when Dillon shook her off she just wandered away, pulling at her own greasy hair. Two had ended up on the news, reported as missing. He'd been careful to approach all of them without witnesses around, as Varick had told him, but he sucked at following orders, and had often been stoned. One day someone might remember seeing him. He wasn't exactly low profile.

There had been times since he'd met Varick when he decided he couldn't take it anymore, when he wanted to get on his bike and leave Varick and Alice in Wonderland and all the creepy shit behind. But there was the H, calling him back before he could even leave. And the bike. He had the feeling that the bike would just disappear from beneath him if Varick decided it should go. He loved his bike.

With the twins gone, and that freak show Romero around, he didn't like hanging around the loft. He didn't know what kind of deal Romero had made with Varick, but he had the feeling that the guy wasn't going to walk away from it in the end. What about his own deal? If he found Amber's kid up in the loft, what in the hell was going to happen? It would be nice to hear what kind of bullshit explanation Varick might give, but, really, how likely was that? Varick had never explained one damn thing to him.

When he got to the building, he saw a few lighted windows scattered around the lower floors, but it seemed pretty much deserted as usual. He went in through the vast, dusty lobby, with its industrial vinyl shades hanging at various angles and the card table set up with a folding chair and old-fashioned dial telephone as though the security guy had just stepped out.

He didn't hear the baby until he was standing in the seventh floor hallway and the elevator door had rattled shut behind him. It was a faint cry, but it was a living, angry cry, and when he figured out where it was coming from he let out a long breath that he hadn't realized he had been holding.

Bending over, he slid the pigsticker out of his boot and moved it into the sleeve of his jacket. Letting someone know he had it was usually enough. But would it work on Alice? Unfuckingpredictable Alice?

There was so much he didn't know. She'd never mentioned coming to the loft before. More important, was Varick with her? It seemed likely, and it would really fuck things up. Varick would take one look at the knife and just laugh. Varick's laugh—so normal, so easy, like the laugh of some jolly soccer dad—scared the shit out of him.

The door to the loft stood open, and he walked inside to find Alice trying to put a pacifier in the crying baby's mouth. The baby lay on the dining table wrapped in a blanket streaked with blood. Amber's blood.

He hadn't seen all that many babies in person. It was tiny, and kind of ugly. It didn't look anything like Amber or even Asshole Thad, but like some bad computer-generated special-effects doll, with a splotchy face and bits of crusty stuff on its cheeks and where one of its eyebrows would eventually be. Still, one of its fists had escaped the blanket and was waving in the air as if to punch away the light that Alice had turned on to full brightness above it, and he wanted to take that fist and work his finger into the middle of it to see if it would grab on to him.

Each time Alice got the pacifier inside the baby's mouth, it screamed and worked it out again, even though it could barely move its own head.

"She doesn't want it," Dillon said.

"All babies need pacifiers," Alice said. "It comforts them." She laughed and forced the pacifier back in again. "Like you know anything." Alice herself had smears of blood on her face and in her bleached-white hair.

"Where's Varick?"

"He'll come back here," she said. "And he's going to take us with him. He just doesn't know it yet."

"What the fuck, Alice? I think you killed my sister." He held his right arm down, fingering the tip of the pigsticker's warm handle.

Now she looked up at him. "I used to buy your sister things. Did you know that? I had a list of what everybody liked, and one year I bought her a really sweet camisole set at Victoria's Secret for her birthday because she said she liked to shop there. That was my thing—buying presents and planning parties. I was good at it. And I bet your sister wore that camisole when she had sex with Thad." She tried once again with the pacifier, but the baby still resisted. "That was really tacky. Your sister is white trash."

"She doesn't deserve to die," he said.

"This is *my* baby," she said. "The one I was supposed to have with Thad. But she's going to be mine with Varick now."

Hearing that she was more delusional than ever wasn't helping him. He tried to think of something—anything—that he could say to her to get her to give him the baby.

"What does Varick want with a baby?" he said. "You can't do anything with a baby, Alice. They eat and sleep and shit and you have to watch them all the time."

"You don't know anything about him," she said. "We don't need you anymore."

He was about to say something about her not being able to clean up her own puke, let alone a baby's, but he left it alone. He put his hand to his sleeve and let the knife slip out.

"You don't want this, Alice," he said. "I know all you want is Varick. You don't need the baby."

But she ignored the knife and simply picked up the baby, who had begun to whimper.

"If I don't need her, then it doesn't matter what I do with her, does it?" she said. Before he could reach her, she was across the room and out the deck door, running across the roof to God knew where.

He ran after her but she was fast and the wind seemed to carry her along faster. He had almost caught up to her when he tripped over a tiki torch that suddenly rolled into his path. But she kept on, and as he got up again, the only thing that he could see ahead of her was the three-foot wall surrounding the roof.

The snow, driven sideways by the wind, blinded him for a moment and he lost sight of her. He screamed her name.

For so long now he'd lived with her, fed her, kept her from hurting herself, cleaned her up. But he had never really known her. If he had been more sympathetic, she might have listened to him now. He thought of the baby falling, falling through the air. He called for Alice again.

The wind died down and now he could see her through the snow. She had stopped, but she still held the baby.

Ahead of them, up on the wall, Varick stood with the snow-blurred lights of the city behind him. He was like some fashion model, smooth and absurdly confident, looking as though he'd just decided to get up there and take a walk or something. He held his hands out to Alice.

"Alice, dearest," he said.

Dillon was beyond being surprised at anything Varick could or would do. Varick just *was*. He knew in that moment that he was no longer necessary to Varick. Up to now he'd been very necessary. Indispensable. Varick had often thanked him for what he called his "services." Varick had wanted Alice, but on very specific terms that had nothing to do with anyone else. But why Amber's baby?

Varick used people. Used them up. But they always made the choices. Not Varick. What the hell kind of choices could a baby make?

"Alice," Dillon yelled. "Give her to me. He doesn't want her, Alice."

Alice looked back at him. The smile that had come to her face when she first saw Varick faded, and she looked worried. Confused. How many times had he seen that look? Once, after being shut in her room with Varick for almost two days, he had found her wandering in the upstairs hallway, unable to find her way to the kitchen. Hadn't he been kind to her then? Hadn't he made her tea and oatmeal and opened up some applesauce because her mouth was full of sores? Didn't shit like that count for anything? Did she have to try and kill his sister? Kill Amber's baby?

Even though the wind had picked up some, he was close enough now that he could hear the unhappy mewling sounds the baby was making.

"Come on," he said, holding his arms out. "Just let me take her." Realizing he was still holding the knife, he let it clatter to the ground.

"I'm not going to wait forever, Alice," Varick said, sounding like he was talking to a child.

"I've done every fucking thing you've asked me to," Dillon said, addressing Varick. "Every. Fucking. Thing."

"And it's been a pleasure," Varick said, making a small bow.

The baby was screaming now.

"He doesn't need the baby, Alice," Dillon said, trying to be heard over the wind and the baby, trying to keep the hate out of his voice. "All Varick needs is you, Alice. Isn't that right, Varick?"

Alice had been looking back and forth between them, still worried, but now her face changed.

He could see that she'd once been almost as pretty as Amber. But she'd never been a nice person like Amber—a real person. Nice people didn't cut other people and leave them to die. But it was all he'd ever heard her say she really wanted: someone who wanted her. She smiled at Dillon and then glanced back at Varick. He knew that all Varick needed to do was to say a single word and Alice would lift the baby up for him to take, or bite off her ear, or throw her off the building.

Dillon waited, his hands and face turning numb in the cold. Every fucking thing in his life had been a failure, and he couldn't do this one thing for Amber. It made him sick to think that the baby had been so close and he hadn't even had the nerve to take a chance and stab the bitch. He felt like Varick could see it, too, across the rooftop, through the dark. Varick knew him. Varick owned him. He was permanently screwed. He had figured out Varick—well, one part of Varick—but he was still screwed.

Then Varick did a funny thing.

He shrugged.

Before Dillon realized what Alice was doing, the baby, still wrapped in her stained blanket, was flying up, up into the air, far above his head. The blanket began to unravel itself so that the wind caught at it, and he was certain that it would carry the baby behind him, smashing her down onto the deck. But he took two steps backward and caught her, letting his arms sink a bit as he wrapped his hands around her tiny body. In the air, the baby had stopped crying, but as he pulled her to his chest, she took in a great gulp of air and began to scream again.

He tucked the ends of the blanket around her so that her head and feet were covered as well. Looking back to Alice, he saw that she had already turned her attention to Varick and he was helping her up onto the wall.

But Dillon didn't want to see any more. Holding the baby close in one arm to shelter her from the snow and cold, he ran back to the loft. He put his hand on the doorknob, but found it had locked itself. Beneath the blanket, the baby made sounds as though she would cry again. Pressing his face to the glass, he realized that the lights inside the loft had been turned off and he couldn't see any familiar outlines: no furniture or light fixtures or even the weird bird sculpture. On one wall, a red emergency bulb was glowing, and in its glow he could see that the room was empty, with the exception of a wheelbarrow and some scraps of wood and empty bags. He tried the door again, jerking it back and forth so that it shook in its frame, but it was no good.

Unzipping his jacket, he tucked the baby inside it as best he could, and started across the roof to the door to the emergency stairs.

CHAPTER 42

Everything that Romero had brought with him from the monastery fit into the black carry-on bag that lay open on the bed. It had been a quick trip from Iowa, with one day in the middle of it spent testifying in front of the grand jury. Now that the grand jury was done with him, there was nothing he wanted more than to get out of the diocese guest-house and back to the place that had become his new home, spartan as it was. He zipped up the bag and—though the action was painful—hefted it to the floor. But he didn't want to ask the housekeeper for help. There were some things he just couldn't bear, and asking for help from a sixty-something-year-old woman was one of them. When he finally made it down the stairs, the bag bumping on its wheels behind him, he was exhausted and almost breathless.

Father Simon, the bishop's assistant, was supposed to take him to the airport, but there was no one waiting in the dim foyer where the stained glass in the front door's transom threw a pattern of muted color across the floor. But before he could reach the bench by the door to sit down, the housekeeper came from the back of the house.

"Father Romero," she said. "Father Simon is on his way to get you. He'll only be a few minutes. And there's someone here to see you. He's waiting in the library."

"Thank you," he said. Another helpful lawyer? Another helpful priest? He'd had enough of helpful people to last him a lifetime. He almost preferred the honest antagonism of the prosecutor who had managed to get Jock Connery indicted for Roxanne's death.

Realizing where his thoughts were headed, he closed his eyes and said a silent prayer to shut down the cynicism he couldn't seem to escape through his own will. He'd opened that conversation again, realizing that he had never completely shut it down. Strangely, he felt no pressure to recover the life he'd left behind so many years before. The monastery was a good place for him to be now. Later, there might be something else. He didn't know exactly what he was waiting for but knew that it would be revealed to him, in time.

"Are you all right, Father?" the housekeeper said. "We have a room down here if you want to lie down for a few minutes."

"You said someone wanted to see me?" he said.

She led him to the library.

"So this explains why Varick kept calling you *Padre*," Dillon said.

While he couldn't say that Dillon had undergone a radical transformation, there was much that was different about him. All of the metal studs were gone from his face and ears, leaving him looking more like someone in a vaguely silly Halloween mask than a sideshow freak. But there was a deep scar on his forehead that dipped down into his eyebrow. He had put on a little weight, too. Romero found himself hoping that it meant that he was off the heroin.

"You're looking well," Romero said. "Setting off fewer metal detectors these days?"

Dillon swept a self-conscious hand across his brow. "Turns out I was allergic," he said.

"Sit down," Romero said. "Someone's taking me to the airport in a few minutes."

Dillon sat on the edge of an overstuffed wing chair, but didn't look comfortable. "What did you tell them?" he said.

"Tell who about what?" Romero said.

There were so many things he might have told the police, or Thad Hudson, or even Roxanne's mother: that Alice almost murdered a woman and child because of something he wanted, that three women who didn't deserve to die were dead because of him, that the revenge that he had purchased had cost Jock Connery a wife and meant that he was eventually going to spend several years in prison. Jock would no doubt be disbarred, his livelihood stolen from him. And Wendy. Whom would the child ever trust? So many things he desperately wanted to forget.

"Amber told me you were back in town to go to court," Dillon said.

"That was about Roxanne's death," he said. "I didn't say anything about you, and they didn't ask."

He had hoped that the grand jury appearance had been the last of it, but they would probably bring him back if there was a trial. The best thing that could happen for everyone would be for Jock to plead the second-degree murder charge down to voluntary manslaughter and get it over with. The worst part of the whole ordeal (*ordeal*—such an inadequate word!) had been the way the newspapers had lauded him as some kind of hero for trying to save Roxanne. He hadn't known that he was capable of feeling such shame. It was the thing that had made him at first refuse the medical treatment the diocese had insisted on for him. The doctors told him that if he wasn't put immediately on regular dialysis, he would die within a few days. His liver was in bad shape, too, his immune system wrecked.

"I can handle the fucking police," Dillon said. He sneered. "Bunch of pussies."

At least some things hadn't changed about Dillon.

"I just told them that Alice in Wonderland had me drop her off at that building sometimes. I said I just guessed that was where she'd be," he said. Then his voice dropped. "It wasn't like they could prove I'd been there before, or anything."

Neither had Romero volunteered to the police that he'd been staying at the loft. Father Simon, the priest sent to the hospital by the bishop, later also agreed that it wasn't relevant to the case of Alice's presumed suicide. Father Simon had shown up late one evening in Romero's room, asking if he wanted to talk. By two o'clock in the morning, Romero had made a full confession, and even felt like he was willing—and ready—to die. But Father Simon had come back the next day and talked him into trying the dialysis.

"No," Romero said. "It isn't relevant, is it?"

"I thought I saw him," Dillon said. "Sometimes, I think I just dreamed that I did, but I'm sure I saw him downtown, getting into the back of a car."

"I don't think so," Romero said.

"How do you know?" Dillon said. "I still have the bike. What if he wants it back? What if it means I owe him, or something?"

Romero laughed. "You don't owe him anything. I think he's finished with you. With us," he said. "I don't think there *is* a Varick anymore." But as he said it, a feeling in his gut told him it was just wishful thinking on his part.

"I don't know if I believe that," Dillon said. "I keep thinking there's something I should do to keep him away. You know, like they do in the movies. I could start wearing garlic or sleep with the lights on, or some shit like that." He shook his head. "That's stupid, isn't it?"

Romero shook his head. "It's just not going to be a problem. But even if I told you to pray, you probably wouldn't do it, would you?"

Dillon looked doubtful.

"You might give it a try. Maybe go to church a few times with your sister. She goes, right?"

"Yeah, she's started to go all the time, now," he said. "She and Thad and Hannah."

When he said the baby's name, his mouth lifted in a small, involuntary smile. He had also said "Thad," not Asshole Thad. This was progress. Romero knew that even if Dillon never set foot in a church, there was hope for him.

Father Simon stopped the car at the small blue and white section marker a hundred feet or so from Roxanne's grave.

"Do you want to go alone?" he said.

Romero saw that there was genuine kindness in his eyes, not the banal solicitude of the diocese housekeeper or the abbot of the monastery to which he was returning. He couldn't help but think about Roxanne, also, and the way she had stood over him in her driveway, trying to scare away the dog that had attacked him.

Why had the Church worked so hard to bring him back into the fold? He had given Father Simon permission to talk to the bishop about the details of his confession. There would be questions, official interviews. Eventually. He was going to have to tell everything he knew about Varick, everything he had experienced. It was going to be ugly, and probably painful. His words would be logged alongside stories of manifestations of true evil going back as far as the beginnings of the Church. As far back as the beginning of time. The Church had the benefit of the long view.

"You have about ten minutes," Father Simon said.

Romero didn't like how enormous and lonesome modern U.S. cemeteries were. The cemeteries of his childhood were crowded, like busy marketplaces for the dead, the white marble and stone markers pressing against one another and the aboveground tombs and crypts like so many people. It gave one a sense of community, of companionship. This impersonal place, The Cemetery of the Immaculate Conception, was spread out over a hundred and fifty acres, and the section that allowed statues and memorials covered only about a tenth of it. The rest of it looked like a lovely park that didn't allow picnics.

The grass here was thick, the ground even. He had been unsteady on his feet in the hospital, and the doctors had urged him to use a cane. But walking the grounds of the monastery had made him somewhat stronger. Approaching Roxanne's grave while leaning on a cane would have been a demoralizing thing for him to do.

•••

It had been a large funeral. He suspected that many of the mourners were only acquaintances of Roxanne's, people who were more prurient than genuinely saddened. He recognized Del's parents from years before. There were two brothers as well, one just a teenager. Alice's funeral had been only two days earlier, and the O'Briens looked shell-shocked, as though they couldn't believe they were there, burying yet another one of their daughter's friends.

Romero met Roxanne's mother, Carla, outside the church. She was small, like Roxanne, and dressed in a calf-length black dress and long fur coat. She looked to be about fifty, but seemed to be fighting it with too much makeup and a too-black dye job. But she didn't appear to be much like the woman that Roxanne had described to him long ago— one who couldn't settle into one faith, one relationship, one job. She looked settled, maybe even prosperously conservative. She had none of Roxanne's fire about her. Her male companion spoke little and looked less grieved than she.

"I'm sorry I don't remember you," she said to Romero. "Were you one of Roxanne's friends?" Her voice was high and childish, but there was no mistaking the note of skepticism in the question.

"We knew each other only for a while," he said.

When he asked if they could talk for a moment, she didn't respond immediately. Roxanne had been dead for almost two weeks. He had been in the hospital much of that time, but knew he still looked half-dead himself. But he had once gotten the impression that Roxanne thought her mother was greedy, and so suspected that she might be curious about what he had to say. Greedy people rarely changed, and he didn't doubt for a moment that she would agree to the memorial he wanted to offer for Roxanne.

The man with her whispered something in her ear. Romero didn't know what it was, but she said that, yes, they could speak.

He hadn't thought to bring flowers. The remnants of some yellow roses bowed their heads over the edge of the vase buried in the ground beside the grave marker. He took them out and looked around for a trash can.

Finding none, he simply moved them closer to the next grave and carefully lowered himself to sit on the grass.

Years before, Father Frankl had tried to make him out as some kind of monster, and, in the end, it had become a kind of self-fulfilling prophecy. He might have come back for her. He might have forgiven her. And she might have forgiven him.

There was nothing to do but sit for the remaining few minutes, listening to the traffic outside the cemetery's gates and the spring birds nesting in the nearby trees. The late afternoon sun was strong, but there was some shade over the grave from the sculpture standing above it, the angel with its white, feathered wings spread wide, watching over Roxanne, guarding her from the things he could not.

About the Type

This book was set in Sabon, a typeface designed by the well-known German typographer Jan Tschichold (1902–74). Sabon's design is based upon the original letter forms of Claude Garamond and was created specifically to be used for three sources: foundry type for hand composition, Linotype, and Monotype. Tschichold named his typeface for the famous Frankfurt type founder Jacques Sabon, who died in 1580.

Isabella Moon

Laura Benedict

Sometimes the past comes looking for you . . .

Carystown, Kentucky, is still scarred by the mysterious disappearance
two years ago of Isabella Moon. Faced with an almost complete lack
of evidence – lack, even, of a body – the case of the missing girl is
still open, and, though the media circus which engulfed the small
town has long since subsided, frustrated Sheriff Bill Delaney is no
nearer a resolution.

In sleepy Carystown Kate Russell has found a refuge from the
horrors of her past and with the handsome Caleb she dares to feel
safe. But in an instant her quietly idyllic life is turned upside down.

Kate knows where Isabella's hidden grave lies, and knows she must
go to the authorities. But before long it becomes clear that she
herself is a suspect.

Kate has long-buried secrets of her own that the Sheriff's enquiries
are threatening to uncover. As she is drawn further into the
investigation, some unsettling truths emerge . . .

'Like digging up an unmarked grave in the gloaming, *Isabella Moon*
is a tense and creepy hunt for the truth about what lies beneath . . .
Laura Benedict's debut will definitely have readers sleeping with
the lights on – if they sleep at all' Lisa Unger, author of *Black Out*

arrow books

Three Junes

Julia Glass

Winner of the National Book Award

Three Junes is a novel about how we live, and live fully, beyond grief and betrayals of the heart, and how family ties (those that we make as well as those that we are born into) can offer redemption and joy.

'*Three Junes* almost threatens to burst with all the life it contains. Glass's ability to locate the immense within the particular, and to simultaneously illuminate and deepen the mysteries of her characters' lives, would be marvellous in any novelist. In a first-time novelist, it's extraordinary.'
Michael Cunningham, author of *The Hours*

'Like . . . Michael Cunningham's *The Hours*, which won the Pulitzer, *Three Junes* won its own prize (National Book Award) and deserves it . . . a highly accomplished and sensitive novel, all the more remarkable for being Julia Glass's first.' *Sunday Telegraph*

'Glass seems to relish depicting her characters' struggles and confusion, after which she skilfully negotiates them through the emotional wilderness as they live, love and grieve. The result is an impressive and moving debut. It's a great read, and yes, the accolades are deserved.' *Time Out*

arrow books

ALSO AVAILABLE IN ARROW

Circle of Friends

Maeve Binchy

Big, generous-hearted Benny and elfin Eve Malone have been best friends growing up in sleepy Knockglen. Their one thought is to get to Dublin, to university and to freedom . . .

On their first day at University College, Dublin, the inseparable pair are thrown together with fellow students Nan Malone, beautiful but selfish, and handsome Jack Foley. But trouble is brewing for Benny and Eve's new circle of friends, and before long, they find passion, tragedy – and the independence they yearned for.

'Binchy's novels are never less than entertaining. They are, without exception, repositories of common sense and good humour . . . chronicled with tenderness and wit'
Sunday Times

'Full of warmth and pure delight'
Woman & Home

'As gripping as a blockbuster, but infinitely gentler and wiser'
Cosmopolitan

arrow books

Black Out

Lisa Unger

'*Black Out* is riveting psychological suspense of the first order.'
Harlan Coben

On the surface, Annie Powers' life in a wealthy Florida suburb is happy and idyllic. Her husband, Gray, loves her fiercely and together they dote on their beautiful daughter, Victory. But cracks are beginning to appear as demons from Annie's past come back to haunt her. It is a past she has no memory of – and it won't let go.

Disturbing events – the appearance of a familiar dark figure on the beach, a mysterious murder – trigger strange and confusing memories for Annie. And as her world starts to fracture around her, she soon realises that she must piece those memories together before her past comes to claim her – and her daughter . . .

arrow books

Sleepers

Lorenzo Carcaterra

An unforgettable true story of friendship, loyalty and revenge

Lorenzo, Michael, John and Tommy shared everything – the laughter and the bruises of an impoverished childhood on New York's violent West Side. Until one of their pranks misfired and they were sent to a reformatory school.

Twelve months of systematic mental, physical and sexual abuse left the boys transformed for ever.

Eleven years later, one of them had become a journalist, one a lawyer – and the other two killers for the mob. In a chance encounter they came face to face with one of their torturers and shot him dead in front of several witnesses. The trial that followed brought the four friends together in one last, audacious stand – and a courtroom climax as gripping as any John Grisham novel.

'A compulsive true story'
The Times

'Undeniably powerful, an enormously affecting and intensely human story'
Washington Post

'Fabulous, unbelievably good'
Entertainment Weekly

'A brilliant, troubling, important book'
Jonathan Kellerman

arrow books

First Love

Adrienne Sharp

A devastating and heartbreaking novel, that captures the joy, pain and intensity of young love. *First Love* is the story of young dancers, and lovers, Adam and Sandra, members of rival ballet companies in New York. Passionate and talented, yet naïve and ambitious, the pair are unprepared for the seductive and demanding world of which they are becoming a part. As Sandra's star seems to be rising their allegiances are tested and she has to make some tough decisions – loyalty to her high school sweetheart Andrew or her childhood dream.

'Spare, evocative . . . *First Love* is . . . harrowing in its on- and off-stage depictions of desire and disappointment, rendered with writing that is hauntingly lyrical . . . Sharp brings to life beauty, magic and all-consuming passion of the professional dance world.' *Los Angeles Times*

'With the nuance of an insider's knowledge, Adrienne Sharp stages the passions of dancers who use and abuse their bodies for art, pleasure, and emotional release, in an excruciating pas de trois of ecstasy and wrenching horror executed step by compelling step in sentences of theatrical brilliance.' *Susan Vreeland*

'Compulsively readable' *San Francisco Chronicle*

arrow books

ALSO AVAILABLE IN ARROW

The Lake of Dead Languages
Carol Goodman

Jane Hudson never thought she would return to Heart Lake. Her years there as a scholarship girl ended in a double tragedy: the drowning of her two roommates. Now she is back, struggling to adjust to her new life teaching Latin and as a single mother. But the events that haunted her memories for so many years begin to recur in front of her eyes. It seems she alone can see what is happening, and only she will be able to prevent a second catastrophe.

Surrounded by the lake that gives the school its name, steeped in history and overflowing with the emotions of teenage girls, Heart Lake guards its past . . . but cannot keep it hidden.

arrow books

The Burning Blue

James Holland

Joss Lambert has always been a loner, constrained by a secret from his past, until he finds friendship and solace firstly with Guy Liddell, a friend from school, and then with Guy's family, who welcome him into their farmhouse home. Joss increasingly comes to depend upon the Liddells and treats Alvesdon Farm as the one place where he feels not only appreciated but also truly happy.

The idyll cannot last. With war looming, Joss is forced to confront the past. He escapes through flying, becoming a fighter pilot in the RAF. But with the onset of war, even the Liddells's world is crumbling. As Joss is fighting for his life in the Battle of Britain, so he begins to fall madly in love with Stella – Guy's twin – but with tragic consequences.

Leaving England and the Liddells far behind, he continues to fly amid the sand and heat of North Africa, until his hopes and dreams are seemingly shattered for good . . .

'Holland skilfully turns the screw of tension as the last months of peace slip away . . . He has joined the few who can bring history to life' *Guardian*

'This beautifully written book is a work of exceptional authenticity' Geoffrey Wellum, former Battle of Britain pilot and author of *First Light*

arrow books

The Flaw of Love

Lauren Grodstein

One moment can change your life forever . . .

Joel Miller's girlfriend has locked herself into the bathroom with a pregnancy test. Joel hasn't planned to be a father, he's not even sure he wants to be one, but as of a couple of hours ago it's a very real possibility.

Lisa isn't the love of Miller's life – theirs is a relationship which happened by accident rather than by design – but Miller realises that he might now be bound to her forever. And so, while his future is decided for him behind a closed door, he tries to make sense of his past. Complicated memories come back, many of them buried for a good reason, of a turbulent childhood and his parents' dysfunctional marriage, of his complex father and difficult, unpredictable mother. But, most of all, he thinks about his failed relationship with the unforgettable, unconventional Blair, the woman he loved most of all . . .

'A compelling novel – a wistful tale of modern love'
Daily Mail

arrow books